Critical acclaim for *The Unblemished*

'His carefully crafted descriptions of horrific images, along with the ability to suggest they are even worse than words can tell, is reminiscent of Poe and the early stories of Clive Barker. Not for the squeamish, but no fan of literary horror should miss it.' *The Times*

'*The Unblemished*, winner of the International Horror Guild's Best Novel award, is cleverly constructed, building relentlessly from intense, intimate terror to something on another scale altogether . . . the ruined London in the closing chapters of this stark gripping novel will stay with you a long time.' *Guardian*

'Top-notch writing skills, poetic vision and beautiful prose raise this way above your Hammer House of Horror . . . unusual as well as highly accomplished terror.' *Sunday Express*

'Williams is so good at what he does that he probably shouldn't be allowed to do it any more, for the sake of everyone's sanity.' *Publishers Weekly* (starred review)

'Williams has built a whole mythology, one that makes the book feel like a cobwebbed relic from another time. Dust it off, if you like. Just do it at, say, ten in the morning. In a crowded room. In a military compound.' *Time Out*

'*The Unblemished* scooped last year's highly coveted International Horror Guild Award, beating off some pretty stiff competition (which included some bloke called Stephen King). *The Unblemished* is a stomach-churning visio̶̶̶̶̶̶mplished and courageous author and definitely not for the f̶̶̶̶̶̶̶ ̶̶̶̶SFREVU

'*The Unblemished* is ̶̶̶̶̶̶̶̶̶̶̶̶̶̶̶̶̶̶̶̶e and doesn't back down. Its unse̶̶̶̶̶̶̶̶̶̶̶̶̶̶̶̶̶̶ts. This is one of the best books tha̶̶̶̶̶̶̶̶̶̶̶̶̶̶̶̶̶̶̶̶al

'Williams' threat emerges from the world like an optical illusion being revealed, then you find that society fell apart while you were looking somewhere else.' *SF Site*

'A terrifying tale of violence and determination to survive. Highly recommended.' *Monster Librarian*

'This book scared the crap out of me ... In my estimation, Williams does so many things so well that there's really not much he can't do. He is one of the few writers working in the area of horror and dark fantasy who has my full attention all of the time. *The Unblemished* is further evidence of his superlative talent.' Jeff VanderMeer

'[A] rich, emotionally engaging and extremely fast-paced novel ... *The Unblemished* achieves the admirable, tricky task of interweaving physical horror with spiritual terror ... an unapologetic white-knuckle thriller.' William P Simmons, *Infinity Plus*

'Conrad Williams takes us on a roller-coaster ride through ancient buried secrets and body-horror invasion into the pulsing gut of apocalyptic British horror.' Christopher Fowler

'*The Unblemished* combines a carefully orchestrated accumulation of paranoid detail reminiscent of Ramsey Campbell with passages of vividly described transformations evocative of early Clive Barker.' Steve Rasnic Tem

'An apocalyptic nightmare narrated with great vigour, clarity and stylishness. Steel yourself for some hideous sadism – there's awe along the way.' Ramsey Campbell

'A tour de force. Awe-inspiring in its sheer unsparing, unflinching, grimly horrifying view. One nasty piece of work.' Ed Bryant, *Locus*

ONE

ABOUT THE AUTHOR

Conrad Williams is the author of the novels *Head Injuries*, *London Revenant* and *The Unblemished* as well as a collection, *Use Once Then Destroy*, and the novellas *Nearly People*, *Game*, *The Scalding Rooms* and *Rain*. Born in 1969, he sold his first short story at the age of eighteen and has gone on to sell over 80 more. He is a past recipient of the British Fantasy Award and the International Horror Guild Award. He lives in Manchester with his wife, three sons and a monster Maine Coon cat.

ONE

Conrad Williams

Published by Virgin Books 2009

2 4 6 8 10 9 7 5 3 1

Copyright © Conrad Williams 2009

Conrad Williams has asserted his right under the Copyright, Designs and Patents
Act 1988 to be identified as the author of this work

First published in Great Britain in 2009 by
Virgin Books
Random House, 20 Vauxhall Bridge Road,
London SW1V 2SA

www.virginbooks.com
www.rbooks.co.uk

Addresses for companies within The Random House Group Limited can be
found at:
www.randomhouse.co.uk/offices.htm

The Random House Group Limited Reg. No. 954009

A CIP catalogue record for this book is available from the British Library

ISBN 9780753518106

The Random House Group Limited supports The Forest Stewardship Council
[FSC], the leading international forest certification organisation. All our titles
that are printed on Greenpeace-approved FSC-certified paper carry the FSC logo.
Our paper procurement policy can be found at www.rbooks.co.uk/environment

Typeset by TW Typesetting, Plymouth, Devon
Printed in the UK by CPI Bookmarque, Croydon, CR0 4TD

For Zachary
All these miles, and more.

CONTENTS

ACKNOWLEDGMENTS

I'm extremely grateful to Dr Christoph Winkler, Project Scientist for the International Gamma-Ray Astrophysics Laboratory (Integral) at the European Space Agency, for his input regarding gamma ray bursts. Paul McAuley also helped with the science (and encouraged me when the idea for this novel was in its infancy). If there are any factual howlers, point the finger at me, not them.

Thanks too to Rob Wilcock for details regarding oil platforms and for checking a couple of early chapters. Alan McGrath also chipped in with anecdotes regarding life on the rigs.

Other people who helped during the writing of this book were Nicholas Royle, Shaun Hamilton, Simon Strantzas, Ethan, Ripley, Zac, Mum and Dad. My superb editors at Virgin Books, Adam Nevill and Simon Lee-Price, made sure I didn't take my eye off the ball. Thanks also to Robert Kirby at United Agents.

As always, Rhonda Carrier read drafts, rolled her eyes, shook her head, but generally infused me with confidence and hope. I love that woman.

'We live as we dream – alone.'

Joseph Conrad

Part One

BIRTHS, DEATHS AND MARRIAGES

1. RAPTURE OF THE DEEP

... and in the morningtime we can drive in the jeep to the zoo and bort tikits and see the munkiz. Our jeep is cool acoz it goz reely fast and plays som grat muzik and its a green car ...

Richard Jane glanced to his left and saw the other divers ranged away from him at ten-foot intervals, ghosts fading into the distance. Visibility was poorer than usual but he could just make out the yellow flashes of Henrikson Subsea's company logo on the dive suits. His breath came in shallow stitches. He could feel his heartbeat where it played in the thin skin of his wrist whenever it pressed against his suit as he applied pressure to the wrench. Another few turns and this section of the clamp would be sound. The fatigue crack, fully three feet long, was a black frown in the scarred weld between the node and its supportive brace. The great leg of the oil platform rose into the murk and was lost. You had to move against the current to get the job done. You had to anticipate where it might try to drag you and plant your stance accordingly.

This deep, the pressure was so great that it could be felt

like a vice around the chest. The first time Richard Jane experienced it, all those years ago during his training – hard, filthy work burning three-inch monel bolts out of the flanges of a rig in the Gulf of Mexico – he thought he was having a heart attack. Breathing was labour. But the complexity and physical demands of his work took him out of his environment, helped him to forget about the risk, or at least keep it at a manageable distance. The ocean was unforgiving at these alien fathoms. Death was in the deep. It cruised around like the shadows of sharks. And like a shark it could smell a drop of blood from miles away. It preyed on the mind after a while, if you let the thoughts settle. No amount of reading or cards or letters home would steer you away after that.

Jane had known two men, in his four years as a saturation diver, who had taken their own lives because of the pressures of the job. He was a veteran already. Few lasted longer than two years in this line. Despite the advances in technology and safety, it still put a drain on your health. Holes in the lungs. Neurological threat. Aseptic bone necrosis. A sense of never being able to escape the cold: helium's thermal conductivity sapped the body of heat. The hot water pumped through the wetsuit was just never hot enough. Sometimes the grand a day he made on these two-week stints seemed insufficient. You spent so long down here you forgot what trees looked like; you'd be forgiven for believing the entire planet looked like this.

The helium mix turned everyone's voice cartoonishly high, but it could only have been Stopper who said, 'Down tools in fifteen. Three days from now I'm going to be suffering from a bad case of boozer's elbow.'

'Better than tosser's forearm, you skirt-frightener.' That was Carver.

Tyldesley's voice, coffeewarm in the control room, nearly a thousand feet north of here, said, 'Cut the banter, you prozzers. Job's not over till you hear the school bell go. Till then, your freezing cold arse flesh is mine, d'you hear me? All mine.'

'Charming fucker,' said Rae, immediately to Jane's left. He was making wanking gestures. There was something about seeing that, 600 feet beneath the surface of the North Sea, 150 miles from Aberdeen – that and Rae's falsetto profanity – that Jane found hilariously funny. He started laughing and could not stop. He felt something pop in his head and thought he might have pulled a muscle. Tears in his eyes threaded his vision with colour. There was a strange sensation of increased pressure, as if a gust of wind had suddenly barrelled into them, and then the soft hiss of the headset died, the heat from the circulating water began to rapidly dissipate.

He saw Rae turn to him, arms outstretched: *What the fuck?*

'Tyldesley? Tyldesley? Are you reading me?' There might have been a trace of panic in Jane's voice but the helium disguised it. He gave three quick tugs on the security rope binding them all together and made a start for the pair of two-man diving bells, twenty feet east. There had been some failure, some catastrophic failure. Fear swelled inside him, like decompression sickness. He had seen a man with the bends once. You don't forget that. All of the limbs withdrawn into a core of impossible pain. The welter of blood at every orifice, fizzing bright red. Bubbles opening in the jelly of the eyes.

He checked back a couple of times on that shambling race for the bells. He could only see Stopper, but the silver streams of bubbles rising behind him suggested that Rae and Carver were at his heels.

Jane reached the second bell and swung himself under. He rose through the open hatch, pulling himself in with arms that felt too weak to support him, or anything else. He was shivering, trying to shoulder off his bale-out bottle when Stopper's head emerged into the wet porch.

'Electrics?' Stopper asked, when he'd levered off his helmet.

'Must be,' Jane said. 'Thank fuck the back-up kicked in or we'd have been sucking in nothing but the taste of rubber.'

'What do we do?'

'I'm calling this an emergency,' Jane said. 'How about you?'

'I second that.'

'We get back to the habitat,' Jane said. 'Decompress. Then kick the cock off whichever twunt sat on the off button. Are the others in?'

'Already ascending,' Stopper said.

Jane sealed the inner hatch and turned his attention to the depth gauge, so it was Stopper who saw the first of the dead fish drifting past the portholes. 'Look,' he said. His large goalkeeping hands kept wiping and rewiping the Zappa moustache that bracketed his tight nervous mouth. Shoals of dead fish – cod, coley, pollack – were raining down around them.

'What's it look like to you?' Stopper asked Jane.

Jane shook his head. Visibility was improving as they rose out of the black of deep sea into the blue surface waters above 200 feet. Blood billowed out of the fish from the gills and the eyes, swinging in the pulses of current. 'Explosion, maybe?' he said. 'Poison in the water?'

'Poison wouldn't put our comms out,' noted Stopper. 'But maybe they're unconnected. Shall I try the radio in here?'

'Already did,' Jane said. 'It's dead.'

'We need to get back to the Ceto,' Stopper said. 'We need to get inside.'

'It's OK,' Jane said, and the words died between them.

'What if there's nobody up there to disconnect us from the stage?'

'Seriously, Stopper, give it a rest,' Jane said. 'What do you think happened? Everyone fucked off and left us on our own? Check the pressure. I don't want us going fizzy.'

'Pressure's stable,' Stopper said. And then: 'Oh my God.'

A human body. And then two, three more. Drifting down through the water, arms outstretched as if they were skydiving.

'Oh, Christ,' Stopper said. 'Who's that? Is that Terry Mead? What's going on?'

Jane joined him at the tiny porthole. Together they watched as what looked like black cobwebs funnelled from the sockets of Terry Mead's face – his mouth hanging vastly open as if it had been dislocated, clouds of blood pumping from it like a belching factory chimney – before he twisted and tumbled away from their field of vision. More bodies sank around him. Jane counted a dozen before Stopper, weeping, dropped to his knees.

'We're dead,' Stopper said, hysteria threatening to take his voice to a point where it could not be heard. 'That poor man. All those poor fucking men. We're dead.'

'It must be an explosion,' Jane said. His own voice was rendered toneless by the panic. 'But then, I don't think so. Look at their clothes. Nothing got torn off.'

'They jumped? A fire?'

'Maybe. Maybe a fire. In the comms room? Spreading to the generators? It would explain the blackout. It would have to be a nasty bastard to make men jump.'

'Jesus,' Stopper said. 'Who's going to plug us in?'

They ascended the rest of the way without speaking. The bell filled with hard hot breath. As they neared the surface they braced themselves. The bell began to rock violently on its hoist wire, more so than was usual when they lifted out of the wet and into the air. The great legs of the platform seemed to be swaying in the current, as if about to pull themselves free of the bed and start walking.

'This is not good,' Jane said.

The bell broke the surface and he had time enough to see the service chopper hanging from the helipad with its rotors torn off. The portholes became caked with a sudden thick black residue. He hadn't seen anybody else on deck and had no idea what had happened to the bell containing Carver and Rae. Their own bell swung about on the end of its cable like a wrecking ball in search of something to hit. The abandon-platform siren was coming to him, shredded by the wind to an ineffective stutter.

Even as he tried to grab hold of something to stop him being clattered around the unforgiving innards of the bell, Jane was thinking of reasons. Electrical storms. Terrorist attacks. Dirty bombs. Chemical agents.

Stopper cracked his head hard against the CO_2 scrubber and fell back against the top hatch, his foot folding under him as if it were without bone. Jane heard something crack dully, like the sound of splitting sapling branches. Stopper made no protest; blood pulsed steadily from a wound behind his left ear. Jane ducked down and propped him against the rack of heliox cylinders, strapped a belt around his chest and trapped it behind the heater. The diving bell jerked back on itself and Jane crashed into the control panel, tearing what felt like a foot-long strip of skin from his back.

But then there was a jolt that seemed unnatural, a punch that had not been dealt by the wind's fist. Water cleared a viewing space in one of the portholes; Jane swung over to it and peered out. He could see the other bell swinging around on its hoist wire and little else through a blizzard of spume. They were level with the decks but waves were crashing over the sides. He hadn't seen that in ten years of working around rigs. He'd much rather not be seeing that while being inside a pressurised diving bell. Again, that feeling of something controlling the bell came back; he heard the cable grind as it was shifted against the direction in which the wind wanted to take it. He felt a tightening, a drawing-in; he realised it must be the motion-compensation system, which meant that someone was supervising their return. He saw the other bell impact against a landing stage, almost crumpling it as if it were fashioned from aluminium foil.

Their own diving bell was stilled for a moment; it was under control. He heard the usual thumps and dings that meant the stage was being disconnected, and another thunk as the bell was mated to the entrance lock of the Ceto, the Diving Support Vessel. He tried to see through the porthole who was rescuing them – at least two men must have survived to be able to coax the bell into its docking position – but he could not make out anything beyond the ceaseless spray and the strange persistent fibrous rain.

He ran a palm over his forehead, pushing his sweaty hair back from his face, and looked through the hatch at the trunking space and the tunnel to safety that it offered. 'How are we for pressure in there?' he asked, but nobody was replying. The readings on the diving-bell gauge were normal but everything else was frazzled; it might simply have frozen. He had to hope that the pressure inside the DSV was equal to that in the bell. Jane thought of his son. He whispered, 'Stanley.'

He spun the hatch wheel and felt his body tense as the door hissed open. Seawater rained on him from the seal as he ducked under the frame and into the Ceto. Blood was smeared across the outside of one of its tiny windows. There was nothing to be seen through that. He ducked back into the bell, grasped Stopper under the arms and dragged him through to their living quarters. He tried hoisting him onto one of the bunks, but all his strength had left him; his muscles felt flabby, saturated by fear. The wound on the back of Stopper's head had stopped bleeding. His breathing and pulse were weak but regular. That was something. Jane wondered how long they would have to wait for help to arrive. Nothing was landing on the helipad while the sea was being whipped up like this. Decompression time for the team would be something in the region of thirty-six hours.

He made sure that Stopper was comfortable, then made his way to the end of the chamber where a window allowed him a view of the second chamber. He could not yet see Rae or Carver, but he could hear the clamour of their diving bell as the winchmen struggled to align it with the entrance lock. Shadows flashed across the porthole and then he could see the other bell as it was hauled into view alongside theirs. As the hatches drew level the tartan headband that Rae always wore became visible.

Rae was crying. His mouth was open; light glittered in the bars of saliva between his lips. Maybe Carver had died. But that wasn't so; Rae's buddy was standing behind him. He was trying to calm Rae down.

What is it? Jane mouthed, but he wasn't sure Rae could see him. The cramped living quarters had never seemed so stifling to Jane.

A letter from Stanley lay on his bunk. Before they had descended that morning – the sky a beautiful unbroken span of coral pink; the sea flat cobalt, not a scuff of white upon it – he had read it half a dozen times. He wrote well for a five-year old. It was in a mix of upper- and lower-case letters, and the spelling relied on phonetics in the main, but it was neat, with little slope. Stream of consciousness, almost. A blurt of detail, as if he couldn't get it out of himself quick enough.

Me and mum went for a peetsa after the fer and I wasunt sic I was big enuf for the dojims this time remember wen you tuck me and I was to smorl.

It had been three months since he'd last seen his boy. He'd moved out of the flat in Maida Vale that he shared with Cherry and Stanley. She didn't like Jane being away for six weeks at a time. She felt she'd been dealt a short straw. *I have to look after the boy 24/7 while you fanny around swimming with fishes?* She wanted to know why he couldn't get a proper job. Something that started at nine a.m. and finished at five p.m. and meant he could put the boy to bed every other night and then eat dinner with his wife. She didn't seem to understand, or refused to. Four months of hard graft on the mid-Norwegian shelf meant they could take leisurely breakfasts for the rest of the year and he could have Stanley out of her hair as much as she liked. But no. She wanted the cliché. She wanted him in a suit and tie. At the bus stop with the other husbands, reading the newspaper, comparing packed lunches, complaining about the boss. She didn't understand the struggle it had been for him to reach the standard he was at. The years of training. The sacrifices. All of that had been before they'd met. She didn't appreciate that the diving was just a way for him to get from A to B. He was a skilled welder; one of the best. He had worked his nuts off to get to this point in his career. Companies requested him by name.

'What happens when all the oil dries up?' she asked him once. 'Where will the work take you then? Halfway around the world?'

'I'll be long finished before then, Cherry,' he said.

'We will be, you mean.'

And she was right about that. She'd missed out on one cliché but nailed another: the failed marriage to the man who was never around.

Bye Dad. I love you. With orl my hart. See you soon.
Bring me sum Ben 10 stickers. And we can have a fight,
just playing fight. And the chum-chiggle-iggle-um-
ching-cha.

No. No. No.

'No.' The word flipped out of him, like a belch, involuntary. 'No,' he said again, louder. He yelled it so hard that spittle flew across the toughened glass of the window. Now he could see what it was that Rae was crying about. The hatch of the bell had been warped by one of the collisions with the platform. The flanges were rippled like the mantle of an oyster; they would not meet flush with their counterparts on the docking hatch. The bell was repositioned and the locking mechanism secured, but fingers of light poked in around the seal.

Jane shouted out again, shook his head, but either Rae couldn't see him or chose not to. He heard the hiss as bell pressure was increased to ensure a seal that could not be made. He saw the wheel on the hatch begin to turn. Jane spun away, flinching at the sound of their bodies as they unravelled into the hyperbaric chamber. When he was able to look back through the porthole he could see how the hatch in Rae's diving bell had been unable to open beyond three inches. Explosive decompression. Rae and Carver had been turned inside out. Tiny scraps of his friends slid through the red gruel on the window.

Jane staggered back to where he had left Stopper. He positioned a blanket over him, then sat on the bunk. He took up Stanley's letter, folded it carefully and put it in his pocket. He realised he was wiping his hands, though it would have been impossible for any of Rae or Carver's blood to have splashed him.

There was tapping at the hatch. Someone was scooping away the muck from the glass. He staggered over to look through the porthole and saw Gordon McLeish, one of the derrickmen. His face was as red as the coat he was wearing; blood was the filling in a sandwich formed by his lips. Where the bones made angles in his flesh, Jane could not see anything but tight shining skin. He might have been inflated. What looked like spoiling cottage cheese was foaming from his ears and nostrils. There were two bodies behind him, face down. One of them had fallen on his hands, as if he had dropped in the act of fastening his coat buttons. Or if that was what Jane thought it was, piled up bloodily next to him, then maybe he was trying to keep as much as he could from slithering out of whatever rents had appeared in his abdomen.

What was it? Jane mouthed at McLeish, but the other man was too intent on other tasks to be able to answer. He punched buttons on a back-up console that had been plugged into the mains; the central computer must have failed. He was beginning the decompression process. Jane stopped rapping on the glass and let him do his job; it didn't look as though McLeish was likely to be around much longer. Blood was drizzling from the end of his coat sleeves, welling out of the eyelets of his boots.

Jane heard a wail, a gasp, and turned to check on Stopper, but he was still unconscious. It had been the wind chicaning through the struts of the oil platform, howling like something animal, something crazed. It had to be savage as hell for him to be able to hear it through two inches of steel.

McLeish was taking too long. Jane could see him slowing down. At one point he dropped the console and swayed as if he was about to faint, but he put out a hand to stop himself. The oil platform was shifting alarmingly. Jane could imagine the black grin in the leg of the platform that they had been trying to prevent from widening. What would happen if that leg buckled completely? It didn't bear thinking about. He had to turn away. He went back to Stopper and tried to rouse him. He wiped his forehead, checked his vital signs again. Stopper was stable, but he'd wake up with a swine of a headache. Jane patted his pocket and felt the flat comfort of his son's letter. He must not lose that, no matter what.

> *Yor not her to kiss at nighttim but I send you one out the window and I love you Daddy. I have nise drems abowt you, Dad.*

A green light on the hatch door. Decompression was under way. Through the porthole – rapidly filling again with that gritty dense grain – he could see McLeish on his knees, vomiting blood and tissue onto the deck. McLeish who was comically cinematic whenever he played poker, wearing sunglasses to hide the signs his eyes might be giving, turning over his cards after a studied pause. McLeish who would fart in the middle of a tense scene during a film in the theatre and ask everyone if they wanted seconds. There was nothing Jane could do, but he whispered a thankyou anyway.

It was doubtful he'd see this thirty-six hours through. There was only one thing worth doing in this situation. Bolted to the wall between the bunks was a khaki-green metal box, fastened shut with eight screws. The words IN CASE OF EMERGENCY were stencilled in white on the face. Jane worked the screws free with a knife. The lid popped open, revealing a litre bottle of economy whisky bought from a corner shop for under ten pounds. *It would have to be some emergency for you to get me to sup that shite*, Stopper had once said. *It would have to be a real soupy bowel moment.*

Jane cracked the seal and started drinking.

2. PRESSURE

He lay on the floor with Stopper. The ceaseless swaying of the chamber was bearable in that position. He could close his eyes and the freak weather's battering of the oil platform became manageable squalls of sound, like remembered arguments or old plumbing, and he didn't have to look at Stopper's pale skin or congealing wounds. It was just him, his whisky and the incremental dispersal of nitrogen from his blood and tissue.

Jane wondered for a moment what effect alcohol had on the decompression process but as soon as the thought was in him it was gone, replaced by others, seeping through him like gas in the blood. Stanley remained a constant throughout. He was a watermark on pages, indelible; not that Jane wanted him out of his thoughts, but some of the others were inappropriate. He didn't want his boy to share headspace when Saskia Sharkey from his sixth-form days – with her large breasts and talented tongue – flitted through his mind. Stanley oughtn't to be there when Gormley, his first boss, was tearing into him about timekeeping and Jane told him to ram his job. And all those girls he had brought tears to over the years. All those regrets, all that sorry. Maybe this shitstorm of blood and wind was down to him: payback time for being a career bastard.

Trimming the fat from his thoughts, bringing them back to the here and now, served only to alert Jane to the headache thickening behind his eyes. Alcohol for a man under as many kinds of pressure as you cared to mention couldn't be doing him any good. But what it did do, while he was decompressing, was compress his perception of time. That was one of the rare beauties of booze. It provided you with a beer Tardis to flip you forward to a point where you could have a coherent say in matters again.

He was slithering around in a puddle of vomit and couldn't work out who it had come from. It reminded him of Stanley, when he'd been three, just before the end of things. He had been violently sick in his sleep, had woken himself up with it, and had cried out, distressed, panicky. Jane and Cherry had bulldozed into the room to find him sitting up in bed staring in dismay at Walter, his toy lion.

'Walter sicked all over me,' he said. 'Walter sicked all over me.'

It must have been Jane, not Stopper, that had vomited. Both of them were wearing it; it didn't matter. Jane pulled himself upright. The stubble on his chin told him what the clock could not. Was he still drunk, or was the platform still lurching? Had the storm not blown itself out by now? The windows were packed with filth. He tried the radio again out of habit, but already he was ignoring its silence, thinking ahead, wondering when, wondering if. Already he was thinking what might happen if there was nobody left to come and let them out. There was water in a five-pint container. There was no food; the food was always served to them through the airlock at mealtimes. He felt a bite of claustrophobia, a fear he had never, until now, experienced or understood. If the weather should persist, if the platform should fail, back to the seabed he and Stopper would go, with little hope of rescue before they suffocated. Maybe it would be for the best if Stopper did not regain consciousness. He was taking up air that Jane could use. Jane could ... Jane could ...

Could what?

He rubbed his lips and called out. *Hello?* His voice, no longer etiolated by heliox, was scratchy and tired. Scared. Keep your mind away from that. Do not touch. Turn away. The clock wasn't working, so why should the mechanism release? Did fail-safe mean that, if *everything* broke down?

'Stopper?' he said. The bristles on Stopper's face seemed too dark for his alabaster skin; he wished his buddy were blond. 'Stopper?'

Let him sleep. Let him just fade away.

No. Not a great option. *'Stopper!'* Jane knelt beside him and lifted an eyelid. The pupil contracted. OK. Good. He pinched the skin on Stopper's clavicle; Stopper flinched. Better. Jane leaned close. 'Wake up. You lazy fucker.'

Movement. A grey edge of tongue. Jane poured water onto a discarded shirt, pressed it against his friend's forehead. He pressed it against his lips and his mouth worked at it.

'Come on,' Jane said. 'Sit up. Have a drink.'

He managed to get Stopper to lift himself up from the floor. He wore an expression of someone angry without understanding why. Confusion, hunger, muddied things. He was trying to speak but only a fudge of sound fell from his lips.

'Something in the water,' Jane heard eventually. 'My God. Something in the water.'

Over the next few hours Jane coaxed his friend back. Stopper was shaking quite badly – they both were – but Stopper's mouth was shuddering like that of a baby plucked too swiftly into the air. 'I need a drink,' Stopper said, but waved away the water that Jane offered him. 'I need a fucking drink,' he growled. There were a couple of fingers of the economy gut-rot left and, even though Stopper eyed it suspiciously, he necked the lot.

'Can you stand up?' Jane asked. 'We have to try to get out.'

'What about Carver? Rae?' Stopper was smacking his lips as though he'd just been quaffing Châteauneuf-du-Pape.

Jane shook his head. 'Let's concentrate on us for a while. Give or take, we should be clean. If we go fizzy after this long, it'll only be like taking a swig from a bottle of piss-warm Coke. But take it from me, there's nobody left. Nobody came to check on us.'

He could see Stopper beginning to get twitchy, as he had done in the bell before his fall, and he laid a hand on the bigger man's shoulder. 'We have to get out of here. I'm not sure how long the platform is going to remain upright. There's a wind been blowing for the last day and a half that'd tear your face off if you looked at it the wrong way. It doesn't sound as though it's going to let up.'

'You don't just slip the lock in these bastards, Rich,' Stopper said. 'You don't just kick the fucking door off its hinges.'

'The windows, then,' Jane said. 'There's got to be something we can do.'

Stopper was shaking his head, but he stood up and tested the bunk bolted to the wall. 'Fetch me one of them spanners,' he said.

Between them they managed to unscrew the bolts and wrench the bunk clear. Jane tossed the bedding to one side.

'Here,' Stopper said, 'turn that round so we can use that nasty-looking corner. See if we can't ram that into the glass.'

They spent ten minutes trying to crack the porthole, but the glass wasn't even scratching. There was no swearing;

they had both known what the result would be. Stopper tossed the bed into the corner of the chamber; the echo of its collision rang dully. Panic unstitched itself once more in Jane's gut. He wanted to breathe fresh air. He didn't want the stink of cheap whisky fumes and stomach acid to be the last odours to sit in his lungs. And though Stopper was suddenly the only thing between him and being alone, he wished him a thousand miles away. He didn't know what was going to happen once the goodwill and the fire from the whisky were all gone and it became just the two of them and the panic stripping them away, layer by layer, to a point where violence was waiting.

They were painstakingly checking the seals at the hatch on the far side of the chamber, in the hope that the explosive decompression Carver and Rae had suffered might have somehow weakened it, when there was a deep sound they both recognised: the chunk of the hatch tumblers sliding free. They stumbled over each other in their desire to be first out of the door, and Stopper's fist was balled, ready to fight Jane for it, when Jane put out a hand to hold him back.

'Wait,' he said, and held up his other hand in a placatory gesture. 'Stopper, let's just take it slow. We don't know what it was did for the guys out there. If it was a gas leak, maybe.'

'There's nothing on the platform that could take out a whole shift.'

'But something did, right? Something did.'

Stopper sighed and let the tension fall out of him; he seemed to dwindle. 'OK. I just . . . if that's the fail-safe, I just don't want it to unfail-safe itself. You hear me?'

'I hear you. But let's at least get some masks on. The suits too. You didn't see . . . their skin, Stop, their skin was sliding off them.'

They shrugged on their wetsuits and masks, gloves and boots. They checked each other's oxygen tanks and gave each other the OK signal. At the hatch, Jane pulled out his regulator and said, 'Stop, try not to look at what's out there too much. Let's head for the OIM's office and see what's what. Quick as we can.'

He didn't hang around to see if Stopper was following, but took off quickly and almost paid the price for his impatience. The wind on deck was gusting so violently that it swept his feet from under him and took him fully twenty feet towards the guard rails. Part of them had been sheared off either directly by the wind or some piece of hardware driven by it. The rubber suit bit at the deck and brought him to a stop six feet away from his death. He was almost too busy looking at the sky, at the chicanery of violet and green and orange, to notice. *Northern Lights*, he supposed. *This far south?* He thought it more likely that it was the breakdown of cells in his own brain as he lay dying. But he wasn't dying. Not yet.

Stopper had tiptoed down to him, hand-over-hand on the guard rail, and helped him upright. Together they shouldered into the wind, angling towards the block that contained the Offshore Installation Manager's office. Bodies were piled up at the threshold of the door. He could feel the panic creeping through him like cold. He felt he must keep moving or it would consume him. Jane led the way inside, hoping that Stopper would give the dead as short shrift as he had. There were more bodies ranged across the corridors and internal stairs. In a canteen, one man sat hunched over a half-eaten sandwich, his cheeks ballooning, his stomach hanging like a Portuguese man-o'-war from his lips.

Jane could hear his breathing quicken through the regulator. He tried to calm himself by thinking how ridiculous he must look in his diving gear. Some of the toolpushers and roustabouts would pull a muscle if they could see him and

Stopper now. *Gas leak*, he was thinking. *Cyanide? Hydrogen sulphide? Could that change the colour of the sky?*

He slowed as he neared the OIM's office. The control room next to it was utterly still and dark; the windows were packed black with debris. Ricky Melling, the Dynamic Positioning Operator, was slumped over a desk, a welter of his blood dried to glaze like a slab of treacle toffee waiting for the hammer. The swelling of his body had split his jacket up the back seam, the jacket he'd described once as a bit roomy since he'd come off the sauce and started grilling his chicken and chops.

Though everything was dark, Jane tried the lights, the TV, the radios. No response. Wind was getting into this module somewhere; he could hear it howling and rattling around the prefabricated units. It was a wonder they all hadn't been torn off their housings. He was about to leave the control room and move further into the building, to the recreation room, when he saw Eamonn Tate, the OIM, sitting against the wall, his hands in his lap. He seemed to be staring down at them, or perhaps at the pale grey slack of his tongue as it lolled against his chest. Though Jane had been expecting this, to actually see the guy in charge, a guy who was as serene and quiet-talking as they come, broken and bent and capsized, was almost too much to take. Jane crouched down next to him and thought about taking his pulse, but shook his head. No survivors. Just Jane and Stopper. He was turning to tell Stopper this, but he realised he would have to take out the regulator to do so. Stopper wasn't ready for the news anyway, by the look on his face. To confirm what he was already seeing was to invite his utter dislocation.

Jane clapped Stopper on the shoulder and gestured to the door. Stopper followed him. Jane lowered his head against the wind as he edged outside and led the way to the lower decks and the bright orange lifeboats. Jane checked behind him when he was shooting open the bolts on the entrance hatch. Stopper was standing loose, head back, watching the queasy swirl of the sky. He appeared deflated, a bottle of something unstoppered, flat. Now Jane wished he could say something. If Stopper didn't keep his mind on what was happening, a rogue gust was going to pick him up and toss him a couple of hundred feet into freezing water. Jane made a grunting noise around his mouthpiece, waved his arms: Stopper slowly levelled his gaze back on his buddy, but Jane doubted it had anything to do with his pleas for attention. Stopper's eyes were wide open but unseeing. Clouds had formed, despite the wind, pinguid and low, like something thick in a mixing bowl, streaked with the colours of decay. The secret colours he had only ever heard mentioned by his mother and her sisters: taupe, mauve, teal. The clouds sweated greasy rain.

Jane bundled Stopper into the lifeboat and swung the hatch shut. He pressed his fingers against Stopper's regulator to prevent him from spitting it clear, waiting to see if any of the granularity of the sky had followed them inside. What there was settled quickly without the wind to propel it. It settled like a weird matte glitter on their clothes, twinkling dully. Scintillas of quartz, Jane thought. Obsidian. Asbestos. He plucked the regulator out and drew a breath.

'Normal service has been resumed,' he said, trying a smile. Stopper blinked at him. Jane gently tugged free Stopper's mouthpiece; a glut of drool followed it out. The other man didn't protest but regarded him slackly, as if every muscle in his face had been injected with relaxant.

'Buckle up, Stop,' Jane said. In the end, he had to do it for him, pulling the straps tight over flesh that felt deboned, as yielding as a baby's.

Jane secured his own restraints and took a few fast shallow breaths. He hated fairground rides, and the times he'd rehearsed lifeboat drops had left him on the brink of vomiting. There was a lurch, but not his guts, not yet: the oil platform. Something had given way, most likely the leg they had been trying to reinforce. He peered through the hatch and saw the deck of the oil platform tilting towards the sea as the supports folded beneath it. Then a hard jolt and the tilt was halted. Jane reached out and hit the release button, but nothing happened. He punched it again and again. No reaction. It would need to be released manually, from the outside.

He unbuckled his harness and went to the porthole. 'Maybe the sea will wrench us clear,' he said, 'when the platform gives way.'

He looked back at Stopper, who had freed himself and was spinning the wheel of the hatch.

'What are you doing?'

Stopper stopped and slowly turned around as if addressing a fool. 'Uncoupling the boat,' he said.

'But it needs to be done on deck.'

Stopper gestured at the hatch. 'I know.'

'But . . .' Jane had been about to say *you'll die* and had to stop himself. Stopper was in shock. He wasn't thinking straight.

'I *know*,' said Stopper. 'I'm not going with you. I'll set you free.'

'What do you fucking mean, you're not going? We're a team. I'm taking you off this platform. Now sit down and buckle up, or I swear' – he unsheathed the fire extinguisher from the wall – 'I'll deck you stone cold with this cunt.'

He turned back to the window. What bothered him most about Stopper's act of bravery wasn't that his friend would die but that Jane would be left alone. He wasn't sure he could face that, especially with the electrics on the boat shot, relying on the violence of the waves to take them to shore.

They hadn't discussed the madness of this, but they had gravitated to the boats because that was what happened in an emergency. It was their only way off the platform, the only hope for survival. At some point there'd be a rescue attempt. Better to be warm and dry in an eye-catching orange capsule than a corpse pinned to the seabed by a thousand tons of steel. Better to . . .

He felt a spray of something hot against his cheek, and Stopper was saying, 'OK, so can I go *now*?'

There was other stuff in the First Aid box. Chocolate, Kendal Mint Cake, a vacuum-sealed pack of raisins. Water. Jane eyed the bandages and plasters and dressings. None of them any use. He was sitting hunched in his seat, surrounded by a slurry of vomit. He had emptied his bowels too, unable to control himself through a fit of retching that he'd thought might turn him inside out. There was a lot of blood sprayed across the walls, a scary amount, given that Stopper had taken just a few seconds to turn the hatch wheel and duck out into the wind. Then the thunk of locking pins being hammered free and the drop into the ocean that he could not now recall, despite his fear of it. The scissors from the First Aid box were rattling around the floor, sticky with the blood that Stopper had cut out of his body. His severed artery had hung like the ragged end of a rubber hose in the exposed meat of his forearm.

Jane had been unable to say anything. Maybe this was all down to nitrogen in his blood. Maybe this was how your brain dealt with things when a million bubbles were expanding in its folds. If only.

Somehow he managed to sleep a little, although he supposed it was more a kind of unconsciousness, a turning away. He was able to sip some water and nibble a little mint cake during momentary lulls in the violence. The sugar fortified him, persuaded him that he wasn't dying, that the iridescent chips in the air were not going to cause his lungs to rupture.

He kept the restraints firmly fastened. The boat was tossed so violently that he doubted he'd survive should he free himself. He couldn't be sure if the boat had turned turtle at all; it didn't really matter. It was sealed. It wasn't sinking. The hull was the same colour no matter which way was up. Nobody had died – as far as he knew – from a surfeit of Big Dippers and Corkscrews. The storm must abate soon. Somebody must come to rescue him. If the oil platform did not topple, the helicopters would see that a boat had been launched. It couldn't be long. The thought of drifting far out into the North Sea and never being picked up he could not host. Nor consideration that a capitulation such as Stopper's was something that would become more attractive to him.

He pulled the letter from his pocket. He struggled to read it in the endless vibration and shuddering of the boat but studied it four or five times anyway. Stanley stayed with him. There could be no letting go while his boy waited at home for him. He would not see his letter lacking a response. The smell of his scalp; the shape of his slim shoulders under his father's hands. Machine-gun laughter whenever he was tickled.

dad, can we tak the tent to the bech soon and hav a picnik lik befor but not get sand in the food. remember we plad futbal and I scord ten gols. can we have a baby soon. a boy I dont lik gerls.

Cherry, flat-line mouth, lifting the boy's pudgy hand to wave goodbye. Cherry, unable to lift a hand of her own. 'You're pulling us down,' she told him. 'I don't want to be a part of a family that has a corner of its triangle missing.'

'I'm not missing. I'm working,' he reasoned. 'Who paid for that leather jacket you love so much? Who bought us the extension to our house? Who bought the Audi you've christened Mungo?'

'It's my house. Dad bought it for me.'

'It became ours when we married, Cherry. We share everything. That's what marriage is all about. Read the small print.'

'Marriage.' She spat the word as if it were something spoiled she had put in her mouth. 'This is no marriage. This is me skivvying at home while you swan off for a piss-up with your Aberdeen cronies.'

He'd been unable to counter that. She must break down and start laughing soon, he had thought. She must just be kidding. 'We can afford to get help in,' he had managed at last. 'You don't have to lift a finger.'

'I'm lifting this finger,' she said, and showed him her wedding ring. She slipped it off and tossed it to him.

'Think of Stanley,' he told her. 'What this will do to him.'

'I *am* thinking of Stanley,' she said. 'He wants a dad, not some lodger who brings him an expensive toy every couple of months. He's growing up and you're missing it.'

'I'm providing for my family,' he said, but the anger had been punched from him. She was right. He was missing it, but it wasn't his fault. It was called sacrifice. You put up with the cold and shitty work and bad food and loss of hearing in order to give your loved ones a better path in life. Why was she unable to see this?

And then Stanley stumbling in, all smiles. 'Hello, Daddy, Daddy, you're a green paste.' And laughter and wrestling and Cherry looking down on them both, lachrymose, statue-cold.

He had talked her round a little. She agreed to a trial separation, that sad old cliché. So he'd ended up moving out, which was what she was criticising him for in the first place, and he took off to Aberdeen and put his name down for as many shifts as he was medically fit to work.

He'd always believed it would be different for him, whenever he had listened to the bitching and the bitterness among the oil platform's divorced club. But he supposed there were always going to be trends, likelihoods, destinies. You work away from home for long enough, then you might as well be a stranger. You were the shadow on the wall, the flicker in the mirror. You were the empty place at the table and the awkward question at bedtime. He could see what it was she didn't like. It was a male world, working the rigs. There was a lot of industrial language. A lot of bawdy talk and banter. Off the helicopter, after a shift, back on the Aberdeen soil, men unwound quickly. You could see them, refracted through glasses of amber, unspooling as if their bodies, if not their minds, were celebrating coming back from the brink. It was as if, at any moment, they might float away into the sky. They needed all those atmospheres of water on their backs just to stay in one place. And there were women, in Aberdeen, all too willing to provide a lap for a weary diver's head.

Jane slept a little, he ate a little, he drank a little. He cried a lot. He screamed when he wasn't vomiting; it helped. He kept one bloodshot eye on the porthole, craving the weathered bow of a rescue vessel, or the beat of a helicopter rotor turning the surface to shivering skin. But instead it was swell after swell of convulsing ocean. He could be anywhere. He could be drifting north towards the Arctic. A pure childish fear had reawakened in him, gripped him to the point of numbness. But at some point he seemed to switch off and everything that had been conspiring to make him feel alive – the fear and hunger, the panic, the hope – shrivelled like a pupil in bright light.

Stanley stood in his red pyjamas at the end of some horribly long corridor, Walter the lion hanging from his tiny fist. His eyes were like the portholes in the Ceto, unstable, crawling. The filth shifted upon them like iron filings on a bed of magnets. He was speaking, but the words were spoiled by the misery in his voice. Sometimes Jane had to sit and soothe him for five or ten minutes when he was like this, until Stanley's chest stopped hitching and he was able to make out what was wrong. It was usually thirst, or dreams of being left behind, of not being able to catch up during a walk to the shop or the park. Sometimes it was that uncomplicated need for human closeness. A hug, reassurance. *Stay with me all night, Daddy. Don't go.*

He felt himself clench inside that he had not always done as his son asked. Little things, really. But important to Stanley, which should have mattered more at the time. He could have stroked his hair, slept with him until morning, but there was always a perceived crisis elsewhere.

He had always believed he carried childishness in him, that he had never truly grown up, but the opposite was the case. He was all too quick to finish the game, pack away the toys, curtail the rough and tumble. There was always something else that needed doing. And now he was near death and his boy was 500 miles away. It pierced him to think there would be no more hide-and-seek or piggyback rides.

Perhaps there had been footage of the storm on the TV and Cherry was either shielding him from it or gleefully pointing out that had Jane found a job on a building site in London Daddy wouldn't be in trouble.

Stanley in the corridor, putting out a hand to the wall to steady himself. His voice shattered by fear. 'Dad? Dad? I'm scared.'

'It's all right, Stan,' Jane said. 'I'm with you.'

3. DEAD CLADE WALKING

He was thinking about beaches on the west coast of France. Long and white and narrow like ivory letter-openers. Stanley no more than six months old, sitting in the sand with a large floppy cricket hat casting a broad shadow. Cherry snoozing on her back in a black bikini, skin shining with sun cream. The heat pressing people into the ground. A blanket and some baguettes, some cheese. A jar of anchovies. Christ, he had been mad for anchovies that summer. A bottle of Muscadet in a cool bag. The air thin and baked, stripping the throat dry. Sweat dried as soon as it escaped the pores. He had watched the sea for a long time, that strange illusion of the horizon seeming to rear up higher than the leading edge of the tide, as if it was a wall of water. He had been wishing he could go diving in water like that, instead of the cloudy, frigid swill of the North Sea.

He remembered the Gulf of Mexico and the fish that came to ogle him while he trained in the clear warm sea. When was that . . . '93? '94? He had worked with a guy called Erubiel, a Mexican from Lagos de Moreno who had not wanted to take over his father's dairy. The smell of milk made him sick. He just wanted to dive and then watch girls on the beaches of Pensacola during his time off. Erubiel was a good diving buddy, if a little hot-headed. He was methodical when it came to checking Jane's gear, but when it came to his own, he trusted to God. 'I drive carefully when I carry a passenger,' he said. 'When I'm on my own? Safety? *Chupame la verga.*'

Erubiel used to tap Jane on the head whenever he wanted his attention. He did it all the time. Tap, tap, tap. He was doing it now. And that was funny, because Erubiel had ended up in a wheelchair. Jane had received a postcard from his father a couple of years later when Jane had been building a reputation with his burning gear on drilling rigs near the Shetlands. There had been an accident on a rig in Campeche Sound. A gas leak. A dozen men had died. Erubiel leapt from the rig and the drop crushed his spine. Now he could sit and watch girls all day, but that was pretty much all he could do.

Tap, tap, tap.

Pack it in, Ruby. Give it a rest.

Jane opened his eyes. His head was slapping against the edge of the chair. But it was more rhythmical now, less violent. Gone was the arbitrary shearing of deep-sea currents, a sickening, jolting pitch and yaw. This was a shallow-water beat. This was land ahoy.

He scrabbled for the harness release and tumbled out of his chair to the floor, which was now the portside wall. He couldn't see anything out of the porthole there; starboard was the queasy flux of the sky. But at least the howling had stopped. He staggered through the ruins of the boat, remembering to snatch up the green First Aid box. His legs felt as though they might pitch him into the slough of filth beneath him; he was grateful to have become inured to the stench hours ago. Hours. How long had he been asleep? How long had he drifted? He checked his watch. Midday.

7th December. Five days since he and his crew had lumbered back to the diving bells, panic at their heels. Where had that time gone? He must have spent most of it unconscious. He checked the gauge on the oxygen tanks and jammed the regulator back in his mouth. Hunger and thirst slapped him around the face while he struggled to spin open the hatch wheel. Steak and eggs and fried potatoes and a pint of best bitter. He pulled on a pair of latex gloves. A last look out of the porthole. He jerked up the hood on his coverall, readjusted his diving mask and pushed open the door.

It took a long time to get used to the still ground. For a while Jane trudged around on the beach where he had fetched up, the uncertainty of his tread in the sand a weird kind of comfort, a training ground for his balance. Part of his hanging around near the boat was down to his not being sure where he was. He didn't know if this was the UK, or Norway, or Nova Scotia. He didn't know what to do. The brutality of the wind on the oil platform had not followed him here, but it was still rough. It was hot, too, like the blast you got when you opened an oven to check the pizzas weren't burning.

He hid his face from the squalls of rain, but occasionally some of it would bite him and he'd have to swipe it away quickly with his gloved hands before it started to burn. Holes began to appear in the latex. He discarded them quickly. What the fuck was this? What the fuck had happened?

After a while spent scanning an horizon that resembled more the jag of an oscilloscope reading, Jane scrambled up an embankment of brown grass. The land appeared to have been sanded back to polished lava. He couldn't see much once he'd breasted the rise; a mist clung to the headland, erasing all but the darkest shadows of the near coast in both directions. He could see a road though, and he hurried towards it. British tarmac, he was sure. He felt a pulse of optimism. He was on home turf, at least. He got onto the road and saw a car parked half a mile to the north, slewed across both lanes as if it had braked suddenly, and hard. He trotted gamely towards it – UK number plate, which was a boon of sorts – but gradually his speed faltered as he saw the passengers. Both had attempted to get out of the car. One had succeeded but was lying on his back about ten feet away, a mousse of lung tissue and blood streaked across his face and shirt. His companion was still buckled in, although the strap had disappeared into the soufflé of her flesh. Her eyes drilled into him, poached, piscine. Her hand was a lobster claw hooked into the catch of the door. Both of them glittered like pixie-dust confections. The woman's head was jerking in the fierce slaps of wind, her charred hair jinking on a red-raw scalp like a fright wig. The tyres of the car had melted into the road. So whatever had killed his colleagues on the platform had done for these too. Not isolated, then. So, what? Nuclear? Was this a nuclear attack? Was this chemical warfare? Was this biological?

Jane reached into the car, hands shaking, and tried not to look at the woman any more. He was glad of his face mask, that he didn't have to smell her. He turned the key, but, as he expected, there was no response from the engine. Backing away, he swung his gaze north, wondering if he should head up to Aberdeen, but his initial impulse was to find immediate shelter, maybe a phone that still worked. Maybe a car or a motorbike. He followed the road south and his heart lifted to find a row of pretty cottages behind a bluff of land. A small harbour with a surrounding stone wall. Small boats had become driftwood. There were bodies in there too, face down. He wasn't sure if he should be grateful for that.

At the first of the stone cottages, he peered through the window, but there was nobody to be seen. He knocked on the door and the sound startled him. The skin on the back of his hands was striated, as if he had thrust it into a bed of thorns. Nobody was coming to answer. It didn't matter how many doors he tried. He rested his forehead against the blistered wood for a second. Closed his eyes. He went around the side of the house to the back. He climbed over the fence into a neatly tended garden. The lawn was a fried brown square. Washing on a line was pitted and scorched. A man was on his knees, toppled over against a chimney pot that contained a plant now little more than a few black tongues. The man's left hand was distended; blood had flowed and dried around the vanishing tourniquet of a watch strap. His fingers were purple, swollen and shiny like baby aubergines. Attached to a kennel by a chain, a peeled thing with too many teeth lay on its side, flanks scorched down to purple bone.

Jane strode past the man and pushed open the back door. The kitchen was halved by light that no longer existed. Whatever had torn across the coast had left an impression of itself here, like the discoloration that sunshine creates on the cover of a forgotten book on a windowsill, only much, much more swiftly. The dining table was a duotone of caramel and coffee. The plastic jug of a fruit-juicing machine had turned into a molten Dali nonsense. Envelopes on the table showed him where he was: Burnmouth, Berwickshire, which he knew to be a good 200 miles south of Aberdeen.

He moved through the house, checking each room, but he didn't know what he was seeking. He saw the shape of a child's bed in a room painted blue but did not dare look inside. Something wrong with whoever lived here. Inhalers and gas cylinders and endotracheal tubing. Tube holders like dog muzzles. Rows of medicines. Bleak textbooks. Volumes of hope.

On a table in another bedroom lay a book of photographs. Smiling faces. Oblongs of love protected by cellophane. A wasting girl in a white hospital gown. Eyes weighted with dark underscores. A smile fought for.

He checked with his fingers for the photographs of Stanley in his wallet but could not bring himself to produce them. It was enough to know they were there.

He felt a moment of mild panic when he thought of his parents. They were in their seventies, living in an industrial town in the north-west. Both were succumbing to the kind of low-level health problems that had increased the number of pillboxes in their bathroom cabinet and visits to the GP's surgery. Both had talked to him, casually, almost in passing, of what he should do if and when. They had set up a trust fund for Stanley. Ash in a vault, now, perhaps. He suddenly felt that he ought to go to them first; they were nearer, they were his parents. Whatever had burned this part of the east coast might have been pegged back by the Pennines. But no – Stanley had to be his priority. Either his parents were alive, or they were dead. He couldn't think that way of his little boy. Stanley had survived this. He must go to him.

There was a bookshelf in the hallway. Volumes about birds of prey. A plate of keys. Maps. He sifted through them and found the village. At the top of the cliffs overlooking the harbour, the East Coast Main Line railway and the A1 ran parallel to each other, south along the Berwickshire coast.

He picked up a phone and put it to his ear but he was no longer listening. Downstairs he opened the refrigerator and checked the contents. Everything was spoiled. He picked through the tins in the cupboard and put some of them in his rucksack. He wanted to spit out the regulator; the synthetic sound of his own breath was a constant reminder of how close he was to losing it. It was too early to see if the ambient air was breathable, but he would have to find fresh tanks soon or prepare himself for an experiment.

Jane went back outside and broke the lock on the shed. Inside he found pricking pots containing seeds that would never come on, a couple of poorly maintained gardening tools and a metal box filled mainly with Rawlplugs and drill bits whitened by masonry. A dusty table with thin legs bore a pile of papyrus-dry Sunday supplements and a coffee cup with the legend *No. 1 Grandpa*. There was a bicycle with dribbling tyres. In a drawer he found a combination lock, a bottle holder and a bracket, and an anti-pollution mask with a packet of replacement filters. He pocketed these and stared at the shelves on the wall, the tools on the shelves. Nothing of any use. Nothing he knew how to use well enough to make it useful. He stared through the cracked, foxed window into the garden, and the dog and the man were softened to a point where they might still be alive. The man finishing off a little work on his hosta; the dog stretched out, enjoying a snooze. If he stayed here long enough maybe he could will the world back into true. Going back outside could only lead to more awful discoveries.

He closed the door and stood in the lane. He kept thinking of the man in the garden. *No. 1 Grandpa*. He imagined a daughter and her child coming to visit and finding him like that, roasted to the bone. He went around the side of the house to the garden and retrieved a spade from the shed. He dug a grave. It took a long time. By the end of it he was sweating so much he could not get a sense of his own skin. His breath churned through the regulator; perspiration pooled in his diving mask.

He dragged the old man to the lip of the hole and drew him into it as gently as he could. He hesitated, the spade in his hand, before arranging the dog alongside him. Then he filled in the hole and smoothed the earth flat with the blade.

He stared at his work, his raw fingers gripping the ash timber handle. He felt eyes on him, a heat on his shoulders, but when he turned the windows were empty. Just the eyes of the house then. Just the enormity of what had happened, massing.

Jane walked along the front of the other cottages, cupping his hands to the glass where it wasn't broken in order to see inside. Only in the last house in the line did he see anybody in the living room, a woman in an armchair, her body swollen into it as if she were a pile of badly fitted cushions. Her head was tilted back so he could only see the inverted V of her chin. He left the street and walked past a small roofed bus shelter and a red postbox on a wooden pole. He began the long steep ascent of the road to Upper Burnmouth and concentrated on his boots, one foot in front of the other. He had not eaten for some time. Fainting here might be the last thing he ever did.

At the top of the cliff the ribbon of the road held hands with the railway as far as he could see. The rails had buckled in places. No birds, no cats, no dogs. He stared at the village and thought about why he had survived. Something had roasted the face of the Earth while he'd been at the bottom of the sea. So what had saved him? Water? Then why so many dead fish? Depth, then. That must have been it. He knew, talking to some of his mates on the rig, that this area of the coast had been a popular landing point for smugglers. The precipitous cliffs and numerous inlets were a blessing to boats bringing in contraband. The place must have been riddled with cellars and secret tunnels. Maybe some were deep enough to survive in. At the very least he might find a serviceable bike.

Jane crossed the railway and spotted a pub on the other side of the dual carriageway. The planes of roofs were like broken solar panels. A tree burned. The mist north of here was thickening, congealing almost, like something that he might have to peel off his skin should he be captured by it. To the south the sky was more fluid. It moved constantly. Cables of rain glittered from it like guys slung to the earth. Out to sea the waves were still churning; their roar a persistent complaint over the noise of his own breath. The mist shifted again, lifting slightly, enough to show him a suggestion of hills to the north, shoulders turned away from him. The mist closed in again as if it were teasing him with glimpses of things forbidden.

Jane hurried across the road. He could hear his breath hissing in the regulator. He wondered if he was panicking or in the early stages of shock, but he couldn't tell; he had no frame of reference. There was nobody to talk to, nobody against whom he could gauge his level of fragility. Nobody to give him an askance look. Not that anybody would be in any fit state themselves to decide what was normal any more. Panic might now well be the new default setting.

He pushed through the door into the lounge bar as the mist sweated in the air behind him, as though eager to assume form. A cleaner lay on the floor in a pale blue pinafore now several sizes too small for her. Her face was that of someone beaten featureless; everything was lost to a uniform swelling. Her cheeks shone, at splitting point. Jane felt the world tilt a little, as if he were in a fast lift that had just begun to ascend. His vision vignetted. He closed his eyes. He must get used to this. There were bound to be others. Christ, where were the emergency services? He felt, like a blow to the gut, the suspicion that this village, maybe even the entire north-east coastline, had been closed off, quarantined. What could have caused this? It was a question that kept tapping him on the shoulder; every so often he felt he had to turn to confront its ugly little face, but he couldn't provide any satisfactory answers. Terrorism, he thought again. If so, they'd succeeded. He was scared beyond feeling. The nuclear power plant at Dounreay? Meltdown? A nuclear sub off Cape Wrath playing war games? Could an exploded sub rip the skin off the face of Scotland like this? He was no defence expert, but he didn't think so. Something natural, then? Some catastrophic event?

He stared at the bruised air streaking by the windows, the glittering sediment piling into the corners. This didn't look natural; this was a storm on Venus. This was Ray Bradbury.

He was on his knees. His left leg was pinning the cleaner's left arm to the floor. The added pressure had caused her clenched hand to open; clear fluid sweated from the tips of her fingers like glue bubbling from the sponge applicator of a UHU pen. He couldn't breathe.

He swung the O_2 gauge in front of his face and blearily registered that he was in the red, sucking on the tank's dust. He fumbled the bicycle mask from his backpack and held his breath, spat out the regulator, took off his face mask and clamped the filter over his nose and mouth. He breathed. There was a smell of burning, and something underpinning it, something chemical. His sight cleared, his lungs loosened. At least there was still something left to breathe in the midst of all this smog.

Behind the bar he drew a double whisky from an optic and gulped it quickly before replacing the mask, relishing the hot fumes that were trapped inside. He moved down a corridor to the doorway to the toilets. To his left was a door leading into the beer garden. Somebody was dead out there. He could just see a pair of legs sticking out from the side of a Vauxhall Corsa. To his left was a door under the stairs. A bolt on it was drawn back, an unhinged padlock hanging off the hasp. He flicked the bakelite switch above the banister without thinking and descended slowly in utter darkness.

Jane called out when he reached the bottom of the stone steps. His voice was loud and flat and scared. Nothing replied. He reached out with his hands and moved into a cool room. His foot clanged against what he assumed was a beer keg. Further on there were crates of bottles and a wooden door. He pushed against it. Inside there were plastic containers, mops, brushes, heavy tins. He felt along the walls for a resting bike, but there was nothing. Light filtered through the cracks in the delivery chute and shapes began to solidify. A chest freezer filled with melted sacks of ice. A fuse box on a wall next to a graphic of a skeleton being electrocuted. A deckchair. A child's scooter.

Jane unfolded the deckchair and sat down. He thought about going upstairs, checking the bedrooms, but he didn't know what for. All he knew was that he would find more bodies, and he didn't want to look at a dead child.

His hand went to his pocket and felt the edges of Stanley's letter. Stanley had been asking for a scooter, as well as a bike without stabilisers, a skateboard . . . all kinds of stuff. His 'I want' phase. There were all kinds of petty aches that broadsided you as a parent. It pierced Jane that Stanley didn't want to watch the programmes aimed at his age group on TV. Dora the Explorer. Pingu. Noddy. A couple of weeks at reception and he was coming home talking about Power Rangers and Ben 10 and Darth Maul kicking people in the face. Guns and punches. He was calling people *stupid* and *poo-head*. He was a boy growing up, that was all, but it was tough to stomach sometimes. Innocence eroding. You could see it in the darkening intelligence of his eyes and the disappearance of his pudgy cheeks. The baby's clean blackboard was filling up with chalk marks. *Dad? When you called that man in the car a tit, what means tit?*

He wondered if London was aware of what was going on

up here. It was such a terrible occurrence, perhaps Whitehall was shielding the public from the truth.

Jane peeled off the gloves and touched his face, his hair. He felt normal, if a little hot and sweaty. He considered how he felt inside. He was hungry, which was a good thing, he thought. He didn't feel nauseous. Apart from the burns on his hands where the gloves had melted, there were no blemishes on his skin. No headaches, or rather, no pains inside his head that couldn't be dismissed by a couple of co-codamol.

He unclipped the lid of the First Aid box and cleansed the skin of his hands with an alcohol wipe. There was an unbroken tube of antiseptic cream; he applied some of that too. Care needed to be taken now. If he fell and broke his leg there was nobody around to cart him off to A&E. And he didn't relish the prospect of any wounds sucking the filth of the sky into them. Slow and sure.

He peeled back the lid on a tin of baked beans and guzzled them straight down. He followed them with a tin of peaches. He found a crate of Pinot Noir and unscrewed a bottle top.

He and Cherry had discussed death, early on, when things had been good between them and dying naturally at an old age seemed something that one of them would do with the other close by. But they had also talked about what-ifs. They had both written private letters to Stanley and sealed them without reading each other's words. In the event that one of them died prematurely, Stanley would at least have a message from his missing parent, a way of making contact with a son who might otherwise have no recollection of a dead mother or father.

Jane fell asleep imagining Cherry handing over the envelope to their son.

4. THE GREAT NORTH ROAD

Jane woke suddenly, into terror. The jolt from sleep was down to some external factor, not a bad dream, not a gradual returning from unconsciousness. He knew this feeling: Stanley grizzling in his cot. Cherry knocking over the pot of toothbrushes in the bathroom. A sound had brought him back. Something near. He sat up in the deckchair and felt his muscles complain. No light in the cracks of the delivery chute. The luminous hands of his watch shrugged at him: ten past two in the morning.

He hadn't thought to equip himself with a weapon, but maybe he needed to. What if there were squads of armed soldiers sweeping the area, briefed with orders to shoot any survivors to prevent the leak of damning information? He clenched his eyes tight. Nothing was too bizarre now.

The sound came again. A scrabbling, a skittering. Like loose plaster. Maybe that was all it was. He called out. His voice sounded nothing like his own. He felt already that he was losing the sense of who he was. He had made a place for himself in the world, defined himself by his job, his behaviour, his appearance. All of that was shot to pieces. There were no rules now. There were no guidelines. For the first time in his life he had no idea of what might happen. Probability had become obsolete.

Jane stood up and there was a responsive scratching noise. Mice, he thought. Or rats. Probably as spooked as him to find something breathing in the neighbourhood. He climbed the steps back into the pub and felt his way in the dark to the foot of the stairs leading up to the living quarters. There was a bathroom here. He tried the taps. Cold water sputtered and gushed into the basin. He peeled off his clothes and the bicycle mask and, holding his breath, splashed his face, feeling the growth of a week's worth of stubble. He towelled himself dry and replaced the mask. He moved through to a bedroom and opened a wardrobe, grabbed a handful of shirts and tried one on. Too large, but at least it was clean. It made him feel happier. He stole some jeans and a belt and pulled on his own boots. A long leather coat and leather gloves. There was a mound on the bed; he left it undisturbed. On a dressing table was a tea light in a red glass container. He lit it with a wax-coated match from the First Aid box. He avoided the bedroom door dotted with Spider-Man stickers and drew his shivering shadow along the corridor to the living room.

The living room was large; a dining table and an upright piano dominated one half. A fruit bowl contained mouldering shapes; their smell was cloying, dusty almost. A woman in black underwear was reclining on the sofa, a magazine opened on the floor beside her. A mug. A bar of chocolate. She glittered at him, her flesh pitted with shards of glass from an exploded window. He went to it and looked out at the silent village. Lightning pulsed in the clouds like something trapped, desperate to be set free. It afforded him views of desolation. Cars turned over in the road, windshields spidered with cracks, tyres gone. Bodies lay in the street. A house burned: restive orange eyes shivering in blistered sockets. Behind him, a page of the magazine turned. He imagined the woman stroking the ball of her thumb across the death-dry edge of her swollen tongue. He removed the mask and vomited hard. He spat and choked against the fire in his throat and nostrils, then rinsed his mouth with water from a bottle. He trudged downstairs and pushed his way out into the street. A bicycle could wait. He didn't want to stumble upon any more nasty little surprises in these homes. *Get pounding. Put some miles under you.*

Jane was grateful of the dark as he made his way to the edge of the village and onto the dual carriageway. Suggestions and shapes and murmurs remained so. The sea was an urgent incessant booming to his left, restless beneath a sky that, even at night, roiled with sombre colours, a melancholy oil painting failing to dry.

The A1 would take him all the way to London. The thought of a ribbon of tarmac connecting this shattered community with his son's feet quickened his blood. He imagined his boy sitting on the doorstep of the flat in Sevington Street, with Walter, grubby and matted, next to him. The big smile when he saw his dad. The leap into his arms. His little boy, so light, as he swung him up for a kiss. The astonishing colour of his eyes. Baize-green with an outer rim of cobalt. Freckles and milk teeth. He could feel his warmth, could smell the magic of his hair, his scalp.

Jane suddenly, reflexively, shouted his son's name. He realised he was running, sprinting, as if he might cover the hundreds of miles between here and Maida Vale before dawn. He wanted his boy so badly that he thought his heart would clench itself into a knot. Tears drizzled across his vision; he had to stop. He dropped to his knees and cried so violently that it felt as though he had pulled a muscle in his chest. He was nodding. Cars and lorries and coaches threw freakish shapes across the lanes for miles in either direction.

He wished he'd been caught in this. He wished he had never left his family. He cursed the moment he had signed up for diving lessons and applied for a job on the rigs. He wished he had been infertile and had never met Cherry. He wished for utter oblivion.

'I know,' he said. 'I know.'

He was fooling himself. This was no isolated event. The whole country had been hit by this. *Depth*, he thought. Cherry might have taken their son on the Tube. He might be safe. He must be safe.

Jane kept his eyes on the ground and watched it disappear under his feet. At the English border he passed three flagpoles bearing flapping black scraps; a blistered sign might have bade welcome to his country. He did not look up. He didn't know how far he had walked before the light changed and began to creep across the rocky coastline and seep through the mist, to bring edges to the darkness. He rummaged in cars, trying not to touch their ruptured occupants, until he found a pair of sunglasses in a glove compartment. All the time he was trying to quell his panic, trying to assess himself for the signs of shock. It would be almost criminal to survive whatever had happened only to succumb to heart failure. When the traffic became too much for him to deal with, he cut across a field to the railway. The rain came again; it never really went away, just a variation between gossamer breath and tropical muscle.

At Berwick-upon-Tweed he climbed up onto the railway station platform and angled along Castlegate. He had to step over the bodies of three people who had dropped dead in the entrance of a Somerfield supermarket. The windows had survived but were little more than opaque mosaics. Rats had been at the corpses' faces and fingers. Rats too had ransacked the shelves. Plastic-wrapped loaves of bread had become culture specimens. Popcorn had exploded out of its microwave-ready packaging and created a foam in the aisle. Racks of vacuum-sealed ham slices were molten twists of biltong. Cans were pitted and scarred. He saw a tooth embedded in a plastic container of washing detergent. The newspapers and magazines were shredded, leeched of colour.

The freezers had all failed. The smell of rot permeated the bicycle mask, but it didn't spoil his hunger. He headed into the storage space at the back of the shop; here there were tinned foods that had survived any damage. He wrenched open the thing nearest to him: a can of pilchards; wolfed them down. He hated pilchards, but flavour and texture meant nothing: he couldn't taste anything beyond the chemical coating that layered his throat. He ate a can of corned beef and a can of pears. He felt the flakiness that comes with low blood sugar dissipate. He welcomed the false optimism that always accompanied a full stomach. He searched the delivery bay at the back of the shop and found a dead man who had been welding a broken railing to a gate. His goggles were by his side; Jane put them on, discarding the sunglasses. He transferred a Stanley knife from the tool bag to his rucksack. He moved back through the shop and found a crate of glass bottles of water, shrink-wrapped plastic torched off. He drank half a litre; it tasted funny – maybe it had boiled inside the glass – but he kept it down. He placed a couple of the bottles in his rucksack.

Jane stopped in the town centre at a camping shop and took a waterproof coat and hat. He found some more gloves; the current ones smelled scorched, were already weakened across the backs where the rain had settled. He thought again about a weapon, not for use against any foe – he doubted that the rats would grow any more confrontational – but as reassurance, insurance. He had the Stanley knife but he didn't think he could use that; it would be too much like an insult to Stopper's memory.

He walked down to the parade of shops, but there was no chance of a gun here. Again he thought of breaking into some houses; surely there were hunters in this bucolic part of the country? His own grandfather had owned a shotgun, and he was from industrial Widnes. But he didn't feel as though he could stomach the inevitable bodies. Or perhaps it was something else. Perhaps it was the fear of finding someone alive.

He shuddered, shook the feeling out of himself. It was just an inevitable result of so much open space. You grew used to the silence quickly, especially coming a little inland, away from the waves. You went beyond that super-attenuated aspect, flinching at every sound, every shadow. You learnt the beats of the humdrum quickly. It would spook him now, to see someone moving through the streets, or hear them calling to him from a rooftop. But he had to hold on to the hope. Accidents happened. People survived. It could only be a matter of time.

No hope here, though. The soles of his feet slapped echoes around the walls. He thought he could hear his own breath reflected back at him but it might have been the churning sea, still audible over half a mile away. Skirls of glistering dust swept along the street, creating little dunes and hillocks where it met overturned cars, doorways, corpses. Behind a bus slewed across the thoroughfare, Jane was shocked and excited to see a horse lying at the mini-roundabout on Marygate, where the West Road reached out across the old bridge. The horse seemed badly injured, but there was life in it yet; it was struggling to get up. Jane hurried to it, wondering if it might help him to cover ground more quickly if he could nurture it back to health. He stopped twenty feet shy of the creature, hope puddling out of him. The horse was dead. What he had thought was life was the writhing of rats animating the horse from within. He turned away sharply and followed the road south, wondering how long it might be before he was given the same treatment.

He crossed the river Tweed via the railway viaduct. He stopped counting bodies in the water when he reached fifty. A train was halted halfway across the bridge. Burnt strips of curtain danced from the left-hand windows. As he neared the train he saw a woman's arm resting casually on the window frame, fingers splayed slightly as if she had been holding an apple. Something, perhaps the rain, perhaps a crow or rat, had stripped the flesh to the bone. He strode past the windows, boots crunching on gravel and glass, and did not look in at the sunken creatures in their seats. He stepped around more bodies that had either been thrown free of the train or had jumped *in extremis*, perhaps with their lungs already boiling up in their throats.

He was beginning to wish that he had stayed on the road, but a glance to the parallel bridge showed him traffic piled up; an articulated lorry jackknifed, hanging over the side, somehow defying gravity. Jane kept his eyes on the horizon, looking for a break in the mist, a return to normal cumulonimbus and cirrus. Already, the thought of blue skies was difficult to remember. The colour seemed too unnatural, too bizarre. Everything was muted, dun. There was nothing to claim his attention: no boats offering rescue, no packs of rescuers hunting through the wreckage for survivors. Only the heat and the diffuse light in those deep-shade zones of rust and ochre, fading now, suggested that it was daytime. Lightning skittered on the underside of the cloud mass, like a white spider clinging to the ceiling. More fires raged in a cluster of houses on the south bank of the river. Smoke rose from others nearby; the rain was doing nothing to check the flames. Jane wondered if its astringent qualities were feeding them in some way.

At the other side of the viaduct he checked his watch. Gone three-thirty. How much ground had he covered? He checked his map. Five miles, roughly. Slow going, but still he was exhausted. It would take a long time to come back from these past five days; perhaps he never would, fully. He didn't want to be walking in darkness if he could help it. A trip might result in a broken ankle, or a bloodied face. He doubted even his basic qualification in First Aid would help him if he was infected with some of the filth swirling around the sky.

Jane found an inn at the fork of Main Street and Dock Road and kicked in the door, wondering for a foolish second if he should have knocked first. Close to rest now, he felt exhaustion turning his sight grainy. His feet were heavy on the stairs. On the first floor he opened doors into rooms until he found one that was unoccupied. The windows were shattered, but the wind coming in from the sea was wailing against the back of the inn. He sat at the dressing table and wiped the mirror clean with his forearm. A wild man stared back, hair greasy and lank, fringing eyes that were deep-set, red-rimmed, grey-socketed. A beard, something he had never previously allowed beyond a day's stubble at most, aged him. He was shocked to find patches of white in the hair around his chin.

He placed his valuables – the keys to the London flat, his letter from, and the photographs of, Stanley, the filters for the bicycle mask – on the table. He drank some water and opened a tin of tuna. Already he was sick of cold canned food. He wondered, very briefly, if the horse might have made good eating. Could anything that had been cut down by whatever it was? He might end up with a belly full of radioactive waste.

Would Stanley recognise him like this? He eased off his jacket and boots and shook plaster dust and pebbles of glass from the counterpane, then he crashed onto the bed. The ceiling was covered in cheap woodchip wallpaper, painted magnolia.

'Looks like rice pudding,' he heard Stanley say. 'Can we have some rice pudding?'

Jane reached for his rucksack and picked through the tins. ''Fraid not, badger,' he said. 'But we've got some custard in here. That do?'

'With sponge,' Stanley said. 'Chocolate sponge.'

Cherry giving him her look, the look that said, *Sugar? At this hour? You deal with the fallout, then.*

The light faded. The pillows were soft, the mattress firmer than he liked, but it was better than the lifeboat. A hammock of knives would have been more comfortable than the lifeboat. He stayed awake longer than he expected to. But he was so tired. He ached in so many places that it was difficult to locate the pain. He listened to the agonised scream of the wind, and beneath that the surge of the ocean. It was like a muscle working itself bigger. He imagined it rising, assuming shapes far more sophisticated than it ought to, flying at the towns and cities on the apron of land like a street fighter with their blood up. Bodies torn to nonsense by their rage. Buildings subsumed. Scarlet spindrift.

The door creaked.

He came out of a sleep he didn't realise he had entered. His head was treacly, unresponsive; he turned to the sound too slowly: now others were joining it. Footsteps, but they were too light, too swift. Surely whatever it was would have cut the distance to the bed long before now. Jane couldn't pull himself out of sleep's suck. Fear helped. He blinked, but though he was ridding himself of sleep he couldn't shake the shadows from his eyes. He thought he felt movement on him, but it was just his body tangled in the duvet. He kicked it away from him, sure there were rats trying to climb onto the bed. He saw the horse's body rippling and could not stop his mind's eye picturing his own body moving like that.

Lightning slashed through the room; Stopper was outlined before him, heralded by a thud of thunder. The footsteps had been made by the spatter of his blood as it drizzled out of the wounds in his arm. Hacked flesh slopped around his exposed tendons like the jaw of a dead animal. More lightning drew Stopper closer. Jane saw things writhe in his emptied eye sockets and he wondered for a moment if it might be the other man's dreams. But then Stopper was leaning over him and trying to cut into his forearms with the blade. He couldn't control the knife, though; the severed muscles in his arms would not do as he wanted.

Stopper's lips, curiously thin, split open. 'Pleased to see me?' he asked, and his breath was foul with oil, with decay. The words were like a cork popped clean of a bottle: shadows welled out of him, blood and seawater and prawns bloated by the feast he had become.

Jane closed his eyes. Stopper didn't leave him. His retina clung to his image, red in the black. 'Stopper,' Jane whispered. 'Jesus.'

When he opened his eyes again, light had returned to the room. He gazed down from the bed, expecting to see the hotel-room floor matted with all kinds of filth, but he could see only his boots and a layer of that invasive, pervasive dust.

He yawned and stretched and sat up. He rubbed his eyes. The howl of the wind and the crash of the sea. Rain was sudden buckshot against the roof tiles. In this strange daylight, though, the weather's menace seemed reduced. He went to the door and peered down the corridor. One time there might have been the smell of breakfast, the sound of muffled showers and doors breathing closed on their hydraulic hinges. Now there was just the wind moaning across broken windows and buckled doors.

Jane went to the bathroom and tried the taps. Nothing but a dusty cough. Out of habit more than need he pocketed the wrapped tablets of soap and the mending kit. He inspected his body in the mirror, checking for cuts or bruises to suggest internal bleeding, but he was clean. He eased his boots back on and turned his mind to the next portion of his journey. He took out the map from his jacket pocket and spread it on the bed. Belford was around thirteen miles from here. Could he do that in a day? Heavy boots and heavy weather? He reluctantly traced his finger further north, further away from Stanley, back towards Berwick. Haggerston. About half the distance. That would be his first target. See how late in the day, how frazzled he was by then.

His hands shook as he folded the map and stowed it back in his pocket. Weak. He lifted the curtain and looked out at the sky. Brooding, thick, low. But at least the mist seemed to be dissipating. Perhaps if he got onto high ground he'd be able to look for survivors. He was thinking of freshly squeezed orange juice, bacon with tomato ketchup, and was moving to the dressing table when he stopped.

Next to his belongings lay a large white-tipped feather.

5. THE SEA EAGLE

Jane picked his way through the sludgy tan moss of the hillside, the rain like the heel of a hand pressing him towards the dead earth. Apart from the astonishing spectrum stuttering across the sky, the world had turned sepia. The meadows were scorched flatlands, the woods so many burnt matchsticks piled in occasional clumps. The exploded bodies of sheep lay in fields like fallen sunset clouds. It was hard going. The path had turned into a sluice; already there was evidence of minor mudslides where plates of the sodden, shocked ground had slipped free. An autumnal smell of decay and cold carbon hung in the air. It was deep in his clothes, his skin. He could smell it rising off his piss in the mornings. He wondered if his bones might smell of woodsmoke.

At the top of the hill he unshouldered his rucksack and rested. He had secured the feather in a strap on the bag. It fluttered now like a reminder. He had thought for a long time about the feather, where it had come from, how it appeared to have been placed next to his things. But that could not be the case. It must have already been in the room, and his movement, or that of the wind, must have caused it to fall. Maybe it had been a decoration, an ornament, a memento collected and then forgotten by the room's previous incumbent.

It was a large feather; Jane couldn't begin to guess what it had once belonged to. He had broken into a couple of the houses at the southern edge of the town and found a guidebook to British birds. He'd also liberated a pair of Nikon binoculars and an unopened bottle of Bladnoch malt whisky. He cracked the seal on that and took a brief swallow before putting the binoculars to his eyes and sweeping them slowly over the view.

East, the sea, huge and black and torrid in the lenses, its surface a choppy coating of spume. The beach was choked with tens of thousands of washed-up fish. Here and there something more exotic: white-beaked dolphins, grey seals, a basking shark, a minke whale. Endless fluthers of jellyfish. He peered through the glasses at the land to the south-west, turning through 360 degrees until his attention was back on the water. Nothing but stubbled countryside and the boiling horizon.

He took another belt of whisky and secured the bottle in the rucksack. He shouldered it, making sure that the straps were not twisted, and headed back down the hill.

'Careful, Stanley,' he called out. 'Mind you don't slip.'

He had climbed a hill with Cherry early on in their relationship. It wasn't lost on him that much of their time together since had felt like the same thing. They had taken a tent to the Brecon Beacons in South Wales. They'd climbed Pen y Fan, a day's trek, and then camped in the great valley beneath it, cooking packet foods in water taken from the nearby lake and boiled, smacking their lips, making appreciative groans even though the rehydrated rice had been appalling. The silence as night fell had freaked them out. That and the depth to the sky, the assault of stars. Their chattiness was cut by the spectacle. They lay on their backs in the grass, awed as stars materialised in the dark spaces between the brighter bodies. There was no limit. There was a point when they both swore there was more light than night in the sky.

They watched the scratches of light as meteors erased themselves on the skin of the Earth. They pointed out the uniform trajectories of satellites. Venus crept across their line of sight. Even though they were exhausted by their long walk, sleep had no chance of settling in them.

'It's amazing,' Jane had said.

Cherry's voice, when she replied, quavered, brimming with tears. 'I feel . . . small, and thrilled, and sad,' she said. 'I can't explain. I haven't the words.' He clasped her hand.

'We're on the edge of a galaxy that's expanding,' he said. 'We're the shrapnel from a bomb blast.'

'If we're on the edge, does that mean we're one of the oldest parts?'

'That would make sense, wouldn't it?'

'So the centre of the Milky Way, that's quite young?'

'Well, relatively, I suppose.'

'Should we take a physics degree now?'

They did not make love that night, the first time in three intense weeks since they had started seeing each other regularly. Jane, whose appetite for her was great, did not notice.

'Those meteors,' he said, as another chalked itself off, 'they're probably the size of golf balls. Maybe smaller.'

'Richard balls?'

'I said smaller, not bigger.'

Once you had become accustomed to the dense scatter of stars, and fastened your eyes to one patch, it was striking to realise how many meteors there were.

'It's beautiful,' Cherry said. 'But I wouldn't want to be out there.'

'We *are* out there,' Jane replied.

'You know what I mean.'

'Yeah. It's a pretty rough place. You wouldn't last a second. Nothing to breathe. Sub-zero temperatures. Radiation. Super-accelerated debris would fly straight through you. Pressure.'

'Perhaps only marriage comes close to rivalling it.'

He laughed nervously at that. 'If anything larger than a golf ball came down on us . . . I mean, considerably larger than a golf ball, like the size of Iceland, say, we'd be in big trouble.'

'I've seen the films.'

'You've seen the heroes save the day. What if one really hit? Came down tonight. If you survived the impact you'd be looking forward to a nuclear winter that lasted years. No sunlight. Death of vegetation. Food chain down. Everything dead.'

'Are you always such a hot date?'

Jane liked that about her, that ability to rescue them from a downturn in mood with a quip. It wasn't the only thing. Cherry was like no other woman he had met. She didn't have a ramrod-straight back and skin so glossy and flawless you could have played curling on it. Her hair wasn't advert soft, thick and tangle-free. She didn't have a hundred pairs of shoes or spend two hours in the bathroom getting ready for a pub lunch. She didn't consider a small green undressed side salad to be a substantial meal. He liked the way she moved during lovemaking, flipping him onto his back, climbing him, pressing fully against him, a steepening of herself to match the growth of her own pleasure.

'What would you do?' she asked. 'If this was our last night? If a meteor were to hit, or the Earth split in two, or a star exploded and drenched us in fire?'

'Burn my pants and take a shower.'

'But seriously?'

'If we survived? I'd shoot you. And then I'd shoot myself. There would be no way forward.'

After that night things changed. There was a soberness. It wasn't as if they didn't have fun or failed to enjoy themselves, but later in their holiday, canoeing in the Bristol Channel or scrambling in Llantwit Major did not inspire the excitement it ought to have done. There seemed a check on their behaviour, as if screaming or laughing in the wake of what they had witnessed would somehow be disrespectful. The enormity of what lay beyond the Earth's meagre pull, the knowledge that they had been staring at stars long dead before the Earth had cooled, humbled them both. Jane wondered if that night had damned them in some way. Instead of opening themselves to the beauty of it, they had taken a left turn and talked about the blanket lifelessness in space and time, other than on this speck of blue-green dust.

They returned home and two weeks later Cherry told him she was pregnant.

The wind around him, harsh and frantic, as if trying to get inside him. The sea a black wall. He remembered a magazine he'd started collecting, years before – he must have been thirteen, into fighter jets and blood – about the Argentine invasion of the Falkland Islands, and the British campaign to get them back. It was one of those magazines whose introductory price was remarkably low, but then reverted to a couple of pounds and went on interminably; he never followed the run through to the finish.

The Marines and the Paras covered more than fifty miles of inhospitable land by foot in bad weather in three days, carrying full pack. 'Marching' didn't do it justice; 'yomping' was more like it.

Treat this as an act of liberation, Jane told himself. *This is not about you. The miles will go easier if you keep your mind on Stanley. You can tell him about yomping when you see him. You can tell him about Goose Green and the Paras, and his namesake port where the final battle took place. He'll love that.*

Stanley had begun to be fascinated by death. But he didn't see it as a permanent thing. Playing with his Star Wars characters, he would 'dead' somebody and after a while they would come back to life. But it was obviously in his thoughts. They went to Brittany for a holiday – their last as a family – exploring the coast of rose-coloured granite, and Stanley had come right out and asked him, 'What means die? What means dead?' Stanley and Cherry had decided on a policy early on, not to lie, not to dress things up, and so Jane had told him exactly what it meant. 'It means you stop breathing, your heart stops beating. Your brain stops thinking. And it's like that for ever. You never come back from it.'

Stanley had digested this, his eyes wide and fixed on the middle distance as they were whenever he thought hard about things, and said: 'Will I die?'

'Everyone dies, mate.'

'Oh,' Stanley said, and his eyes turned glassy with tears. 'Will you die?'

Jane nodded.

'Before me?'

Jane had almost said *I hope so* but thought that would confuse him. 'Yes, Stan.'

'Oh, Dad. I don't want to die. I don't want you to die.'

'I don't want to either. But don't worry. It won't be for a long, long time.'

Stanley had become a little more clingy than usual after that. He woke up in the night and called for him and he would go, sensing Cherry stiffen beside him. 'I luff you with all my heart, Dad. I luff you for a five hundred million hundred three minutes.'

Cherry seemed to resent the attention Stanley was giving Jane. And he was at a loss to explain why his son was favouring him. 'It's just a phase,' he suggested. 'A male thing. It doesn't mean he loves you any less just because he doesn't tell you. Boys can be awkward sods.'

Cherry rejected this. She claimed Jane was encouraging Stanley's ambivalence, using it as a wedge between him and his mother. Jane had been shocked. 'Why would I do that? Why would I want to turn Stanley against you?'

'Because you want custody of him.'

He remembered the impact of that, how it had floored him, numbed his tongue. She had that ability, to throw something into an argument that was unexpected, that didn't follow the fight's trajectory or logic. How had he responded? He could barely recall it in the wake of her face twisting, the demand that blasted out of her. He must have said something like 'But I don't want a divorce.'

No, but I do, Richard. I do.

The compression of distance through the binoculars was difficult to cope with. It disorientated him sometimes when he saw some flash of difference in the brown reaches of burnt land and removed the glasses to check its position in relation to him to discover that he couldn't see it. Then he didn't know where to aim the binoculars in order to find it again. Once he had it back in his sights he was more careful, and discovered that it was much farther away than he had believed. He had never used such powerful lenses before: all the binoculars he had ever tried previously had been weak; toys, really.

In the main, these flashes he saw were tangles of fleece snagged on barbed wire, or fragments of plastic, or on one occasion a bottle-green sequined dress stuck against a fence post, arms waving hysterically in the wind. Every sighting caused a palpitation in his heart. He desperately wanted it to be someone, but he didn't know what that might mean. If this was some kind of assault from an aggressive country, there was every chance that an invasion was under way. He didn't want to be clapped in irons and sent to a concentration camp, or shot dead on the spot. He also didn't want to be hampered by an injured companion, or have to tend to someone who might be slowly choking to death on their own lungs.

He walked. He was back on the A1 now, the tarmac swollen and broken, melted and resealed in strange lava patterns. It reminded him of a river's currents frozen in a snapshot. He stopped thinking about the binoculars and the possibility of survivors for a while and ate up some ground. His boots were comfortable; no blisters yet. He felt stronger. He ate little and often. He had filled a three-pint water bladder from bottles in the cellar of buildings just south of Scremerston and stowed them in the water pouch of his rucksack. It was a heavy pack now, but he kept reminding himself of the troops yomping from Carlos Water to Teal on East Falkland. They never gave up, and there was death waiting for some of them at the end of it all.

There were countless fields on either side of the dual carriageway. The haze made all that acreage of black-brown tremble. There were sections of the road that had not been barred by vehicles, but there was a surprising amount of traffic. He averted his head when he walked by, but something wasn't making sense. He snorted a little, mildly amazed that he could think like this in the middle of an entire situation that wasn't making sense.

The day passed quicker when he was intent on the road. He bypassed Haggerston with barely a glimpse at its castle. Further east lay the causeway connecting Lindisfarne to the mainland. The Holy Island was beyond reach now. The sea would have erased that link for ever. Maybe the island itself was drowned. He looked through the binoculars but could only see a riot of ocean and sky, as if the two elements were wrestling over a prize. He walked on, developing his rhythm. He started chanting Stanley's name, and his own, and Cherry's too. A triumvirate to spur him on, even though he knew there were only ever likely to be limited permutations of the three by the time he found them. But you never knew ... a national disaster, a child in peril, estranged parents reunited. It happened all the time in Hollywood.

Stan-ley, Cher-ry, Rich-ard. Stan-ley, Cher-ry, Rich-ard. Stan-ley, Cher-ry, Rich-ard.

As a child he'd attended Scouts a few times. Hadn't stuck it. There was something about uniforms after school that sapped the enthusiasm from him. That and the dumb tasks they set at this particular hut: *you and two friends are going on a three-day camping expedition, so how many boxes of cornflakes are you going to need?* He had to get home by himself afterwards if his dad was on nights and had the car. He'd alleviate the monotony of a long walk back in the dark, often accompanied by rain, by doing the Scout jog, which was twenty paces running, twenty paces at a fast walk: the fartlek before its time.

Stan-ley, Cher-ry, Rich-ard. Stan-ley, Cher-ry, Rich-ard. Stan-ley, Cher-ry, Rich-ard.

Jane was intoxicated by the distance he'd managed. His heart was pumping hard and he was alive. He was alive. He stopped to rest and lifted the Nikon glasses to sweep the area south of Alnwick. Newcastle was a knot of wet iron in the distance. He could make it in maybe four days, if he marched hard. The road was not flat, but it was not so undulating or jagged as to hamper him too greatly. The dried meat and dried fruit he had found in a farmhouse cellar was keeping his spirits up; he'd even lucked upon a couple of slabs of dark chocolate in a tin marked *IZZY'S STASH – KEEP OUT!* He wasn't wanting for energy. But finding such food, such good food, made him wonder a little about the future, despite his intention to keep himself focused on the present. The vegetation frazzled, the food chain compromised. No animals. No food. How much of this kind of thing was going to be buried treasure in the months and years to come? He could see himself stumbling, cadaverous, through villages, his clothes flapping on him, too weak to unscrew the top from an undiscovered jar of jam he might come across in a forgotten pantry. What about water? An image, unbidden, of vultures sitting on the shattered street lamps of Oxford Street, the birds' beaks stained crimson. An image of himself, a scarecrow, shambling beneath their keen eyes, calling out for his family, calling out for anybody, but there was nobody left. Just six million corpses mummifying in the furnace blast of a storm that would not cease.

Jane forced his thoughts outward, and his eye caught the feather nestled into his rucksack. No birds. No nothing. No people.

He snatched up the feather and studied it. He retrieved the guidebook and savagely flicked through the pages, looking for something that might help him identify its provenance. The pictures of birds calmed him, even though he knew they were eternally trapped between these pages, that he'd catch no sight of them here. A big wedge-shaped feather it was, edged with broad sections of creamy white. He held it to his cheek, felt the fragile, firm ruffle as he ran his fingers along its edge, then tried to scent something of the bird via the quill, but there were no smells beyond that of the burned, congealed sky.

He thumbed through the book until he found the large predators. He had to look away from some of the pages, the ones of photographs of raptors rending their prey. The slashing talons, the hooked razor beaks. The eyes were the worst, though. Angry, feral; alien colours. Piercing. He had always been squeamish. Jane tried to imagine being the focus of that unswerving attention as an eagle came at him, claws outstretched, great wings spread in some sacrilegious cuneiform aping, but thankfully it kept sliding away at the crucial point.

He found what he was looking for. The white tail. A yellow beak. Insane, intent eyes. Even as the rain squirmed across the paper, discolouring it, he read that the sea eagle was either a dedicated loner or a loyal partner. Once hunted to extinction in Scotland, it was now mainly confined to the west coast, having been reintroduced to the countryside in the latter decades of the twentieth century. So what was it doing here, east coast, many miles south of its natural habitat? He must have made a mistake, but the diagram of the feather in the book might have been a copy of the real thing clenched between his fingers. An ornament in a hotel room. That was all. A gewgaw. A knick-knack.

It was placed there for you.

Jane dropped the feather suddenly, as if it had turned hot. He stared at it and thought about what he'd just suggested to himself, what that might mean if it was true. Then he picked it up and threaded it back through the elastic ties of his rucksack. It seemed somehow profane to leave something so beautiful to decay into this grim landscape. Gift or find, he would keep it. Perhaps it would bring him luck. At the very least it would make an exciting present for Stanley.

He walked until the low cloud definition began to increase. Shadows building. The sun going down. He remembered flights out of gloomy airfields penned down with rain. Jets jostled by weather, nosing for the cloud banks. The fog of them, dense against the windows, then the sudden break into astonishing, lovely blue. He thought now of a cloud cover without break, constantly mashing and folding against itself as it greedily smothered the world. Which way was this going? Nuclear winter or greenhouse? He realised he'd stopped walking. He was staring at the underbelly of cloud and its greasy gamut of colours. They changed as if inspired by moods. His, maybe. Industrial colours sometimes, alchemic: a range of molten smoky hues. Burnt gold, white-hot slag, the cold blue of steel. Sometimes the colours of pathology, of disease. Or mildew and smog, oil slicks and blood. They contained a look of something seriously damaged that could not be fixed. The rain that slashed out of them was muddy orange, like rust in water. He had to keep swiping the back of his gloves across the black Os of his goggles; his view was perpetually gritty, streaked. He wondered how long the rain would take to eat through the lenses.

And then he saw that he could not see because he was crying. He had to bend down, to rest on his knees, otherwise the shaking in his body was going to topple him over. He unshouldered the rucksack and let it fall to the floor. The sudden sense of liberation, the lightening at his shoulders, highlighting the claustrophobia he was feeling. He couldn't breathe. He ripped off the bicycle mask and the goggles. The wind driving into his face was delicious. He tore off his shirt and trousers, kicked away his boots. He ran naked through the slime of dead grass, angling up along a line of rocks embedded in the mud like rotted teeth in a black gum. He was crying and screaming and howling. The jouncing glasses on their strap around his neck cracked him hard in the chin and he tumbled, off balance, fetching up three feet away from the elongated rictal skull of a sheep, its hollowed eye sockets brimming with mud and rain. His breath flew from him; he scooted back on his knees. Mud oozed through his splayed fingers, stark white against the bruised earth like fallen stars.

He stood up, the wind instantly punching into him. He felt the rain already, stinging at his flesh, tasting him. He put his hands on the barrel of the binoculars and raised them to his eyes. He performed a slow, clumsy pirouette. He never completed it.

6. TRESPASS

... *Hi, I'm Jane. Yeah, I know, I know, a girl's name* ... *but it's my surname. My first name is aw, fuck it* ...

... *Richard Jane. Pleased to meet you. And with whom am I now engaged in conversation* ... *with? Shit* ...

... *Hello. My name's Richard. Any idea what happened here? Here's a plan. Let's stick together* ...

... *HOW DID YOU SURVIVE? WHO ARE YOU? HOW DID YOU FUCKING SURVIVE?*

He lay on his back in the grass, desperate to sleep but unable to until they decided to rest too. And they did not look likely to be resting any time soon. He had followed them through the afternoon, deep into evening. He was shattered and suddenly making no progress. They appeared to be moving in circles, as if they had lost something on the ground that they were eager to recover. But he recognised shock and exhaustion when he saw it. He looked again now, rolling over and pressing the rubber cups of the binoculars to the goggles. They were about half a mile away, trudging through a shallow valley. Two figures in matching red waterproof jackets, hoods raised. One of them was smaller, leaner than the other. A woman? A couple? He had watched them approach farmhouses and then back off, as if too afraid of what they might see should they open a door, which suggested to Jane that they had seen human bodies. They were drifting, passive, hopeless, waiting for something to force the pace. It gave him confidence.

But he had not yet attempted to make contact. He tried to understand why. They obviously needed his help and could use some company, but he held back. Perhaps it was because he had not talked to anybody for over a week. He was mistrustful, both of the situation and the fact that he had discovered survivors where he had seen none before. Who were they to have emerged unscathed from whatever had happened? What if they were infected? What use would it be to survive a monumental disaster only to be struck down by some concomitant disease? He wasn't thinking straight. Anything they had, he had, especially after his foolish streak earlier in the day. God knew what he'd breathed in, what had wormed its way into his pores. The mask was back on his face, complete with a fresh charcoal filter. *Remember that, when you make yourself known*, he thought. The vision of a man with ragged hair and ten days of beard, looking like some post-apocalyptic serial killer, would have them scarpering for the forests before he'd got within quarter of a mile of them. He must wait until the time was right. He must wait until his own fear was checked.

What he'd just considered. *Post-apocalyptic*. Was that what he was in the middle of now? Was that what this was? He had known all along, of course, but putting the words into the centre of his thoughts, that was something new. Maybe he was no longer grieving for his crew, for the not-knowing about his family. Maybe he was coming to terms.

Jane followed them back to a small cottage, somewhere off the B6353 according to his map. Once the cottage might have been pretty, but now the thatched roof was gone, the paint peeled, the hanging baskets scoured by flame. What was left of a woman had sunk to her knees, carrying a tray fused into her hands by immense heat, face flash-burned of any expression into a tight cellophane mask. He watched them go inside. A sign was visible through the broken glass of a window. NO VACANCIES.

He was loath to leave them now that he had found them. What if they should move on during the night? But somehow he didn't feel this was likely. The way they had moved through the dead meadows did not speak to him of high ambition. They were lost. They were scared. He hoped. There was still that niggling doubt. They might be part of the group responsible for what had happened, if this was some kind of chemical or biological strike on the country. But that didn't chime with any master plan he had read about in the past. Raze the UK, then invade Northumberland?

Jane pitched his tent in the field next but one to the cottage, at the leading edge of a wood. From here he could see the cottage and the driveway connecting it to the road. He built a small fire, taking care that the flames would not be seen. The smell of woodsmoke didn't matter; everything smelled of woodsmoke. He heated a can of baked beans and spooned them down. The pork sausages included with the beans made him smile. Stanley loved them. The boy had trouble saying the word, and his face creased with concentration when he tried. *Shoshidge* was about as close as he got. *Podgidge* was another, whenever he was asked what he wanted for breakfast. And he struggled to separate the vowels in 'orange' with that initial 'r'. *Orrrnj*. So cute it made your teeth itch. But Stanley was getting older. Five now. He no longer made such mistakes. He was in a rush to grow up and watched older boys and men for visual and verbal pointers as to how to behave. He was keeping secrets. His love was no longer unconditional.

Jane brushed his teeth. His gums felt swollen, irritated. Too much sugar and not enough with the Oral-B. He wished for a cup of coffee. Instead, he drank water from the bladder in his pack and read the letter from Stanley until the light was forcing him to strain his eyes. The paper was getting ever more creased and greasy. He didn't know what he would do if it tore, or if he smudged the ink to the point where he could no longer read it. He folded it carefully and slid it back into the plastic compartment of his wallet. He checked his eyes and drew his sleeping bag around him and sat at the lip of the tent's entrance, watching the cottage. There was candlelight in the window. He raised the binoculars and saw the shadows of the figures moving around the room. Maybe they were talking. Maybe they were arguing. They were restless, whatever. He tried to remember the body language he had shared with Cherry at the time things started to turn sour, but all he could remember were the words. The invective. The peeled-back lips and bared teeth. The finger pointing. The tears. He saw the shadows come together. Then, as one, they sank out of view. The candle remained burning. Jane was asleep before it died.

Jane wakened to a storm. It was dark, but he could sense the clouds low in the sky. The pressure at such times always gave him a headache. Rain was pummelling the fabric of his tent, a deafening wall of noise. The violence of it must have turned over the fields because there was an acrid, rank odour of death and earth and shit; it reminded him of walks in the woods with his father when farmers were grunting around the fields on their tractors, muck-spreading. He checked through the binoculars but he could not see the cottage, despite the occasional detonations of lightning that flirted across the underbelly of cloud. He checked his watch. Six a.m.; he had been asleep for seven hours.

He rolled up his sleeping bag and wadded it at the bottom of his rucksack. He breakfasted on dried apricots and a can of carbonated apple drink. He waited for another hour to see if the storm would pass over, but it seemed to have settled here, and intensified, if anything. But at least there was light seeping through now. He could make out the shape of the cottage. He doubted they would emerge until the weather improved, such as it could.

He pulled up his hood and left the tent. He walked into the wood a little, grateful for the scant shelter that it afforded him. This might once have been a thick, attractive copse, before its heart was burnt out. No trees meant nothing to absorb carbon dioxide and replenish the oxygen in the air. Cheery morning thought. He pissed long and hard into the loam; his water was dark but not bloody. He was grateful for that, at least. He washed his hands back at the tent, and absently prodded and poked at his teeth while he watched the edges of the cottage emerge from the dark and the mist.

It was another hour before he spotted movement, a naked figure shifting past the window. He could not tell if it was male or female. Twenty minutes later the door opened and the two red jackets emerged. He saw faces this time. Pale. Pinched. One of them heavy with a beard. They did not seem enthusiastic about moving far from the building. The man sat on the edge of an ornamental cart, which must once have been brimming with flowers and grasses. The woman hovered and dithered nearby, like a nervous dog on a short leash. Jane wondered if they had breakfasted; they seemed jittery. Every so often the man would raise both his arms in a monumental shrug, or an expression of pleading. They were at the end of their tether.

Jane raised his hand to his face and heard the rasp of his own beard. He ought to clean himself before making himself known to them. He didn't want to scare them, although they must surely expect others to look the same. But it didn't work that way. It had shocked him a little to see such a haunted, thickly bearded face, enough for him to put down the glasses without a more sedulous inspection. He had missed whether they were carrying weapons, but the pensive aspect to their movements suggested that they were empty-handed. He couldn't say for sure, but he felt very strongly that they were foreigners. And as frightened to death as he was.

He pulled his rucksack close and delved carefully in one of the compartments for his razor. There was a tube of cream and a badger-bristled brush. On his knees, watching the house, he splashed his face and rubbed the cream in, working it into a stiff lather with the brush. He hacked at the beard, having to use his fingers to find purchase as he did not have a mirror to help. He kept his eyes on the couple – red, indistinct blobs at this distance. He was grateful for his stone-coloured tent, the muted cement shade of his jacket.

When the beard was down to a close stubble he took more care with the razor, rinsing it regularly, moving it tentatively over the contours of his face as if for the first time. He unbuttoned his shirt; poured water over his head and chest, tried to subdue the sour odours of fear-sweat. What he'd give for a hot, deep bath.

He pulled the shirt back on and finger-combed the knotty tangle of his hair. He no doubt looked filthy, hunted and mad. But at least he was cleanly shaven. Suddenly he thought that might make him look worse. What maniac took time to shave when sanctuary was to be sought? He pulled out the bottle of Bladnoch and took a few big swallows. Better. He started extracting tent pegs but then paused, thought about it. He left the tent where it was and stowed his rucksack in a corner, filling his pockets with dried fruit strips and canned hams. He would go to them as denuded of threat as it was possible to be. At the last, he picked up the whisky and shoved it in the back pocket of his jeans.

He began to trudge over the solid furrowed field, trying not to stumble, trying not to look like some shambling terror hot-footing it over for a first warm meal in weeks.

He slowed as he approached the cottage. They still hadn't spotted him, or they were doing a good job of bluffing if they had. He heard her voice first, scratchy, raised, Australian: 'But what the fuck, Chris? I mean, what the fuck?'

'There's no need to swear.' Big shrug: throwing imaginary confetti into the air. 'There's no need to fucking swear.'

Their bickering carried on a little longer, then they fell silent and Jane knew they had seen him. They didn't say anything; he sensed a withdrawal. Perhaps they were trying to shrink into the shadows to improve their own chances of not being spotted. He almost looked up, but he felt it would be better if they believed they had made contact first. It was a stupid game – he knew that they knew that any stranger would want to check out the cottage for inhabitants, or food – but he didn't want to scare them away. All of the doubt that had squirmed through him had been misplaced, or misread: he desperately wanted company.

He carried on trudging, head down, as if he was lost in the ruined patterns of the earth. When it seemed he had left it too long and must own up to his charade, the girl saved his face.

'Hey,' she called out. Her voice was no longer the spunky come-on she'd been provoking her man with earlier. It was all breath, almost a whisper. When he turned to face them he knew he would be all right. There was no threat here. He was staring at ghosts. They were watching him, plate-eyed, waiting for a reaction. You couldn't pretend to ignore strangers any more, or at best offer them a lukewarm 'Good morning'. Every person warranted scrutiny.

'I'm Richard,' he said, and his own voice sounded so alien that he almost turned around to see who had spoken.

'Chris,' said the man. 'And this is my girlfriend, Nance.'

'Short for Nancy?'

She nodded. She glanced at Chris, then back to Jane. 'Do you have any food?'

They were five weeks into a six-month tour of Europe. They'd flown Korean Air from Sydney to Madrid, spent a fortune on tickets, but all they had was a couple of packs and a tent. They'd spent the first month exploring Spain but had decided to spend December in the UK before moving on to France, Germany, the Czech Republic. Chris had been keen to climb Europe's spine, up along the Baltic States to Finland, a place he had always wanted to see. Nance had favoured turning south after Prague, heading down to some beaches and some heat, maybe as far as Greece. They meant to hitch where they could, but they had some money for the train and weren't averse to putting in some hours behind a bar to make a little extra.

'Then back to Sydney,' said Chris. 'Get a job. Get married. Have kids. Lock down.'

Nance seemed less enamoured of this idea, although Jane realised she could just be tired. She was pale and glassy-eyed, twitching whenever the wind pressed its face against the windows of the living room. He supposed it was difficult to contribute anything to a conversation, even a sceptical expression, when your mind was filled with *What the fuck?*

She possessed a fragile beauty, the kind that didn't cope well with sleeplessness and stress. She seemed a person for whom the word 'wan' had been invented. Everything about her was pale: her watery grey eyes, her sandy blonde hair, the colourless arc of her mouth. Even her clothes were wanting for colour, as if leeched by her neutrality. That red coat would end up a washed-out pink before long, he thought.

From here, Jane could just make out the shape of his tent in the trees, but you would have to really know what you were looking for. Chris and Nance were sitting almost primly on the edges of wing-back chairs, chewing dates and trading glances as if they were prisoners trying to swap silent messages of encouragement. A layer of pink dust had settled on everything except the bed, which was a knot of duvet and pillows. A novel was spreadeagled on the bedside table next to a shrivelled banana skin.

'We were wondering about the air,' Chris said. 'If it was safe to breathe.' He wore an expectant look; he seemed to be seeking approval all the time, as if he needed to break out in a huge smile but could not because of some unspoken code of conduct. He was heavy-jawed, the beard only serving to emphasise the spade-like aspect of his head. His eyes were a dark, almost dirty green, and they did not stay still.

'I was using a mask for a while, but unless you've got a proper filtration unit strapped to your back it doesn't matter. What's out here is in us now. If it kills us, well, it just means we were a little late getting to the party.'

Chris nodded, looked at Nance as if for confirmation. She wasn't offering any.

'What did you see?' Jane asked.

Nance put down her food and stood up. She brushed the crumbs from her jeans and walked past Jane to the bedroom. She closed the door.

'She can't ... she's not ready to ... process what happened,' Chris said.

'Are you?'

'How about you first? What's your story?'

Jane told him about his experience on the seabed and the violent deaths that had followed. 'I don't know what happened. I wasn't around to see it. But you ... you were on the surface. How did you survive it? Did you even see what it was?'

'I don't know. We were walking out in the fields. Long walk. We were tired, and we were looking for a place to sit and have something to eat. We found these tunnels, concrete tubes just coming out of the hillside. I don't think they were meant to be open, but the grille on them was all broken and rusted to hell. There was a sign, burnt white, rusted. Could hardly read it but you could just make out NO TRESPASS-ING. I don't think the tunnels had been used much recently ... whatever it was they were for.'

'Maybe a decommissioned lead mine,' Jane said. 'We're in the right part of the country for them.'

'Lead. OK. Whatever. So anyway, we went in. We had a torch with us. It looked like it might rain so we had our packed lunch inside. When we'd finished we felt better, you know, so we were shining the torch deep into the tunnel, asking each other how far it reached. We were always going to have a look, but we were dicking about, daring each other.'

'You went in? Deep?'

'We walked for about twenty minutes. Straight in. It went on for miles. It got colder. At one point I turned the torch off, having a laugh with Nance, pretending the batteries had gone flat. It was so dark you couldn't see ... you know the colour of your own blood behind your eyelids? None of that. Nothing. Nance freaked out. I freaked out. Torch back on.

We decided we'd pretty much had enough after that. There was that worry – what if the batteries *did* fail? What if I dropped the torch and smashed the bulb . . . so we were just heading back when this enormous tremor hit us.'

Jane waited. He had held his breath. He let it out now in a steady quiet stream, not wanting to interrupt Chris's flow. Chris was looking at his hands; his too were tigered with thin, sore-looking weals, as if they had been stung with a whip. He picked at the dry flaking skin around the marks.

'It put us on our arses. I thought the tunnel was going to collapse on top of us. We were both screaming, and I think that put us in more of a panic than what was going on. After it had stopped we were still screaming. It took a while to realise it was over. We weren't hurt. Maybe a bruise or two. And then we felt this enormous heat. It just came charging down the tunnel. Where it had been cool, cold even. Damp. Now it was roasting. It was like being in a sauna. Steam everywhere. We started running. We just wanted to get out.'

'What did you see when you got outside?' Jane's voice had become a narrow choked thing. He kept thinking of Stanley. Maybe he had been on the balcony when the tremor hit. Five flights up. Maybe he had fallen. Maybe not. Maybe he had been burnt to a crisp up there. His lungs turned to leather.

'What you see now,' Chris said. 'Only there were fires in the woods. The sky was on fire too. Sheep were still standing in the fields, but they were burning. The whole place was burning. I thought we'd bought it. We hid at the tunnel entrance, trying to breathe. After a while – I don't know how long . . . hours maybe, maybe only minutes – there was a difference. There was rain. Horrible, burning stuff. Like acid. Oily and orange. But the fire in the sky went out. There was just this disgusting coloured smog. It got everywhere, coated the back of your throat like lard. Nance was sick.'

Chris picked up his penknife and fiddled with the hinge. He did not look at Jane. 'We came back here. We buried a farmer we found in the car park. He was ... Jesus. He was ...'

'Yes,' Jane said. 'I know. It's OK.'

'It's *not* OK, though, is it?' Chris asked gently. 'Nothing's OK. I mean, how big is this? I tried using my phone to call 999. To call home. No signal. Nothing is working. No TV. No radio. I mean, how fucking huge is this thing?'

'I'm revising my estimates almost every day. Upwards.'

They sat in silence for a while. Eventually Nance came out of the bedroom, pausing at the threshold as if to check on the content of their conversation.

'Did you see any other survivors?' Jane asked.

Chris shook his head. 'I thought we should head for Newcastle, but Nance ... she isn't ready yet.'

'It's a good idea. Newcastle. Hospitals. Someone must have survived there. From what you described, it seems that exposure was the danger up here. In Newcastle there's more shelter.'

Chris seemed infected by his enthusiasm. 'If it even reached that far,' he said. He got to his feet. 'It's got to be localised. Some awful offshore fuck-up. A nuclear sub. Those things carry heaps of warheads, don't they? Hiroshima times ten or something. We're just wrong place wrong time.'

'I don't think so,' Jane said, quietly, shooting a look at Nance. Her attention volleyed moistly from one man to the other. 'It doesn't matter,' he added.

'I can handle it,' Nance said. 'You'd rather I was standing here giggling?'

'It's just ... well, there'd be help by now,' Jane went on. 'It's been a week. Over a week. This place should be crawling with Hazmat suits and outside broadcast units from the BBC.'

Chris sat back down. 'Yeah, you're right. My God.'

Nance said, 'So what now?'

Jane spread his hands. 'I'm headed for London,' he said.

'Why?'

'My little boy is there. I have to find him.'

'Family,' Chris sighed. 'Shit. My dad is in his eighties. He's got diabetes, angina . . . Lovely little combo.'

'He's in Sydney, right?' Jane asked. 'OK, so calm down a minute. It might be that this is localised after all, a UK thing. We don't know if it's global.' It hadn't occurred to him for a moment that it might be.

'If it's global, it isn't terrorism,' Nance said. 'It isn't "oops, I pushed the meltdown switch" at the power plant.'

'It can't be global,' Jane said.

Chris turned his head to the window. 'Fire in the sky,' he said.

They agreed to accompany Jane as far as Newcastle and assess the situation there. Chris had rebuilt his optimism and was convinced they would walk out of the danger zone into green grass and fresh air before they reached the city's outskirts.

'There's nobody come to help because they looked at what happened and didn't expect any survivors,' he said, and he would not be shifted on his stance.

Jane led them back across the field to his tent. They helped him dismantle it and pack it back in the rucksack.

'Which way?' Nance asked. Sweat stippled her upper lip. She was clenching and flexing her fingers fast. He could see the tendons in her neck pulling the skin tight.

Jane pointed south. 'Just keep the sea on your left and we can't go wrong,' he said. Nance was looking at Chris, signalling something with her eyes. 'Go on,' Jane said. 'I need to take a leak and get this pack on. I'll catch you up.'

He watched them cross the road and sink out of view into the next field. Nance was talking intently, not allowing Chris to respond. Her head jerked towards him at the start of every sentence. Jane couldn't work her out. She seemed utterly uncoupled by events, but in the little bubble that she shared with her man she was determined, unshakeable, domineering. Jane had met a few people like that over the years and he didn't like them at all. They were often suspicious of other people and had a small circle of friends, if any at all. They never offered any solutions, never took the initiative, but behind the scenes they connived and agitated and planted seeds of doubt, usually with the one person they knew best, often a spouse who was so far under the thumb that they owned a flat head.

He gave them a few moments to allow her to get whatever it was off her chest, then made to follow. But something held him back. He scanned the area where he had pitched the tent in case he had forgotten something, but there was nothing. He closed his eyes and tried to understand the feeling. Something was askew. Not the nude, scorched trees. Not the electricity of finding someone alive. Something else.

He opened his eyes and wondered how he could have missed it.

7. 2500°C

They walked across the fields, boots scuffing on brittle furrow-slices, sending plumes of brown dust into the air. Chris and Nance quickly moved ahead, and Jane watched the argument they carried thickening between them, pushing them apart. Nance pecked at the air and Chris raised his arms as if to describe the size of some mythical fish he'd hooked. Jane left them to it. Despite having been alone for so long he didn't want to talk. The wind was beginning to alarm him; it was not any longer the hard, constant heel shoving him in the back, denting his eyeballs whenever he turned to look at the sea. It was becoming shapeless, directionless. Little tornadoes were fizzing up from the dusty fields. If he opened his mouth the wind stole in and made him gasp. The sky to the west had darkened, although it was still early morning.

His fingers worried at the tiny curved cranium in his pocket. He wondered who might have left it for him. He ran his thumb over the horny beak sheath, and thought of its hue, and that of the chambers within, stained the colour of mahogany. Jane imagined litres of hot blood jetting through the pores in the bone over its lifetime. The skull was remarkably intact. The thin forked *vomer* was in evidence in the upper beak, as were the quadrates, which gave articulation to the lower jaw. No tissue clung to the bone at all; it was as white as if it had been bleached. Whoever had cleaned this had done so with care and respect. Love, even.

He took the skull out and inspected the great circles of its orbits. He blinked and something in the light allowed him to see the fierce, fixing yellow glare of what had once turned within those sockets. The focus, the deadly intent. It chilled him that something so small could be so violent. It had been built for the purpose of death. It had nothing in it other than the instincts of procreation and killing. He felt something stir inside him and suppressed laughter. He'd felt a sudden bond with the creature, with that way of life. He supposed it was in all people, that flicker of race memory, the hunter-gatherer mentality. The so-called civilised lifestyle had rubbed its edges away over the centuries. But it was still there, the romance of it, the grizzly part of you that got a thrill when you picked up a fishing rod or headed into the forest with a sleeping bag rolled up on your shoulders.

He put the skull back in his pocket and hitched his pack tighter around his shoulders. He gave one last troubled look at the sky and hurried after the others. There was a marked disintegration in their mood when he caught them up. They had stopped snapping and talking over each other. Now there was a grim silence and a distance between them. Chris seemed crestfallen; Jane wondered if Nance had finished their relationship. He felt like laughing. You survived the end of the world, fate dumping you, and you get all mopy because your girlfriend tells you to lump it.

It was Nance who drew his attention, however. She was still sweating, still doing that weird flex of her hands, as if she was suffering from a muscle spasm or a trapped nerve.

Chris noticed it too, but although he kept shooting her looks he didn't say anything.

'We'll hit the road soon, then we can pick up some speed,' Jane said. 'I've been making good time. It's all about rhythm. And making sure the weight of what you're carrying is well distributed.'

They didn't appear to hear him. He put his head down and concentrated on walking.

They'd covered around five miles through the dusty expanses of meadows and fields and forestland, all of it layered with ash and limbs of charcoal, the heat causing them to gasp and swear; Jane could feel the burn through the soles of his boots. This land would be a long time cooling down. The road was not worth considering. It had bulged and buckled; it looked as if some giant hand had gripped it further along and yanked it like a strip of carpet. Crash barriers and fallen street lamps created further obstacles. It was tough going on the farmland, but at least it was level and consistent. Up ahead electrical pylons had crashed to the ground. Hopefully the road would be fit for walking before they had to navigate those. He didn't want his discovery that the country's electricity had died to be a bad mistake.

They were coming to another stunted reach of incinerated wood when Nance shrugged her rucksack off and started running for the road.

'Hey,' Jane called.

Chris was already trotting after her. 'We won't catch her. She ran for her school. She had state trials.'

'Great,' Jane spat. They both lumbered in her wake. It must have been a good three miles to the dual carriageway and she just kept diminishing into the distance. Jane saw, before she skipped like a goat across the burst lava mass of blacktop, that she was wearing running shoes.

Five minutes later they were at the road too. Jane took his backpack off and rested it against the warped ribbon of a crash barrier, colour side towards the sea so that he'd spot it against the grey when he returned. Both of them were breathing hard. Jane thought the years of slog on the seabed, fighting currents, might have improved his fitness, but he guessed his lungs must have been damaged to some degree.

They tripped and skidded across the tarmac and followed Nance along a B road past a battered grain merchant's. Its grounds were host to dozens of silos, all of which had been lopped like boiled eggs. Tons of grain had been swept by the wind into drifts against brick walls and the burnt black skeletons of lorries. Beyond that and the railway, the earth sloped towards the sea.

'Where the hell is she going?' Jane cried.

Chris didn't answer but Jane received a reply when they started to run past items of her clothing. Chris gathered them up in his arms. He was calling out to her, but she would not stop. By the time they reached the coast, a further three miles away, Jane thought maybe his heart would burst. His clothes squirmed against his body, a layer of sweat sandwiched between them.

They staggered across a bluff of volcanic rock and onto the beach proper. An immense flash of heat had turned it into opaque leaves of obsidian: black, dark green, firebrick red. Their boots chinked and clinked. The sea was a horrendous churning stew. Bodies rolled upon the surf. Far away to the horizon, when the waves allowed them to see, they could see huge tankers upended.

Nance was naked, standing at the edge of the black froth of the breakers. Her feet were bleeding but she didn't seem to notice. They approached her carefully. Chris said her name but she didn't turn around. Her hair was lashing around her face. They couldn't see her eyes.

'I'm going for a swim,' she said.

Jane said, 'Not a good idea.'

Chris touched her on the shoulder and retracted his hand quickly, as if he'd been burned. Jane saw his confusion. He didn't know how to deal with her. She was wild, you could see it in the sweat that swicked off her, creamy as that of a racehorse. It was in the tension of her muscles. Jane reached for her arm and she was hot iron. She pushed him away. Her body gleamed as if she too had been turned to glass in the furnace of the beach.

'Nance,' he said, trying to keep his voice low and calm but able to be overheard above the torment of the waves and the howl of the wind. 'Nance, look at the water. Look at the steam coming off it. Look at the bodies. You go in there and you won't come out again.' Jane had never seen the sea appear so impenetrable. It looked as though it wore a skin, shining and thick, that would need to be pierced before you could submerge yourself. It was the molten tar that ran off the roads into the gutters. There was no sense of depth. You couldn't see the shadow of bladderwrack within it, or of sand churned up from the bed.

Nance's body glittered with dust. She resembled an exotic dancer with sequinned flesh, pumped up and ready to do her shift at the pole. Her breath came quick and shallow. Jane took off his coat and put it around her shoulders. She didn't make any attempt to squirm away. She turned quickly, within the temporary circle of his arms, and pressed her body to his. He held her, conscious of Chris's incredulous expression. He wondered if he would say something. There was that strange feeling with Chris, that he was involved in some silly domestic game of one-upmanship. He had the slouched, downturned look of someone who is in a perpetual sulk about one thing or another. It was an insult to the people who had died to see him here now with the pilchard lip, deflated by Nance's need. He couldn't realise that it was directionless. If it had been the Yorkshire Ripper standing here, she'd have fallen into his arms instead.

Jane led Nance back up the beach, away from the sea. Chris followed, dragging his heels. Jane held Nance by the arms while Chris dressed her. She had slackened somewhat, but her eyes still ranged across the horizon. It reminded him of *Treasure Island*, a book that had terrified him as a child. She was Billy Bones keeping constant watch for the seafaring man with one leg. By the time Chris had pulled her coat on and zipped it up, glancing at Jane as he did so as if to show him that this was his woman and she was now closed to him, Nance had lowered her gaze. She was shivering. Jane turned away. His eye caught the trembling line of tobacco sky to the west. The colour had deepened since dawn, and it had spread. He chewed his lip over it. Maybe it was another wave of poison, or fire. They would not escape it this time.

'I think we should get back on the road,' he said. 'We should try to find some shelter.'

'We'll never swim again,' Nance was saying. 'No sand-castles. No ice cream if you're good. Playtime's over, isn't it? We all have to wear serious faces for the rest of our shitty little lives.'

Jane was about to try to bring the subject around to Newcastle, to retrieving his pack, anything, when they heard the whistle.

It was an SOS. Three short blasts, three long blasts, three short blasts. Jane thought he could see its author, standing against the volcanic fist of rock beneath Bamburgh Castle. *What about me?* he thought bitterly. *What about someone answering* my *mayday?*

He left Chris and Nance to their inevitable row and trotted through the slag towards the figure. The shrill blasts of the whistle were becoming more frantic, now delivered to him so clearly that the blower might have been standing nearby, now whisked away by the wind so that their patterns became lost. He saw the figure, a white head on a thin blue body, slump to its knees. The whistle stopped. When Jane reached him a few minutes later he saw it was an old man. He did not look up, even as Jane's feet crunched loudly towards him. Jane turned back and Chris and Nance might well have been infected by all the obsidian on the beach and become glass sculptures; they had not moved from their original positions. He could see the ovals of their faces turned towards him as if waiting for some signal from him to animate them again.

Jane wondered if the man would not look at him because of how alien he must seem. His breath sucked and rattled behind the bicycle mask like in a child's nightmare. The man still had the whistle in his mouth and it tooted pathetically as he exhaled. He let it fall from his lips. He said, 'She's dead.'

'Who's dead?'

'Ella, my granddaughter.'

Jane didn't know what to say. He was itching to get away, to retrieve his rucksack and get back on the roads and rails south. Every minute spent putting sticking plaster on wounds here meant another minute away from the needs of his boy. He sensed movement and turned to see an elderly woman making her uncertain way down the mounds of bare land abutting the castle ramparts. The old man stood up and went to her. They bussed against each other, like clouds, yielding, finding each other's shape with the surety that comes from years of companionship. Jane envied them that. He and Cherry had been together for seven years. Prior to that, his longest relationship had fizzled out at three. He had longed for the kind of security he could see being played out here in front of him, albeit born out of grief.

'Where was your granddaughter?' Jane asked.

The old man cast a glance up to the battlements, but either the light or the painfulness of glimpsing the place of her death caused him to avert his gaze. 'She was playing. We said it was all right. You shouldn't clip a kid's wings, despite all the paedophiles and murderers. You can't stop a life from being lived.' He choked a little on the irony of his words.

'It's all right, Brendan,' the old woman said.

'Anyway. We were down in the castle keep. She said she wanted to go and have a look at the view. Angela here, she's got emphysema. She's not in great shape at the moment. I didn't want to leave her on her own and she couldn't climb to the top. So I told Ella she could go on her own as long as she was careful. She was a good girl and I knew she wouldn't cause any bother.'

The old man didn't go on. He kept opening his mouth to say something, and then there'd be a quiver in his face and he'd shut it again. His eyes were large and pale grey and very wet, like something from a fishmonger's slab. His skin was blotchy and sagging; his hair blown by the wind into a shivering grey meringue. His wife was huddled into her coat. Her lips seemed too loose for her face. They gathered together, a smudged scarlet slick. She kept pursing them, as if she were sucking at a sweet, or keeping badly fitted dentures in position. Most likely, Jane thought, she was trying to keep the lid on her rage or her grief. There was an almighty storm piling up behind those defences. Jane closed his eyes. The more survivors he came across, the more stories like this he would have to listen to.

'We felt the heat down in the keep,' Brendan said. 'I mean, the chappie, guide fella, had only just told us the walls were ten feet thick, and we felt it. Like an oven it were. He took off as soon as he heard all the screaming. I never saw him again. We just sat in the keep, huddled together, shouting

Ella's name. We got drowned out by the roar of this thing. Like a jet engine at full throttle right next to your ear. I thought we were going to die.'

The old woman put out her hands as if she were about to grab her husband's face. Her eyes widened. She was snatching at her breath. 'Oh, Brendan, what about Anne and Stephen?'

'Oh, bloody hell,' Brendan said. 'Bloody, bloody hell.'

It turned out that Anne and Stephen were Ella's parents. They had gone to The Lakes for their wedding anniversary. Brendan and Angela, Stephen's parents, had offered to look after Ella for the weekend.

'She was only six,' Angela said. 'She was going to be seven next July.'

Jane said he would go to the battlements to find the body. Angela blanched and shook her head. Brendan touched Jane's wrist. 'Thanks, son. But I've been out there. I've seen . . .' He glanced at his wife and checked himself. 'Nothing could have survived.'

'We did,' Chris said. He and Nance had somehow made it across the glass without Jane hearing, or more likely he'd been so horribly engrossed in Brendan's tale that he'd not registered their approach. Jane shot Chris a look now and the two of them shared secretive glances. They'd obviously made up on their way back. Chris put a protective arm around Nance. Jane felt like telling him that he was welcome to her.

'I'm heading for London,' Jane told Brendan. 'These two are coming with me as far as Newcastle. We're hoping that whatever hit us – meteor, solar flare . . .'

'Wrath of God,' Chris said.

Jane ignored him. 'We're hoping that things might be better the further south we go. Maybe we can find a hospital in Newcastle that can treat your wife. Maybe there'll be some kind of emergency rescue post. If we survived, then there must be more. Who knows,' he said, working some optimism into his voice that his heart would not back up, 'we could set off and in five minutes there'll be Red Cross helicopters buzzing in from the hills.'

'Hospital would be good,' Brendan said. 'The wife's got an inhaler and it's almost run out. She'll be in a right state if we don't get her some more. We've spent long enough in that bloody castle, wringing our hands over what to do. It's time to face up to things.'

They kept giving Nance nervous glances and now Jane saw that her feet were still unshod and they were bleeding badly. She was still glassy-eyed from her crazed little jaunt.

'I've got a First Aid kit back at the road,' he said. 'We should get you sorted out. An infection is not something you want.'

Four of them started to walk the short distance to Front Street while Brendan hurried back to the castle to collect their things. It was slow going. Angela had to keep stopping to catch her breath. She didn't so much inhale as seize at the air, her head jerking back as if she'd been punched. Nobody said anything, but Jane could sense Chris and Nance's dismay. He felt like rounding on them, pointing the finger, telling Nance that if she hadn't lost it they'd have walked right by and Brendan and Angela would most probably have starved to death in each other's arms, afraid to re-engage with a world that had burned itself out around them.

Brendan was much more sprightly when he returned. A plan had stiffened him. His eyes no longer seemed like rain made flesh. He had two coats – thin, flimsy affairs – and a canvas bag that held a couple of books and a make-up bag. Jane checked their feet. Brendan wore brown brogues; Angela a pair of deck shoes. He fished out a bicycle mask and handed it to the woman. She put it on and looked at him over the edge of it with expectation, as if this alone might cure her of her disease.

'We'll find you some proper clothes and shoes as soon as we can,' Jane said. 'All of the cars have been knocked out of order. Electrics fried, or something. So, we have to walk.' He looked at Angela. 'Can you manage that?'

'I'll try,' she said, but then she turned to Brendan. 'Maybe I should stay here. You can come back for me when you get to Newcastle. Find help.'

Brendan was shaking his head almost at the moment she started speaking. 'No way, love. No. We all go together. We stick together. I'm not leaving you.'

Jane sighed. If they didn't find some way of transporting Angela they'd be stopping every few minutes. It would take them weeks to get to Newcastle, a distance of around forty miles that he'd have been able to march in four days. He silently cursed Chris and Nance. And Angela and Brendan. He felt a sudden impulse to just take off, to leave them to sort out their problems. He had a son to find. Stanley might be injured. His mother might be dead. The thought of him alone, crying for his daddy, knifed Jane every time he thought of it. There was no build-up of resistance where children were concerned. You didn't get over the stifling worry, the cotton in the mouth, the frantic slam of the heart. It was the price you paid for love, he supposed. He wanted to articulate this to the others, to offer an apology, when Angela reached out and held his hand. Her skin was surprisingly soft and cool.

'Thank you,' she said. 'Thank you so much.'

'That doesn't look right, does it?' Chris asked.

They were a mile from Front Street. It had taken them three hours. Jane was considering picking Angela up and carrying her. She took a few puffs from her inhaler but the canister sounded as though it was empty when she shook it. Jane was about to ask Chris which of around a million not-right things he could possibly be referring to, when he saw how the sky had assumed a closed aspect. It didn't look as granular as it had earlier in the day. The sickly brown colour had deepened. It appeared solid, but as Jane stared he saw that there was movement; the wall bulged and shrank infinitesimally, like the slow explosion of storm clouds.

'There was a mist, a fog, first few days I landed,' he said. 'Maybe this is that in a different form. Dirtier. Maybe it's fog that's become polluted. A pea-souper.'

None of them were agreeing with him. Nobody was saying a word. They stared at the dimpling umber wall as it came on. Jane dropped his gaze to its foot and saw how fast it was really moving; it ate the ground. He'd once seen footage of a pyroclastic flow after Mount Unzen had erupted in Japan. A cloud of superheated ash hurtling down the mountain at over two hundred miles per hour.

'That's not fog,' Brendan said. 'That's a dust storm.'

Now Jane did pick up Angela. She squawked her indignation and started berating him, but he ignored her.

'Come on,' he shouted, and headed for a large farmhouse at the edge of the field. It was in bad condition. Fire had gutted it; the roof was partially caved in. But there was one corner that looked relatively solid despite the lack of windows.

'Get your tent ready, Chris,' Jane called.

'But it's only a two-man job.'

'Get it fucking ready.'

Jane could feel the first grains stinging his face, like grit churned up in the wake of a bus or a lorry in the high street. He was glad of the goggles and the mask. He could hear Chris and Nance and Brendan swearing and spitting. Angela had stopped shouting at him, perhaps because she could see the seriousness of the situation, or her lungs would no longer allow it. They reached the eastern wall of the house as the dust storm boiled up around them. Jane felt his breath sucked from his throat as the ferocity of the wind vaulted over the dented inverted V of the roof. Nance and Chris both yelled. Jane kicked at the sagging door and it rocked in on its rotten hinges.

'No,' called Angela. 'It's not safe.'

'Get inside!'

'No. The wall will come down. We'll be crushed.'

Chris got the tent down in what seemed to be a large living room. 'Where do I hammer the pegs?' he shouted.

'Just get inside!'

They all piled in as the dust storm's muscles flexed against the house. Even above the howl of the wind and the grapeshot of dust and grit against the tent fabric, Jane could hear the suck and blow of Angela's lungs and her prayers to the Almighty. There was something else too, and no matter how hard he tried to bend the sound to the logic of his mind, he could not. It was obviously the savage, blood-keen cry of a bird.

8. ZOMBIES

'If it was going to come down, it would have done so before now,' Jane said. Angela would not shut up about the wall. He closed his eyes to the headache hatching behind his eyes, and wished for a long cold beer. He tried to step back from his irritation; she was just focusing on that to keep her from the fright of the storm, or the dust storm in her own lungs, that was all.

They had begun desultorily to help pack away the tent but everyone could see it was a pointless task. The skin was punctured in numerous places. Chris called a halt and threw it away. 'We can get another one in Newcastle,' he said. 'Top of the range. No expense spared.'

Everyone seemed a little put out by the sudden relief of a task; they looked at each other with a mix of puzzlement and doubt. Jane supposed there was a concern that the storm might return; three times it seemed to have drifted away only to return, like a dog tied to a post. And there was Angela too. He wondered if Chris and Nance were waiting for her to fall back on a stock disaster-movie trope: *You go on without me . . . I can't make it*. He had no doubt they would gladly piss off, yet the awkward truth was that he too wished he could leave her behind. Leave all of them behind. He couldn't rid himself of that bitter longing. It stayed on like the crackle of the dust against the tent's laminated plastic.

They filed out of the building into a coffee-coloured desert. Nance, her feet bound with strips from a torn shirt, winced at every step. The sky appeared to have been coated with another layer. Dust hung against the background of the clouds like swarms of insects looking for a crop to decimate. They felt it furring their hands and clothes. Jane remembered one time during his childhood when he wakened to red dust coating the cars outside, sand borne thousands of miles from the Sahara on a freak wind. This could have come from anywhere, any desert, any steppe, any prairie. Jane had a vision of the world turned opaque; just another dead planet to anybody looking down from outer space, a cold stone masked by a caul of toxic gas.

He looked north, along the raised strip of road. His pack would be gone, or so buried in dust it might take a lifetime to find. His shoulders felt naked without its weight. He had a good two litres of water in the bladder, food to last a couple more days, the First Aid kit, his own one-man tent, his maps. He did not share Chris's *que sera sera* attitude. Yes, they could replenish their supplies in Newcastle, but they had to get there first. They had no shelter. No provisions. If another dust storm came they would have to hope they were near enough to some kind of dwelling. If they were caught out in the open, they were dead.

He didn't say any of this out loud, but he saw that he didn't have to.

'Shall we?' he said, turning south.

Darkness was upon them before they knew it. They had walked for so long in something akin to a midnight sun, the light soapy, ill-defined, that they had not noticed the day tipping away from them. The temperature plummeted. There was nothing to do but keep going until they found a house where they could rest until dawn. Angela's breathing seemed to have levelled out, despite the exertion. He guessed the mask was helping. Maybe the cold did too.

Half an hour later they came upon what seemed to be little more than a beat-up shed for cattle. All the straw within it had burned to ash and been blown away, the shed's walls painted black by fire. A charcoal smell lingered. The walls and roof were intact, the columns supporting the open bays stout, undamaged. It had been built carefully, to last, by craftsmen who knew something about storms. A trough was filled with water that resembled molten lead. A little way off, bones lay in the dust, roasted curves partially buried. A large skull tilted onto its side, fat burned to black upon its surfaces, grinning as if floored by the irony of dying so close to shelter.

They huddled together under shared coats in one corner, like kids during playtime. None of them slept. The darkness became absolute. The baying of the wind was an animal trapped in a cage, trying to find a way out. Jane couldn't hear his own breathing above it. When he thought he might fall asleep after all, when the cold in his muscles seemed to reach a plateau, he felt another body, smaller, nestling into him, snuffling for warmth.

'Hi, Stan,' he said.

'Hi, Dad. Budge up, Dad, I'm freezing cold.'

'We've been colder than this. Remember when we went to Skye?'

'We've been in the sky in an airplane, Dad. It wasn't cold.'

'No, the Isle of Skye. Where we went fishing. We took your mum to clean out her sinuses after she had that awful cold that lasted so long.'

'I caught a fish.'

'You did. You did catch a fish. And it was massive.'

'It was as big as me, wasn't it, Dad?'

'It was, Stan. I thought it was going to eat you.'

'I can't get warm, Dad. You're not giving me any warm.'

Jane reached out but Stanley was no longer there. There was a sense of fingers brushing against soft cotton, of an opportunity missed. He felt a flutter of panic in his chest; he would lose him in this dark if he wandered away. He half called out to him and only just managed to disguise it as a cough.

'You all right, son?' Brendan's voice was warm, concerned. Jane was glad of its Lancastrian underpinning. It made the words somehow more genuine.

'I'm fine. I suppose I had a nightmare, but I don't feel as though I was asleep.'

'You can't tell, it's so dark. There's no telling how long we've got till morning. Could be hours yet. I've lost all track of time. My watch packed up the moment it happened.'

Jane saw the invitation to talk, but he couldn't accept it. Stanley was still too close. He knew it was an illusion, but he wanted to concentrate on his immediate proximity, in case the feeling of him returned. It was a poor substitute, this truffling for his boy's ghost, but it was all he had. Brendan, to his credit, did not pursue the conversation. After a while there were other half-shouts of alarm or bewilderment. The dream became the living moment became the nightmare. You reached a point where you did not know what path to follow in case it dissolved into a new, a different sort of reality.

Morning was later, rather than sooner. When it did arrive there was barely a change. Shapes grew out of the shadows. The sky paled only fractionally.

A mile further on down the road they reached a village. Chris groaned. 'If we'd put a spurt on we could have been sleeping in beds last night,' he said.

They broke into a house and found good coats that fit Nance and Angela. There were some stout walking shoes too that were the right size for the old woman. Her feet were blue and stiff when Brendan eased off her deck shoes, and she bit her lip in pain. Jane glanced at Chris to see if he might get a message from that but the other man was busy going through cupboards and drawers. There were some canned goods in the kitchen and Jane peeled them open and passed them around. They guzzled the contents where they stood, too hungry to talk or set a table. In the fourth house that they tried they found a coat and boots for Brendan. They also found a new canister of Ventolin. Angela almost cried when Nance handed it to her. She fired a few puffs down her throat and closed her eyes. When she opened them again they carried an extra sparkle.

'I'm ready to go jogging,' she said. 'Who can keep up with me?'

There was a wheelchair in the next house and Brendan rolled it out onto the road, deaf to Angela's protests. The rubber had melted away from one rim completely and was a bubbled mass stuck to the other, but the wheels turned, noisily. 'Last resort,' Brendan said, and Angela acceded.

There were no tents, and although they had been on the road for less than four hours Chris was keen to spend the rest of the day in the village.

'We need to recharge our batteries,' he said. 'A good night's sleep in a proper bed will give us something to smile about.'

'This isn't a holiday camp,' Jane said. 'We need to put some miles on the clock.'

'*You* need, you mean,' Nance said. Jane tried to remember if she'd ever said anything without that trademark snarl of hers.

'Yes, I need. You want to stay here, be my guest.'

'You're not my fucking captain,' Nance said.

'I refer you to the answer I gave some moments ago,' Jane said. He turned to Brendan and Angela. 'You with me? I'm sorry, I don't care all that much one way or the other. But I have to crack on.'

Brendan nodded. 'I understand,' he said. 'We're with you, and – I mean it – if you feel we're keeping you back, you go on and floor it. We're better off already for knowing you. You got us off our arses. We'll be all right.'

Chris and Nance went with them, but not without a volley of tuts and hisses and sighs. Jane heard Nance say something to Chris about sleeping out in the open again over her dead body. He wrestled with the urge to say that at least it would keep the damp out of Chris's clothes.

The griping stopped eventually. The slog of the journey and bodies becoming visible in the fields like soldiers downed by gunfire worked as an excellent conversation stopper. Angela improved steadily throughout the day. He saw in her the woman she must have been before emphysema dragged everything south. Some people, no matter how old they became, carried within them that essence of youth. It was like astonishment, Jane thought. A way of looking at the world that was all *wow*. Such people never became bitter or cynical.

They spent that night in a farmhouse. Bodies in the kitchen. Everyone had a bed to themselves. *Happy, Chris?* Jane found a new rucksack. Brendan found some maps of the north-east, but they couldn't work out how far they had come. It didn't matter. Knowing you were twenty miles or 120 miles from Newcastle didn't detract from having to cover that distance. Ignorance was bliss, in a way.

The days tumbled into one another. Jane couldn't be sure if it had been three or four or five since Bamburgh. Angela's breathing began to become more laboured, no matter how much Ventolin she took. But at least the road wasn't so bad and Brendan could push her in the wheelchair for fair stretches before she had to get out to circumnavigate a damaged section. Eventually there seemed to be more and more villages. Jane could sense a picking-up of pace. It was as though they were going slightly downhill. Conversation became lighter. Angela laughed, a wonderful sound. Even Nance was more gregarious.

The last night they spent before entering the outskirts of Newcastle, Jane awoke to the sound of screeching. He thought he'd dragged the sound with him out of a dream, but after a few seconds of hard breathing, and staring through a window opaque with heat discoloration, he heard it again and knew that it was outside, that it was following them. He sat up and pulled on his coat. Everyone else was asleep. He went downstairs and stood by the front door, his ear to the wood. The cry came at regular intervals, as though it was from the kind of creature that targeted its prey via sonic rebounds. He opened the door a little and felt the wind try to muscle it wide. He found himself trying to overlay the sound of Stanley crying over this, to try to make the sound that of his boy, so that he could do something. But it was nonsense. He remembered waking in the night as cats yowled in the street, thinking that it was a baby in trouble, but this sound was at the same time too bestial and too intelligent for that.

It was a hawk of some kind. Or an eagle. Or an owl, even. He wished he could differentiate, but he had never been much of a twitcher. Stopper had been a member of the RSPB. He always took his binoculars with him wherever he went. 'Goes a skua,' he'd say one day and you'd look up and see this shape in the distant sky. A while later: 'Goes a guillemot.' And there didn't seem to be an awful lot of difference.

Jane thought about going outside to see if he could spot it, but it was too dark. He'd only get lost and then he'd be in big trouble. He closed the door. Nothing had survived the Event, as far as he was aware, apart from a handful of people who had been shielded from its impact. Surely all the birds would have been wiped out. Which meant that whatever was making the noise was a human survivor. Or an approximation. What was it? An invitation or a warning? An all-clear?

Irritated, he wandered around the house. There were no dead here. The furniture was functional, the decoration spartan. It reminded him of a stage set for a one-act play. He sat down at the kitchen table and wished for his turntable, his records. A cup of tea and the sound of Stanley upstairs playing with his toy keyboard. The thoughts would not shut out the terrifying screeching coming to him from across the fields. He looked out at the dark and imagined the kind of throat that shaped that noise. He thought he could see the glare of yellow eyes and the controlled madness that burned within them. It had not occurred to him that other survivors might not be as community-spirited and would seek to harm anybody who crossed their path. Surely they were a long way from squabbling over the last tin of beans in the land. Some might not see it that way, of course. You can't reason with an animal when there's food in front of its face. And maybe that was the thing, maybe they weren't people any more. It was time to regress. Everybody was an animal, after all.

He fell asleep with his head on the ravaged wooden surface. Liberal parents. Naughty kids. *Granma smells of wee*. Don't we all, he thought.

The fields gave way to thickening villages. The villages became more and more built-up at the outskirts of the city.

The A1 curved west, as if cowed by the sight of it, happier to bypass it altogether and leave the entrance to lesser roads. They moved towards Gosforth; Brendan had found reference to a hospital there in a newspaper the previous night. It was a little unnerving to find themselves walking streets again. Jane had been expecting to see people, perhaps some kind of patrol group set up on the northern perimeter to watch out for survivors. He'd expected army trucks and soldiers in fatigues. Hot soup and the best medical attention that Britain had to offer.

Within fifteen minutes they were wading through acres of dead.

'This way,' Chris called. 'It's less . . . busy . . . this way.'

They steered a course through the bodies, trying not to look, trying not to stand on anything. Angela kept her hand to her mouth. Some of the people had died with their hands fused to the handles of their doors, trying to get outside. Others had been partially incinerated; shadows of disappeared body parts remained against walls, like *anasazi* hand prints.

They reached the hospital and stood watching it for a while. Jane couldn't understand why there wasn't any activity. It couldn't have destroyed everybody, could it? He glanced south for a moment, imagining London like this. Utterly silent and still. Spending years rooting through the bodies until he found that of his boy.

He must have flinched because Angela took his hand, asked him a question with her eyes. He nodded, shrugged the moment away. To avoid any more inquisitive looks he strode away from them, over a mound of landscaped earth to the main entrance. The car park was like a dusty, hot garage forecourt of woebegone bangers.

'I'll not be going in there,' Angela said. 'I don't think I could bear seeing dead people in a place meant to help you. If that sounds daft I can but apologise.'

'It's all right,' Jane said, although privately he was irked that this diversion was for her benefit. 'Just tell me what you need and I'll see if I can find it.'

'Salbutamol, like the Ventolin inhaler I've got now. Or Atrovent. As many as you can carry. And if you see any steroids like, oh, what is it Brendan?'

'Cromolyn? Is it?'

'Cromolyn, that's the one. Or I think there's one called Tilade, something like that.'

Jane nodded, eager to be away. A goodie bag of drugs, a kiss, a handshake and *all the best* and it was him straight to the nearest Millets for a stock-up on camping supplies and off. Chris and Nance came with him, but he wished they'd stayed with Brendan to look after Angela.

They pushed their way through the revolving doors of the hospital entrance. A security guard was swollen into his black serge suit so completely that he had split its seams. It hung off him like a soiled superhero cloak. A porter in a luminous orange vest drew attention that ought never to be paid. Nurses in once-white uniforms were marbled with all the colours of the vital rainbow.

There was an arrow pointing to the pharmacy. Jane headed for it quickly, hoping to put some distance between himself and the bickering Aussies. He tried to avoid looking at the figures slouched in wheelchairs, or on gurneys from which they would never rise. He imagined all the *Do Not Resuscitate* signs on the ends of beds. He thought of the morgue. No need for a discreet room now. Or body bags – the whole country was doing that job now.

A short corridor led them past the radiology department. A man with a pair of crutches and his foot in an orthopaedic shoe was waiting for an X-ray. His face was covered with a towel. Jane stopped.

'What is it?' Chris asked.

'Where did that towel come from?'

They couldn't answer. There was the slightest creak. Jane turned to see the heavy door to the X-ray room widen, a grimy hand with split nails white upon its edge. Before he could raise his hand, a woman with wild eyes came out of the darkness and slammed the end of a desk lamp into the side of his head.

Jane touched the compress to the lump above his ear and winced. 'What are you doing here?' he asked. They were in the X-ray room. The woman had apologised profusely, assured him it was a case of mistaken identity. A boy sat in a plastic chair, his arm in a muddy-coloured cast. He watched Jane with big hopeful eyes, a child who has seen Santa unmasked and doesn't want to accept the truth.

'I work here,' the woman said. 'I'm a radiographer.'

'What happened?'

'I don't know. Fire. An explosion.'

'How did you and the boy . . .?'

'The shield we use, for the X-rays. Aidan here, I was showing him what I do, to calm him down. I was showing him the buttons I needed to press before giving him his X-ray. Then there was this flash. I thought it was the machinery. A malfunction. But there was thunder in the corridors. I thought the whole building was going to come down.'

Jane told them about his own experiences, toning it down for the sake of the boy. The woman shook her head throughout. He thought maybe it was in astonishment, but it turned out to be a rehearsal for her answer when he asked if she and Aidan were ready to leave.

'I haven't been out since it happened,' she said. She gave Jane a loaded stare, gesturing lightly towards the boy. 'Not sure how good an idea it would be. Maybe best to wait for help.'

Jane drew her to one side and lowered his voice. 'What's up with him?'

She shrugged. 'He's been having a series of tests. Doctors are worried he might have some kind of blood disease. It's early days.'

'And now, what? We won't know?'

The woman shook her head and turned to regard Aidan. He was flicking switches on the malfunctioned control panel. 'He's always been a sickly child, according to his reports. Maybe things will iron themselves out over time. Maybe not. There's no help for him now, if it's serious.'

'It might be that we're as much help as you're likely to see,' Jane said. 'There's a lot of . . . casualties out there.'

'But we're fairly safe, secure here. There's plenty of food and water. Medical supplies. People will come to the hospitals. You proved it.'

'If there are people, they will come.' He lowered his voice. 'I'm not sure how many people are left.'

Aidan watched them owlishly. He seemed fascinated, as if he were being read some amazing bedtime story. Jane wondered about the boy. About his parents.

'I'm on my way to London,' Jane continued, as if that alone might be inducement enough.

'Long way,' the woman said.

'Have you been out at all?' he asked.

She shook her head. 'I prefer to stay with what I know.'

'What about home? Family?'

She shook her head again. He could tell she resented having to explain to a stranger, no matter the extraordinary circumstances. 'My parents died when I was in my teens,' she said. 'I have brothers and sisters, but nobody local. I never married.'

Cruelly, he imagined her shaking her head whenever she was asked.

'What about you, Aidan?'

'Mum and Dad. Kerry, my sister.'

'You tried to get home to see them?'

He shook his head. 'They're here.'

Jane felt the air stiffen around him. 'OK,' he said.

He wanted to move on, but Aidan was making things difficult. He felt perfectly happy about leaving the others to fend for themselves, but Aidan was Stanley's age. He couldn't abandon him without making some effort to get him safe.

'What about looters?'

The woman sighed. She still appeared nervous, uncertain about Jane. Her gaze flickered to Chris and Nance, who were dithering by the door, trying not to look at the stiff, shrouded body in the waiting area.

'A couple of days after it happened – I think, perception of time all messed up – I heard a bunch of people come in here, running around the corridors. I thought help had arrived, but they were screaming, laughing. We hid. They must have been pissed or drugged up. Plenty of free goodies on offer now, I suppose.'

'You saw them? They still around?'

'They moved on,' she said. 'I think they were just kids.'

'What did they take?'

The woman shrugged. 'The pharmacy has been raided. A lot of uppers and downers gone. The snack machines have been emptied. I saw a lot of empty wallets and purses lying around.'

'You can't buy anything, actually,' Aidan said. 'Actually, they're just idiots.'

The woman laughed, a little too breathily, a little too close to tears, but it broke the mood. She realised she was still holding the crutch and tossed it to one side.

'How's your head?' she asked.

'I think I need an X-ray.'

Jane liked her despite the assault. It wasn't just the Pavlovian response a lot of his oil platform colleagues displayed when confronted by a woman, although it had been a long time since Jane had enjoyed female company. There was something about her that nibbled at him. Maybe it was the way she had selflessly protected Aidan – the latent mother come to the fore – or maybe it was just the way she was decked out. She wore simple clothes – a short-sleeved white blouse, jeans, leather sandals and a long amber necklace. She had an easy physicality about her. She was slender, long-limbed, but not gawky. He liked the way she turned a rub of her forehead into a slow trawl of her long shaggy hair. He'd always liked girls with a thick mane on them.

'What's your name?' he asked. He was thinking, *Jesus, hit me again.*

'Rebecca,' she said. 'Becky. Becky Bass. It should be like the fish, or the brewery, but I prefer it pronounced like the guitar.'

A cough from the doorway. Chris said, 'This is fascinating, really. But we should get back to Angela and Brendan.'

'Do you know if anybody else survived?' Jane asked. 'Anyone from the hospital?'

The shake of the head. She had it down pat – a skill no doubt learned in childhood. You could say no all you liked with eyes as beautiful as that.

Becky agreed to accompany them on their search for supplies; Jane saw it as a start. She looked as though she wanted to go but the professional in her was the anchor.

'There's nothing to be done here,' Jane pressed.

'Survivors,' she said.

'They'd be here by now.'

'You weren't.'

'We've been on the road for days. I was thinking of Newcastle survivors.'

Becky turned to Aidan, as if silently canvassing for support.

'You can't stay here,' Jane said.

In the pharmacy she led them to a few of the shelves where stock had been ignored. Painkillers and antiseptic, syringes and penicillin went into Jane's rucksack, along with bottles he didn't recognise.

'Isn't that for diarrhoea?' Chris asked, intercepting a phial of potassium permanganate.

'Yes,' Becky said. 'But mix it with this' – she brandished a bottle of glycerin – 'and you get fire.'

Jane did his best to shield Aidan from the casualties as they made their way back to the entrance – a quadrangle was heaped with bodies wearing bloodied, rain-scarred hospital gowns – but Aidan did not seem affected by the atrocity. He kept batting away Jane's hand and asking, 'Is he dead?'

'He's been doing that for a week,' Becky explained. 'On the X-ray bed he was asking, *Will it hurt? Will I die?*'

It was probably the ideal age for a child to be caught up in an extinction-level event, Jane thought. Any younger and it would be non-stop crying. Any older and there'd be catatonia. Five-year-old boys and death were a fine match. In years to come, though, there could be some serious fallout in store for Aidan. Some enterprising young therapist, if there were any left, would get colossally rich on the back of this one day.

Brendan and Angela were in the same position in which they'd left them, holding on to each other as if afraid that one of them might defy gravity. They regarded Becky and Aidan with a naked pleading.

'We found some portable oxygen canisters,' Jane told them. 'And enough Ventolin to clear out Kong's chest.'

Brendan asked Becky: 'Are you a doctor?'
Aidan said, 'Am I looks like a doctor?'

They were readying to leave, Jane making his final appeals to Becky who was shaking her head, backing away, feeling for the entrance to the hospital behind her. A klaxon went off, dopplering through the blistered, blustery sky like the appetite cry of some fantastic beast. Jane swivelled on the step. He could see nothing beyond the thick ranks of cemetery cars. Dust had turned them all the same colour. It was piled thickly on the windscreens, obliterating any views within.

The klaxon came again, closer. Was this the sound they had heard in the nights on their approach to the city? Jane doubted it; that had been more organic – this was compressed, synthetic, impersonal. It had the air of code about it; he imagined a gathering of weaponised shadows closing in around them. Spies on rooftops coordinating an attack.

'I don't like this,' he said.

'What?' Chris said. 'Survivors? Like us? Are you worried your trip down to London is going to be delayed even more?'

'It doesn't feel right,' Jane said.

'That's because nothing *is* right any more,' Nance said. Chris curled an arm around her, trying to disguise his surprise at her support.

Jane's eyes were fast on a road filled with shadow, fifty yards or so away, opposite the car-park entrance. Something had moved within it, he was certain. Now he saw it again. A figure peeled itself away from the shelter of an overturned ice-cream van. A white scarf clung to the lower half of its face. Jane squinted, confused. It looked like a child, no older than nine or ten. There was something wrong with it. Its pallor was waxen, unnatural. He might have guessed this was some kind of sculpture, a fashion dummy escaped from the shop window, had it not been for the movements it made.

The klaxon made itself known again through the treacly air. The child's head snapped to the left; Jane followed her lead, again distracted by the apparent failure of her physicality. Was she sick? Was she disabled in some way? She raised her hand and he frowned and felt a tip of the tongue moment, a thing observed and then forgotten at the moment he noticed it. But all this was dismissed from his thoughts when he saw a half-dozen heads bobbing past the procession of naked trees at the far end of the car park. Steel flashed.

'We ought to leave,' Jane said. 'Is there another way out of the hospital?'

Becky led them back through the corridors. Jane heard something slam behind them. A crash. A cheer.

Chris said, 'Survivors,' but made no other attempt to get them to return. They were something other than survivors. They were drunk on that survival, or cursed by it. They had things on their mind other than finding family, or swapping tales of how they had dodged the breath of the devil. Survivors didn't knock about city streets clutching weapons, insanity flooding out of their wide-open mouths.

They were trying not to run, trying not to admit the panic in their legs, but they weren't far off it. Angela's breathing was shallow, irregular, edged with pain and fright. Brendan ushered her into a wheelchair and Jane didn't know what was worse, the protest of her lungs or the squeal of a loose castor.

'Did they see us?' Jane asked.

'I don't think so,' Nance said.

'Maybe they're coming here to stock up on pills,' Becky said. 'Maybe I ought to stick with you after all.'

The noise of pursuit carried on after the point where they would have reached the pharmacy.

'I get a feeling they saw us,' Chris said, risking the ire of his girlfriend for contradicting her.

Now they were running. Becky led them to a reception area on the east side of the hospital. A café was filled with patients and visitors obese with death. A security guard's hand was splayed on a visitors' book, his ravaged eyes downcast, tongue protruding as if in revulsion over his swollen, polished fingers. His skin was like paper, the heat had driven out the moisture from his bones. He was little more than a pillar of salt in a uniform.

They filed out, heads snapping this way and that as they searched for a path to safety, or somewhere to hide.

'Keep moving. Let's try to stay close and change direction as often as we can.'

They made their way through houses and shops, café kitchens into back alleys, hotel lobbies – Nance was eager to hide out in the rooms, but Jane's flesh tightened whenever they went indoors.

Eventually, with Angela close to tears and Brendan in need of oxygen himself after pushing his wife for so long, Becky asked if they might be safe now.

Jane stood still, looking back the way they had come. He waited a long time. Something in him, some diver's sensitivity to pressure change, suggested they were being followed.

'OK,' he said. 'I think we can rest for a while. But not too long, yes?'

'Well, that'll be for us to decide,' Chris said. Jane noticed the change in him, how he became cockier, more aggressive, when the number of companions increased.

'Of course,' Jane said. 'But if you're coming with me, I want to crack on.'

'We haven't decided what we're going to do yet,' Chris said.

Jane snorted. 'I'm sorry. I'm finding it hard to care. But in ten minutes, I'll be leaving. Anyone who wants to come along is welcome. Whatever you do, seriously, good luck.'

Chris wouldn't be mollified. Nance was egging him on with her eyes, with her body language. Jane gave him every opportunity, backing off, turning away, but Chris was at the point where any kind of retreat would be seen as cowardice. Nance would gut him for it later.

'Every step of the way you've been laying down the law,' Chris said. 'I'm not used to being ordered around.'

Jane couldn't suppress his laughter.

He felt Chris's hands on him, a push, a provocation. He felt fingers tighten on his jacket, turning him around.

'Maybe things can change a little bit,' Chris said, his fury spitting between clenched teeth, empurpling his face.

'You can be in charge all you like, Chris,' Jane said. 'Look around you. The world is all yours. Build an army. Go on a rampage. Conquer your enemies. Shout at their dead faces. Call them names—'

Chris hit him. The sound of the punch was flat and pathetic in this dead space. Jane felt a brief flare of pain in the lower left side of his jaw and thought he heard a distant scream, like those that had haunted them on their last few nights in the countryside.

Angela and Brendan turned away. Becky and Aidan watched with open mouths. Nance seemed excited, turned on almost, but confused too; perhaps she had been expecting a fight. Jane's pacific reaction was not in her copy of the script.

Jane readjusted his goggles, removed the air filter from his mouth and spat. Clean.

'What are you thinking, Chris?' Becky asked. 'We survived this terrible thing. There are hundreds of thousands, probably more like millions of people dead, and you're giving someone a slap because they said something you didn't like? Jesus.'

'Jesus,' Aidan said.

Jane kept his mouth shut. He stared at Chris, seeing the fight crumble out of him. Chris held up a finger; his hand was shaking violently: all that adrenaline crammed into his muscles and nowhere to go.

'A warning,' Chris said, but his voice could not invest in the weight of what he was trying to say.

They weren't safe.

As soon as they moved on they heard whooping noises again. Sounds of joy taken by some as yet unknown quantity into the realms of nightmare. These were violence sounds, death sounds. They carried on the wind currents like vengeful ghosts. Angela pushed herself up from the wheelchair and cried out: 'Leave us alone!'

Jane put a hand on her shoulder but it was too late. The whooping had stopped. Now they could hear determined footsteps slapping towards them.

'Keep your heads down,' Jane said. 'Don't make eye contact. Give them what they want. Don't give them an excuse to hurt us.'

There were six of them – five men and a girl, all of indeterminate age – and they came sprinting out of Castles Farm Road. They did not look good. Their heads had either been shaved to the quick or burned back almost to bone. They looked like something peeled and bruised and sore: too pink, purple and moist. Their blasted faces carried eyes that were overly bright, too intense. Jane wondered if they could focus properly; it was clear they had taken drugs of some sort. And then he saw the melted eyelids, the skin hanging off them like strips of torn material, and he understood why. They were not going to live for long.

'You!' one of them screamed, and they all swerved towards Jane, like starlings at dusk.

Jane again cursed their lack of a weapon, especially when he saw the ice axes hanging from their belts. He hoped that a lack of obvious threat might work in their favour; Angela and Aidan too. The gang didn't stop moving, even when they were within metres of their quarry. They prowled and twitched and spat and perspired. Nobody said anything until Angela again rose.

'Sit yourself back down!' the girl screamed. Metal studs poked out of her shoulders. Her shaven head was pockmarked with razor scars and slashes; it was difficult to guess if any were deliberate.

The girl wore a T-shirt bearing the legend *I LOVE GIRLS THAT LOVE GIRLS*. Some of the men wore knuckledusters. The pain they felt was there in their eyes; you could see it beyond the gauze of narcotics, you could hear it in every laboured inhalation.

'We have painkillers,' Jane said.

One of the men, a tall bull-shouldered figure with lips so dry they had blackened, laughed and unclipped one of the ice axes. He buried it to the hilt in his own thigh. They knew they were going to die.

'We have water too,' Jane said. They were clearly dehydrated. They were high on whatever they had injected or swallowed, but also on the natural chemicals with which their failing bodies had flooded their bloodstreams.

'Fuck your water!' The girl again, stabbing her head into his airspace like a weapon. '*What are you doing here? This is our sweetshop. You been stealing sweets?*'

Jane licked his lips. Carefully he said: 'We took some painkillers. Some inhalers. That's all.'

'That's all?' asked the man who had injured himself. He hobbled around them, each stamp of his foot on the ground pumping fresh blood up around the blade embedded in his thigh. 'The fact is, you set foot in our sweetshop. Without express permission.'

Another of the men ducked towards them, squat, box-headed, his teeth bared, gums bleeding a scarlet wash across them. 'Shoplifters,' he said, '*will* be prosecuted.'

'We didn't know,' Jane said. 'You can have it all back. We'll go somewhere else.'

'No. You won't,' said the girl, her words turning to ash. Her eyes were on Jane's throat. She was unhooking her axe; they all were.

Jane could see what was coming. He drove his fist into box-head's face and shouted '*Run.*'

He saw Becky drag Aidan away. Brendan was flapping at the girl's hands, trying to get her to drop the axe. Chris's hands were up in an appeal. Nance had ducked behind him, her hands holding on to the waistband of his jeans. Angela was leaning over her knees, praying or crying or trying to catch her breath.

Jane heard movement behind him and turned to keep it in front. As he circled he saw Angela lift her head, concern folding into her features. She raised a hand. He didn't realise she was reaching for him until he felt the blow on the back of his head. Suddenly he was on his knees, warmth trickling down his nape. He tried to stand but he couldn't feel his legs. Cold filled them. He vomited, put out a hand, but his eyes couldn't measure how far he had left to fall. He heard someone shout, 'No, Chris,' and then a cry: avian, shrill.

And then blackness.

9. THE PLUCKING POSTS

Blue sky. Such a searing science-fiction blue that he thought it must be a screen and looked to the horizon in case he could see its edge. He was lying on his back in a field. His arms were outstretched. Stanley's hands were touching his. They wrestled with each other lightly, fingers interlacing, interlocking, prodding, stroking. Jane turned his hand into a claw and froze it in mid-air. He began to move it jerkily, like a crippled crab:

Chum-chiggle-iggle-um-ching-cha . . .

No, Daddy, Stanley cried out, his voice a mash of giggles and pretend fright. *No.*

Jane moved his hand closer to where he imagined Stanley lay, looking up in gleeful terror as the probing fingers drew nearer. There was a tickle at the end of it all, when the suspense became so great that he was convinced Stanley would come apart at the seams with unbearable pleasure.

A shadow flitted across the rearing perfection of sky. A jet, Jane thought. But it returned, or was followed by another.

Dad?

Jane was twelve when he went fishing for mirror carp with his best friend at the time, a boy called Carl from his class at school. They'd cycled to the gravel pit, mist-covered and grey this particular winter morning, with rods already set up and baited, pieces of corn infused with vanilla extract speared on their hooks. Jane had told Carl that vanilla extract was a bit gay, but Carl said the fish liked it, that they wouldn't spit the corn out because of it.

They ditched their bikes next to the pit and pitched a tent. They made their casts and sat watching the tips of their rods. Soon Jane dug into his rucksack and started divvying up their breakfast. Morning rolls spread with peanut butter and mashed bananas, cold crispy bacon wrapped in kitchen paper, a flask of hot chocolate. Jane was bored after a couple of hours. He wasn't the fishing nut; he'd simply agreed to come along with Carl who had a passion for carp. It had sounded like an adventure. It was just cold and dull.

He told his friend he was going to do a round of the pit on his bike, maybe see if there was anywhere to do some jumps. Carl waved him off. Something made Jane turn to look back at his friend when he was on the opposite side of the pit. A figure, slight and pale, wearing a Lord Anthony covered in *Star Trek* badges and jeans so faded they were almost white.

Almost immediately he heard the sound of cows lowing. He turned toward the noise, nervous. He didn't like cows. He didn't like their thick pink tongues licking at too-wet nostrils. He didn't like their swollen udders and the caking of shit around their tails. They stank. They attracted flies. He drove his mother berserk because she was worried he wasn't getting enough calcium inside him.

There were no cows in the field. He could hear the groan of morning traffic rising from the main road, a couple of hundred yards away. And this lowing.

He scrambled through the sludge of rotten leaves and mud, splashing cold, dirty water all up the back of his cords

– his mother was going to clear his lugholes out over *that* when he got home – and found his way barred by a fence. Behind that were a couple of parked cars and an open door to the building beyond. The sound was coming from that.

Jane thought to go back to Carl and ask him about it – he knew this area better – but instead he dumped his bike and climbed over the fence. He went to the door and peeked inside. There were five men in white gowns and helmets, like a team of weird construction workers dressed up as ghosts. One of them turned around and Jane was aghast to see an apron slicked with blood. He stepped back out into the cold air, glad of it in his lungs, smacking him in the face. He thought about getting back on his bike and cycling to a phone booth, calling the police. There was murder going on here.

He had to make sure. He ran around the back of the building, where lorries were backed up against open bays. He heard the cows again. And other noises. Screams and squeals. This sounded nothing like the deaths that occurred on *Kojak*. Through a window he saw cows being led to pens. A man with what looked like a large black wand bent over them and pressed it to their heads. There was a hiss, a deep *ka-chunk* sound, and the animals dropped.

He didn't know whether what he felt then was relief or sickness. It was another kind of murder, after all.

He was thinking of bacon sandwiches, and whether he would miss them if he decided to become a vegetarian, when he heard another scream. This one was altogether different. It was high-pitched. Somehow *wetter*. It suggested a knowledge of what was happening to its owner.

He ran back to the windows, thinking of intelligent animals, wondering crazily when the British public had developed a taste for dolphins or octopi, and saw a long steel trench with lots of metal teeth turning within it. Someone had been piling indeterminate cuts and wobbling, shiny bits of offal from a plastic chute into one end but had got his arm trapped. His mates were running towards him and the man was screaming *Shut it off, shut it off.* Thankfully, Jane couldn't see his face. He didn't say anything else after that, because the auger ground him into the trench and he was killed. Jane heard the scream cut out as if the man had flicked off his own power switch. He'd heard, even at this distance, through the glass, the pulverisation of thick bone. He'd seen the teeth of the machine impacted with flesh and torn clothes. The man's face had risen from the trench, scooped up by a blade, like a bad horror mask on a pound-shop hook.

Jane was sick where he stood, violent and without warning. It was as if someone had punched it out of him from within.

He didn't remember climbing back over the fence, collecting his bike, or returning to Carl.

'Where have you been, you bone-on?' Carl demanded. 'You nearly missed this.'

He stood back to allow Jane a look at the mirror carp lying in the grass. It was enormous. It seemed deformed. Its skin was olive-coloured, there were maybe four or five scales, dotted near the tail and the dorsal fin. Its eyes protruded, its huge mouth gawped, gasping in the air. Jane felt suddenly detached from nature. Atrocity was in front of his face and at his heels. He couldn't understand how this thing could still be living, how it could have come into being in the first place. There was this sudden impact in his mind about the outrageousness of animals. He had sucked up science-fiction films since the age of five and stared out at the night sky wondering if aliens truly existed without giving any thought whatsoever to the bizarre creatures that lived on his own planet. Elephants. Rhinoceros. Squid. Mirror carp. Here was as weird as you could get. He saw Carl for what he really was, a network of organs, blood vessels, bones and nerves. A brain with ganglia. Meat. The boy in the snorkel parka was gone for ever. Everything had changed.

'I have to go home,' Jane might have said. He didn't remember cycling back.

He woke up with Stanley's name on his lips and his cheeks wet with tears. The back of his head felt as though it had not risen with him; tentative fingers tripped across the lacquer of his own dried blood, but despite a large lump he believed there to be no fracture.

He was alone, but had not been left where he fell. He fretted over that for a long time. Their attackers had meant to kill him. Perhaps they thought they had. So then why move him? He looked around. He was by the door of a fast-food restaurant. A plastic yellow signed warned: CAUTION, WET FLOOR. People had died queuing for burgers. People had died in the process of eating them. A man was sitting with his face in a cardboard carton, a whitened newspaper before him. The smell of old cooking oil, the greasy light on lengths of chrome, the plastic locked-down seating made Jane feel sick.

He pushed himself upright and staggered outside, fumbling for the bicycle mask dangling around his neck, and the welder's goggles, which had remained on his face but become displaced. He wondered how long he had been unconscious. It felt like a long time; the blood on him was long dry. He was hungry and thirsty. He thought he should look for the others; he couldn't guess how events must have developed after he had been knocked out, but he wouldn't accept that some of the others had failed to get away.

He checked his position. He had not been moved far. He walked back to the hospital and almost immediately found Angela and Brendan. Angela was still in the wheelchair. Like Jane she'd received one blow to the head, but this had proved catastrophic. He could see how Brendan had tried to protect her: defence wounds split his hands. His back was a patchwork of punctures.

Jane covered them with a tarpaulin liberated from a skip in the hospital car park. That the others were nowhere nearby gave him hope, but then, he thought, neither were the attackers. He patted his pocket, suddenly hollowed clean by fear that Stanley's letter had been taken. He realised he was moving in circles, reluctant to move beyond the self-imposed perimeter he'd created with the tarp. Staying with these known dead was his safest option. He knew where he was. He knew what the score was. Moving on meant that he might find the others dead. And he'd had a bellyful of it. Moving on was one step, one second closer to his own demise. Maybe it was time to let the misery come and find him for a change. Walking only ever seemed to lead him into danger. Though he'd been suspicious and impatient with the survivors he'd come across, he realised he liked it better with the sound of them griping alongside him. Hell might well be other people, but hell was also solitary confinement.

He took out Stanley's letter and read his closing words.

Hug you till yor branes com out yor ears Dad and boges com out yor noz. xxx

After a while he carefully folded the paper and replaced it in his pocket. He continued walking south.

He couldn't look. A second it had been, if that, to understand what he was seeing, before he tore his gaze away. But he knew the image would stay with him until death. Christ, maybe even longer.

They were all there, it seemed, arranged for him on the bank of land where the Angel of the North stood like an appeal at the foot of the dead city. Chris. Nance. The deranged killers. Strung up on telegraph posts, chests shredded, their tongues hanging from slashes in their throats like badly knotted school ties.

Jane had not happened upon any more survivors, despite checking the shopping malls, the football stadia, police cells and train stations on his way to pick up the A1 where it left Newcastle in motorway form. Whatever had broadsided the country seemed to have hit harder in some places than others. Perhaps it was to do with topography, the amount of land exposed to the sky. Perhaps it was just bad luck. He had to hold on to the possibility that survivors had massed and, like Jane, were marching on the capital, looking for the country's leaders to provide answers, protection, recovery.

He trudged by, head low, eyes on the road, always on the road, trying not to be too grateful that Becky and Aidan had escaped the kind of death visited upon the others. Trying not to think too much about who had committed their murders. Trying not to think about why.

There were other things to try not to think about. But the nearness of the Angel meant that he could cast his mind a little way back, to the road tunnel under the Tyne, and the girl in the car. The horror of proximity had receded, been trumped by other things.

He thought of the girl almost in sepia tones. It was as if it had never happened:

Cars mashed into each other. Darkness and ash. Every vehicle burned, matte, crumpled. No glimpse of road. Sometimes a jackknifed lorry meant that he had to climb down from the emergency footpath at the side of the tunnel and clamber over the bonnets and boots. He caught his hand in the shattered frame of a windscreen and hissed and swore, but he was lucky the skin had not been broken. Already he was worried about the break in his scalp. About what might have entered his body along with the edge of the axe.

Bodies hung out of windows or made abject shapes between cars. Everything carbon black. The smell of burning still in the air, cold, inescapable. This was what the air had become now. This was the smell of Earth.

Midway through the tunnel he heard water. Heavy water trickling, tapping hard on the ruined cellulose of the cars. The river coming through. He had to watch it. What use was he to Stanley if he was to survive the mother of all solar flares only to throw a seven drowning on river water? Despite the note of caution, he hurried on, slithering over the vehicles in his way, hoping that the darkness would not become absolute before he had picked a way through the tunnel.

He pushed his way past contorted bodies, grateful to the heat for disfiguring them to the point where he could not discern facial features or limb shapes; they were just nightmare trees, ugly and forbidding but easily avoided.

And then, insanely, a still point, a miracle. A car untouched by the flames, all of its glass intact. Torched, shattered shells of cars lay around it but had not come into contact with this one. There was a single occupant, a small girl perhaps aged ten or eleven. She was frozen into position on the back seat, a novel clutched in her hands. Next to her was a neat pile of comics, a hairbrush and a bag of chocolate éclairs. Her skin shone. Her hair was neat and long, the fringe held back with a green clip that had been fashioned to resemble a dragonfly.

Breath trapped in his throat, Jane stood by her window for a long while, waiting. He reached out for the handle but it was locked. All of them were. Parents gone to look for help? No, one parent. It would be one. Otherwise one of them would have stayed with her. But in that case why not take her too? And then he thought maybe the driver had been dragged out of the car and his last act had been to lock the doors. But if they were desperate enough to do that they'd be more than prepared to smash the windows. He puzzled over the problem, knowing the answer was there but refusing to countenance it.

He found a car jack and stove in the front passenger window. The smell that lifted out from the car was of fresh peaches. He unlocked the door and clambered in, careful not to scrape his leg against the chunks of glass on the passenger seat. He sat down in the back next to her. She was dead.

He touched her and she was stiff. Her eyes were open, the irises the colour of ivory writing paper. He tried to wrest the book from her hands to see what it was but her grip was colossal. She wore an expression of hope. She seemed to have died from the inside out, and her body had been incapable of going through with it when it met her beautiful shell.

'I won't abandon you,' Jane said to his boy, and he almost jumped because she seemed to move. But it was only his breath in her hair.

He walked hard, concentrating on his rhythm and his breathing. He tried to walk angled forwards, as much to cope with the weight of the new rucksack as to prevent himself from seeing anything else bad that day. He walked past pubs and houses and shops and did not glance at them. He stepped around the bodies in the road, avoiding their fixed stares, if they had been allowed even that. He walked until the pain in his legs became a constant and his lungs roared like the surf at the shore.

Next decent place, he thought, and kept on until the clouds lost their definition and turned from coffee to steel grey to slate to black. He thought of the figure he had seen, the child wearing the white scarf, appraising him intently. An omen or a warning. A ghost. Something about her.

There was a hotel set a little way back from the road. Whatever sign it once displayed had been torn down by the wind. Some of the glass in the face of the building was intact. Darkness was its only living inhabitant.

He crunched through the lobby. The reception desk was deserted. A floor plan explained the hotel layout. The lift was open; darkness prevented him from seeing anything other then the soles of three pairs of feet. He took the stairs up to the top of the building, the darkness solidifying around him at each landing until he could barely see to put one foot in front of the other. There were two honeymoon suites up here. He checked them both and rejected the first because rain had found a way in.

He dumped his rucksack on the bed and stretched. He took off his boots and socks and let his feet sink into the deep pile of the carpet. It was cold, but at least it was dry. He placed his clothes over the radiators in the hope that the sweat would dry out of them by the morning. He lit candles and placed them around the room. In the bathroom a wild figure ducked out at him and he almost shouted. He stared at himself in the mirror, at the rings of black that the air filter and goggles had marked, at the thickening beard; he went hunting for a razor.

To his astonishment, the monsoon shower worked, after an age of groaning and gurgling and retching. Jane positioned himself beneath it and quickly scrubbed his skin clean. He was appalled to find a great many patches that wouldn't shift so readily under the soap: bruises. He shampooed his hair, gently working at the matted cake of blood at the back of his head. He winced as he fingered the knot of skin there, and watched, dismayed, as the water turned black around his feet. How close had he been to death? How much harder did he need to be hit before it accepted him? He couldn't understand why there were people left who wanted to do harm to others. Fear ought to have ended with the blast that eradicated so much life. It was hard enough to think about survival without having to worry about being attacked too.

He soaped his arms and chest and genitals. He closed his eyes and thought of his honeymoon with Cherry. They had been unable to go away for a proper holiday. Cherry was heavily pregnant and Jane was expected on the rigs within a week and a half of their wedding day. They promised each other a luxury break to the Bahamas as soon as they could find the time. Instead they had booked a night in a huge room at a boutique hotel in London with views of Waterloo Bridge. They had drunk champagne and made love on the balcony. Later he had whispered to Stanley in his mother's tummy in the dark while she slept in a bed so large he thought he might lose her.

The water sputtered. Jane quickly rinsed the rest of the soap from his body as the stream became a stutter of drips. He was sobbing and hardly realised. He always did his best crying in the shower; he'd done a lot of it back home. It meant that Stanley couldn't tell there was something wrong if he wandered into the bathroom.

He shaved by candlelight, rinsing his razor in a bowl of drinking water poured from the plastic bladder. A man he didn't recognise emerged. Thin. Eyes couched in soft grey pouches. Skin blistered and pale.

There was plenty of food but his body craved something green. Salad. Steamed French beans. Peas thumbed out of a pod. Buttered asparagus spears. A sour apple. His stomach complained. He turned to what remained in his pack. Hot-dog sausages in brine. Spam. Tinned fruit salad. Condensed milk. A tinned strawberry-flavoured protein shake. He could feel the food sitting heavily in his gut before he'd taken a spoonful.

He left the food on the table, peeled four paracetamol and codeine tablets out of their blister packs and dissolved them in water. He swallowed the draught down, grimacing at the bitter taste and the sediment at the bottom of the glass. He unwrapped a waffled bathrobe and a pair of slippers. He was still a little cold but there were spare blankets in the wardrobe. In the mini-bar he found four miniatures – vodka, gin, whisky and rum – and a half-bottle of Australian Merlot. He lined them up on the coffee table and snapped open the ring-pull on the first of the tins. He forked meat into his mouth and now the hunger didn't care whether it was processed slabs of meat or the finest pâté or if there were any accompanying vegetables. The best part of two weeks spent guzzling cold canned produce didn't half put a muffler on your taste buds.

Jane finished the wine with indecent haste and set about the shorts. The pain in his head had dulled; it felt as though he were enclosed within cotton wool. He was warm and full and a little high on the codeine and booze. He wished he had the means to boil some water; a cup of coffee would pretty much set the seal on a perfect end to a shitty day.

He thought about Becky and Aidan. He hoped they had managed to put some distance between themselves and their attackers and, if they were safe, that they had not seen what he had seen. He wished them a warm, comfortable retreat, some food, some hope. He tipped his bottle to the oily scamper of clouds beyond the smeared windows. He was asleep before he'd sealed the toast with a sip from its mouth.

He was chased through interminable hotel corridors by something with deep, dripping red jaws that were unstable, unravelling, leaving teeth the size of boning knives like mantraps to fox any hope he had of return. Shreds of white scarf dangled from them like flags of surrender. He was running out of routes. Becky's voice was somewhere, exhorting him to *turn this way, turn that way*, to *come on, for Christ's sake*. To *move*.

Light chanced across the way ahead; he arrowed for it. He could hear the rage and the upset in the throat of the thing that hunted him. He crashed through a revolving door that gritted and scraped upon lumpen shapes that threatened to block him in for good. But they did not catch and he was through and safe.

Here there was no stinging red rain or lightning or random fires. The ground was flat and there were animals grazing, swinging their heads up to regard him almost with bland amusement. The sea was topped by only the most occasional tilde of foam. He was no longer being pursued, but there remained the awful pressure of something at his shoulder, some presence demanding that he turn and sate the curiosity that was burning a hole through the back of his head.

He would not do it.

He felt a hand on his hair, pulling, scratching, trying to gain purchase on the ugly scar where the ice axe had glanced against his skull. A fingernail caught on the wound and he felt it loosen. He felt the matter inside him shiver like a barely set custard. He was going to come spluttering out of that gash, turned inside out like the contents of a plane's fuselage punctured at 40,000 feet.

But the hand only wanted him to turn and look. To acknowledge.

They had all been lashed to great posts of wood driven deep into the ground. Their arms had been broken behind them, tied against the wood so tightly that the canvas strips had bitten into their wrists. Their legs dangled. He could see where the heels of some of them had scraped into the wood as they tried to gain purchase, tried to lift themselves up enough to take a breath as they suffocated.

Something had been at them. Their bodies were torn and pecked. Their eye sockets were ragged holes. Their lips turned to purple scarecrow cross-hatchings where the integument was stabbed away.

The ground around them was a stew of feathers and blood. Their eyes swivelled to follow his progress beneath them. Open mouths struggling and failing to suck in the air they needed to cry for help or condemn him.

Jane jerked out of sleep, his mouth trickling with blood, his tongue filled with bright stitches of pain where he had bitten it. Had they been alive? Could he have helped any of them at all?

He sat up in bed. The slurry of rain at the windows. The dark hanging in the rooms like a poisoned cloud. The sheets were a tangled mess; he'd kicked them to the floor in the night. He could feel his heartbeat, very close, so close he almost mistook it for someone else's and sat there shivering, fists to his eyes, certain that someone would reach out and touch him in a moment. Someone whose blood was too cold and still to be deserving of such a heartbeat. He heard padded footsteps on the carpets in the halls. He heard the snuffle of his boy asleep, the occasional nonsense he would sometimes speak as an unknowable dream flitted around his mind: *Spiky crawns ... Bye, George! Bye! Spiky crawns ... you can't eat them.*

Nance's jeans had been torn off her; the skin of her legs hung like badly adhered wallpaper. Chris's face was black, swollen to twice its size. The killers' meatless grins; fear shining through the narcotic haze in their eyes.

He shrank away from his own thoughts, dug his fists deeper into his eye sockets as if he could threaten the images away. It was past five a.m. There was no way back into sleep. He tried the water in the bathroom again but the spigots only breathed at him – they were dry. He dressed quickly and shouldered the rucksack. The room no longer seemed so inviting. The pile was too springy, it reminded him of walking on body parts in the Tyne tunnel. Too cold, too dark. A smell of staleness, of life in stasis.

Jane hurried down the stairs, his neck prickling as he imagined shadows leaping out behind him, begging him not to go, to stay in the hotel for ever with them because what was the point of trying any more? Death was thrown into ever more excruciating detail now, you couldn't focus on anything else. Surviving this only meant you wouldn't survive that, or the next thing, or the next. Death was queuing up to get you.

10. PICA

Jane got back onto the A1 and stretched his legs, found a rhythm and stuck to it. The shape of other dead towns grew firmer in his sight as his eyes accustomed to the dark. The chimneys and rooftops were depressing in their numbers. Endlessly replicated streets of punched-in windows and terror in every sitting room. These were not houses any more; they were mausoleums.

The pattern repeated itself. He walked. He fed. He slept. He restocked his supplies. He found new boots and clothes. He replaced the filters on his mask. He broke down at the side of the road and screamed and cried and wished things were different. He wished himself dead. His checks on conurbations he passed through became less thorough. He didn't want to pick up any more dependants.

He turned and looked back at the way he had come. He used the binoculars to see if he could find evidence of the figure he had seen in the white scarf. Already he was beginning to think it had been an hallucination. Nothing shifted on the horizon. It was as if he were dragging oblivion in his path, erasing everything in his tracks.

He wished Stanley dead.

He broke into a pub and drank himself into a stupor and woke up in some half-melted bus shelter apologising over and over and over . . .

Jane opened his eyes one morning to find he had overslept for the first time in weeks. He could feel illness sitting in his chest like flame just failing to catch on damp tinder. His breath was soggy, painful. He felt chilled to the bone yet saturated with perspiration. The light lanced him despite the tinted goggles.

He knew enough to drink plenty and often and was glad he'd recently replenished the fresh water in the bladder. But it quickly became obvious that this wasn't just some niggling cold. He developed a cough that soon began to saw in his throat; it sounded like some avian warning signal. He spat into the verge at the roadside and his waste was thick and green. Infection.

He was no longer exactly certain of his position. All of the road signs had been bleached white or burned black. The map was no longer of any use if he couldn't picture himself on its green dual carriageway, snailing his way south.

'Hi, Dad.'

'Hi, Stanley. You need a wee?'

'No.'

'Then stop fidgeting. You could fidget your way to Olympic glory, you could.'

'What means linpic?'

'Never mind.'

'What your doin', Dad?'

'Walking.'

'I'm tired.'

'Me too.'

'Can I go on your shoulders?'

'No. Carrying a bag up there.'

'Aw.'

'Come on, you're a big boy now. You can walk.'

'Where's the car?'

'Broken.'

'You broked it?'

'No. Something happened. All the cars broke.'

'What about motorbikes?'

'Them too.'

'Are motorbikes faster than cars?'

'Some.'

'Are motorbikes faster than cheetahs?'

'Oh yes.'

'Are cheetahs faster than swordfish?'

'We'll never know. Where's your mum?'

'I don't like girls.'

'You might, one day.'

'Boys are best.'

'We have our moments.'

He looked down to his side where Stanley was walking, but he had gone. Jane inspected his hand, as if he might see some ghost of his son enclosed within it, but there was just the usual network of filth and blisters.

He could no longer hear the ocean. He doubted he ever could, beyond its persistent echo in his thoughts. You lived and worked on the sea for long enough you heard its call when you were in the deepest parts of the inner city. You never forgot its voice. He had stopped. He was looking towards the coast, which was lost behind some urban pile that might have been Sunderland, Hartlepool or Middlesbrough. The only thing that shored up the misery was the way in which the land was condensing; there were fewer open tracts between cities. The bucolic sprawl towards Scotland was giving way to the industrial claustrophobia of the North-East.

He sat down in the road, listening to the squeak and burble of fluid in his lungs. He thought of eating something and his stomach flinched. He kept walking. His eyes streamed so that the view through his smeared goggles was of a world of splinters that he had to fight to keep vaguely horizontal. The wind bullied the clouds along, but there was never a break in their ceiling. The sun was a piss stain on a grey blanket. The ceiling lowered; its colour deepened. After an hour he saw lightning stab the earth maybe twenty miles to the west. Thunder concussed the air around him. He sensed rain building long before he felt it. When it came it was tropical. Large bullets pelted him. He took refuge in a barn on the edge of a field where rape might once have blazed but was now only so much ash and stubble. Farm machinery stood like some pathetic exhibition of past glories. Already the shape and purpose of such vehicles struck him as faintly ridiculous. He couldn't remember the sound an engine made. The howl of the wind and the memory of surf was a white noise that erased all others. He poured water from the bladder into a metal cup tied to one of the rucksack straps and added four soluble painkillers. He downed it before it was ready, crunching on the tablets and feeling them fizz on his tongue. Almost immediately a coughing fit caused him to bend double; he had to put out a hand to steady himself against dizziness, the scatter of light seeds across his vision. He hawked and spat. No blood, at least. Not yet.

He forced himself to eat: a small can of macaroni cheese, a small can of pineapple rings. The food rolled uneasily around; he lay on his side in swatches of straw that, if he pushed his face in far enough, smelled of childhood. He closed his eyes, concentrating on not vomiting. After a while he felt better, and realised that he must have slept: the fingers of light were pointing a different way through the cracks in the barn door. He sat up and a gruel of heat behind his sternum spread through the base of his lungs. It was a strange feeling, an itch deep inside him. He wondered if this was cancer's beginning; after all, he couldn't expect to escape every kind of physical repercussion.

Jane checked in his rucksack but there was nothing to help beyond the painkillers and a packet of blackcurrant-flavoured throat lozenges. Tired of cold food, he cleared a space and built a fire out of straw. He broke off some decaying slats of wood from the apron of the barn and positioned them above his kindling. He poured a little of the glycerine and potassium permanganate onto the straw. A couple of seconds later they combusted. He felt a tremor of the thrill he used to get as a child whenever he saw good magic being performed. 'Good work, Dr Becky,' he said. The words came out on razor wire.

He punched holes in the lids of cans of potatoes and stewing steak in gravy and placed them on the edge of the fire. He thought of hot baths and warm beds while he watched the food bubble, and ate with his fingers, juggling the scalding meat around his mouth and blowing out his cheeks. He blistered the roof of his mouth, but it was a good pain. He ought to cook more of his food; it improved it no end and it gave a brief illusion of normality.

He sucked his fingers clean and lay back in the straw. He watched the flames turn to embers. He was asleep again before the embers had lost their blush.

Jane woke up cold and stiff. There seemed to be no change to the burning in his chest. At least he had suffered no nightmares in the night, or he had failed to remember them. He palmed some water from the bladder and washed his face, his hands scraping against stubble. Bearded again soon. He gingerly felt the wound in his head. It seemed to be healing well. He refreshed the dressing and carefully pulled the beanie down over it.

He shouldered the backpack, repositioned the mask and goggles, and opened the barn door. He looked out at the bewarted, bewitched landscape and ran his tongue over furred teeth. The rain was still there but it had lost its muscle. Skeins of it hung like barrage nets. Hills slouched away from the road like the bellies of downed comeback boxers. Pylons marched into the mist, their cables impotent. A febrile, feral country now.

The sky seemed a little lighter towards the south. He rejoined the A1 and fixed his eyes on a point on the ground four feet or so further on than the extent of his step. He did not look up for three hours.

Jane's coughing had worsened. Each convulsion caused a flare of pain in his chest. He thought that if he contracted pneumonia he would die.

He got off the road and made his way to the black crust of a town. Rooftops shivered with soot. A church steeple had been shattered; buckled ribs thrust out of it like the exposed frame of a burnt corset. Tree limbs and human limbs lay in his path, burnt into solid, fissured cords of carbon. Arse-end retail parks. Computer palaces offering any combination of frazzled, corroded processors and silicon chips. Deep-fried chicken for deep-fried customers. A supermarket the size of a small airport.

Jane trudged, coughing, across the car park. Litter wheeled around him. A dent in the wall suggested that the wind had lifted heavier things in the recent past. Something thin grinned at him by the trolleys like a portion of hide draped on a chair to dry out in the sun. He paid it no heed. He bypassed calcined ranks of dead whose last act had been to queue for lottery tickets. *It might be you.* It was.

The supermarket had been rifled. The perishables had cooked, melted and rehardened into their plastic baskets. Most of the tinned produce was gone. That which remained was fouled in some way. He got on his knees and checked underneath the shelves. He fished out some cans that seemed fine. Sardines, mushroom soup, tomatoes in herbs. He put them in the rucksack. He found more canned goods in the infant section that had been ignored or more likely unseen. Puréed spinach and apple. Apricot and vanilla custard. Sweet potato, rice and butternut squash. He was aiming to reach the top of this aisle and turn into the next when he heard a boot grind into glass. To his right, a little behind him. He snapped his head that way, and pulled the reins on a cough. He froze.

After a few seconds he heard another step. Something shadowing his movements. Jane immediately turned and began creeping back the way he had come, his head turned to the left now, eyes burning into the empty shelves as if he could see his pursuer through the moulded steel. He tried to remember if he had made any noise beyond the gentle clacking of cans as he stowed them in his rucksack. He shot a glance towards the end of the aisle, panic rising, certain that he was surrounded. He had to face the possibility that not every survivor was a potential ally. Desperation drove people to do extraordinary things, not all of them laudable. He had made a mistake, been too blasé. He must be more diligent in future, if he had one.

He reached the end of the aisle and risked a look beyond its edge. Nothing. He turned and kept his eyes on the other aisle's far end as he backed out of it. A shadow lengthened on the wall. One arm much longer than the other. Jane stepped out of sight before the shadow could shed its host. He moved as quickly as he dared, scanning every aisle around him as he drew alongside them, trying to work an angle to enable him to check the entrance for a sentry before he was on top of it. He thought of the Falkland Islands and the battalions who'd had to clear out the villages on their way to Port Stanley. He wondered if the soldiers sent into those houses had felt as soft in the middle of their bodies as he did now. Fear was fuel, he thought. Fear was good. Strangely, he did feel better than at any point over the last three or four days. The cough was in abeyance, the fire in his chest subsumed by the spike of adrenaline.

Jane hurried through the car park, feeling terribly exposed. At the exploded wreck of a tree stump he hid, watching the entrance. Nobody appeared. He waited for a long time, more than half an hour, and was beginning to doubt what he had heard and saw. He was shifting the pack into a more comfortable position, readying himself to move away, when the darkness within the entrance changed, and he could make out the white scarf concealing the face of the figure he had seen in Newcastle, before their encounter with the mob that had attacked them. Jane's heart put a spurt on. The figure did not emerge fully, but hung back a little, as if aware that it was being observed. Pale, thin; even at this distance he could tell it was trembling. A fledgling fallen from the nest. There was something both repulsive and weirdly comforting about the figure. Its anatomy was all wrong; Jane wondered if it might be injured in some way, but that didn't feel right. The shape of illness was in it. A body racked by convulsions; a physique drawing into itself due to the suck of failed lungs. Bad blood. Change and compromise. His mind flirted with images of mutations. He wondered if what had flashed across the surface of the Earth might also have damaged the little genetic kinks that made us human.

Jane was convinced now that he was being followed by the figure, but to what end? He didn't feel threatened by it; he believed the appearance of the attackers at the same time to have been a coincidence. He wondered if the figure had something to do with their deaths, but then that would mean it had done for Chris and Nance too. Again he wondered why he had been spared.

The figure moved back inside the supermarket and Jane waited and watched for another quarter of an hour before moving on.

As Jane had expected, the travails of the day had an adverse effect on him. He could feel his strength sapping at each step. The fire had returned to his chest, with interest, and each breath bore a damp, rattling coda. If he looked up from the rhythm of his feet the edges of the road were blurred, and he felt he could no longer blame that on the mist, or the goggles. He thought he might be dying.

'Stanley?' he called out, but his voice wouldn't rise above a bubbling whisper.

He couldn't summon the sound of his boy's voice, or his face from the grain that was writhing behind his eyes. He panicked, thinking that his mind was already shutting down, the brain cells switching off, and that any memory of Stanley he might have clung to *in extremis* was lost to him.

There seemed to be no towns or villages within reach. The wind was building; the storm he thought he had left behind was circling, coming back. He pitched his tent by the roadside but was too weak to bow the poles into position. He crawled into the tent as it was and chewed on co-codamol tablets till their foam parted his lips. He pulled out a tin but couldn't read the label. He fell asleep squinting at it.

Footsteps gritting on the road. The tang of a shovel as it bit the ground next to him. If he reached out he might be able to touch the gravedigger's boot.

* * *

A smell of cold, burnt fat. A hand in his hair, pulling it back. Rain on his face. The sound of something querulous, unsure. A glimpse of white scarves.

The smell of cooking, of fresh, hot meat. He saw firelight through the drizzled mess of his vision. Figures moving through it, like the winks and kinks of perspective in a mirage. He was handed a bowl and he took it, but stared only at the space above it, where the hand that proffered it had been seconds before. A pale, elegant hand. Long fingernails sharpened to claws. Feathers stitched into the skin of the hands. He ate the food in the bowl, a delicious stew of dumplings and what tasted like roast pork, but he knew he was dreaming when he got to the end of his meal and found a strip of meat with a crisp coating of tattooed skin attached.

The fire extinguished. The figures moving away. The hoot of an owl somewhere; an answering call in the distance. A blanket for his body, a pillow for his head. Hands on his face, soothing. A smell of cloaca. Something sharp pressed into his palm; his fingers gently closed one by one, locking it into his grasp. That querulous sound again. A soft trilling on the breath. A question or a comfort. Then gone and the hard acres of sky pressing down on him.

Something was darting around above them, too far off to be identified. Occasionally the swiftness would change to a slow circling. *They birds, Stanners? Can you see?*
Dad?
Jane reached for Stanley's hands again, hearing the panic building in his son's voice. He could see the birds now. Birds of prey. Owls and buzzards, kites and hawks. But there was something wrong with them. They spiralled, falling, not diving; they were struggling to stay aloft. And now Jane

could see why; they were destroyed, their wings parting from the patagium. They seemed able to remain airborne, yet void of any counterweight they spun like seeds to the earth. There were hundreds of birds. It was like weather, of sorts.

Jane grabbed his son's hands. 'They're going to hit us, Stan,' he said. They would have to gain shelter, fast, if they were to have a chance of evading the talons and bills of so many plummeting birds.

He pulled and it was too easy. He rolled and the hands rolled with him. He glanced back and froze. Stanley's hands ended at the forearm. What remained of the bone was socketed in the wet sleeve of flesh. The great chiselled bill of a foot-high raptor came suckingly free of Stanley's opened chest. The screech it loosed as it gulped down bits of his son jagged along Jane's spine like a curve of broken glass.

Voices. Whispered, urgent. Happy. Sad. *No, don't move me.* From a sort of warmth to definite cold. He felt himself being lifted. He could do nothing about it. Something hard and edged and cold beneath him. He slithered into it. A sense of movement.

The scratch of a needle in his arm. The sound of water. A smell of wood burning. *They will scald me first. It will help them to pluck the hair out. Will they kill me before they cook me?* A warm blanket. A cool flannel.

He was tensed to the slash of a hunting knife at his throat. He kept waiting for the rage of a smoking griddle to tiger his skin. The spit and crackle of his own fat. The rending of open mouths unable to wait for the meat to cook through. These things were inevitable, but they never came.

Instead, by degrees, he felt the fire in his chest dampened. The pulses and jolts in his head evened out. The irritation in his lungs disappeared so swiftly it was as if someone had reached into his windpipe and plucked it free. He looked down at his fist, opened it. Stared at the thing within.

'The tent fall on top of you while you were sleeping?'

He turned to see Aidan looking at him. He held a toy in his hands. A plastic figure disfigured by heat. Aidan's plaster cast was dark grey, fraying at the end.

'It must have done,' Jane said rustily, unable to keep the wobble from his voice. 'What you got there?'

'General Grievous,' Aidan said. 'He's in *Star Wars*. The third film. My dad won't let me watch it because he says it's too scary. He's got a cough nearly as bad as yours.'

'Your dad?'

Aidan rolled his eyes. 'No. General.'

'It's really good to see you again,' Jane said.

'Do you want a hug?'

'I'd love a hug.'

Aidan came to him and put his good arm around Jane's neck. Jane was unable to stop himself from sobbing. He closed his eyes as the tears came and Aidan patted him gently.

'You might want to keep that cast away from me. I don't want to catch anything nasty.'

'Lick it,' Aidan said, pushing the bandage into Jane's face. They were wrestling happily together when Jane realised they were being watched.

'You need to rest,' Becky said. She was smiling. He smiled too.

'Where are we?'

'Sunny York,' she said. 'You've been asleep for nearly twenty hours.'

'I feel better.'

'You had a chest infection. You were so hot. The sweat was flying off you. It was really worrying.'

'I didn't mean to alarm you.'

'I pumped you with antibiotics. Good that you did this now, while they were still effective.'

'How do you mean?'

'Drugs have a use-by date, just like food. Their efficacy wears off after a while.'

Jane sat in silence, digesting the significance of this. Aidan quietly swapping his attention from one to the other, a trait Jane noticed he fell back on when he was unsure of a situation, or how it might develop.

'I'm moving on,' Jane said. 'I can't stay here.'

'We'll all go,' Becky said. 'No more Scooby-Doo shit, right?'

11. HIBAKUSHI

They talked while the tarmac disappeared beneath their feet. Sometimes when Aidan grew tired Jane would give him a piggyback, or they took it in turns to push him in the wheelbarrow Jane himself had been carried in when he'd been found. Aidan was in there now, asleep, his arms over his head as if he were playing hide-and-seek.

'Where did you find me?' Jane asked Becky.

'We were looking for you. You said you'd stick to the A1. It was Aidan who saw you. Lying on a bench in the Shambles. I thought you were . . . God, this is awful to say . . . just another dead body. But he recognised you even though you'd been . . . swaddled.'

'Swaddled?'

'Wrapped head to toe in blankets. You looked like something parcelled up. Or an offering.'

He didn't like the sound of that.

'After we were attacked . . . after you got away,' he said, 'did you see—'

'Yes, we saw.' And her tone put an end to that.

'I think I'm being followed,' he said.

Jane could see in the shape of Becky's face that she had

thought about that, perhaps considered the wisdom of taking to the road with him again. She said, 'We can't be the only ones who made it. There's no telling how many survived, up in the mountains, say, or, like you're hoping, in the tunnels, the Tube. And there's no telling how many of them might be nutcases. Born mad, or turned mad by all this.' She cast her arm at the firestormed city. 'Maybe you are being followed, and maybe they're friendly. But we should suspect otherwise. I don't ever want the decision of how I bow out taken from my hands again.'

They walked in silence and Jane stared at the boy, not knowing how to phrase his next question. Becky noticed it in him and understood what he was working on. 'It's not something we need to discuss now,' she said. 'It can wait.'

He could not help but compare her to Cherry. Cherry's insistence had an edge to it that said, pester me about this at your peril. Becky was firm, but he could see the cracks. There was pleading there. He wondered how Cherry would deal with their situation. He thought about how it might change her. Maybe the cracks in her shell would be showing too by now. It bolstered him a little to think that she might welcome his arrival.

If she survived, kiddo. Big fat if.

The way that decay wormed its way into the structures that people in love built around them. He couldn't pinpoint a moment when he noticed that his and Cherry's lives had soured. He guessed it was the same for all doomed couples; a gradual disaffection. You suddenly found yourself spitting and sneering at each other, arriving at some awful location without remembering the route. You couldn't turn back or consult a map; the road behind you seemed to erase itself. There were other routes, but they never quite arrived back at the place where you were most happy.

Jane remembered being in a pub in Stoke Newington one afternoon. Cherry and Stanley had gone off to visit her parents in Reading. He'd been flicking through a magazine, wondering whether to have another pint or wander down to the Keralan restaurant for lunch, when he noticed a couple sitting on a sofa in a far corner. Something in their body language that wasn't being replicated by any of the other couples caught the eye. A distance. Defensiveness. He was trying to mollify her; everything about her talked of barriers. Crossed arms, crossed legs, her body angled away from him. Her eyebrows knitted, the flatlining mouth. He would say something, his arms open; she would shake her head. He was crestfallen. She was determined.

It was painful to watch, but enthralling too. How did things get to such a point? When did the smiles and the butterflies and the quickening heart become a folding inward? How could something as positive as love become dread? And then Cherry came to his thoughts, reading out the grim list, her breath hitching in her throat as she rushed to get it all out before he could argue a point.

You got older, there were resentments and regrets. You felt stifled, unfulfilled. You felt trapped by the person you'd thought you'd go to the grave with. You were tired all the time. You had more important things to think about than curling up in front of the fire to read or watch a film together, to make love.

He turned away from her furious, strangely triumphant features, and saw the girl stand, shrug away from the beseeching hands. Jane could see this was the final summit, could see it in the crumbled look of the boy. He'd played every card and was left holding the Joker. Sitting near the door, Jane had watched the girl leave. She'd drawn herself upright, lost the tightness that drew her features together before she'd crossed the threshold. She appeared reborn. He wondered if there was another man she was already on her way to. There was a catalyst, he supposed. A sweetener. He considered, idly, on the point of sleep, whether Cherry's head had been turned by someone else, someone closer to home who chatted to her and Stanley, who didn't go off to the rigs every six months. Even now, when he thought he'd been immunised to every kind of pain there was left to know, the thought pierced him. Jane no longer had his map. But he wasn't so desperate to know where he was all the time. The road would take him where he needed to be, as long as he stayed on it and kept the paling sun to his left at dawn, right at dusk. When his watch stopped he felt a blip of panic, but it soon passed. He didn't need to know the time. He didn't need an alarm. It no longer mattered what date it was. It was liberating. He was paring away all the dead wood, the better to focus on his son. Sustenance, shelter and progress, that was what it all boiled down to.

And these shades on your heels. Don't forget them.

Jane ground the thought under his heel and upped his pace. He had developed a feel for distance and wanted to improve his daily mileage after his sickness had reduced him to a snail's meander. Becky didn't say a word but fell in step with him. The jolting of the wheelbarrow eventually wakened Aidan, but he didn't speak either. He watched Jane as if unsure of who he really was, or trying to assimilate him with the thin figure he had spotted on the bench, rattling in his sleep.

They stopped at a place where the M1 and the A1 split into separate roads. West of here was a town. Jane found some hiking boots for Aidan, who was wearing trainers that were beginning to unravel. It was difficult to shield him from the worst of the casualties but in the end Aidan just told him it was OK. Dead things didn't scare him. It was the living he was worried about.

Some of the dead bore unusually specific injuries, as if the heat had been focused on a plane. Jane thought about that a lot. It suggested something other than a random explosion or explosions. A woman whose clothes had been incinerated off her body had been burnt across her back, but there was an unaffected line of skin next to her spine, as if that scimitar of bone had shaded it from the fire. Other people were burnt only on their hands or faces. But it had not been this flash that had killed them; an ambient heat had cooked them from the inside out, like a microwave oven.

They found a supermarket but Jane told them to wait a while before entering; they sat on a wall and watched the door. The shelves were packed with bad food. Thousands of tins that had been compromised in some way: splits and pits and punctures.

'What happens when the food runs out?' Aidan asked.

'It's not going to run out,' Jane said. 'Think of all those millions of houses. All those millions of tins.'

'There isn't much here,' Becky said 'And a lot of the stuff we've found in the houses so far has been damaged. Exploded because whatever it was that hit us cooked everything inside the tins. Getting the shits from a dodgy meal isn't funny any more. It can kill you.'

'There's plenty. We just have to think.'

Aidan said, 'The shits.'

Jane led them along the aisles and checked underneath the bottom shelf. Only a tin of broad beans. 'See,' Jane said. 'Everyone else missed this one.'

'Or left it on purpose,' Aidan said. 'I don't like beans.'

Jane led them to a curtain of plastic at the back of the supermarket. It had melted from the doorway and resolidified into a weird polymeric puddle. They crackled across it and into the delivery bays beyond. An articulated lorry was parked outside. All of the pallets in the bays were empty. A fork-lift truck lay on its side, whatever it had been carrying incinerated. Jane unclasped the hitches on the canvas flanks of the artic and threw them back.

A smell, sweet and rank, hit him like a fist. He recoiled. Nothing good in there. He saw the soles of feet, maybe half a dozen people sitting up against the back of the lorry. Everything on the pallets already taken or spoiled. Back in the delivery bay there was nothing but a large lidded yellow skip, some cleaning fluid and mops. A radio that didn't work.

'We'll find something at the next one,' Becky said. 'And all those houses. There must be tons of food.' Her face clouded at this, though. Jane could see how appetites might be tested if they had to resort to wading through bodies to get to their cans of button mushrooms and new potatoes.

They were heading out but all Jane could think of was the skip. 'Wait for me here,' he said. 'I need to check something.'

'But Richard—' Becky protested.

'Please, let me do this,' he said. 'Think of it as training for the future.'

He thought that maybe she muttered something like '*What future?*' but he didn't stop to argue the toss.

He went back to the delivery bay and pulled a shopping trolley over to the skip. He tipped the trolley over onto its side and stood on it. The lid of the skip was secured with a padlock. Vents showed him how things were thrown in. He stepped off the trolley and looked around him. He saw a sign in the neighbouring car park. He walked to the back of the delivery area and clambered over a bowed diamond-link fence. He crossed a wasteland of aggregate and glass and cindered chickweed. Another fence led into the garden area of a DIY megastore. Everything black and cowed. Great twenty-litre packs of obliterated compost. Hostas and acers and rhondodendrons in large earthenware pots. Bamboo like cross-hatchings in a grim cartoon. Plastic garden furniture bent and bubbled by heat. Concrete statues reaching to the heavens, blinded by soot. He touched one of the hosta leaves and it collapsed to dust.

Inside he found a collection of lump hammers. He hefted one, then looked around for anything else he might be able to take with him. Everything that could be used as a weapon had been lifted. Axes. Ball-peen hammers. Cold chisels. He rifled the pockets of a dead staff member. A few coins. A travel pass. Nothing. He stared at the man lying on his belly. He put his foot under him and levered him over onto his back. Jane had to look away when most of his torso stayed where it was on the floor. A Leatherman multi-tool and a Stanley knife were attached to a large key ring with lanyards. He cut them free and put them in his pocket.

He carried the lump hammer back to the supermarket delivery bay. It took three strikes to knock the padlock off its clasp. He stepped onto the shopping trolley and with the heels of his hands pushed the lid up and off.

Inside the skip were piles of waste. Nylon ties cut from pallet loads. Broken glass. Cardboard cylinders from till receipt rolls. Great wads of shrinkwrap. Bricks of polystyrene. And dozens of cans. He carefully picked out some of those nearest to him and studied the labels. Some of them didn't have labels. Some were punctured or rusted; these he discarded. The dented cans he checked more sedulously, pushing the tops to see if any air had got inside. He scooped up an armload of cans he thought were safe and carried them inside.

They ate in the pet-food aisle. Mystery cans that turned out to be apple-pie filling, meatballs in gravy, kidney beans in chilli sauce. It didn't escape Jane's notice that all of the tinned cat and dog food was gone.

When they'd finished, Jane wiped his mouth and stood up to get more for their rucksacks. Aidan rolled onto his back, belched and patted his belly. 'Dee-licious,' he said. 'I doff my cap to you, sir.'

Jane thought he might laugh all the way to London.

They walked maybe another three miles before the clouds began cosying up overhead again. A motorhome, a four-berth Fiat Mooveo, had come to a stop by the central reservation. Its occupants had crawled from the cabin to die; it was impossible to tell what gender they were, so denuded and leathery were they. Jane opened the door in the side and ducked in, checked there were no nasty surprises in store. He ushered them inside quickly, just as the first fat drops began to pound against the roof.

Aidan was uncertain at first, hanging back by the door while Becky and Jane looked around. Jane wondered if he might have suffered an unpleasant shock recently. An unexpected body in a house, maybe. Just because Jane was tensed to see corpses at every turn didn't mean the boy had to be. Or should be. The whole country seemed to have turned into a house of horrors, jangling skeletons in every shadowed corner.

It took a while to work out how the space ought to be used. There was a bunk above the driving area. You pulled a strap and it folded down. There was a harness system to prevent you from falling out. A mattress and pillows. There was a smell of burned plastic; the moulded air-vents on the roof of the motorhome had been melted out but there was a blind with a bolt that could be pulled across and locked. It would keep out the rain at least. At the rear of the motorhome was another bed. Behind the passenger seat was a folding table and behind the driver a small sofa. There was a cooking area too, with a hob. And a toilet and shower beyond that. The shower didn't work. Jane tried the gas and a burner jumped to life.

'Oh, yes,' Becky said, and leaned into him, pushing her forehead gently into his chest. 'Please tell me there's some tea?'

They searched the cupboards and found some sticks of granulated coffee and a tin of tea bags. Sticks of sugar. A couple of packets of chocolate powder.

'No milk,' Jane said, but Becky couldn't have been happier. She boiled water and made them all hot drinks. They sat around the table. There were another two or three miles in the evening if the rain eased off, but there seemed tacit agreement that they would stay the night here. Aidan, now that the door was locked and he had a mug of hot chocolate, had kicked off his boots and was laying claim to the bunk.

In a cupboard above the sofa they found books, a pack of cards, a board game they didn't recognise and that had no rulebook. They ate heated tins of pork sausages and baked beans on plates with forks, and played snap until the light faded and Adrian was nodding.

Jane undressed him and hoisted him into the bunk, pulled the blankets up to his neck and secured the harness. He lit candles and poured whisky into the rinsed mugs and handed one to Becky.

'Some music would be nice,' she said.

'Not that you're a hard woman to please.'

She laughed and sipped her drink. 'Music, though,' she said. 'I think this must be the longest I've ever gone without hearing any.'

'Yeah,' Jane said. 'Although in my line of work, I have to confess I'm glad for the respite.'

'Your line of work. Diver, right? Sounds interesting.'

'Kind of.' He told her about his work, how it was much

like any other hard, risk-filled labour once you got beyond the technicalities. 'Saved my life, though,' he said.

'Fate throws us in or pulls us back,' Becky said.

Jane watched her in the candlelight. She was gazing into her mug as if she might find a solution there. Aidan's breathing was like the soft hiss of an oil burner. It was soothing. It was something to alight upon other than the tragic wail of the wind.

'Do you have anybody?' Jane asked. 'Anybody at all? We could check on them.'

She was shaking her head. 'Even if there were someone, I wouldn't go to them. I don't want to have to remember them dead for ever.'

'It might not be like that.'

'No, you're right. I hope you're right. For you, above all. But I can't hope. It's not in me.'

'Where are your family?'

'Abroad, mostly. I have relatives in Canada.'

'Quite a journey, if you decided to go looking.'

'Yes,' she said. 'Something tells me I'll have a little trouble booking a flight.'

They sat and digested this. It was another jolt; Jane hadn't considered what might have happened at the airports. All that fuel. It didn't bear thinking about.

Becky took a drink, the slightest sip; she'd done little more than moisten her lips. 'I remember one day, our teacher took us to the TV room. We were all excited. No proper lessons. We just get to veg out in front of the box. He put a tape in the machine and switched it on and left the room. He actually left the room. Everyone started monkeying around, and then the programme started. An atomic bomb going off. Mushroom cloud. Buildings turned to dust in the blink of an eye. Everyone went quiet. Sat down. Watched it. It was the mid-1980s. Cold War paranoia. Every siren you heard was a four-minute warning, every plane going over was filled with plutonium.

'There was a woman on the screen who looked like a piece of rubber that has been left too close to the fire. She was writing her story and it was read out to the camera by her daughter. How she became pregnant by an American. There were some living there in Japan before the war started. He was eventually interned. She never saw him again. The daughter was born a couple of months before the attack on Pearl Harbor. The mother worked as a teacher. Towards the end of the war she moved around a lot. She was offered work at a school in Hiroshima.

'She left her daughter at home with her parents, who had moved with her too. They lived in a traditional wooden house near the mountains. Their house overlooked an island. I remember her talking about deer. About how they used to walk through the streets. The mother used to collect wood and bring back fruit for the family breakfasts. Every day she would walk miles to the train station and get a train to the centre of Hiroshima. On the morning of the bomb, she was helping to organise the morning assembly. There was a flash, and the colour of violet. And then she doesn't remember anything until she was aware of something dripping on her face. She thought she was in heaven. There was dust over everything. She could hear singing. Girls singing the school song. Later she realised it was because the children had been forbidden to cry for help. She was able to stand up. The school was gone. She had been standing half a mile from the nuclear blast. She was the only teacher to survive. She tried to save others but the voices singing went out one by one. Four children survived.

'She nearly died. She turned black and her hair fell out. Her nose bled constantly and she was unable to keep food down. All she wanted to do was drink water. She never spoke again. Her vocal cords had been seared together.

'I watched that programme and I could barely speak for a week. It felt as though I had experienced it. And now I have. I have.'

They finished their whisky in silence. Jane was all for pulling up the table and throwing down a mattress but Becky told him not to be silly. They undressed and climbed into the bed. It was cold. She moved against him, her head on his chest, and he was reminded of how long it had been since he had felt someone as close as this.

He somehow fell asleep with the maddening smell of her hair and a hot, chaotic thought of stumbling through limbs, trying to find where his face had landed while fire raged 200 feet high all around him and his son sang a song that turned to ash in his throat.

In the night he turned and saw the face at the window, its lower half concealed by a dirty white mask. The eyes were as black as to not be there, shadows, sockets punched out of coke. Hair lashed the forehead. A hand left a greasy imprint on the glass. Then the face was gone.

A lull. It woke him, spooked him. He lay in the darkness feeling certain that if he moved he would tumble into a chasm so deep that it would have no end. He would die of thirst before impact. He reached out and Becky was next to him. She made no sound while she breathed. She responded to his touch, though, rolling over and slipping her hand into the waistband of his boxer shorts. He stiffened immediately, felt the blood leave his head so quickly that an ache took its place as if he had swallowed an iced drink too swiftly. But he was too distracted by the face at the glass to be able to think of anything else. He turned to look at Becky but the darkness wouldn't soften. He edged away and swung his feet to the floor. The motorhome creaked as he picked his way to the door. He opened it and stepped outside. The wheelbarrow carrying their provisions was where he had left it. He wondered if he should have rooted around for his mask and goggles before leaving the vehicle. The sight before him wiped the thought immediately from his mind.

The clouds had parted. There was a patch of the universe visible through it, about the size of a football field. The stars seemed packed within, as though so desperate to be seen they'd shifted their positions. He watched until the cloud knitted itself together again. It was as if it had never happened. The wind stirred his fringe. Soon it might be howling around them again. What was this? Eye of a storm? He could hear thunder coming up from the south. The familiar pulses of silver. It was warmer outside than in. He knelt and placed his hand against the tarmac. Residual heat. He wondered if it was from the event itself. He thought of his parents in their tiny garden, sitting together doing the crossword and drinking gin and tonics before dinner. He hoped that oblivion had reached them as quickly as it had those in Hiroshima. He couldn't cope with the thought of them surviving and struggling.

Black, burned bushes at the side of the road. Scars in the embankment where cars had collided and rolled. He looked at all the dead vehicles, dozens of them, and wondered if they could ever be fixed. If something electrical made now by someone with know-how would work, or whether there was some atmospheric gremlin in the air that would not allow it.

He walked around the motorhome to the off side. He peered into the dark. Another four hours until light, or its approximation. In the centre of the road was a diagram, scratched into the tacky skin of filth with a chunk of rock.

It was a picture of a hand with six fingers and, within it, a stick figure.

He remembered the bowl of meat. How he had scooped up the hot, greasy contents, chewing the skin which crackled under his teeth. The flavour of it rose in his throat now and he was sick, a thin gruel of whisky and soup. The tattoo. What had they given him?

He looked up at the motorhome. On the window above the kitchen sink was a handprint.

12. BREAKING AND ENTERING

In the morning Jane broke into a barn and found a keeve filled with broken bottles and jars of fermenting pickle. There was a wooden chest filled with junk. He sorted through it but there was nothing worth taking although he did see a toy boat, painted blue and white, with a broken mast, no sail. He put it in his coat pocket. He emptied the keeve, wiped it clean with his gloved hand, and lugged it back to the motorhome. He used a pan to scoop up dirty water from a nearby brook, filtered it with a sieve and heated it on the burner. It took a while but the promise of a hot bath was worth it.

'Go ahead,' he told Becky when she'd risen. She was standing at the door in her underwear, her hair tousled, looking down at the grey, steaming bathwater. 'A gift from me to you. A thank-you.'

He took Aidan's arm and guided him away. They walked along the carriageway and Jane showed him the cats' eyes set into the middle of the road. He wanted to show him how the fixed rubber dome they were set into wiped the glass clean when it was depressed, but all of the rubber had melted. He picked one of the eyes out with his knife and handed it to Aidan. The mist wouldn't allow them a view south further than two hundred feet. It looked like something from a war photographer's portfolio.

'I've never been to London afore,' Aidan said. He was scratching the top of his plaster cast. Jane hoped the break would heal well. If they couldn't find anybody good at setting bones they would either have to find a textbook and learn or walk around wrapped in cotton wool. He'd done his mandatory First Aid courses. He knew how to perform cardio-pulmonary resuscitation and dress a wound with a piece of glass sticking out of it. But what if Becky severed an artery? What if Aidan fractured his skull?

'London's great,' Jane said. 'Especially for people who don't live there.'

'What's in London?'

'What isn't?'

'Are there helicopters in London?'

'Yes,' Jane said. 'And a big zoo. And parks so big it would take you a day to walk across them. And a big wheel that you can ride on.'

'How big? As big as the Earth?'

'Nearly.'

'Woah,' Aidan said. He was thoughtful for a while. 'Dad took me and Kerry on a big wheel at the fair.'

'This one is much bigger than that.'

'How do you know?'

'Trust me.'

They turned and made their way back to the motorhome. Jane could see Becky wrapped in a bed sheet, drying her hair. He whistled and waved so that she would know they were on their way back, although he supposed privacy was the least of their worries. The land either side of the road was wreathed in mist. He shook away a conviction of creatures in white masks just beyond its margins, watching them intently. He oughtn't to have left Becky to bathe alone, but something about these pursuers told him that it was all right. They were too timid. They seemed, for all their menace, to be in thrall to him, if that was the right word for it. A thought occurred to him, of protection, but he couldn't move beyond that inclination. He had surprised himself with it. It seemed an absurd notion. But the image of the bodies hanging from those great posts in the ground. The injuries they had sustained. It was like punishment. A statement, or a warning. Chris had physically attacked him, and he'd ended up on one of those posts.

By the time they got back to the motorhome, Becky had made breakfast. Mugs of tea, tinned fruit, a box of cheese crackers she'd found at the back of a cupboard. Aidan got into the bath and Jane remembered the boat. He tossed it in after him. Aidan pushed it around on the water, pretending there were people on board falling into the sea and being eaten by sharks. He got out, shivering, and Becky wrapped him in a bed sheet.

'Is there anything we can take with us?' Jane asked.

'Can't we take the motorhome?' Aidan asked.

'Afraid not,' Becky said. 'The engine's kaput.'

'What means "kaput"?'

'Broken,' Jane said.

'Dad says "knackered".'

'Knackered works.'

They ate breakfast and rifled the drawers and cupboards. Aidan pointed at a door under the rear bed that opened into storage space.

'Good boy, Aidan,' Jane said. 'Nice work.'

They found a case of shrink-wrapped mineral water, a tin of Quality Street chocolates, blankets and waterproof coats. A tripod and a camera bag. Jane unzipped the case and pulled out a pre-digital Nikon SLR. It was loaded with film.

Three exposures taken. He thought about taking it with him, but he didn't know anything about development. Enlargers wouldn't work any more. Safelights wouldn't work any more. He had never been into photography before. And it wasn't as if the world hankered for a couple of family portraits while it smouldered to cinders and ash.

He tossed the camera back into the cabin.

'Look,' said Aidan. He'd been at the glove compartment and found passports, a bunch of keys, and a wallet.

'Mr and Mrs Lewis,' Jane read. 'From Plymouth.' The wallet contained one hundred and fifty pounds, credit cards, photo-booth snaps he didn't look at. He put it all back.

They rolled the blankets up, stuffed them inside black bin liners and strapped them to the top of their rucksacks.

'Thanks, Mr and Mrs Lewis,' Aidan said.

They walked south.

The things they saw.

A woman in a lay-by wrapped around a child, their ribcages fused together.

A man in a car, its windscreen blasted and molten, reset across his face in a syrupy gyre of bone and slag.

A dog on a leash impaled by what looked like part of a human femur.

'I'm hungry,' Aidan said.

'Can we stop for a while?' Becky asked. Something in her voice made Jane look up sharply. He couldn't tell if she were angry, or scared. Or both.

They got off the A1 and followed a track through a field to a farmhouse.

'Where are we?' Aidan asked.

'Yorkshire,' Jane said. 'Britain's largest county. Home of the pudding. And tea so strong you could arm wrestle with it.'

'I've had Yorkshire pudding,' Aidan said.

'I should hope so,' Jane said.

'And that thing you put on it. Brown juice.'

'Gravy.'

'Yes. I like that.'

'I'll make you some. I promise.'

'Richard.' Becky was frowning at him. 'Don't promise.'

'But I do. One day I will make you a roast dinner. I absolutely promise you.' He was about to say that it would be good meat, with a trustworthy provenance. No tattoos. But he kept his teeth clenched on that. He thought there and then that he might have gone a little mad. And why not? Who could go forward, given what had happened, without insanity shadowing them? He doubted everything he had seen, even as his hands moved through the thick furring of ash on a gatepost, or he hopscotched a way through the broken pieces of the dead. He wondered if the ghosts that pursued him were of his own imagining, and if the awful deaths of Chris and Nance were illusions too. That, or done by his own hand during a fugue that he'd believed was the result of a crack on the head.

For the first time he thought of abandoning Becky and Aidan. Perhaps they would be safer without him. He didn't know himself well enough to trust his actions any more. He doubted how the future might play out. Every possibility was edged with black, with blood.

They moved through a garden that sloped up to the farmhouse, their feet scratching through the thin bristle. Black remnants of haycocks dotted the fields around them. A rusted disc harrow embedded in lifeless, impacted soil, twisted and cracked augers, their spiral inner teeth spilling free, the tines of a shakaerator broken and bent as if set to work on earth turned to stone. The roof of the barn was punched in; a wall bending out from one corner, as if holding on for grim life. All of the machinery bore fresh pockmarks, as if it had been peppered with pellets. He turned back to the house. All the windows on the upper floor nude, framing black. It would have to've been a powerful air rifle if it had been fired from that distance.

'Let's have a look in the kitchen,' Jane said. A door flapped in the rising wind, providing a beat that their feet marched to. Jane held up a hand and they hung back a little once they were near. Jane waited, checking the broken windows for movement. The kitchen was magazine rustic. Wheatsheaves burnt to fingers of charcoal on a cupboard made from recycled scaffold planks. Crisped cushions in an inglenook. An Aga. Welsh-slate floor. Shaker-style cabinets. Copper pots. A Belfast sink filled with bloody water. Jane hesitated over that, feeling the warning signs begin: the skin gathering at his nape, the hairs rising on his arms.

They checked the drawers and cupboards. There was basmati rice in an old coffee tin. Dozens of cans of plum tomatoes. Spices stored in tins that had once contained Assam tea. In the cellar Jane found a freezer with its own generator. He opened it and recoiled at the stink of rotted chickens sloshing about in a defrosted broth. Another fridge containing bottles of wine, cans of bitter. No longer cold, but who cared?

Becky and Aidan got a fire going in the porch, where they were shielded from the brunt of the wind. Aidan was given a pestle and mortar and shown how to grind the spices to powder. He worked at their names as he did so, struggling at first, but reciting them like a mantra to the rhythm of the pestle. *Cor-i-an-der. Cu-min. Car-da-mom. Fen-u-greek.* While Becky drained tins of chickpeas and new potatoes, Jane made his way into the hall. A rush-seated stool stood in an alcove beneath a coat rack crammed with coats of varying sizes. A restored Bakelite phone on a stand. A shoe rack with muddy wellington boots. There was a living room off to the left. Inside it Jane found bodies lying under torn-down blinds and a plastic shower curtain. A man, two boys in pyjamas, one maybe five, the other seven. And a baby girl. All had been shot in the head. The eldest boy had a gunshot through the palm of his left hand. Where was the wife, the mother?

He closed the door, wishing there were a bolt he could shoot or a key he could turn.

He went back to the kitchen, considering what to say, but Becky and Aidan were engrossed in their cooking. Instead, Jane made his way upstairs. He stood for a moment on the landing, looking out at the field below. A good view of the dual carriageway from here; they could have been tracked easily as they approached the house. Someone with a gun would have made themselves known by now, surely? Warning shots? *Hands up. Turn around. Leave.*

Dead, then. Or long gone.

Jane entered the front bedroom. The man was lying in a pool of blood. He could have been any age between twenty and sixty. A gunshot wound had opened up his thigh; he'd cut his trouser leg up the seam and the two halves of fabric hung off him like grey skin. He'd stitched himself shut but the wound had become infected. His head seemed dented. Blood had flowed and coagulated there; it sheened the shoulders of his biker jacket and it cracked whenever he moved. His skin was as pale and lustreless as wax. He was scut-bearded. A silver hoop glinted in his earlobe. He viewed Jane through a curtain of white, ratty hair. Jane wondered how much blood he'd lost. The walnut stock of a rifle was buried in his armpit. The barrel pointed at the floor. His bloodied fingers lifted and rested, lifted and rested on the trigger, the polished thumbhole. His other hand played in the fans of blood, drawing shapes, fingering the crassamentum. That bothered Jane more than the weapon.

'That's a nice gun,' Jane said.

'Too right. It's even got a ventilated butt.'

'It and me both,' Jane said.

The man laughed. There was death in it. He coughed and Jane saw him taste it, what was coming to him. It caused his face to screw up.

'Those prison issue?' Jane asked, nodding at his clothes.

'Yeah.'

'Where were you?'

'Lindholme. About fifteen miles from here. If you're travelling by crow.'

'What were you in for?'

'Stealing sweets off kids.'

Jane waited.

'Rape. Manslaughter.' He pronounced it *man's laughter*. 'I was bored. It was something to do.'

'How did you get this far?'

'Walked.'

'In that state?'

The man coughed, shook his head. 'I was attacked,' he said. 'Fucking crazy bitch comes running out the farmhouse, carrying this gun. She was screaming. I ran off but she shot me in the leg. She'd killed everyone in her family. Husband, two sons. Baby daughter. Claire. Told me that she'd always wanted a girl and it was their last try at it. Meant to pull the trigger on herself next but couldn't bring herself to do it. Told me that if I didn't shoot her, she'd kill me too.'

'You didn't kill them?'

'I didn't kill them.'

They regarded each other for a while. The man was in too much pain for Jane to gauge his honesty.

'So you shot her?'

'I shot her, yes. What else could I do?'

'So where is she? There's only four bodies in the room downstairs.'

'Outside.'

'Mind if I check?'

'I'm not lying.'

'Still . . .'

'Knock yourself out. Down in the barn.'

Jane bit his lip and eyed the gun. He'd be dead before he made one step to wrestle it from the man. 'I'll be here when you get back. I'm not going anywhere.'

He was turning to go when the man said: 'You been here a day earlier, could have been you she got hold of. Think about that, lucky fuck.'

Downstairs Jane pulled Becky to one side. Aidan was scooping rice into a pan.

'There's a guy upstairs,' he murmured. 'He doesn't know you're down here, I think. He's in pretty bad shape.'

'You want me to help him?'

'He's beyond it. He has a gun. I think he's dangerous, but he won't be able to make it down here. I need to check something out. I'm going to the barn. If you hear anything, movement upstairs, you shout at me, loud as you can.'

'OK.'

'He shoots me, you take Aidan and fast out the front door. Not the back. No trying to save me. OK?'

'OK.'

Jane went straight outside and moved fast to the barn. His back seemed to expand. He wouldn't hear the shot; but there might be enough time to see his heart as it exited his chest. He glanced to his left just before he met the collapsed barn wall and thought he saw skulking figures down by a clump of Corsican pine trees. Inside the barn he found the woman almost immediately. She was sitting up against the far wall, a photograph album in her hands. A single gunshot to her left eye. Jane looked around for something to cover the body but there was nothing. He noticed half a dozen big rats eyeing him and wondered whether they'd got started on the woman somewhere he couldn't see.

'Jesus,' he said, and picked her up. He blanched at the stiff, cold weight of her. The sudden change of position drew a sigh from her lungs that brushed his neck and made him cry out, but he did not drop her. He made to take the album from her hands but it wasn't going anywhere. He heard the scamper of claws as he took the body outside but the rats would not follow him into the field.

He got into the kitchen and Becky was saying, 'Oh, Richard.' And Aidan was saying, 'Who's she? Is she dead?'

'Don't let him in here,' Jane snapped as he kicked open the door to the living room. He put the woman next to her baby and covered them both. Could he have done to Cherry and Stan what this woman had managed to do to her family? No. No way. He didn't have it in him. He could kill himself, he reckoned, but not his boy. You survive and you think you're chosen for something special. You can't believe your luck. And then you find yourself envying the dead.

He closed the door and told Becky to wait with Aidan.

'I want to come with you.'

'There's nothing to see. Get dinner ready.' As if he could eat anything now.

Upstairs the man had died. His position had not altered. He stared at Jane but whatever it was that made life so beyond doubt was absent now. A sheen to the eyes. Elasticism.

A memory from childhood. Lying in bed, getting Dad to play his favourite track from the *White Album* one last time, before lights out. *Hey, Bungalow Bill, what did you kill, Bungalow Bill?* Such memories had not impinged as much as they might. It was understandable now, he supposed, yet when he had been on the rigs he had often thought of home, when he was a toddler, usually when he was struggling with a job in the gelid deep. The family garden had been large and well tended. Dad was proud of his lawn, trimmed regularly with his Webb mower so that there were pretty stripes patterning the grass. *What do you think, Rico?* His dad would ask him, sweating over the handles. *Wembley or Wimbledon?*

They had grown all kinds of fruit and vegetables in that back garden. Carrots he'd eat straight from the ground. Gooseberries. Beetroot they chopped together for pickling.

That's glossy, Jane remembered saying of the succulent slices. *Like a magazine.* His dad had been impressed with that. *Glossy . . . get you.*

Memories. Pain. He supposed it was because it might mean a link to Stanley that was too painful to experience. It might also lead him to thinking that Stanley might not remember who he was, or the things they had done together. He thought of photographs stored on hard drives now no more than irretrievable ghosts of code. There was nothing beyond memory. The painful thing was trying to come to terms with the possibility that before too long he'd discover that was all he would ever have.

He pulled the gun from the man's hands. He clicked the safety catch on and checked the breech. One pellet spent, but otherwise fully loaded with .22s. Jane checked the man's pockets and found cigarettes, a lighter, two boxes of ammunition. There was a folded photograph of a woman, topless, reclined on a sofa, her arms outstretched. An inscription. *Hi Loz. Waiting for you, babe. x* Heartbreaking stories everywhere.

He took the pellets and the lighter. He looked around him. A single bed covered in dust and dead insects. A chest of drawers contained nothing but a few wall hooks and a laminated copy of the Lord's Prayer. There must be more boxes of ammunition somewhere.

He slung the rifle over his shoulder and went downstairs. The smell of curry from the kitchen was good, but it didn't inspire hunger. He doubted he could eat again after the last hour or so.

In the cellar again he took more care over his search. There was an old pine cabinet pushed against a wall where all the white goods were arrayed. Inside were tools, all well cared for, clean, oiled, free of rust. Trays of nails and screws sorted into different sizes. Rawlplugs. Drill bits meticulously cleaned of plaster dust. All useful. All useless.

But then he found a drawer that wasn't meant for the slot into which it was embedded. Instead of a handle, double loops of shoelace had been stapled into the front. Inside was gun oil, barrel brushes and jags, cleaning rods. A screw-in silencer that didn't look as if it had been used. The drawer was only half the length of its neighbours. Jane pulled it all the way out and ignited the lighter. Boxes hidden in the gap at the back. He fished them out. Six boxes of .22 pellets. Six boxes of .177 pellets. He pocketed everything.

They ate in the kitchen but though it was the most flavourful meal he'd eaten in weeks – months, if the dishes scarfed under pressure in the Ceto were included – he didn't taste any of it. He kept gazing at the ceiling, expecting the man's blood to blacken the paint, to come seeping through the boards. Or he'd hear the turning of the doorknob and the woman poking her perforated head around the corner, breathing in stitches with words struggling through it all: *My, that smells good.*

He put down his fork and pushed back from the table.

'I'm going to reorganise the packs,' he said.

Aidan was playing outside with some toy cars he'd found in a box under the stairs. Becky came to Jane while he was sorting through things they could do without.

'Don't worry,' he said, gesturing at the clothes. 'I'm not going to just bin it. We'll put it to a vote.'

'It's OK,' Becky said. 'It's not that.'

'What, then?'

She squatted next to him. 'All I'm asking, suggesting really, is that you keep us in the loop.'

'I'm trying to protect you.'

She smiled. 'There's nothing you'll see that I need to be protected from. I mean, really. I used to work in a hospital.'

'OK. But Aidan. He doesn't need to see everything.'

'Agreed. But let me in. I can help you. I know guys like you. This alpha-male shit. There's no need for it.'

'All right. So from now on we only check things out if we all agree?'

'Yes.'

'And if we're starving?'

'Yes.'

'Every house, every place we see. There'll be people hiding out, maybe. Maybe not. We'll have to take chances eventually. Because I'm not thinking about just now. I'm thinking ahead. Three years. Five years. Ten. You think we can just waltz into the supermarkets every day and pick out a few cans for supper?'

Becky couldn't reply. He saw it in her face. The future opening up before her like a rotten gourd. Suddenly she seemed to understand the unhealable nature of things, the struggle ahead. He saw her realisation that she was a young woman who might die long before she became old.

She made to say something but nothing came. She walked away. Jane finished packing the rucksacks. Nobody complained about what he had decided to leave behind.

'Can I take these?' Aidan asked, holding up the toy cars.

'Of course you can,' Jane said, trying to swallow the bile, trying to cap a raging voice that wanted to ask if a couple of Matchbox toys meant more than an obliterated family lying under plastic in a room already sweating and stinking with decay.

He moved off at a smart pace, not waiting to see if the others were coming with him. They'd spent far too long at the farmhouse; it sickened him that they'd been preparing fancy food, filling their stomachs while bodies grew cold around them. He thought of all the meals he might eat in the future, however frugal, however pathetic or desperate. And he wondered about all the people who would watch him while they did it, with blank, unblinking eyes.

13. TRACHEOTOMY

Jane woke up reaching for someone who wasn't there. He could feel his slender shoulders beneath his fingers, the fabric of his favourite pyjamas. Words from books they loved to read together fragmented in his mind, falling away as though incapable of being remembered without the vital missing ingredient. *Daddy Island. Frog Finds a Friend. Dad Mine.* Titles Jane could hardly give voice to without the prickle of tears.

He sat up. His breath came in plumes. The climate was like that of a desert. Hot days. Frozen nights. Thin plaques of ice matted the canvas. He broke a piece off and sucked it. A taste of metal and chemicals. He spat. He wondered if dreams of Stanley had wakened him, or something else. The others were breathing steadily in the tent. He gripped the rifle stock loosely, glad of the weapon, but wary too, worried that it might inspire violence in others. He gazed out over the rooftops and countryside, the swollen, haphazard road. He had suggested finding a big house to stay in, or a hotel, but Aidan had begged them not to, preferring the tent.

'I don't want to see anybody,' he explained. 'I don't like how their faces look soft. Like they're asleep but they're not.'

It was too dark to see anything beyond the shapes of battered houses and factories, broken fingers of mills, the great shoulders of hills muscling up against the town. Again, he wasn't sure where they were. *Somewhere between north and south*, he told Aidan, and Aidan had been satisfied with that.

There was a distant thrum, a brief vibration. Jane thought he felt something in his feet, but couldn't be sure. The horizon they had left behind contained a burnt orange smear. His mouth went dry at the thought of some power station having finally reached tipping point and gone into meltdown. It was inevitable. Maybe life on Earth from now on would be dictated by whichever way the wind was blowing.

He moved away from the tents and leant back against the badly crumpled bonnet of a car. The engine block had rocketed into the driver's zone, lifting the top of the man and depositing him in the back seat. Oblivion. Out like a light.

The idea of death had caused Jane many moments of panic as a younger man. Newspaper articles about random attacks: samurai swords in London churches, knives on Manchester buses, guns in Liverpool nightclubs. People set on fire. People tortured and gut-shot. Left for dead. But death didn't go on. Your nerves were incinerated beyond use by fire; your lungs filled with water. The struggle to survive was out of your hands. You were insensate before the end. Death came and calmed you down. And it could only happen once. He was no longer scared of death. He didn't feel he had the right to be, not after what had happened to Stopper and the others. But he was scared for Stanley. He wanted to be able to assuage his son's fears, hold his hand, show him there was nothing to be frightened of beneath the bed or in the wardrobe. Because Dad was here and everything would be all right.

He thought he sensed movement a way back off the road. Shadows congealing, dispersing. But it could just be the colour of the night, writhing in his eyes.

Something came sailing past him, riding high on the wind. A piece of clothing, perhaps. A plastic bag or the remnant of a flag. 'No standards left,' he said, and coughed a bitter chuckle. An ache was building around his teeth, an itchiness. His gums bled whenever he brushed his teeth. They bled when he bit into food. He wondered if it might be gingivitis. A friend of his mother's had lost all her teeth to gingivitis in her twenties. He half-wished Becky was a dentist instead of a radiologist.

He was tired, his feet, back and neck ached, but sleep played games with him. They were averaging, he guessed, between ten and twelve miles a day. Good going, with such a small boy in tow. Jane suspected his exhaustion was down to pushing Aidan in the wheelbarrow, but there was also the rain to contend with, and the diminishing food supplies. Some days he went without so that Aidan and Becky did not. While they slept he went hunting for cans, but it was alarming to discover that there were few to be found. Already the stockpiles had been rifled. There were survivors in their houses – maybe half a dozen so far – who said nothing as he approached, but showed him the grin of something sharp in their hands. They would not talk to him. Once he had been shot at.

He found a jar of pickled red cabbage in an end-of-terrace hovel taken over by rats. A skeleton sat in a squirming armchair, a china cup and saucer at its feet. There was a tin of bamboo shoots in a flat where someone seemed to have melted into the floorboards and left only his clothes behind. He had thought, *Fuck bamboo shoots, you might as well can rabbit tods*. And then he'd knifed the lid back and eaten it all there and then. It had been delicious. The supermarkets had become ghost buildings. Everything taken apart from DVDs, household electrical items, barbecues. Where were all these people? Where were all the survivors? Was everyone on the A1 ahead of him?

He wondered about his leisurely pursuers. He wondered if they were pursuing him at all. Maybe they were stripping provisions from his way ahead, pushing him towards some kind of test. He thought of the meat in the bowl. He thought of Becky and Aidan. God. The way your mind worked when you were up against it. All that trickle-down shit. A confrontation was ahead, he thought, one way or the other. Before they made it to London, perhaps. Or once they were ensconced there. He wondered what that meant, the moment it occurred to him. Just because he had lived there before didn't mean he had to stay there now. He would find Stanley and Cherry and they would leave, try to make it across the Channel to France, somewhere where this fury had not touched, if there was anywhere like that left. He wasn't going to spend the rest of his life fighting over crumbs in Kentish Town larders and carrying the gun with him every time he took his boy to play in Coram's Fields.

His throat ached for cold beer. The whisky was too strong to drink greedily, and he could do a good session, he felt he deserved a night on the lash. Thirsty, he went back to the tent and drank from the bladder. Becky and Aidan were in the same positions he'd left them. He heard the scrabble of pebbles loosed from a bank of earth, the hush of dead vegetation kicked to dust as bodies hurried by it.

'Show yourselves,' he whispered. 'Talk to me.'

He fell asleep sitting upright, in an awkward position. Aidan nudged him awake as he hopped from foot to foot, trying to unzip the tent's entrance so he could go out for a piss. Jane's neck flared with pain. He stood up, rubbing at it. Cold had seeped into his bones.

'Where's Becky?' He blinked, looking out at the pale morning, finding it hard to believe that he had been asleep for any length of time; the darkness, and the sounds, and his uneasy thoughts seemed to have been the product of only a few seconds previously.

'She said she was going to try to find us some breakfast. She said she was sick to the back teeth of dried apricots. She said don't worry. She said she was going to do things and buy a book.'

'*By the book*,' Jane corrected. 'So much for democracy.'

'What?'

'Never mind.'

Aidan helped him take down the tent and pack it in the rucksacks. They sat together on the rucksacks, feeling the temperature climb, waiting. They talked about books. Aidan liked *Where the Wild Things Are*.

'Do you still like it?' Jane asked, but Aidan didn't understand what he meant.

The thought of books had stayed with him. He supposed there would be no more. Not for a long time, at least. He thought of all the books he had read over his lifetime, a great deal of them in those prison cells of hyperbaric chambers where there'd been little else to do. Were they still important? Maybe yes. Maybe more so than ever. Aidan had not been read a bedtime story since they'd found him. That wasn't good enough. It was time to remember the stories Jane had been told as a child, or make up some new ones. It had been a while – he remembered singing silly, off-the-cuff songs to lull Stanley to sleep – but it was in him; it was in everyone, like the skill to make fire, or love.

Becky came back empty-handed. He was harder on her than he should have been, perhaps because of that.

'I just looked in a corner shop,' she said. 'I waited a long time to make sure there was nobody inside.'

'But that's not the problem, is it?' he asked. 'It's people on the outside, watching you, waiting for you to make your move.'

'Well, I'm here aren't I?' she snapped.

'Have a dried apricot.'

They walked most of the day in silence.

'How many minutes until we get to London?' Aidan asked.

'I don't know,' Jane said.

'Ten?'

'A bit more than that.' But he wasn't really listening any more. Up ahead, maybe a mile away, there was a strange glinting on the road, as if someone were sending messages by reflecting light off glass.

'What's that?' Becky asked. They had all stopped.

'I don't know,' Jane said.

'Code?' As if she had read his mind.

'Maybe. I don't like it. Let's get under cover somewhere for a while.'

They scampered down the embankment to a ploughed field. They had to leave the wheelbarrow. Jane dumped it in a ditch and they hurried across the field, dust pluming up from every footstep and lifting from their clothes, their hair, as if they were made from the stuff. At the far end of the field they climbed over a charred fence. There was a lake beyond it, dark and flat as a lithograph.

They lay down by the fence and watched the road. Their dust ghosts rose too slowly, but were then whipped away by the currents of wind. They had barely dissipated when the first of the figures appeared.

It was like looking at a mirror image of themselves. A man led the way for a woman pushing a young child in an old-fashioned pram. The child was too big for it, legs hanging over the side, jouncing at every bump and crater. He seemed to be wrapped from head to toe in shiny material, similar, perhaps, to the reflective insulating blankets that marathon runners wrapped around themselves at the end of a race. Was that what he had seen glinting earlier? Jane thought the child must be injured, or sick. He wanted to go to them, to ask them if they had come from London and why they were heading north, but there was something he didn't like about the senseless motion of the child's limbs.

'Is that a little boy?' Aidan asked. 'Like me?'

'I think so,' Jane said.

'Can we play? He can have my boat. I've played with that enough now.'

'Let's just watch them. I'm not sure if they're friendly.'

Jane could sense Aidan's scrutiny of him. He hated having to seed his mind with doubt. Boys of five shouldn't have to be saddled with issues of trust when it came to other children. He didn't want him growing into a suspicious, lonely man. But he didn't know what else he could do.

The pram – not the best mode of transport for such an unpredictable road – hit one pockmark too many and the woman struggled to right it. The child slid out on to the surface; they heard the dull crack of its head, or Jane imagined he did. The man turned and started haranguing the woman. Two more figures appeared, as though rising out of the road itself. Men. They picked up the child – one of them grasping it by the hair – and dumped him back in the pram. There was no cry of objection, from the child or the woman.

'Becky, I think maybe you should take Aidan down to the lake for a while,' Jane said. 'We don't need to see any more.'

Becky tugged at Aidan's sleeve. The boy resisted. 'But I want to play.'

'Aidan, it doesn't look good. I think—'

'NO!' Aidan said, his chin thrust out in determination.

Jane glanced back at the travellers and saw how they had turned towards them. He saw the first man's stance alter. He saw his knees bend slightly. He saw his shoulder recoil.

'What—' began Becky. And then the fence to her left disintegrated, the bolt the man had fired from his crossbow burying itself in the dead bark of a tree with a dull *phut!*

'Let's go,' said Jane.

Aidan was pulling toys from his pocket. 'He can have this if he wants. He can—'

'Now,' said Jane, and grabbed Aidan's hand.

His back to the road, he felt the air move. Something punched past his ear, missing by a matter of inches. There had been some practising going on. He slipped the rifle off his shoulder and headed for the lake. Jane rued the lack of shots he had taken himself. He hadn't even tried the gun out yet, thinking it better that he conserve his supplies of ammunition. He thumbed the safety off as they ran. Before the shape of the land took them lower than the level of the road, he glanced back. The three men were coming across the field. He felt his throat turn cold and swollen; he couldn't swallow and for a moment he thought he'd been shot through it.

The lake stretched out, grey and uninviting, gnawing against pebbles so cold they might crack if you held them for a while. No boats to launch from the jetty, which was half collapsed, bending into the water. The trees thinned out as they approached the edge. Their breathing was fast and shallow; the breath of fear. The men would soon breach that fence, the last line of trees, and they would be targets easily picked off.

To the left, maybe two hundred yards away, Jane glimpsed the exposed spine of a drystone wall. They had to get beyond that, and quick, but there was no way they could make it before the men reached clear ground. He urged

Becky and Aidan on ahead of him. Someone shouted out. They were splitting up: two men were following the route they had taken; the third – the man with the crossbow – had broken left and was taking a long, curving route to cut them off.

'Stop looking around you,' Jane urged. 'Get to the wall.'

They were at it, folding over it, exhausted, when another bolt hit one of the stones; chips of granite peppered Jane's face. He felt blood wetting his cheek, the taste of it. He was blinded in one eye, but there was no pain. *Just blood*, he thought, blinking it clear. *I'm all right*.

He could hear the man now, his thundering stride, the rasp of his breath. He could hear the collision of wood and metal as he notched another bolt into his crossbow. Jane twisted hard to his right, falling back as he raised the gun, and shot from the hip. He no longer knew where Becky and Aidan were. Mouths full of burnt grass if they had any sense. The pellet struck the man in his left shoulder and that and his own velocity spun him violently; Jane heard the crunch of cartilage in the man's right knee as his position suddenly changed. Pain was boiling in the man's throat, a tethered, growling sound, but it couldn't get beyond his clenched teeth. His eyes were too large for his face: he pushed himself upright and lifted the crossbow. Jane shot again out of panic, his aim wild. The pellet caught the man in the throat and the growl was replaced by an awful choking as he began to drown in his own blood. Jane kicked away the crossbow and turned to see the two other men descending on him. One of them carried an iron bar, the other a ceremonial sword. Jane shot the man with the bar in the middle of the chest; he collapsed as if all his tendons had been cut at once, with no apparent regard to physics. The other man was upon Jane before he had a chance to swing the barrel of the rifle his way. The sword came down in a desperate, choppy arc, but it was too shallow, the action of a man who visualises what he wants crucial seconds before the physicality behind it can be achieved. Jane felt the tip describe a curve across his chest. There was a sting, massive heat, but the damage was only superficial. If anything it enlivened him. He was utterly, joyously conscious when he shot a round into the man's open mouth.

Jane lay on the ground hearing only the slam of his heart and the torture of his lungs. *This is the clamour of life*, he thought. *This is the noise of the spirit*. Every time he breathed he felt the split in his chest part. Blood welled in his left eye. It was running into his mouth, making him cough and splutter. The taste of it. He'd not tasted anything so fine in such a time.

He rolled over and was sick. He was shaking like a nervous dog. He felt hands on his back, tentative, nervous, as if there was some reserve there, the fear that Jane was running amok, that he might blindly strike out at anyone within reach.

Gradually his breathing calmed. Blood had turned black the pale green shirt he'd put on that morning. The shakes would not abate, however. He could feel his mouth turning dry.

'Get me warm,' he told the shapes he could not quite see but that he hoped were Becky and Aidan. He heard Becky say 'Shock.' She knew what she was doing. She worked in a hospital. Even X-ray people knew how to deal with emergencies. He blacked out.

It seemed that he revived almost immediately.

He felt a sudden deep pain at the realisation that Stanley had never seen a dragonfly.

'Sorry, Stan,' he murmured. He was crying now. The likelihood was that dragonflies would not come back. How could evolution go that way again? How could you fluke the weirdly beautiful twice in a row?

'I saw them,' he said.

'Quiet, Richard.' Was that Becky? He saw a figure hunched over fire, bringing a pan of water to the boil. 'You need to rest. Just take it easy.'

'But I saw them. Dragonflies.'

Sobbing. The boy. His boy. No, not Stanley. Aidan. Sobbing into his cupped hands. Taking peeks at Jane, then sobbing some more. *Do I look that bad?*

'We were fishing,' he said. 'Place called Tabley Mere. Knutsford. North west of England. Lovely place. Me. Dad. Grandad. Grandad . . . one of those people who don't have much time for little boys. Gruff. Sombre-looking. Bright blue eyes. Hair white. Hawkish. Sunken. He said maybe two dozen words to me before he died. I was thirteen by then. Miserable fucker, all things considered.

'I'd started to get into fishing. I was only six or seven. But I could set up a rig. I knew about baiting a swim. I knew the difference between a roach and a rudd. We didn't catch a thing. Dad and Grandad both fell asleep. I went for a walk, took my rod with me. Over a stile. Through a field to some trees. There was a gravel pit beneath them. I caught roach after roach, or maybe it was the same one. And then I realised I was being watched.

'It was like a window of stained glass had shattered into a thousand pieces and they were all hanging in the air behind me. It was a little scary, but I knew they couldn't sting me, they weren't like wasps. They didn't come near, as if they were attracted to you. They hung back. Hundreds of them. Maybe it was birthday for dragonflies, this particular day. You look at a dragonfly for a while, then everything else seems so dull afterwards.

'I wouldn't know how to tell him. I wouldn't know how to describe it to him. How do you describe a dragonfly to someone who hasn't seen one? You might as well be blind.'

Jane slept again, or fell unconscious. When he came to, he felt stiff, immobile. For terrifying seconds he thought he had been captured by his pursuers, ravened from the inside and left nailed to a post for the birds of his nightmares to tear strips from. But he was only lying on a blanket, his arms above his head – the way Stanley had slept as a baby – his midriff bandaged tightly, professionally. His head felt warm, treacly, his *veins* felt warm. He thought that if he closed his eyes he could visualise his entire circulatory system, map it in his head, every junction and branch and bend.

Gradually, the real world began to impinge. The wind skirled above their heads, cheated out of them by the high tops of lorries on either side. Their canvas skins thumped and fluttered and creaked. The woman and the child, the dead child in the shopping trolley, were gone.

Becky must have manhandled Jane into the barrow, got him across that macerated field and onto the road again. She was sitting by Aidan, stroking his hair, leaning over one arm, a blade of hair hiding her eyes from him. She looked spent.

Perhaps she sensed Jane's inspection, or heard the slightest shift of his arms as he repositioned himself; she looked up. Her eyes were red-rimmed, her skin sallow.

Aidan said, 'I want to go home.'

Jane resisted the urge: *You are home.*

'We've nothing to eat,' Becky said. 'And it's weird. It's not that I feel tired, I mean I do, I'm knackered. But it's just . . . there's nothing in the tank. I'm depressed just at the thought of having to lift that pack onto my shoulders again. And it's not as if it's all that heavy.'

Jane sat up. He felt light-headed, but otherwise OK. He felt guilty that he had rested while the others had not. But he would pay them back. There was no danger of that not happening. The pain drew his eyes closed, but he didn't cry out. The bandage seemed to muffle it somehow, that and whatever Becky had slipped into his arm while he was out of it.

'Lorazepam,' she admitted when he asked her. 'Just to take the edge off. You deserved it, after what happened.'

'How much have you got left?'

'A couple of ampoules. For special occasions.'

'It's good. It's very good.'

He felt honey-coated, bubble-wrapped. He looked around him at the cars and lorries, some super-magnified child's game in the moment of its abandonment. His head beat with the lack of sugar in his blood. But he tried to think. He'd seen something that teased him, like a scab not quite ripe for picking. He looked at Becky and Aidan. He looked at the lorries. The cars. A red car, maybe sixty yards down the road. Dented, windscreen cracked, layered with dust, but it had a sheen about it, an immaculateness that was missing in the others. *Lady driver*, he thought. *Careful owner, full service history*. He stood up, shakily.

'Richard,' Becky said, in *that* voice, that nurse's voice she had down pat.

'It's OK,' he said. He wondered if he'd lost much blood. But the wound had only scored his chest. No major blood vessels there. Perhaps just a fine fighting scar on his ribs to impress any bonehunters of the future.

There was a shrivelled figure in the driver's seat, ageless, sexless, dwarfed by heat. There was a pair of softened crutches, bowing over a singed passenger seat. Something plastic on the dashboard wrinkled to a coin-sized disc. Disabled badge?

He checked the odometer. Less than 15,000, although the car was over three years old.

Where were you going?

Jane went round to the back of the car and tried the boot.

Locked. He lifted the back seat but there was no jack to be found. He replaced the seat and rubbed his face.

Where had you been?

Between the seats was an armrest, folded into a well. He put his finger through the loop and pulled it into position. In the well was a plastic tab. He opened it; a little door to the boot, handy access to bits and bobs to save you from stopping mid-journey.

Just a little runaround. Something to get me down to the shops.

Cardboard boxes. Maybe half a dozen of them. He called to Aidan. 'Come and help. I need a super-strong boy with little hands.'

Two of the boxes were filled with perishables. Vacuum-packs of ham, beef, chicken. Yogurt. Butter. Milk. Bread. Ice cream. The stink of it made Jane's eyes water. 'Ripe Christ,' he said. 'That stuff is ready to make an evolutionary leap.'

Aidan said, 'Ice cream,' as if he had never heard the words before. 'I like ice cream.' He began to cry.

The other bags contained tins. Lots of them: beans, spaghetti hoops, red salmon, Toast Toppers, pineapples, tomato soup, Coca-Cola, 7-Up, Stella Artois. There was a box of Rice Krispies. A pack of sugar. Energy bars. Jane stopped Aidan's tears with a can of strawberry-flavoured long-life milk.

'Nearly as good as ice cream, yes?' Jane asked him.

'Actually, yes,' Aidan said. 'Actually. Very refreshing.'

They ate until they felt stronger. The sponge of their muscles receded. The vignetting in their sight disappeared. They could breathe more deeply, more freely. Even breathing could become too much effort. A bad sign, if they needed one, Jane thought, replenishing their packs.

They walked on into early evening. It began to rain. They pitched camp. Jane slept so deeply that he could remember

ONE

no dreams when he wakened, although his eyes were crusted and there were tracks through the glaze of blood on his cheek: he had been crying in the night. Almost as soon as they had packed up and were moving on they found a road sign that had been uprooted and was face down on the hard shoulder. Aidan helped him to lift it.

'My God,' Jane said. 'My God.'
LONDON 38

14. DESCENT

Aidan skipped across chevrons at a slip road. Becky walked a little way ahead of him, to his right. Jane brought up the rear, pushing the wheelbarrow. He was itching to get rid of it. There was no need any more. Their packs were full, the road was coming to an end. Within three days they would be in London.

He was hunched over the barrow, his breath coming in short, shallow scoops. Becky kept admonishing him, telling him to stand up straight and breathe normally, but the pain in his chest wouldn't allow it. One foot in front of the other. Twelve miles a day. Three days. He imagined Stanley standing at the balcony, watching out for him. *He will be here, Mummy. He will.*

Whenever he felt his mind bending towards dark things he rescued himself with thoughts of Stanley. In this way he believed he was confirming Stanley's survival and reminding himself what it meant to know order, to be human. He thought of taking his son to the fair in Hyde Park. Stanley must have been around three. Jane had been disgusted by the prices, but to see his son laughing to the point of losing control was worth ten times what he had paid. He had decided to let Stanley be in charge after that. They would otherwise have gone home and watched TV, but he didn't want to be locked inside with Cherry tutting and shaking her head all afternoon. They had walked – slowly, very slowly – for miles. They stopped often, to look at the scrollwork on the iron frame of a bench, to watch the kites being flown, to trace the pattern of bark on a tree, to honk at the geese on the Serpentine and dodge the squirrels who barred their path aggressively, expecting nuts. They played peek-a-boo at the statue of Peter Pan and Stanley demanded to be picked up so he could pat the head of the bear at the end of the path near the Italian Gardens. They played on the pirate ship and Stanley made Jane laugh so hard when he said 'Shiver me timbers' that Jane's nose began to bleed.

They stopped off at Baskin Robbins for ice cream on the way home. Stanley was nodding into his raspberry sorbet. Blond hair. The cowlick over his left ear that would not stay down. 'Daddy, um, when we get home which toy do you want to play with? Walter or red Power Ranger? You can have Walter if you like, but I love Walter the best.'

He was snoring almost before he finished his sentence. Jane scooped him up and carried him onto a bus. They got off at Maida Vale and Stanley was deeply asleep, head on Jane's shoulder, melded to it, as though this configuration of muscle and bone had been waiting all these decades for just this one boy.

Cherry had been at him the moment his key found the lock. *Needs his sleep. Worn him out. A three-year-old boy can't. A three-year-old boy shouldn't. You. You. You.*

He'd let it all slide past him, moved slowly past her and put Stanley to bed. *Best day of my life, Stanley. Thank you, mate. Night-night.*

They followed the hard narrative of the road, navigating their way around its punctuative tragedies. Jane found himself thinking how it had gone for them, these car-bound travellers, long-distance or quick hop, going to or returning from. No time to get away. They must have seen what it was, perhaps had the vision melted into the back of their skulls before life was struck from them. He remembered an old annual he had been given for his birthday, something that had bothered him greatly when he was a boy. It was supposedly filled with adventures and excitement, but all he saw were nightmares. Nuclear war. Man-eating polar bears. Innocent aliens hunted for sport.

There had been a story about a man who tests a dream machine; his dreams are relayed to a screen for scientists to view. He dreams he is on a spaceship moving faster than anything in the galaxy. He reaches the end of space and sees what is beyond it. But something goes wrong. There is an explosion. His body dematerialises. The scientist dies and his assistant, blinded by the explosion, calls out vainly to find out what was revealed, but, as the last panel explained, *It was not for living men to tell.*

The scientist's body had been in close-up, his mouth open, his eyes open, strangely pimpled. It had stayed with Jane for months, that image. It was with him now.

What did you see?

There had been those oily miasmal colours, impressive even at the depths Jane had experienced it. What must it have been like at the doorstep? He felt a pang of envy, despite knowing that to have seen it would have been to die. These people in the cars flash-fried, brains scrambled, the upholstery of the seats in which they perished barely touched in many cases. It must have hit like a tidal wave, tearing the breath from everything in its path.

He stopped in the road. Aidan had tired of his skipping game and was walking alongside Becky, his hand enfolded by hers. The broad green bandeau she was wearing glittered with dust. The bodies in the cars, lying on the floor swollen, split and black, like baked apples left too long in the oven. The rats wouldn't touch them. They ate only the bodies they found indoors. They didn't eat what was outside. The dust, was it some kind of appetite suppressant? And something else. He had been blind.

'Becky?' he called. She turned in the road, swinging Aidan around with her. He was still giggling when Jane asked: 'Why is nobody decomposing?'

They found a veterinary surgery in Stevenage's industrial area where it cosied up to the motorway. A small laboratory was connected to it at the rear, where cages contained dead animals that had tried to bite their way through the wire mesh. Boxes of drugs were stacked in a cupboard. Someone had been here before them. Drawers had been pulled out and tipped empty: laryngoscope blades and draining tubes; worming treatments and syringes. Refrigerators and cupboards had disgorged their contents, none of which were of any use to desperate people. Watchglasses of agar. Test tubes and flasks. Injectables. Liquids, powders and pastes. Dermatological oils. Becky pocketed a skin stapler and some removal forceps as well as some pads and tape and a sealed pack of suture needles.

A microscope had been knocked over but Becky checked it over and it seemed all right. She prepared a well slide with the dust added to a few drops of quieting solution and clipped it to the stage. She was quiet for some time, alternating between the coarse- and fine-focusing knobs.

'Any news?' Jane asked. Aidan was inspecting a broken centrifuge, when he wasn't glancing at the evidence of the animals' frenzied attempts to escape.

'I . . . I'm not sure,' Becky said. She lifted her head away from the eyepiece. 'It looks . . .' She sighed. Shook her head. 'Well, it looks . . . cellular.'

They camped that night on the fairway of a golf course west of Welwyn Garden City. Large amounts of litter were sweeping through the air. London's love letters to them. Some of it plastered against the face of the tent. A *Washington Post*. Sheets of unintelligible data. An airline sick bag. They could see the motorway from their tent, through a clutch of famished trees. Aidan hadn't said much all day. Jane wanted to talk to him, bring him out of his shell and find out what was wrong, but he was still digesting the revelation in the laboratory. He couldn't understand what it meant. And it was doubly confusing to think that it might mean nothing. Cells. Dead spores on dead air. Just another thing that had shot its bolt at the end of the world.

Only Becky had not said they were dead. She'd told him that she'd read about cells that had survived for millennia, trapped in ice.

'But the soil. It's too dry. Anything good in it has been blowtorched out of it. It's dead ground.'

'I know,' Becky had said. And chewed her lip, looking at him with that mix of worry and compassion.

She was still wearing it. He watched her shape soften as darkness came on, as if she were losing the edges of herself to it.

He said, 'You're thinking that whatever this stuff is – cells, seed – it doesn't necessarily need earth for germination.'

'I don't know what I'm thinking,' she said.

'Aidan, what about you? What do you think?'

'I miss my mum and dad,' the boy said. His eyes were metal discs. They both went to him and held him. He cried hard and for a long time. By the time he had stopped he was asleep and the darkness was complete.

The way a child develops. Playtime and learning and meals and sleep. Aidan no longer had a timetable. It was walk and eat what you could and fall down exhausted and then walk some more. No time or space in which to read stories about animals. There were no more animals. No latitude for being scared about the things that didn't matter. This was adult worry and adult fear all the way. Five years old and he was looking at beasts who'd shredded their muzzles to mince in their desperation; the agonies of people steamed in their own liquor. Five years old and he knew what the face of painful death looked like.

Jane laid Aidan's head down gently on a folded coat. 'I'm going out for a while,' he said.

'For a walk?' He could imagine the smile on her face.

He touched her shoulder. 'Just a bit of me time. I won't be far.'

She held on to his hand when he made to duck out of the tent. Her face came up from the shadows. She kissed him, clumsily, on the mouth.

The wind had abated again. Maybe the storms had circulated, were laying siege to other parts of the planet. They would be back, though. He knew that. This wasn't a winding down, an underscore. A time to patch up, take stock and forge a way forward. It would take more than he had, in terms of effort and lifespan, to see the Earth back to anything like its normal self. Although he realised that this was what the Earth had been like for billennia, before the first life forms uncoiled themselves from their pits of sulphur and nitrogen.

Movement. The snap of twigs. He saw figures flitting through the trees, white scarves flashing like the tails of fleeing rabbits. Without thinking, he took off after them, sudden anger fuelling his muscles. He was tired of playing this game of hide and seek, or follow my leader, whatever it was. But they eluded him easily. They were more agile, sleeker, more athletic. He ran until his chest was too tight and hot to continue. He stood in a field, hands on thighs, coughing. He sensed them around him, watching, gauging. He jerked upright when he heard a stream of noise that was too ordered to be anything other than a voice. Not that it contained any word he could understand. He heard other noises. Something heavy falling, being dragged. His mind flashed up images of holes being dug into the ground, of posts being hoisted.

She emerged from the gloom, a spectre with a deep cartoon smile. It was only the mask, covering her mouth and chin like a rustler's disguise, hanging down to her chest. She wore little other than tribal swatches of cloth, tied around her limbs like filthy bandages. She was maybe seven or eight. Her limbs swarmed with curlicues and cross-hatchings, tattoos depicting a world and a people that had been hidden from him, from everybody, until now. Survivors. But they looked as though they knew all about how best to do that.

'Who are you?' he asked. She stopped about ten yards away from him. Something in her eyes told him she was smiling. She didn't answer.

'Where are you from?' he asked. 'Why are you following us?'

She held up her hand. She disappeared back into the darkness. He heard footsteps, quickening. By the time they'd hit full stride they were already too distant to hear properly. He was alone again.

He turned and there was the polished skull of a raptor lying on the ground. Tiny, basilisk, fragile. He picked it up, a weight that was almost not there. It was like holding an origami conceit. He inspected the boss and the bill and the eye sockets, turning the skull in his hands delicately, feeling its egg-shell thinness flexing beneath his fingers. He could feel the hot stare of intent yellow, smell the blood of its prey, so much of it gushing through these chambers that had it had crept like a stain through the porous bone, its own kill badge.

Jane lifted the skull to his face and breathed in the air that was trapped in the fossae of its nasal cavities. He thought he caught a flavour of what it meant to be wild, untrammelled. A killing machine, something designed solely for the purpose of death.

He got lost on the way back to the tent. He couldn't find it, no matter how often he looped back or measured his progress against the road and the lines of dead trees. He didn't call out. He lay down in the sand of a bunker, burying himself in it. At least he was sheltered from the night's breath. He fell asleep dreaming of the skull. How it was positioned looking away from him. The grind of spine as it rotated his head to look at him. Eyes behind the sockets, accusatory. Stanley's eyes, rendered by this alien juxtaposition into something freakish and chilling. The bill opened to howl his name and blood began to gush out. He put out his hands to plug it but there was no stemming its ferocity.

When he wakened, he smelled the copper of blood and saw that the tent was less than twenty yards away from where he had bedded down.

Aidan had rallied. He was eating dry Rice Krispies from the box, supplying his own *snap, crackle, pop* sound effects. The raptor skull didn't look quite so savage in the daylight and, after a moment's pause, he handed it to the boy.

'Keep it safe,' he told him. 'For luck.'

He saw Becky bite on some admonishment that she might have been considering. Aidan wouldn't have been put off; he was fascinated by the skull, once he'd established that the bird was dead, although it meant that Jane had to field a series of questions about the bird's skin and feathers and where they had gone and what, exactly, did *decomposition* mean?

They walked the A1 until lunchtime, when they stopped to eat. A blue shirt hung in the leafless branches of a tree. A brown shoe stood by the trunk, as if waiting for it to come down. Large, glittering worms hung and spun in the air: scraps of tape and insulating foam, and what looked like shreds of metallic paint.

Aidan munched his way through three hot dogs in brine, relishing the disgust on Jane's face. 'Look, I'm eating widgets,' Aidan said. Jane covered his eyes and pretended to be sick.

The wind brought the smell of the city to them. A foul fossil smell of oil and rendered tallow and cadavers and standing water. There was mildew in it, and something faecal; something old and defeated, like the smell you got when you opened the wardrobe of a dying grandparent who no longer combed his hair or brushed his teeth. It was the smell of capitulation.

The road was blocked.

'Holy fuck,' Jane said, his voice full of awe, both at the horror before him and the fact that he could still have the wind punched from him, there were still sights to be seen. Aidan looked up at him quizzically, perhaps about to ask him about the bad word, but he too was distracted. Becky simply stopped walking. She sat down in the road and bowed her head.

Jane told Aidan to wait with her, but he refused. Together they approached what was left of the airliner. The M25 stretched its arms out before them as if offering a hug, or a shrug, unspoken sympathy for the disaster it had witnessed. One engine remained, as far as Jane could see. Debris was spread all over the road and across much of a large field, north-west of Junction 1 of the A1 motorway road. Around two hundred yards away they could see the deep black gouges in the blacktop where the aircraft had hit. Perhaps the aircraft had tried to land on the A1. Perhaps it had just been battered down out of the sky by the fierce strike of incinerated air, a newspaper swatting a fly.

'It was a big one,' Jane said.

'How big? As big as a elephant?'

'Oh yeah.'

He pointed out the immense crippled landing gear. 'Look, see? Six wheels. That means it was a 777. Big plane. Big engine. If there were three of you inside standing on top of each other, you might just reach the top.'

'How many people could it carry?'

Jane looked around at the wreckage. Little remained of the fuselage. Curved aft sections. A portion of wing. A portion of the great tail. He didn't recognise the livery. Something from the Far East, most likely.

'I don't know. It depends on the route, I think. And the time. Three hundred and fifty, maybe. Maybe as many as five hundred. A little more.'

Aidan spread his arms wide. 'About this many?'

'Yes, that's about right.'

Although the fuselage had disintegrated, there were sections of the interior that had survived the impact. Some passengers were strapped into their seats, bolted to the floor. One man, decapitated, held on to a plastic cup, imprisoned between clenched fingers. Most of the bodies, or body parts, lay in the field; some had hit with such force that they had partially buried themselves. Suitcases and handbags, wheelchairs and buggies. Someone had once told him that whenever you took a flight, the chances were there was a coffin in the hold. The shining dust from the crash skirled around the debris as if reluctant to leave the construct that had produced it.

Aidan had found a laminated emergency procedure sheet. He stared at it for a long time before tucking it under his arm. He seemed thoughtful, as if he'd done something wrong. Looking at children sometimes, Jane thought, you could almost see the cogs shifting.

They found what remained of the cockpit: instrument panels and throttle levers, the pilot's chair. Miles of wire and hydraulic cables hanging out of bulkheads, like some lost ungodly page from *Gray's Anatomy*. Nothing of use. Everything in the galleys broken or crushed. Jane found an ugly mass of metal and a great deal of blood but couldn't work out what it was. There were hard impact marks – deep scars in steel – that suggested there had been some almighty meeting of surfaces. He saw the edge of a small plastic number plate and realised: the seats at the front of the aircraft, maybe four or five rows, had concertinaed into a compressed block barely a foot deep. There were people crushed paper-thin inside that. He saw tufts of hair. Little else, thank God.

'I've seen enough,' he said. They went back to Becky, who was playing with her bracelet, staring resolutely at the ground.

'Think of how many aircraft are in the skies at any one time,' she said, and he saw her shudder, an almost reptilian reaction that moved slowly through her body from her head to her feet. It was as if she were trying to slough her skin. 'There's just no end to this. No end at all to how low things can get. No end in sight.'

Jane didn't know what to say. He muttered some bland platitude about survival, how she had to go on because she had no choice. But he didn't really believe it. She stood up. She had either swallowed what he had to say – which he doubted – or decided to move on anyway. It was all for Aidan. Jane wondered what she might do if the boy wasn't there. He felt almost guilty that he had Stanley to keep him motivated. How empty was your own life if you had nobody living in it?

The three of them picked their way through the wreckage and put the M25 behind them. They were within its circle now, and Jane knew that somewhere within its borders, somewhere within this 800 square miles, was Stanley. He thought it would give his gait added swing, but instead he felt more and more enervated. He couldn't concentrate on anything but that great circular concrete road, how it seemed like a trap, a slip-knot that might close around them at any moment, trapping them for ever.

They bade farewell to the A1 where its motorway name-sake crossed beneath it. They headed south-west across Edgware to the A5, the ancient Roman Road that would lead them, straight as a rule, to Marble Arch. The nearer Jane got to his goal, the slower the going. The bodies had been increasing in number ever since they passed into the northern environs of the city. In some places they had to double back and find a different route; it seemed as though every person in the street had come together in a mass huddle to die.

Jane tried to leaven the atmosphere with jokes, but his delivery was exhausted, deadpan. He looked into Aidan's grey emaciated face and saw himself there. Nothing for the boy to grow into; he was old before his time. Where could you go from here? Back to Toytown and Sodor and Nutwood? What was there in those places for a boy who had seen heads without faces; death in every possible position and permutation? You couldn't reclaim your youth after that, no matter that it was only a third lived.

He had to gee Aidan along; he was complaining of being tired. 'We're nearly there,' he said. 'Stanley. He's going to love you. You two are going to be great mates.'

'What if he's dead?'

Jane's stride faltered. Becky said: 'Aidan.'

'It's OK, Becky,' Jane said. And to Aidan: 'He's not dead.'

'How do you know? Everyone else is.'

'You're not. Becky's not. I'm not.'

'Everyone else is.'

'I can't explain it to you,' Jane said. 'I can't make you see. But he's not dead. I promise you. Now let's get cracking. Get a wiggle on.'

They followed the road past places Jane had never visited before, names he knew only because of the Tube map. Colindale, Hendon, Kingsbury, Dollis Hill. Aidan fell asleep in the wheelbarrow. Darkness was racing Jane home. He was tired too. He wondered at the irony of collapsing with exhaustion seconds from his doorstep. He glanced at Becky but she was a wraith, much too thin for the clothes she wore; a belt was cinched tight around her waist. She seemed to be fading into the grey of this north-west street.

Cricklewood. Mapesbury. Brondesbury. Kilburn. He didn't recognise anything. Buses and cabs and cars choked the road. Bodies were folded over each other as if they'd been competing to die first. It was fully dark by the time they reached the borders of St John's Wood and Maida Vale. Here were fall-back shops that he'd sometimes trolled out to if they'd been out of milk or bread and nowhere else had been open. Pubs he'd met friends in. Parks where he had taken Stanley on his scooter. Here came the roads he'd walked every day. The shape of things became known to him. The juxtaposition of trees and fences and street corners. He recognised a car that belonged to a friend and it shocked him so much that he thought he might be sick. Dead friends all over the country. Dead friends so much riddled flesh in the North Sea now.

At last he stopped. He was expecting the smell of dogwood and rosemary. The bark of Major at Number 9. Maybe a top-floor window open and a stereo playing music too loud: Interpol or Elbow or White Stripes. The hum of traffic. Female heels tapping on a pavement.

None of that. No street lamps. Just the grey trench of his street and dozens of dead sprawled up it, like procumbent weeds.

'Come on,' he said. He stopped outside Number 7 and shook Aidan awake. Jane could hardly speak for the pistoning of his breath, the hammer of his heart. 'Come on.'

He led them to the door, which was hanging off its hinges. Stanley used to pummel that door like a maniac whenever he got home. 'Stan?' he called, but it crumbled out of him, barely a whisper. He ushered the others inside, his eyes blurring, his fear mounting, his excitement hollowing him out until he thought he might float up the stairs. 'Stan?'

In the street, a dead thing twitched and sat up.

Part Two

LAZARUS TAXON

15. CITY OF CODE

Jane edged his way out of the alley, casting glances up and down a road that might or might not have once been called White Horse Street. Its sign had been prised off the wall years before. He checked windows and doors, rooftops, shadows. Shops here were long abandoned. Word had percolated through the city that the tiger had been seen in this area recently. He stopped outside a hairdresser's. Dust covered every surface inside. Hairdryers lay on counters like science-fiction weapons. Foxed mirrors reflected a throat of stairs to the rear of the shop that he did not investigate. His white breath measured a pulse rate of fear. Black snow lay in drifts against doorways that had lacked for years the wood meant to fill them. It formed a slush that ran and refroze in the roads, creating strange shining curds of pitch. It fell in soft obliques against the dun of the cloud ceiling: slow black bullets, every one of them hitting their targets. The cold reached fingers under the cuffs of Jane's coat and caressed his skin.

He couldn't keep his eyes off those backstage city shadows. It was like seeing a car crash occur in front of you, or a Skinner uncoil within its epidermal prison for the first time. *What if?* The question had died in him long ago. *Maybe? Just think* . . . All of it had withered like a basil leaf scorched by frost. The secret slots and pockets of the city were too dangerous for casual checks these days. Leave it to the flushers. *If he crops up, he crops up. Old enough to look after himself now.*

Ahead of him lay Shepherd Market, a tiny enclave with neighbouring pubs and an alleyway between them leading to Curzon Street, if memory served correctly. To the left, curving away from him, more restaurants, chichi fashion boutiques, jewellers and chocolatiers. People sitting inside a Polish-Mexican bistro at pretty tables waiting for a meal that would never arrive, time having drawn deep runnels into their superdried faces. Nothing moved. He made his way towards the alley, keeping an eye on the oily windows of the pubs.

He walked down Curzon Street past the Mayfair cinema where he and Cherry had watched some Japanese horror film centuries ago. Afterwards, they'd walked home, a fair hike miraculously shortened by the excitement in their conversation and proximity. Love could do that to you, he thought, staring at the broken cinema entrance. It creased time and distance, put you in a bubble. He wasn't going in there either. Not without a flame-thrower and plenty of back-up. And it was another two weeks before he was on incineration detail.

A gust of wind drove a blast of black hail into his face. He flinched from it and pulled the collar of his coat up around him, checked the positioning of his goggles, cycling mask and helmet. He had never grown used to the smell of sunblock; it stuck in his craw like the dense stench of a rancid dairy. He tucked himself into the doorway of a café while he went through his backpack, habit lifting his head to check the various approaches every few seconds. There was a bottle of water, a tin of emergency rations, a First Aid kit, a sheaf of tracing paper tucked into a plastic wallet and an Ordnance Survey map of London from 1968. He ignored these and picked out a battered notebook. Loose leaves, old tickets, photographs and torn pieces from maps were tucked in among its pages. Notes to himself. Reminders. Warnings. White spaces on the A–Z he had yet to explore. The city according to him, decked out in highlighter, pencil and paper clips.

The light was failing. He had to find shelter before it vanished completely. Some had taken to riding bicycles around the ruins but he preferred to go by foot. He didn't like the way a bicycle switched you off. Your senses were dulled by the rush of wind and the exertion. You could coast around a corner into any amount of trouble. One step at a time. Stop, look, listen and think. Stay alive.

Jane thought of the places he had slept in over the years. He'd stayed in a bedroom in Buckingham Palace that he was pretty sure had belonged to Queen Elizabeth II. He'd slept on the grand old table in the Cabinet Office at 10 Downing Street; a lovely blue sofa in the United States Embassy in Grosvenor Square. But the novelty quickly wore off and he became more careful with his choices. He stayed in rooms close to well-connected roofs in case he had to make a quick getaway. Whenever he found a secure place to hide out, with excellent escape options, he marked it by the front door with a stick of orange chalk, making sure he found a spot that the sleet couldn't get at. Orange marks crossed with blue meant that a previously good place was now infected, unsafe. You didn't go there unless you had a canister of kerosene strapped to your back.

He moved now through Mayfair but paused at Berkeley Square, where he could see masses of bodies that had not been burnt piled up against railings. That would have to be reported. He made a note of the location and doubled back on himself, not keen to invite trouble by trying to pick a way through them. Not this late in the afternoon, anyway. He crossed Piccadilly and jinked up Jermyn Street. A sign in a window: *Quality Cooled Offices*. All the buildings failing in some way. Rain sanding the concrete back to reinforcement rods. Teeth marks where Skinners had, like leeches at fish-tank glass, sucked away the animal grease of fingerprints and sputum laid upon the stone by human beings over the decades. The venom in their saliva had reacted with the building materials, producing ugly seams of black decay that wormed through brick and breeze-block, like cavities in a tooth going unchecked. There could be only one outcome. Already some of the more recent constructions were sagging like sots at a happy-hour bar. Terraces made stovepipe shapes. Millionaire waterfront properties tossed up in the 1980s were throwing themselves into the river.

There were a number of hotels sharing space with classy formal dress shops. Mannequins in the windows had not changed their outfits in a decade. Those that had not melted looked more human than the people he saw every day, himself included. He caught sight of his reflection in the glass that remained in its frames. Long hair. Wild beard. He looked like a shabby mountaineer. All the razors were as blunt as a bad comedian's punchline. Hillaby had taken to sharpening his old blades with a strop and shaved religiously, every day, but life was too short, way too short, for that kind of behaviour. One nick from those blades and there was no telling what might tumble into your bloodstream.

Jane stood and watched the entrance to a hotel at the Regent Street end of the road. Orange chalk mark on the steps leading to automatic doors long dead. Ornamental bay trees crumbled to ash in their grand marble pots. A man in a black suit and top hat lay dead just inside the entrance. He had fallen awkwardly, his left knee bent unnaturally, causing his shin to splay. Jane always felt a twinge of sympathetic cramp whenever he saw a body crumpled like this; felt the compulsion to straighten things out, give the body some dignity, some illusory comfort.

He panthered into the lobby and paused again, felt his skin prickling as he strained to hear noises that might give him a reason to leave. He hated this. Every night, the necessity of a roof over his head. It was like shutting yourself in a coffin, but statistically it was safer than a night spent treading pavements, ducking, hiding, trying to stay one step ahead. The reception area was empty. He took marble steps carpeted with red up to the top floor. A long corridor with subtle lighting that had not worked for ten years studded in the ceiling. Jane had forgotten what electric lighting was like. Sunlight too, for that matter. It would probably scour his eyes out.

He listened at the doors of all the rooms. Silence from within. He chose a room at the end and delicately closed the doors behind him, gritting his teeth at the soft, barely audible click of the lock. He listened for a while. Wind growling in the old city lungs. Snow spittle lashing glass and steel.

There was a body on the bed. A skeleton in ragged pyjamas with a white floss of hair. Most of the bones were still connected by leathery integument; he picked up the pyjamas like a bundle of faggots and tossed it into the wardrobe. He heard the scrabble and scratch of claws in the walls and sat on the bed, smelling the musty, rotten stench of ancient serous fluids rising from the mattress. It was rare to escape the filth. Occasionally he'd crack open the seal of a room that seemed never to have been occupied. A virgin territory, spotless, ghost-free, that breathed the faintest odour of new carpet and paint upon him as he entered.

Mostly, though, he spent his nights in bedsit crypts and hotel-room mortuaries, clearing the beds of cringing bones or stiff, withdrawn bodies like so much unwrapped beef jerky.

He checked the exits. On the corridor there had been a fire escape next to his door. It would take him down to the ground floor and up to the roof. There were any number of options up there. The double-glazed windows didn't open that far; they were on a security catch, but they were weak, shot through with cracks. A judicious blow would clear their frames.

Jane went to the wall separating this room from the next and pressed his ear against it. The journey of air through the hotel's pipes and gutters and gulleys, little else. He returned to the bed and stripped the mattress. He lifted one corner but the body had emptied itself into the filling. It was rotten, the springs coming through the fabric as he inspected it. Good only for burning.

The sofa was a better option. It was a two-seater, which meant his legs would hang over the side, but it was better than the floor. He positioned his pack by the cushion where he would lay his head and placed his rifle alongside it, safety off, within easy reach. He lighted the stub of a half-inch candle and dripped wax on the dining table so that it would sit fast. The light didn't matter; Skinners couldn't see. He kicked off his boots, unzipped his sleeping bag and got into it, fully clothed.

From the pack he pulled a packet of chocolate buttons he'd found at the back of a fridge in a Holland Park kitchen. Best Before: over five years ago. They were white with age but they were delicious. So sweet he worried that his stomach might reject them. He unzipped a compartment in the top flap of the rucksack. A blister pack. Omeprazole. Protein-pump inhibitors. He pressed a bright yellow capsule into his palm and swallowed it. *Twenty milligrams a day keeps the incubus at bay*. What a chipper line Liggett had dreamed up; one that Jane could not shift from his thoughts every time he swallowed his medicine.

He lay back on the cushion and sighed. He felt age settle in his bones. What was he now? Forty? Give or take. His muscles would seize up by morning and he'd struggle to get his boots on. He thought back to a time of lying in hot baths while listening to the midweek football commentary on the radio. A glass of beer and the newspaper. Stanley lalling from his cot and the chatter of Cherry's sewing machine as she worked the treadle. Maybe imagining his face under her foot. Some Thai food on its way from the local restaurant. Christ. Thai food. Close to sleep, he felt his mouth fill with saliva at the thought of prawn crackers and sweet chilli dipping sauce, curried chicken, jasmine rice.

Distant screams rose in the night. He knew what that was all about. He shut his eyes tight to it, and thought only of his son.

The candle was out when he wakened. But it was only recently extinguished; he could smell its acrid last breath. He heard the scratching in the plaster between the walls. He sat up, his hand falling to the stock of the rifle, which filled his hand and gave him a surge of confidence. There was a shocking, high-pitched cry, so loud he thought the rat that had loosed it must be upon him. He swung his feet out of the sleeping bag and they landed, not on his boots, but on the greasy, bristling backs of countless squirming animals. They recoiled before he did; he jerked back onto the sofa and pointed the barrel of the gun at the floor. He fired. Something screamed. There was the sound of bodies, an avalanche of bodies, falling over one another to get away. But then he realised he'd hit something and they weren't trying to get away, they were fighting over the booty, they were tucking in.

Jane flipped over the back of the sofa. No light. No boots. Maybe a hundred, maybe two hundred rats in the room. Rats that he'd watched get fat and get thin again over the years, once the carrion ran out. Rats who had lost their timidity; he'd watched hunger push that right out of the rat set-up. *Shit.*

He leaned over the back of the sofa and snatched his rucksack towards him. He held it to his chest, and yelled out when a warm, bony body scuttled out of it, over his arm and away. A different rat might have buried its jaws in his throat.

There were three glowsticks in their wrappers tucked into an inner pocket. He tore two open and shook them awake: sudden acid-green light reflected back at him from dozens of eyes. More rats were pouring through a hole in the door beneath the desk. Fear turned him sluggish; his bladder slackened and he leaked piss. The sudden whiff of released chemicals sent the rats into a frenzy, but defocused them. Jane slammed the butt of the rifle into the window. A fist of wind did the rest of the work for him.

He felt claws at his feet and looked down as a rat attacked him, bared stained incisors shredding the leg of his denims. Its glistening fur seemed to ripple with pleasure as it inhaled the stink of his fear-sweat. Jane couldn't shake it off. Another rat got a piggyback off its mate and launched itself at his eyes. Jane twisted his face away so violently that he felt a muscle pull in his neck; blindly he swung an arm and batted the rat away. He beat at the rat on his foot with the butt of the rifle. The rat continued to gnash at the air even as it was stove in.

Jane got a leg out of the window and, straddling the frame, fired three shots into the room. A squeal suggested he'd hit something, enough time to get out while they fought over the remains. He stood on the windowsill, grateful it was too dark to see how far down he would fall if he lost his footing. To his left, below the edge of the sill, was a ledge that ran to the end of the building, a distance of less than ten feet. A drainpipe waited for him there: another twelve feet above that and he'd be on the roof.

He sat on the windowsill, hands on either side of him, and inched along, using his palms to lift his bottom and swing himself incrementally towards the end. The wind plucked at his clothes – it felt to Jane as though it were assessing his weight, gauging how much it would take to drag him off into the night. He paused at the end of the sill, thinking how best to make the drop. How far life could take you, he marvelled, how far away from what you deemed to be normal could you be transported. Cups of tea, the cross-word, a phone call home, all of this seemed as bizarre in the same way as what he was doing now would have appeared to his old self.

He anchored his hands as best he could to the windowsill and lowered himself towards the ledge. Almost immediately his muscles began to tremble. The breath hammered out of him; he was going to fall. But then his foot found concrete and he leant his weight upon it. The surface felt about as solid as a pack of muscovado sugar. He sidestepped as quickly as he dared to the end of the building, his hands flat against the wall by his sides, creeping along, giving him the illusion of control.

There was a hiss; rats were pouring like oil onto the window sill, sinuous, jet, intent. He grappled with the drainpipe, feeling his hold on the rifle slipping. As he reached around to secure the strap on his shoulder he felt the drainpipe lurch towards him. A great chunk of stone containing the screws that attached the top section of pipe to the masonry had come free, weakened by the corrosive drizzle. Jane shrugged the backpack from his shoulder and let it fall. He looped the strap of the gun around his neck and scrambled up the pipe until he felt close enough to grab the edge of the roof, but his fingers were a couple of inches shy.

This is it, he thought. *The moment of my death*. And he was not afraid; he felt a little foolish, that he had dodged the hammer blow that marked the end of humankind only to be snuffed out by a pratfall. He closed his eyes. The rats could have him, but not while he was breathing.

A gust of wind caught him, fed him to the wall with a smack. He snatched at the parapet and was dismayed at how the coping stones shifted under his fingers. Thankful for the first time at how much weight he had lost, he managed to hoist himself onto the roof before the stones slipped free. He paused for breath and took off, scuttling onto the rooftops of Regent Street before descending at Piccadilly Circus. He circled back and picked up his rucksack; the ledge writhed with shadow. It put a chill through the girdle of bone around his groin to see how far up the window was.

He took a detour around to the front of the hotel and with a blue stick of chalk slashed the orange mark with shaking hands, thinking all the while that the open doorway would suddenly bloat with the slithering bodies of millions of rats. Then he began walking north-west.

Every morning was a different route, more or less, to the same destination. He must have trodden the streets around W9 to a point where he'd be able to see his own path worn out of the pavements. Hunger, exhaustion and a build-up of lactic acid in his muscles conspired to bring him to the point of collapse. That and the projected disappointment. But he could not give up on his son. He would never give up.

His fingers strayed to the pocket of his jeans. The letter was there; he could make out its edges. It had become so worn by his constant folding and unfolding over the years, the salt and oil from his skin, that he'd ended up sealing it in a plastic wallet that he'd found in the Cabinet War Rooms under Whitehall. He felt cheated somehow, as if the closeness to his son was reduced by these microns of polythene. His fingertips could no longer press against the ink that had been so close to Stanley's own. They could no longer feel the faint pattern of words in the paper that had been shaped by his son's brain. He felt as if he were being gradually detached from him, like the dovetail join in two pieces of wood that has begun to fail over time.

Each step he took was accompanied by a crunch of broken glass; the boots he'd found on a platform at Paddington station had become studded with splinters picked up as he crossed the basin and its density of office blocks that was now little more than a desert of glittering scimitars and framework skeletons. He hurried under the Marylebone Flyover, shadowing the water, so aware of the pools of darkness that he felt himself involuntarily shrink, as if he were trying to withdraw like something crushed on a beach, retreating into a shell that was no longer there.

The bodies crammed into the basin had turned it into a slurry of rotting clothes, hair and fat. It disguised his own smell. You had to grasp that wherever you could, despite the inevitable unpleasantness. He skirted Little Venice and its houseboats, all of them floating coffins with their blinds drawn on secrets he wanted no knowledge of. People at a café were tumbled over their empty plates as if drunk, dull bones and mirrored grins, everybody having a whale of a time.

Stanley wasn't home. Jane waited outside the door, kidding himself that he could hear Stanley playing with his battery-powered trains and wooden track or pestering Cherry for a beaker of apple juice. He stood at the door, listening. He stood at the foot of the stairs, listening. He stopped at every landing and waited. The building was empty.

He pushed his way into his son's bedroom. Plaster and glass on the floor. Part of the ceiling was bowed and cracked; water created stalactites at its lowest point. The posters on the walls had been bleached to white oblongs; he could not remember what had hung there.

What do you want to be when you grow up, Stanley?

Lying in bed, this tiny boy, the duvet up to his chin. Hand on his soft blond hair, the heat of him rising through his fingers. A smell of soap. Sleepy-eyed. Some toy, some cheap piece of plastic that was his current favourite twisting in his fingers. Warm. Happy.

Umm, I want to be an actor in Star Wars. *Because I want a real light saver.*

Would you protect your mum and me if you had a light sabre?

It's light saver, *Dad. But yeah, I'd cut Darth Vader's head off if he tried to hit you. And then push him off a clift.*

A cliff?

No, I said a clift.

Good to know, Stan. Thanks.

He could convince himself that Stanley's pillow bore an impression of his head or that his smell lingered in the room. It was easy to convince yourself of anything if you needed it badly enough. He checked the note on the table. He couldn't distract himself by thinking that if Stanley were still around he'd probably not be able to read it, no matter that he was fifteen now. No schools. No teachers he knew of. Precious few children left to attend classes if there were.

Stanley. I come here every day. If you see this note, wait
for me. I'll be with you very soon. I love you. Dad. x

Jane closed his eyes and felt nausea swelling. He staggered
out to the hall and was as sick as he could be.

The rest of the flat displayed its unremarkable ghosts to
him, as it had every day for the past ten years. There were
some who were irked by his behaviour; others who envied
his dedication and faith. He knew of people who had lost
partners or children and who would not countenance
thoughts that they were still alive. They were easily given up,
the alternatives too horrifying to tolerate.

He sat by the window and looked out at the dead gardens
behind the row of houses in the next street. The houses were
losing their shape, brick and stone crumbling, steel rods in
reinforced concrete becoming exposed. Edges were rounding
everywhere. One day there would be no house to return to.
A solid yellow puddle was a plastic football. The frames of
cloches burned away covered patches of ground where
rhubarb or strawberries might have grown. The flavour of
cream itched at his memory, but he couldn't summon it.
Nothing growing anywhere now. No dove to release; no
green leaf to bring back.

A group had taken off, though, for the Continent shortly
after he'd made contact with the capital's survivors, people
who had already invented a name – The Shaded – for
themselves. Jane remembered two of the expedition team:
Hinchcliffe and Henderson, because they had the same
names as his accountant and his secondary-school head-
master respectively. He couldn't remember anything of the
other ten or twelve. They had set out for Dover, intending
to steer a boat across the Channel to bring help back. They
were like the Flat Earth Society, refusing to believe all
evidence to the contrary, that this affliction had done for the

entire planet. *Wouldn't help have arrived already if it was the UK alone that was suffering?* was a question they refused to consider. Nobody had seen any of them ever again.

Something snagged on Jane's vision, something that didn't move when he did. At first he thought it was a flaw in the glass, or a shadow falling, but when he angled his head he saw the tiny, greasy remains of fingerprints. He stared at the patterns in those pads, drawing closer until he could make out the whorls and curlicues, the signature of his boy, a hello from across the years.

16. SKINNERS

Dawn was always a hurdle. The break of filthy yellow light over the city, like a diseased yolk, heralded a reminder of what lay in wait for anybody who had lasted this long. *We are but dust and a shadow*, Jane remembered, *and some of us aren't even that.* London was shored up with bodies. They lay in drifts at the mouths of Tube stations and shop fronts. They foamed from the pits and ginnels of the cluttered interior, thickened the roads like browbeaten demonstrations. It was ceaseless, monotonous, Auschwitzian.

Jane gazed up at the bent and bowed and broken street lamps, the electrical wires, the dissolving architecture, and half expected to see vultures eyeing him, waiting for him to fall. But there weren't any vultures. Everything that had had a heartbeat was lost for ever. You could only goggle at bones, or try to remember. Hunger was causing people to forget. Jane often worried about that. The scrabble for food was erasing every other trait that made them human. How far into the future before it was all scrubbed clean and they were falling upon each other? It had already started, he was sure, among some of the other splinter groups that were dotted around the city. It was galling to think that you had to keep an eye on your neighbour as well as the Skinners.

He plodded towards the base of the Shaded, through the corridors of Regent's Park and the interstices of Somers Town, home to ghosts of diesel oil from the long-defunct termini of Euston, St Pancras and King's Cross. Regent's Park itself was a redzone. Short cuts were becoming a thing of the past. He turned north, along the old Caledonian Road, now marked only with painted black skulls on the walls. He had to wait at the railway bridge. A Skinner was prowling in the shadows. Jane watched it and wondered about its name. Who had come up with it? Olly Easby, was it? Or Lynn Botting? It was childishly simple, yet accurate. They might have stuck with something a little less graphic, that was all. It was unpleasant having to refer to them by way of a noun that also served as the verb for their actions. Although they wore evidence of that too, like jewellery, like trophies; there was no escaping what they did.

It was unusual to see a Skinner up and about at dawn or so soon after feeding, as this one undoubtedly had. The remains of a meal were strewn about its feet like some broken human jigsaw puzzle. Jane cast glances all around; they usually moved in packs of three or four, sometimes more. They weren't fast, but they had some intelligence. They knew how to orchestrate a successful hunt. He hoped this was a rogue specimen. It swung its head from side to side like a distressed elephant in a cage. The ancient, tanned face that masked its own features shook and jiggled as if threatening to slide free. The eyes that sat in those chokers of biltong were nothing of the sort. They were the decoy flashes found on the fins of fishes. They were vestigial: un-eyes. But these animals compensated, he knew that. They were snakes when it came to smell; cats when it came to sound. There was something almost supernatural about their ability to find warm living things, as if they knew the flavour of thought, or the flares that leapt human synapses.

Eventually the Skinner moved off, sloping left up a dusty access road to the trackside where it began to follow the rails west towards Camden. Another city redzone. Jane let his breath out. There was no telling how keen their senses were; breathing – Jesus – *blinking* might make enough noise for them to begin a dogged pursuit. They didn't give up when they had the scent of you in their nostrils. They would stalk you for weeks, long after you thought you were safe. Shaded advice now was, if you've been chased, consider yourself a hot target and do not touch any bases until you've been scrubbed down by medics.

Jane paused at the railway bridge to watch the hulking figure as it diminished. A final check, and he was through the crumbled perimeter wall of the prison, trotting towards the middle of the radial arms. Part of the wall here was caved in too. Inside he saw Linehan with a sub-machine gun.

'You don't have to point that at me,' Jane said. 'Do I look dangerous?'

'You smell dangerous.'

Jane pushed by him into the corridor. All of the cells were locked. Dead men sat or lay inside them. There were claw marks on the walls, teeth marks on the bars. Most of these men had starved to death, their cries for help having gone unheard. Still nobody had found the keys to release them, to give them a burial, or cover their faces at least.

Jane's boots rang out on the metal walkways. In the office at the front of the building he found Gerber, Simmonds and Fielding sitting around a table playing cards. Ombre. Gerber versus the others.

'Hi,' Gerber said and lifted a hand. He was a man of around sixty who had once been very large. He kept his hair clipped short and oiled, and did the best he could to keep his facial hair in check.

'I saw a Skinner outside,' Jane said. 'Body, too.'

'Loner?' asked Simmonds. Simmonds was in her forties. She had large eyes that gave her the look of a St Bernard, always sad, expecting admonishment.

'Yes. Just outside here. Just by the railway bridge.'

'Gone now, though, yes?' Fielding still hadn't looked up to acknowledge Jane's presence. He fiddled with the fan of cards, getting them in a neat line under his fingers. Then he'd tap them together and fan them out again.

'Yes.'

'So?'

'So I thought you should know we've got fucking Skinners on the doorstep of the base.'

'Base changes site tomorrow,' Fielding said, handing him an envelope: this week's cipher.

'Time enough to have new holes eaten into your arse,' Jane said. Fielding wound him up like a cheap watch.

'I wouldn't worry,' Fielding said. 'And anyway, we could be sitting pretty before too long.'

His phrases. Jane could hit him sometimes. They were all emaciated; hunger was dragging them down. But Fielding had this optimism that made it all sound as though it was little more than a rainy day. It would blow over soon. It would all come out in the wash.

Jane wanted to eat. He had squirrelled away maybe a week's worth of tins for himself, Becky and Aidan by going without for a whole day, once in a while. It left him perilously close to fainting, and he knew that if he did that he would die – food for the Skinners. Or maybe someone else. He hadn't thought that way at all before, not even in the most desperate moments when he could feel his own famished body feeding off itself. It seemed a taboo too far.

He would never do it himself. But then there had been a meeting among the Shaded, or some supposed faction of theirs. Hollow faces sitting around a table. Steepled fingers. Furrowed brows. Chins stroked as they debated whether to enforce euthanasia on those that were draining supplies but not giving anything back to the community. The mentally handicapped. The lame. Babies. There was calm talk of what to do with the bodies. There was mention of recipes.

Jane had not been there for the meeting, and rumour was as slippery as ever, more so now, so he wasn't sure what to believe. But he had to entertain the possibility. You keep the most dangerous option in view and it was one more safety measure, another peeled eye to keep you whole.

'What is it?' Jane asked. He hated having to probe and pry for information. Fielding was no further up the chain of command. There was *no* chain of command. 'One of the gardens suddenly full of shoots?'

'Would that it was. No, this is unsubstantiated . . .' Jane felt the flare of excitement dimming already. More rumour. '. . . But there have been enough mentions, from disparate sources, to give it credence. Or at last make it a concern that deserves independent exploration.'

It was like listening to a formal speech. He'd never really talked to Fielding about his background but Jane wagered there'd been some ambition towards public office there.

'What is it?' he said again, patiently.

Fielding stopped fanning cards and blinked. In that moment his gaze switched from the suits to Jane's eyes. Very theatrical, Jane thought. Very Fielding. 'Have you ever heard of the raft?'

'The raft? No. What about it?'

Fielding shrugged. 'Conjecture, at the moment. But a picture is building up. Some say it's a military op. Some refer to a ragtag group of engineers, architects, carpenters and metalworkers all pooling resources. But whatever, pretty much every report talks of a floating sanctuary being constructed off the Kentish coast. Self-sufficient. Currently anchored but with a crude propulsion system. Sheltered from the elements. And, um, capable of transporting a hundred people.'

'A hundred?' Jane spluttered. 'On a raft? Get some grub down you, Alex. You're delusional.'

'It's what we've heard.'

'Well, it's what I've heard too, now, and I think it's bollocks.'

'We have a duty to check it out.'

'Right. Is this the same duty we have to follow the rainbow to its end, or put a tail on someone who may or may not be a leprechaun?'

'We've got men on it right now. There's a reconnaissance team on its way to Kent. Another doing the rounds here, collecting evidence.'

'Evidence? Hearsay, you mean.'

'We're trying to ascertain where the rumours are originating.'

'And then what? Punish the kid who's been making this stuff up?'

'It might be true. And even if it isn't, it's a good idea. We've got the manpower and the smarts. We need to be more proactive, Richard. We're getting overrun.'

Gerber and Simmonds had quietly placed their cards on the table and removed themselves from the room. People tended not to chip in when Fielding was in full flow.

'We have options open to us here,' Jane countered. 'We have secure bases all across the capital. We know the zones where the Skinners tend to congregate. Surely, once they discover that this place is not the free buffet they thought it was they'll move on.'

'Secure bases, you say?' Fielding mugged, one eyebrow raising. Jane felt like an opposition politician who has let slip a crucial piece of information. He felt skewered. 'Let me show you something.' He led the way to what had once been the prison governor's office. Any decoration – bookshelves, paintings, framed certificates – had been removed. The floors and walls displayed a series of pale parallelograms where things had once been. There was a map of London spread out on the floor, anchored at each corner by a shoe. Much of the centre of it had been whited out with Tipp-Ex.

'Our main base at Elephant and Castle was attacked last week,' Fielding said. 'We've moved out. Burned it down. Their net is closing, Richard. We're vastly outnumbered.'

'And the answer to that is to play cards?'

Fielding did not look up from the map. He sighed. He was a big man, or had been once. Everyone was a shade now, a blueprint of what once was. 'I just finished a twelve-hour shift burning dead bodies and scouring bad zones in south Tottenham. I watched Alan Poole get trapped in a loop of fire of his own making. Burned right through the oxygen hose on the tank on his back. We pulled him out – he'd been breathing fire for twenty seconds. He's going to die. At the moment Doctor Sinclair is making a decision as to whether to let that happen without painkillers, as we really can't spare them. Go down and have a listen to Poole breathing and then tell me what I should do to take my mind off things instead of playing cards.'

Jane chewed at his resentment. 'I'm sorry,' he said.

'Forget it.' Now Fielding raised his head, and there was spice in his eyes as he regarded Jane. 'What have you been doing?'

Spoken as if he was in charge. The implicit needle: *Whatever it is can't be as important as what I've been up to.* Jane felt disgust rising. The best part of sixty million people dead and here they were playing office bitches.

He tried to keep the resentment from his voice as he said: 'Recon. We have a vermin problem in Mayfair. No more than anywhere, I suppose. No Skinners that I saw.'

'And how about Maida Vale? Skinners there?'

'Not my patch.'

'No, it isn't. So why were you seen there? Three times in the last week. At least.'

'You know why.'

'We need you elsewhere. We don't have the numbers. The resistance has many weak spots. Only by adhering to the tight disciplines and schedules we've set ourselves can we hope to keep ahead of the Skinners.'

'Spare me the team talk, Alex. I do my job. Anything outside of that I do in my own time.'

'But you have to face up to the facts. It's been ten—'

'Shut up. I'm warning you to shut up. I haven't slept well. I haven't eaten today. I am in no mood for this discussion.'

Fielding gazed at him, his face a serene blank. Jane waited. He could see this inspection was meant to unsettle him. Let Fielding make his silent judgements and evaluations. Let him report back to his stupid committee with its imaginary powers.

'The pills are running out, Richard,' Fielding said. His voice had cracked – it was nothing like as calm and assured as the face that delivered it. 'The booze is running out too. Someone – a Skinner, I hope – ransacked one of the warehouses. There's nothing left: no grain, no barley, no potatoes with which to make any new stuff. There's nobody with the knowledge, or the machinery, to synthesise new prophylactic drugs either. When we run out, we've had it. And I don't intend to hang around long once that happens. Our only chance is to get off this island, find someone, a health team that can cure us, a surgeon who can cut this out of us, I don't know, but staying here is sitting in a waiting room for a GP who isn't coming into work any more.'

The soft *tang* of footsteps on a distant walkway. Jane thought about the cells. There was dried blood on some of the bars where inmates had tried to squeeze through or tear a way out. He could almost believe that the echoes of their cries were flying around the heights of the prison, like trapped birds.

'How can you stand it in here?' he asked, but he was only filling the silence. Fielding knew that. There was no answer to the question. Anywhere was better and worse than the place where you were. You'd still be trapped inside yourself, with yourself, with what you were likely to become. 'I haven't heard anything of these rumours. You mentioning the raft just now, that's the first I've heard of it.'

'It could just be a rumour, like I said. We have to take it seriously. But if it exists I don't want us sitting on our arses here while people are paddling to safety. We have to hope it's real and we have to hope that anywhere other than here is a safer, better place to be.'

'It might be worse.'

'I know you have more optimism in you than that, Richard.'

'You want me to find out what I can?'

Fielding nodded. 'We've got the whole of recon on this. Depending on what you dig up, we could be out of this shitpit within two weeks.'

'Or up to our chins.'

'There you go again. You know, this unremittingly sunny disposition of yours is beginning to get me down.'

Jane had to smile, despite his feelings towards the other man. He kept trying to convince himself that it was in order to prevent the muscles of his face from atrophying.

'Come and find me if you get any leads,' Fielding said. He curved his lips into a cold smile and held out his hand. Jane shook it. 'Come and find me if you don't.'

* * *

Jane struck north-east, consulting his bible. There was a much folded and annotated patrol map of the city glued into the back cover. He opened it on the lam and studied the zones he had whited out. No real rhyme or reason to their location, other than a preference for areas that contained Tube stations, especially those that serviced the deep Northern Line. There were a lot of Skinners in Camden, Oval, Kennington and Leicester Square. They congregated too in open spaces; pretty much all the parks were off-limits. But rogues had been spotted too. Including the tiger. There was talk of the tiger being a leader, but there was no understanding of who he was leading, or to what end.

Jane visited buildings across Crouch End. He found a terrace of boarded shops near Finsbury Park. Behind the blinds of corrugated iron and chipboard were empty rooms. No rat spoors. No evidence of Skinners. He chalked the walls orange and moved on. It was getting dark. Another day lost to fear and suspicion; work was the only way to carve a way through the hours without dropping to your knees, screaming and crying, immobile until the moment they came and drilled their fingers through your skull. It seemed pointless sometimes. This was no winnable war. It was running from shadows and shivering in the dark until morning, hoping you weren't uncovered. It was hide-and-seek played for unspeakable stakes.

Jane was shivering by now. Cold had found the weak spots of his clothes and yanked them open with its insistent, powerful fingers. He felt it burning under his shoulder blades, in his knees and neck. A damp pain that would take a long time to shift. No hot showers. The luxury of a bath took far too long to create. He'd be little more than something serving itself in its own broth for the Skinners the moment he stepped into it. He wondered if all his years of diving had somehow made him more prone to feeling the cold; maybe his bones were less dense, therefore more sensitive to these sinking temperatures. Or maybe it had something to do with the drugs that he and everyone else were taking: a side effect, maybe. There were alternatives to these gastro-resistant capsules. Hard booze worked well, and many cleaved to it easily, but you had to drink a lot and keep topping it up; Jane didn't like the associated loss of control. The omeprazole was a bind only insofar as he had to remember to keep taking it, but that was no hardship considering the penalty you paid if you missed a dose or two.

He remembered the panic in London when it had become clear that the seed that had been laid down by whatever cosmic wind had swooped upon the planet was germinating not only in the ready fertiliser of the dead but in the living too. People vomited blood and felt a searing pain unwrapping itself in their guts, in their lungs. Jane had never seen a case of what some bleak wit had termed a 'moving-in party', and he didn't want to. There was a rumour that you could feel the shape of the body that was growing inside you, slowly devouring you from the inside out before you died. An inner shadow worming itself into your hollows and crevices like a hermit crab tucking into a new shell. You'd feel the unholy pain of your bones melting, your organs gnawed; a contained explosion. Creatures filled the casing of your skin, growing to whatever limits surrounded them: cat, horse, man. If they had blossomed within the remains of a cadaver, the Skinner would look like some animated scarecrow; you'd see the rumours of its true physiology through the ruins of what had gone before it. Jane had seen a mangy dog trotting in the night, looking for carrion, breath labouring through the holes in its hide. On one morning of noxious mists in Alexandra Palace he'd stood transfixed in awe as the broken silhouette of a stag clattered through a blasted coppice, its antlers like frozen black lightning, matted, slavering, skeletal.

Becky had been on the medical team who conducted emergency medical trials. Take-'n'-shake wards were set up in gutted churches, municipal offices, school halls. Pills of every kind were shovelled down the throats of men and women desperate to prevent or delay the fatal invasion. Nostrums were embraced. Self-harm. Self-help. Fervent prayer. They found that alcohol worked, but only in doses that rendered you insensate. A breakthrough was made with drugs associated with heartburn. Pharmacies were raided for their stocks of omeprazole, lanzaprazole. Those at risk swigged antacids from flasks. People were mugged for Rennies and Gaviscon.

Jane was grateful for the air filters he had used since day one. He was low-risk. What moved in him was little more than the juices of fear.

Jane hurried along Camden Road, one long thoroughfare of orange marks, one of the few places in London where he felt safe despite the road being topped and tailed by white areas: Camden to the south and north, Holloway. Perhaps it was a subconscious alertness to do with this new job; he always felt energised by some new task. Now he felt a tingle in the small of his back at the sight of the petrol station. He had passed this way so many times before without a pause, but now it radiated danger, or at last its potential. Jane tried to see where the threat was emanating. Like many buildings – especially one whose structure was a cheap amalgam of plastic and neon – this one had suffered from the initial blast and subsequent weathering; the shop was little more than a collapsed cabin, the forecourt a black scree of exploded fuel, glass and vehicles.

It took a while to work out why he felt so jumpy, but then

he saw the service hatch in the ground; it was off-kilter, no longer flush with its housing. The explosion might have caused it to come off, but if it had it would have turned it into a weapon, flinging it a great distance through the air. This was a lid replaced by someone who didn't want something to be found, or dragged back into position by someone hiding inside. That thought loosened him a little, and he crouched, trying to quell the melting feeling in his bowels, knowing that to shit or piss here was to bang a dinner gong.

He had to check it. What if it was as he had first thought, a cover for something meant to remain secret? That could only mean food. He would take a bite, just a little to keep him going, and leave a message for whoever had secreted it, telling of a safe place where resources were pooled and a resistance was being established. Maybe the people who used this den were dead and he'd find a treasure trove that he could later lay claim to. If he didn't, someone else would.

Jane scanned the road north and south again, and peered at the houses of Tufnell Park that rose behind the petrol station. He held his breath so that he could hear more acutely over the suck and blow of his breath in the bicycle mask. No movement. Fear opened up in him like a black flower in poor soil. He picked a way through the rubble of bricks and concrete. Rain fell like something forced through an atomiser, adding faint noise to the picture before him. A hand went to his chest. The wound here that the man down at the lake had inflicted with that sword of his was healed as well as it ever would, but adrenaline was like a wormhole to that moment, opening him up with the memory of pain.

Jane thought of the letter he had begun, years ago, in reply to his son. He had yet to end it and knew that it would never come to *Take care, all my love*. He kept the latest pages on him, along with a supply of fresh sheets, so that he could add more whenever he was faced with a long wait or a sleepless night. When he felt lonely, or afraid, he found that it helped to shape the part he was working on. Stanley became his distraction and his saviour, although there was really no 'became' about it. He had always played this role.

Where was he up to? The delivery room. He had been describing the moment of Stanley's birth.

Hey Stan, you know, your mummy burst into tears when I told her you were OK, and that you were a boy. I cried myself when the midwife put you in my arms. I sat with you while they took care of Mummy and even then, minutes old, you had your own little characteristics, your own set of expressions. I had to shade your eyes because the sunlight was streaming into the delivery room. I held your tiny hand in mine, and smelled the miraculous scent that was rising from your head. I will never forget that moment for as long as I live. I loved you all through Mummy's pregnancy, even though I didn't know what you looked like or how you might behave. In the second when you were born, I knew that I would do anything in my power to protect you from harm.

You will discover music, books and art, things that will sometimes move you to tears with their beauty. There will be friends of your own, and people you will love. There will be great happiness, and some sadness too, but even that is a good thing, an important thing to experience. I can't wait until you are old enough so that I can play football with you, and laugh and joke with you, and show you all the amazing things there are to see. I'll take you diving on the Great Barrier Reef. You won't believe it.

Jane had his fingers under the edge of the hatch, lifting it, thinking of moon wrasse and morwong and blue puller, when he realised that its cack-handed replacement was nothing of the sort. It was a deadly come-on, the bait filaments jangling on a devil fish's head.

He heard something lurching within and he felt himself hoping it was just his own limbs readjusting to cope with the weight of the hatch, but the sound was all wrong, too deep, too fast, too out of rhythm with what he was doing. He was stepping back, feeling his back give with the strain, about to drop the hatch and run, when a ragged, striped cuff shot out of the shadow, peeling back to reveal a claw, giraffe-tongue purple, each curved tip as sharp as a ceremonial blade thinned almost to invisibility on a whetstone.

Jane felt it grip him and jerk him towards the place of his death.

17. STALL WARNING

F ear made Jane laugh and vomit. He ran hard for maybe two miles, until he was so shattered he could barely stand and had to drop to his knees in order to breathe. He was shaking violently; he could still feel the claws on him squeezing as though to assess his tenderness. He wasn't sure where he was; he hadn't really paid any attention to direction. Away was good enough. Now that adrenaline was draining from his muscles he began to become aware of his surroundings. It wasn't exactly the fire after the frying pan, but it was close. He was on the fringes of Hampstead Heath, the southern tip, where part of Gospel Oak train station, including the railway bridge, had collapsed into what had once been known as Mansfield Road.

They liked to congregate in this great park. Maybe something in its wintered desolation called to them. The desiccated trees against the sky like black fractures in unclean ice, agonised, all the sap bubbled out of them and rehardened like angry amber boils. The scorched, stubbled acreage of earth. The ponds filled with bodies: huge bowls of chilled consommé for them to guzzle. They crisscrossed the heath – Jane had watched them from the safety of a

Highgate rooftop with his binoculars – like mendicants folded into their rags, deep in thought. Sometimes they dragged partially denuded victims along behind them by the hair, or a limb, to be stowed in the earth on Parliament Hill, or around the Vale of Health, for consumption later.

Jane struggled to think. The cold was freezing his head, turning him sluggish. It was a constant ache in his temples and nape; it had burrowed under his shoulder blades where it burned in his muscles like a slow blue fire. He remembered there was a bolt-hole in Belsize Park. Ten or fifteen minutes from here. It would mean cutting up by the Royal Free Hospital – hospitals were other places where they liked to bed down – but he had to get inside. The Skinner had gripped him so hard he was worried that the skin might be broken.

He ran up through Pond Street to Haverstock Hill and up past the hospital. There was no sign of anybody. Come night-time, though, this car park, this forecourt and street would be a scrum of bodies. He couldn't bring himself to think what the hospital interior must be like. Belsize Park, once a desirable enclave of London, with its beautiful Georgian houses and broad leafy lanes, was now a demili-tarised zone. The smell of copper was in the air; buildings were thickly painted with blood. Whatever fighting had happened here had been intensely one-sided. Bins rolled around, pushed by the ceaseless fingers of the wind. Glass teeth ringed grimacing black jaws in every single window along the parade of shops. He hurried as best he could through the obstacle course of felled lamp-posts and tele-graph wires. Until he reached England's Lane. At the top of this street was a pub that had been gutted by fire. Inside he saw figures hunched against each other in a corner, under a leaning beam of wood that was mackerel-striped with deep burns. He left them alone. He knew from bitter experience that sometimes such quaking, craven types were really Skinners trying to trick you into coming closer. Sometimes the figures were human, and not as shy or fear-beaten as they seemed. It was best to leave well alone or suffer a pre-emptive attack. Nobody wanted any comfort any more. Another trait that made humans who they were gradually erased from the banks of race memory.

On Fellows Road Jane paused, listening for movement. He checked behind him but of course the tiger wasn't there. It would be shambling after him, perhaps having made no more than a hundred yards, but it was coming on and coming on. It had Jane's stink in its nostrils and it would not be shaken from its pursuit of him. It had the pit-bull grip on him no matter where he was.

It had come out of that chamber like something being born. Mewls and whiffles and whimpers; breath shuffling in its deep wet throat. He had tried to move back but had felt the blades of its claw pinch his flesh and he had halted, knowing that if his skin were pierced he was dead, if not from infection then from the bloodlust that would be triggered by any open wound. The jaws of the tiger stretched wide, its teeth like twists of black glass. The coke-coloured pits of its eyes were ringed with a dry cake of pus. Its fur had long since lost its gloss; now it was like a thin coat, burred, plated with muck, with a novelty pattern picked up for pennies from a charity shop. There was no hint at the power and grace that had once swaggered within it. He'd dropped the heavy hatch cover, trapping one of its legs as it rolled over the lip. It was too much to hope that he'd broken the limb, not that it would matter; nothing seemed to put a check on their movement, except fire.

Once Jane was sure that he was safe he cut down past the side of the third house on the left to the rear where a large garden had once played host to children. A rusted swing with chains hanging free where a plastic seat had once been tethered; the circular frame of a large trampoline now nothing more than a silent mouth open to the sky. He had spent a lot of time, in those early months, searching for his son and finding evidence of thousands of other children. It was like cataloguing grief. There were scorched photograph albums under beds; children's rooms; playthings torn into nightmare shapes by the heat and the weather. He had found the remains of boys Stanley's age. Some of them were huddled into the far corners of their rooms, the flayed skeleton of a favoured toy in their famished hands. Teeth clenched on a final word, bitten off by pain. *Daddy*. He had to stop. It was so deeply sad. He wasn't sleeping but whenever he managed to it didn't last long: there was always some blistered bug-eyed thing slinking about in the shadows of his head, limping and stumbling towards him on limbs half devoured by fire.

Jane checked the wall next to the back door. Orange. Inside he moved through a dark hallway almost to the front of the house, his fingers trailing against the failing wallpaper. An edge. He stopped and put his hand to a point halfway down the wall. He pressed hard and fast and felt a magnetic shutter sink slightly against its seal. When he let go, the edge sprang clear of its flush join with the wall: the jib door opened, breathing its musk against him, a smell he never grew tired of sampling. That air had been trapped in here for decades. It was the whiff of safety.

It was really little more than a false wall, but the space was big enough, and long enough to contain a fold-up camp bed, a chair and a narrow table. Jane had a candle burning on the table now. Next to it he'd rested his naked foot; he was prodding the tender flesh of his ankle. A purple bruise encircled it. In places the black indents of claws remained.

He had been mighty close to being punctured, but all seemed OK. Regardless, Jane cleansed the skin – revolted by the memory of its filthy entrapment – with alcohol wipes and bandaged it. His foot wrapped in startlingly clean cotton, his fright and exhaustion allayed somewhat by a bracer of vodka, Jane rubbed his eyes and reached for his bible. The Ordnance Survey map was folded tight and secured in a home-made flap in the back cover with elastic bands. He spread it out on the table and plucked the envelope from his wallet. The candlelight shivered for a moment, as if shuddering in sympathy at the tedious task ahead of Jane. Sometimes it took mere seconds: the shape of the paper almost drawing itself to the conjunction of roads that formed its boundaries and from which it had been traced. Other times he would sit blankly for hours like a man with a piece of a jigsaw puzzle that he was convinced belonged to another box. Now he slowly slid that cipher across the map with the tip of his forefinger. Everyone who was committed to the resistance had a copy of this map, published in 1968, or a facsimile of it; teams of copiers had spent days tracing the streets and key features onto sheets of paper. He'd been treated with disdain when he suggested that all maps would contain the same basic shapes. Why not use those? *Because* they *won't have this map*, the Shaded told him. *And what's wrong with being as cautious as you can be?*

This particular fragment reminded Jane of a dog in full flight, its legs off the floor, its head out flat and intent. Three black dots signified buildings. One of the dots was circled with red ink: the next location for the temporary head-quarters. Sometimes there were complaints about what appeared to be an overly cautious knee-jerk response to the threat of attacks that didn't necessarily occur. What was the point of this constant seven-day scramble for a new HQ when the old one was perfectly safe, perfectly serviceable? Jane knew it was all cosmetic, a façade to keep people busy, to keep their minds away from the open sore of a future not worth living for. None of the gardens they had tried to cultivate was coming on. Food was scarce. All of the talk at the meetings, of trying to grow phytoplankton in the ocean to absorb the carbon dioxide in the air, of building a machine to either blow away or suck in the cloud, countless other geo-engineering options from the possible to the outlandish, had come to naught. People had already spurned the rations offered by the resistance and had moved out of London, hoping to find richer pickings in Bristol or Birmingham or Manchester. Everyone was aware that to walk now was to go to your death, but that didn't stop people. There was the illusion of positive action. It was better than hiding out with a fistful of crumbs, not knowing if you were going to wake up in the morning with some vibrating shredded head trying to gnaw a path to your vitals.

'Got you,' he muttered as the piece of paper found its echo on the map. Some bright spark had decided to take everyone for a hike. Jane wished someone had decided to limit their travels to the A406 ring road rather than the larger ripple of the M25, but there had been a clamour for a greater range of options. There was the feeling of being constricted. That damned circle. A feeling of a noose around the throat.

'Heathrow it is, then.'

Jane napped briefly and woke up to find most of the night gone. He shifted in his chair, hoping it was the wood and not one of his own joints that was creaking. Fear cosied up to him and he stood up, wincing at the familiar aches and pains. He thought of that shambling tiger on England's Lane. *Softlee, softlee, catchee monkey*, the tortoise to his hare. He felt his skin pucker.

He had been dreaming about Fielding. A fan of cards that had steadily drizzled blood across the man's fingers as he spoke in his maddeningly calm monotone. Behind him the illuminated wings of the prison had darkened, block by block, the light snapped off as if someone were flicking an array of switches. Fielding kept talking despite night's casual pursuit, despite the clatter of locks as the cell doors were sprung and whatever had died within them came staggering out onto the walkways.

Something Fielding had said about hoping Skinners had invaded the warehouse chimed with deep suspicions of his own. He thought of the rats piling into the room. An aspect that had needled him. There was a hole in the door, but it had not been there when he went to sleep. Surely. He always double-checked the doors, made certain they were secure. Maybe fatigue had caused him to miss this, but he doubted it. He didn't know what that might mean.

Jane folded the map and tucked it into his bible; he stowed everything in the backpack and shouldered it. The wind was hardly heard in here. It was a surprise sometimes, not necessarily a happy one, to be able to hear the labour of your breath, or the riot of your own thoughts. But the moment you considered the wind, it was there in the background, like the breath of a baby in a cot, as if inspired to increase its volume by virtue of your mind snagging upon it. It moaned in the gaps of the houses and called out from the open mouths of flues. It carried the grief of the city's destruction.

Walking those sagging, abject streets you could almost begin to take the damage for granted. Years of listening to the glass crunching underfoot and the groan of battered timber finding alien positions in which to settle softened your reaction to it. Like the stone edges of buildings dissolved by the rain, you became blunted, you curved away. You kept your eyes on the pavement while the jagged fingers of scaffolding and fence posts and foundations beseeched the sky. He was no engineer, but he knew they could not stay in London indefinitely. It was a muscular city only for so long as its pals stuck around to help out: the Thames Barrier, for example. Who was maintaining the flood defences now that most of the capital's population were so much rat food? He woke up in cold sweats thinking of overheated rods in nuclear power stations melting concrete and spewing tons of radioactivity into the shattered sky. Would they even notice?

Jane closed the jib door and checked that the edges were concealed. He trod through the house to the back door and let himself into the garden. He waited, assessing, gauging.

Eventually he moved back along the side of the building to the road, the aches in his legs reawakening already. He walked south, skirting Primrose Hill on the west side. He was back in Maida Vale without realising his feet were taking him that way. He stood outside the house and called softly to Stanley, staring up at his window. He could still see that cheeky face with its arresting green-brown eyes. There was no effort in his recalling it; he seemed to wait, a good little boy, at the edges of his Dad's thoughts until he was needed.

He waited for a while, feeling his hair whipped by the wind and filling with grit. The foul cake mix of the sky folded in scoops of cobalt and charcoal. He thought of the raft and wondered who had begun it – either the building of it, or the baseless rumour – and imagined himself sitting in a crude boat next to Stanley, holding hands, heading on gentle swells to a gap in the clouds where the sun was peeking through. He took that image with him, empty-handed once again, back onto the A5, ghosts clamouring, that hopeful road upon which he had entered the city ten years before, straight as an arrow shaft, cutting through his fear and doubt, slamming into a bull's-eye so insubstantial that the arrow was still in flight, looking for a target. Anything.

He turned left onto Crawford Street and walked as far as Upper Montagu Street. The windows looking in on the children's area of the library at the end of the road were boarded up. He could just make out the play of candlelight in the cracks around the chipboard. A side door was nailed shut with thick planks. On Marylebone Road he hurried up the steps, feeling woefully exposed in the twilight, and gave a patterned knock on the heavy main entrance. A woman wearing glasses with thick scratched frames let him in. He swept across the marbled hall and down the stairs to the children's library. Becky was sitting in the corner drinking from a tin cup. She rose when she saw him, spilling her drink across her sweatshirt. They embraced and he felt her heart through their clothes, beating hard enough for both of them.

'I missed you,' she said. He nodded and smiled, kissed her. He missed her as soon as he was with her. It seemed to catch up with him. It was difficult when you were in the city. You were so busy trying to avoid Skinners, assess bolt-holes, keep a step ahead of the tripwire of your own dark thoughts that there was little time or space for others to share.

'Is there any food?'

Becky shook her head. 'No, wait. I saved you something. I haven't seen you for days.' She led him away from the small bookshelves furred with dust into the staffroom. He didn't like the children's library. It was too close to what he was all about. She dug out from her pocket a tablet of chocolate wrapped in silver paper.

'What about you?' he asked.

'I'm watching my figure.'

Jane took the chocolate and broke it in half. He placed his half under his tongue and felt his mouth become immediately awash with drool. He pressed the other half against her lips. 'Go on,' he said. 'Be a devil.'

The sweet served only to make his appetite more keen. If you kept busy enough you could forget about hunger, or at least press it into some ancient part of the brain, that lizard knot of slow thought. He was about to suggest going out to hunt for some real food when she told him about the body found that morning at Pentonville. Intact, which meant it was definitely not a Skinner attack.

'Who?'

'Fielding,' she said. 'Throat cut.' Her voice stumbled over the violence in the words.

'Suicide?' Jane asked, but Becky was shaking her head before he'd even begun to shape the question. The dream he'd had tapped him on the shoulder.

'This was a thorough job. And there were wounds inflicted after he died.'

Jane didn't know how to react. Murder had become a thing from history; compared to what was going on today it was almost a polite crime. That fellow survivors had resorted to killing their own during an ongoing crisis seemed a behavioural aberration.

'Do we know who did it? Did anybody see anything?'

'No. Fielding was just clocking off. He said he was going to check out some buildings in De Beauvoir Town before calling it a night. He'd forgotten his chalk and his medipack. Jamie Cosgrove went after him. Found him near the Essex Road train station.'

'Did we check this Jamie Cosgrove out?'

'He was spotless, Richard. Unless he'd had a shower after slicing him up, he had nothing to do with this.'

'I know, I know. I'm just thinking out loud. Jesus. I only saw him last night.'

Becky sighed. 'Yeah. The prison is shut down now.'

'I know. We're moving west. Where's Aidan?'

'He's at the river with his chemistry mates. Testing acid levels.'

'That's helpful.'

Becky jolted his arm. 'He's learning,' she said. 'You never know, he might be one of the people who pulls us out of this mess a few years from now.'

'It's being stuck in the mess now that's kind of a pain,' he said. 'We've got enough eggheads scribbling equations. We could use Aidan on recon, or working the library.'

'He does his share.'

Jane could feel a tension building up behind his eyes. His gums were sore and his tongue kept worrying at one of his molars; he was convinced it was loose. 'All right. Look, I need to get out of here. I don't like this place. I don't like sub-street level. There's nowhere to go.'

'It's secure, Richard. It's safe.'

'Nowhere's safe,' he said, and wished he hadn't. 'How are you, anyway?'

'You're not the only one who wants me to move on. I'm staying at a safe house in Balham from tomorrow. Word is that there are Skinners drifting south from Camden and the parks.'

'Well, then, that's good.'

'What do they want with us?' she asked him, her voice suddenly pressured, cracking. He was reminded of the Ceto; his mates in the chamber all trying to equalise as the pressure piled against their sinuses. Squeezing their noses and blowing, trying to yawn. The first sign of the heliox mix pulling their voices into falsetto.

She didn't mean *us* as in everyone, she meant the women. He knew that. Why did the Skinners choose to hunt the men but abduct the women? Together they'd watched it in the early weeks after their arrival. They'd seen a group of girls pulled from the ticket barriers at Shadwell and dragged away screaming by things that had once been men but whose skin was now swollen with the knuckles and ribs of something that didn't quite fit inside. Black joke eyes staring out of dead holes of bone, a mimic with cheap props. They'd been strangled almost to senselessness, then flung on to the backs of tethered, invaded okapi. Steam had come off the frayed bodies: they'd looked like ghosts fading into the night. Nobody had said anything at the time. People still didn't. You could posit all you liked, but it came down to the obvious in the end, and the obvious, if it was so repellent, so horrifying, was always ignored, concealed, skirted. He could answer her right now, but the question was a squeak from the safety valve. She didn't really want to hear it. She knew what was going on.

'I thought maybe we could walk down to the river, find Aidan, go on up to the power station, bed down there.'

'It's late. And it's a long way. We have beds here. We can go up to the research rooms if you want.'

It wasn't just that he was feeling cabin fever in a place that made Jane uncomfortable and nervous. He didn't like Aidan going off on his own even though the river was generally safe and he was among friends. And Jane still had motion in his joints. He wanted to be on the street, tracking down the gossip about the raft. He didn't like Fielding, but he was sorry to hear of his violent death. The threat of it was like a storm cloud that had slipped inside the building and was clinging to the ceiling, getting fat, building up the pressure on everyone beneath it.

Becky's hands on his shoulders. He thumbed off the bicycle mask and the goggles and stood blinking in the candlelit room. She gave him a little half-smile; she knew she'd won. She slipped a hand into his. 'Come on,' she said.

They took the steps up through the oak-panelled stairwell and pushed through a door into an area filled with old bookcases. Some had collapsed against each other and had not been righted. Magazine racks were loaded with newspapers and glossies bloated and dulled by time and water that had coursed down the walls from a crack in the roof. Ranks of PCs with shattered screens sat on tables cluttered with cups and mugs and soup bowls.

A circular window in the dome of the library was filling with shade. Candlelight flickered from the far end of the room. They bypassed the loans desk and headed for the light. Sleeping bags were wadded into the gaps between the bookcases. There was a silence of deep sleep, the kind of sleep that punched people unconscious as soon as their head hit the pillow, the result of little food and much exertion.

There were two empty sleeping bags in the corner. Becky's bag and coat marked her territory. She undressed quickly and slipped into her bag, pulling the corner up over her body, but not before he saw the rippled sandbar of her ribs, the deep shadow of her stomach. She patted the space next to her. Jane smiled. He looked out at the Marylebone Road as it sought the heart of the city. Figures drifted across it or along it. A fog was rising, or the clouds were sinking. Everything grey. Somebody screamed, far away, and he almost didn't register it. You got to a point where you didn't hear the tragedies unfolding around you. Wasn't it always this way?

Becky unhooked her bra and he touched her breasts haltingly, as if the lambent light around them was being manufactured from within. They made love quietly, although Jane doubted whether anybody would have been roused had they given their fucking full volume. Jane withdrew at the moment of his climax and she held his penis as he came on her stomach. He didn't look. She wiped herself clean and fell asleep almost immediately, her head on his chest, the smell of their sex rising from the sleeping bags whenever she moved. Bitter thoughts of Cherry. A shameful wish that she might walk in on them like this.

He raised himself up slightly and balled a coat and put it under his neck. He pulled a dead mobile phone from his pocket and dialled the number.

'Hi, Stan,' he said. 'What you doing?'

'Colouring in. I done a Batman but it got boring because he's only blue and grey.'

'What did you have for dinner?'

'Pasta. And parmigiano.'

Jane laughed. He'd taught Stanley to say 'parmigiano' at a very early age, with a cartoon Italian accent, and it always tickled him when he said it.

'You had a bath? Brushed your teeth?'

'Roger, roger.'

'Sleep tight, then. See you soon.'

'Night, Dad.'

Jane was about to press the end-call button when a sharp bill shot out of the casing in an explosion of brushed steel and embedded itself in his cheek. He smelled the cloaca of the bird, and the carrion of what it had last dined upon. But he was so tired, so exhausted, that the nightmare could not impinge. He slept, looking down on himself, disinterested, as the bill stripped away the flesh of his face to reveal a thin white bowl filled with dust.

18. RAGCHEW

In the early morning the tiger broke down the library door and killed two men who tried to stop it from cantering up the stairs. Jane saw it happen. He'd been coming down to use the toilet and to check that Aidan had made it back from the river. The tiger swung its great spoiling head his way as Jane pushed his own scent down the stairs before him. There was a frozen moment, almost as if the air pressure they each produced had caused them to be still as it collided. Jane backed off; the tiger approached. Blood from the broken men in the foyer had created large fans across the floor. It appeared solid; you might lift up an edge and it would all follow, like a confection set to dry on baking parchment.

The tiger moved more circumspectly now that its quarry was in sight. Its bluster was spent; perhaps it was exhausted after expending so much energy on the door and the men. Perhaps it was wary of Jane, who had bested it once already. He heard movement behind him and Becky's voice: 'Oh.' She kept the door open for him and it was only as they were pulling down filing cabinets to block the entrance that the tiger charged. It hit the swing doors and half a dozen squares of glass punched out of their frames onto Jane and Becky's

backs as they shouldered more furniture in front of the door.
A paw came through, stinking of shit and rot, and almost
swiped off Jane's face; he felt the wind from it move the hair
of his beard. The other sleepers were up now, and hurriedly
grabbing the things they valued most: food in the main, but
also thick winter coats, old stained albums of photographs.
They made their way silently to the stairs, veterans of any
number of emergency evacuations in the past. Nobody
screamed any more. Too tired. Too knowing.

'I shouldn't have come here,' Jane said. 'I put everybody
at risk.'

'Shush,' Becky said. 'We can do all that later.'

They hurried to the small lift at the back of the room.
During the years it had worked it had taken three people at
most, and clanked as if about to disintegrate into a welter of
hinges and screws. Jane had used it once, then stuck to the
stairs. Now it had been hollowed out; a rope ladder hanging
from the defunct overhead sheave. They descended it quickly
in darkness, Becky going first. At the bottom they had to
lever open the doors with a crowbar that was hanging by
wire on the wall. They burst out through the fire doors into
Salisbury Place and did not stop running until they were out
of breath, leaning on each other. Spit dangled from Jane's
throat, quicksilver mined from the pits of his lungs. It was
so cold he felt as though he was running on the stumps of
his shin bones.

'We should find Aidan,' Becky said at last.

'Maybe he'll be at Plessey's. It's worth a look. I can't think
where else he might be.'

It was rare to see women on the streets, unless they were
part of some captured chain being led off to the Western
Avenue. Rumours filtered through that they kept the women
in Wembley Stadium, but nobody had ever travelled that
way to check. There were some zones that were off-limits

because of the sheer weight of numbers. Any reconnaissance party or rescue squad would be decimated before they reached Willesden. Jane remembered, though, around three or four years ago, a woman who came limping down the A40, naked, her skin torn like strips of errant wallpaper on a well-sized wall. She had been struck dumb by shock. It was in the silver colour of her hair and the owlish protrusion of her eyes, as if she'd seen something of a magnitude too great for her brain to process. Her mouth had been messed around with: there were strange scars pitted in the cheeks, chin and jawline. Most of her fingernails had been torn off; people wondered if that was torture, or something that had happened during her bid to escape. People tried to talk to her. Some of the Shaded wrapped her in blankets and gave her what food was available, and in such a state as to be easily digested. You didn't want to be thinking of chewing your food when shock was threatening to put a brake on your heart. She ate some soup and was getting warmer by the minute, but she didn't say a word. Not then, not for the next five days, after which she died in her sleep.

Jane looked around. He didn't recognise these streets. No signs. No buses bearing destination boards. A row of skulls in rags leered at him from the melted plastic bench under a bus shelter like a comedy audience in between laughs, waiting for the next gag. The buildings had lost any detail that might have pointed to an era or an architect. Blunted, edgeless edifices. Polished office blocks of steel and glass were now riddled dark monoliths, floors bowing with rain.

They moved quickly, hesitantly, dashing to doorways in a bid to find some plaque that would tell them where they were, or a forgotten piece of post behind the door bearing an address. Jane hated the way they scurried around, like mice knowing there was a predator on the wing.

Behind one door was a lipless drop into a benighted chasm that Jane almost toppled over. Becky's hand on his belt saved him a fall that might have lasted minutes. It was like staring in on his own nightmares.

Eventually they hit a series of junctions that pulled at Jane's memory. He took a turning, then another, came back, stared and thought and went another way. With each step he felt knowledge return. It gave him the same sense of relief as an accident missed by inches.

'This way,' he said.

'Where are we?'

'Good news, I think,' Jane said. 'I thought we might be heading towards the Tower, and trouble. But we're further north than that. I think Liverpool Street Station is up here. Which means we're close.'

The shattered forecourt of the station announced itself moments later. They bypassed it on their left, mindful of the baleful stare of figures hunched into the glittering cave of an old coffee shop where coals burned cherry red and something indistinct turned on a makeshift spit. They crossed the road and turned right. A web of ginnels and alleys where small restaurants and wine bars had once enjoyed brisk business at the weekends when the old Spitalfields Market had traded were now host to slouching gangs drinking red biddy or wrestling in the icy mud on the cobblestones. There were others, still and emaciated, sitting on kerbs at the very end of life, blood leaking from their eyes or smeared across their faces as it seeped from noses and gums. They were paper, these people, all but ready to be blown entirely away by the tireless winds. You could see the grooves and notches on their bones through the skin. The recessions and tugs in throat and stomach at each drawn breath was so pronounced that it seemed they must implode. You could hear the suck of it over the muted roar of weather, like something being rescued from thin mud. Becky and Jane moved silently through them, eyes averted whenever possible, knowing that this was them in time.

'Where do we find Plessey?'

'He's inside,' Jane said, gesturing with his chin at the sacked remnants of the old market. Much of the façade was caved in; the ironwork frame remained, albeit malformed by fire, along with dozens of roasted trestles, warehouse trolleys, roll-cage containers and lampblack scaffolds. 'Or he should be. I've only ever seen him here. Aidan likes his shop. Lots of stuff to look at.'

They moved through the wreckage like vacationers at the beach searching for rock pools. In a far corner of the great hall was a shop with its windows boarded over, reinforced with sandbags and razor wire. Faded gold lettering on a purple awning heralded HOUSE OF CLASS.

Jane threw a fallen bracket from the scaffolding at the board. There was a dull clang. They heard a voice call out. Jane said, 'It's me, Richard Jane. Have you seen Aidan?'

There was the sound of bolts shooting back, fully half a dozen before the door cracked open and a small crushed face looked out from a ring of shadow. Plessey ignored the two of them and ranged his gaze over the rest of the marketplace.

'We weren't followed,' Jane assured him.

'Inside,' he said, and left them to forge a path through the obstacles.

Once they were in, Jane closed the door and rebolted it. It was sepia-dark in the shop. Buttery light was reflected back at them in soft-edged rectangles from burnished copper, foxed glass, mottled tin. A smell of naphthalene. Jane felt a known claustrophobia, the kind of stifling he had felt whenever he went to visit his grandparents as a child. Small rooms containing too many things, not least the people who lived there, barnacled fast to ancient, heavy rocking chairs, like pilots in a steampunk story, all anti-macassars and brown tartan.

Plessey had moved ahead. He was busy with a teapot and a tin of leaves. The smallness of his face was explained by his ubiquitous peaked balaclava; Jane had never seen him without it. Perhaps it protected some injury caused by the Event. Perhaps he was just cold. They followed him along a narrow corridor, columns of things from the past crowding in from either side. Scratched dusty gramophone records of dull shellac. Mountains of old cracked lacquer boxes for fountain pens. Rusting tins that had once contained boiled sweets. A cigar box overflowing with tickets for trams, trains, dance-hall events, coupons and vouchers for rations never obtained. Horn-rimmed spectacle frames. Sheepskin coats. Every smell was brown. It was tobacco and tannin, leather and corduroy, heavy, oppressive. Jane felt sweat rising through his skin. At any moment his grandmother would bring him a bowl of stodgy suet pudding and custard, Camp coffee made with condensed milk. Chocolate lipstick bleeding into crow's feet. Dusty haloes shining in the floss of her hair. The metronomic beat on the mantelpiece of a clock presented on their wedding day and ageing alongside them. Oak and ormolu. The grind of the rocking chair. Slow, inescapable punishment.

'Are you all right?' Becky asked.

Jane nodded. 'Just forgot how much I hate this shop,' he said.

'I haven't seen Aidan for at least a week,' Plessey said. His voice was as soporific as the things he collected around him; he sounded as if he were just getting rid of something rich in his mouth: fruit cake or port or blue cheese. Wet sibilants. Contentment.

'Fielding is dead,' Jane said. 'Murdered.'

Plessey didn't reply. He turned from the water he was boiling on a small gas ring and widened his eyes. Jane could imagine what he might have said, camp, theatrical: *You don't say.*

'We haven't got anybody for it. It was something of a surprise.'

'No telling how we might behave when we're thrust into the bear pit, hey?' Plessey said. 'The centre cannot hold. Falcons and falconers. Mere anarchy and all that.' He stirred powdered milk into china cups with a silver spoon. The cups rattled briefly in their saucers as he handed them over. 'I apologise for the absence of a little something to go with this. Fresh out of brandy snaps and macaroons, I'm afraid. No sugar, either. And there probably won't be any for a thousand years.'

'Fielding,' Jane went on, 'just before he was killed, he was talking to me about a rumour. Something about a raft. A way out, or forward. Something.'

Plessey tapped his spoon three times on the edge of his cup, placed it in the saucer and took a sip. 'Not half bad,' he said.

'I thought maybe you'd heard something.'

Plessey sipped again, then gazed at Jane as if trying to assess him for trust. Jane felt impatience riddling him. He liked Plessey, but there was always the sense of you being part of his audience. Mention of falcons had made Jane twitchy.

'Come with me,' Plessey said.

They put down their cups and saucers and followed him through the shop to a hatch in the floor with an iron ring bolted into it. Plessey lifted the hatch and looked into their faces again. Then he disappeared into shadows.

At the bottom of the shaft was a series of rough cases made out of pallets, wine crates and what looked like banister posts, all held together with pins, braces, staples or twine. There was more stock here for the house owner who liked the vintage look. Wooden grooming sets inlaid with nacre. Glass boxes containing silver earrings and pearl necklaces. A corner filled with old transistor radios and their component parts: valves, connectors, wires, knobs. It was to these that he took them now. A workbench was covered in coils of copper wire and small lengths of planed and sanded wood.

'What's this?' Jane asked.

'None of the valves work, of course. We're still struggling with electricity. God knows what's been going on in *EastEnders*. But I've been making crystal radios for the last six months.'

'Why?'

'Something to do, for one thing. When you find yourself on your own it's good to keep busy. But also in the hope of making connections.'

'You mean you've been broadcasting?'

'God, no, dear boy. I don't have the face for radio. I've been searching, looking for signals.'

'You made a radio that works?' asked Becky. She wore an expression almost of disgust, as if he had admitted to messing about in a laboratory and creating a lethal plague.

'After a fashion. It's very simple. You wind a coil of insulated wire around a cylinder – in this case, a plastic bottle – and strip away a little of the enamel coating from the loops. Solder a diode to the bottom of the wire. Solder one of the wires from a telephone handset to the diode and the other to the wire at the top of the bottle. Then you clip a grip to the antenna, that long piece of wire there, and clip the other end to one of the bare pieces of wire that we exposed. Then you earth the radio and theoretically, depending on which part of the coil you touch with your alligator grips, you should pick up different signals.'

Jane scanned the workbench. 'And did you? Pick up different signals?'

'Well . . . one, at least.'

'Show us.'

Plessey sat down on a rug-covered office chair and pulled open a drawer on a heavy desk next to the bench. From it he pulled a shoebox. Inside this was something that resembled an abandoned physics project from school.

'How do you power it?'

'That's the beauty of a crystal radio. You don't need to power it. That said, there's a big chest with a duffel bag filled with thousands of dry-cell batteries. I spent the best part of a week going through it, sorting the possibles from the ones that have leaked and then testing them all. I found maybe half a dozen that work. But they won't last for ever. I've been very sparing with my midnight vigils.'

There were no lights to indicate that the radio was on. No frequency display. Plessey handed Jane the receiver and he placed it to his head. He touched a clip to the exposed wire and the soft, crackling nonsense sounds of the cosmos played tinnily through the earpiece.

Jane's breath caught in his throat. A nothing noise, the voice of the void, but it had been so long since he had heard anything like it that he might well have been listening to his mother saying hello across the years. It had beauty and an immensity, despite the lack of rich amplification. He handed the receiver to Becky.

'I don't hear anybody,' Becky said, and thrust the receiver back at him. Jane felt a stab of irritation. The man had made a radio, a working radio, and she wanted the shipping forecast.

'Patience, my dear,' Plessey said, and the performer in him was at the fore again. He moved the rod to a point on the coil that had been marked with blue felt pen, and this time Jane heard a distinct difference. The white noise was reduced. There was a rhythmic sound, a weird, percussive sound that Jane couldn't identify, until Plessey, at his shoulder, said, 'That . . . I think that might be hammers.'

Now that he'd said it, Jane couldn't understand how he could have heard anything but. After about ten minutes, they heard something else. It sounded like a chair being scraped across a wooden floor.

'Here we go,' Plessey said. 'Bang on schedule.'

Jane had to sit down himself when he heard the voice. It was female. It sounded as though she was from Wales. There was a musical undercurrent to her words. He barely registered what she was saying, he was so tied up in the moment of hearing a voice that wasn't in the immediate vicinity. But she repeated it:

This is Radio Free UK calling all survivors. If you are out there and you can hear this – I know it's a long shot, but what can you do? – then please do not give in. There is a way out of this. There is safety. You will find us off the south-east coast. Coordinates as follows: 50°, 54', 37"N, 0°, 58', 55"E. The raft exists. There is an escape. We are anchored off Dungeness, Kent. We launch in a week. We can take a hundred people. The raft exists.

The sound of footsteps moving off. The sound of the wind across an open doorway.

'They repeat the message every quarter of an hour,' Plessey said, switching off the radio. The disappearance of the sound was a wrench for Jane; he jerked towards the unit as if he was about to try to switch it back on. Plessey didn't notice. 'Sometimes it's the girl you've just heard. Other times there's an older woman, sounds like a newsreader – received pronunciation, you know. And there's also a chap, sounds as though he's from the West Country. They've never said, but I get the impression they've already got a fair-sized group down there.'

'Why?' asked Jane. He was thinking of Stanley, left behind in the city of butchers while everyone escaped.

'A raft,' Plessey said. 'For one hundred? Hardly the work of a carpenter and his gofer, no?'

'It's a trap,' Becky said. 'These people are being forced to lure survivors down there. They'll be waiting for us. With the fucking salt and pepper.'

'I don't think so,' Plessey said. 'They're doing well enough in the city, slowly picking us off. How many of us are left, do you think?'

'It's hard to say.' Jane shrugged. 'Latest estimates put us at around three to four thousand, give or take. The main survival hot spots are at Angel, Victoria and London Zoo.'

'They're running out of food and they know it,' Becky said, her voice becoming edged with panic and indignation. 'They're chasing us to the corners of the country.'

Plessey shook his head. 'Not the case. There's a stiff cordon of Skinners all across the southern city limits, ditto north too, building across the North Circular. They're tightening the noose, preventing escapes. There's no evidence to suggest they're moving out, hunting survivors in other parts of the country. Remember, they don't need to. Wherever we are, they are.'

'We have to make a break for it. As many as possible,' Jane said. 'If they can make one raft, they can build more, or come back for the stragglers.'

Becky was rubbing her hands together hard enough for their rasping to cut through his words. He had noticed this always happening whenever plans were discussed, change considered. She was frightened of any challenge to the status quo, and frightened of the status quo too. She recognised this paradox within herself, but it didn't make it any easier to deal with.

'What about Aidan?' she said. 'I know he likes to do his own thing, but he's been away longer than usual. I worry he's been . . . I think he might . . .'

Plessey shut away the radio in the desk drawer and lightly clapped his hands together.

'Look,' he said, 'would you care to stay here tonight? I insist, really. It's far too late for you to get back to the centre, and anyway, why would you want to? I have some mushroom soup, a large tin I'd like to break into, but much more than I can eat by myself and I wouldn't want it to go to waste.'

Jane woke in the night and he was crying silently. Candles burned in their makeshift bedroom, a small kitchen in which the erstwhile staff could have taken their breaks and eaten lunch. He could hear Becky breathing next to him; she held a swatch of blanket tight in one fist. Plessey's snores carried from the heart of the shop; he seemed to complement the creased, tired things that surrounded him. Jane could imagine him always being here, gradually melding with the furnishings and knick-knacks to the point where he would be camouflaged by them.

He had dreamed of sitting in Plessey's office chair, the crystal radio assembled before him, switched on. It had hummed with potential; even the valves unconnected to the body, strewn across the workbench, had glowed with some arcane intent. He touched the rod to the tightly coiled copper wire and at every contact there exploded from the amplifier a terrible screech, the unselfconscious cry of a child in danger, scared and hurt, a boy with death only seconds away from him.

'Stanley,' Jane called, even though there was no transmitter. 'Stan, it's me. It's Dad. Tell me where you are and I'll come for you. Tell me where you are. Please.'

Stanley kept screaming. The sound of something familiar in the background, a weird, metallic, percussive beat. Each time Stanley paused for choking breath Jane heard it, a spastic, robotic infill. He realised with a euphoric pang that he was with the others at the beach, waiting to board the raft. In two days he could be reunited with his boy. He was dressing hurriedly, trying to pack his bag in poor light, wishing Stanley would stop screaming, calm down, say something, when the nature of the screams changed. If anything, they grew even more frantic. The hammering had stopped, or rather it had lost its metallic beat. Now it had increased its tempo but it was landing on something far less resistant that metal or wood. Jane stopped rushing around and dropped to his knees. He covered his ears but Stanley was behind them and even by the time he had begun to realise it was a dream it wouldn't release him.

He woke up much later. Plessey was gluing pieces of wood together, a box to protect his precious radio. Becky was helping with another batch of batteries, throwing the ones encrusted with salt into a metal waste-paper basket. She was doing it with enough force to suggest she wasn't fully engrossed in the task.

'Oh, I'm sorry,' she said, 'did I wake you? How thoughtless of me.'

'I was awake anyway,' Jane said, levering himself upright. 'You forget that most of my working life I slept through worse noises than that. Once, a friend of mine called Carver was beating sheet metal for two hours not six feet away from my sleeping head. I didn't even change position.'

His voice faltered at the utterance of the word 'beating' and both Becky and Plessey caught it, shooting him a look. But nobody asked any more; everybody had nightmares. Everyone had something that stuck in their craw.

'The others, they'll want a demonstration,' Jane said,

'before we can even think about planning an exodus.' He stood up and began to get dressed.

'I'll nip over to HQ later today,' he said, and Jane thought, *Yeah, right. Nip on up to Heathrow. It'll take you the best part of a day.*

To Becky, Jane said, 'We should try some of Aidan's haunts. See if we can find out why he's not turned up for so long.'

Becky went back to her batteries. 'If Aidan likes it so much here then I'd rather be around when he turns up. I think I'll stay here for a while, if that's OK with Daniel.'

That Plessey didn't look at her when she said this told Jane it was already a done deal.

'Of course, my dear,' said Plessey.

Becky nodded. 'I've decided.'

'All right,' Jane said. 'And if I find Aidan I'll bring him over here, yes?'

'He's not my son, Richard,' she snapped, and flung a battery more forcibly into the bin. 'I'd prefer it if you stopped trying to compensate for . . . for . . .' She broke off. Her shoulders hunched; she put her head in her hands and began gently to shake.

Jane left her like that, unable to cope with her sudden change of mood. Plessey caught up with him just as he cleared the buffer of razor wire. Something had been in the market the previous night. Clothes and bones and almost an entire human skin were spread across the hall. The signs of a scuffle were drying into the poured-concrete floor, along with human blood, Skinner blood, Jane wasn't sure. It was black, there was a lot of it. A familiar sight, a familiar smell.

'She's a little raw, Richard,' Plessey said, taking in the devastation. Out of his cosy bolt-hole and with his balaclava off for the first time since Jane had known him he looked too pale, waxy. His hair was a beige scrim grafted onto a sweating pate. 'Aidan . . . it's not that she doesn't care. You can see that she does. But—'

'But she fears the worst.'

'I think so. I think that's the case, yes.'

'Plessey, I've been fearing the worst for the past ten years. But it's the not knowing that's the killer.'

'I'll pass that on,' he said. 'That will help, I'm sure. She'll come round, eventually. She's strong. People like her don't give up easily.'

Jane looked away, in the direction of Commercial Street. He thought there was trust, some love, even, between himself and Becky, but her dismissal of him, her preference for Plessey's nostalgic comforts indicated that there was no space for sentiment now. You took what comfort you could from people and you moved on. He supposed it was a kind of evolution. He would learn from it.

'What about you?' Plessey asked him. 'Where are you going?'

'I'll see if I can find Aidan at my Library.'

'You're carrying on with that pointless job? When we've got this cause for hope gifted us?'

'We have to make the effort,' Jane said, not believing it for a second. 'It's the decent thing to do. Some of us want to carry on. Some of us want to keep busy.'

He didn't mean it as a slight but he didn't doubt that was how Plessey would take it. 'Let me know what the Shaded think of the broadcasts,' Jane added. He started for the road, then thought of something. 'Plessey, one thing. The Skinners. Could they intercept those signals? Understand them?' As soon as the question was out he thought it witless. Of course they couldn't understand; they didn't speak, they moved as though they had the brains of dinosaurs. They were driven only by hunger. But something in Plessey's expression spoke of his not having even considered this possibility. Now he seemed to, and he began to shake his head, but the gesture was without conviction. They stared at each other, Plessey halted by the razor wire, his skin sickly white against the dark tweed of his jacket, a vampire in hawthorn.

19. FOETAL ECHO

The Library was wherever you wanted it to be. Jane liked to take his journals with him to Trafalgar Square. If the rain had paused he might climb to the top of the ENO building and sit under the dead neon letters of its tower, looking south past the amorphous, dissolving statue of Nelson on his column towards the great roads of Whitehall and The Mall. You could write anything as long as it was connected with the Event. Your experiences, fears, hopes. You were encouraged to write about what you knew of the Skinners, and the way they made you feel: reportage as therapy. You could write about how they killed, if you were up to it, or more prosaically, what your work had consisted of since you last were the Librarian. But you only had one day on the job. Someone had decreed, some psychologist *manqué*, that it was too damaging to dwell for any longer on the agonies of how you got here and what might yet come. There was a greater likelihood of burn-out this way, it was argued, than there was in cleansing the city of its corpses.

The words were designed to be a gift to whoever came after. A warning and a set of guidelines. How to survive. Parallel to Jane's Event work (he usually wrote diary entries expanded from brief notes he made at the end of each day), he continued with his letter to Stanley. He guessed it must be around five thousand pages long now. All of these he kept in a series of fireproof suitcases in the boardroom of a boutique hotel in Covent Garden, fully intending to pass them on to his son one day.

Aidan liked it up here too. But he was not on the rooftop today. Jane looked out across the ceiling of London but could spot no other figure. The possibility that Aidan had been taken was strong, but he doubted it, somehow. Aidan had grown to be a tough, resourceful young man, despite his sickliness. He knew places to hide that Jane would ordinarily have walked right by. He could melt away like shadows on a cloudy day.

The skies around London had lost definition. Where once there had been a strange miasmal fog as black as sea-coal and thick *mammatus* hanging from the base of vast storm clouds, and the teasing of crepuscular rays suggesting that the sun still hung beyond and had not forsaken the planet, there was now a featureless blanket. The cloud was not leaving, merely retreating into the heights, as if aghast at the behaviour of what lay beneath it. It was becoming dangerous now to travel across the city's ceiling. The persistent hungry rain had eaten away the waterproof outer layers and was tucking into less resistant parts of the rooftops. Already some older, less well-tended buildings had collapsed. Some of the warehouses on the banks of the Thames that had missed out on renovation were now little more than scruffy lines of brick dust on the wharves and dockyards nestling against the river. Fires were still breaking out in some buildings as gas pipes corroded and released pockets of fuel. Jane had been close enough to an explosion in a pizza restaurant in Waterloo East some years previously to have felt the ends of his beard crisp.

The grand plaza of Trafalgar Square was awash with dirty water, like a shallow lido that had been neglected by cleaning staff. The great bronze lions at the foot of Nelson's eroding granite column had developed a patina of verdigris and sat hunched like moss topiary. Screams flew out of the city, confused by distance, dopplering towards or away from him like weird sirens, calls for help that were rarely answered. Although there were jobs to be done, there weren't enough live bodies to cope with emergencies. You could hardly term it an acceptable level of collateral, but there were no feasible alternatives. There were no rapid-response units, no electric-blue lights or souped-up engines. Nobody warned you about the dangers; everyone knew the score. The people screaming were either slowed down by injury, or the weight of the things they were carrying, or, Jane wrote: *because they want to be caught*.

He looked at the things that he took with him everywhere. Once it had been a wallet, a shoulder bag for his bottle of water, newspapers and novel. Now money meant nothing and he himself was the news. Reading novels seemed offensive, somehow, in these times; an insult to the people who had been killed. Books had once seen him through many a grim hour flushing his system of nitrogen on the Ceto, so long ago that to think of diving was to somehow question his own sanity. Hundreds of feet deep, wearing only a thin rubber skin and a helmet? It was work from nightmares. It was behaviour from one of the science fiction novels he'd read.

The mantra he had once uttered, getting ready in the morning, had been *keys, money, bus pass*. Now it was *rifle, mask, goggles*. The rifle, its walnut stock having changed its shape minutely over the years where he'd held it so that it might fit his own hand better, was an old friend; he felt as naked without it over his shoulder as he would if he'd forgotten to put on his boots. Filters for the bicycle mask. Sunblock. His bible. The new essentials. Not heavy now, but maybe they would be one day when age was piling into him, or a muscle strain had halved his walking speed.

I no longer know what day it is, Stanley, or what time of day. I know when it's time to wake up and when it's time to go to sleep. It's kind of nice. I remember everything being geared to the clock and the watch when I was younger. Everything was an appointment. Getting you up and to nursery on time, if I was off duty. Picking you up in the afternoon. Tea by five, bath by six, bed by seven. Do you remember the game we played once, Stan? Last man on Earth, I called it. But you said you wanted to call it One. You said it was more serious to do that. More grown-up. You were really into your numbers. What's a hundred add a hundred add one, you'd ask me. And I'd pretend to struggle, and you'd tell me the answer.

And I asked you, what would you do if you were the last person on Earth, the One, and you said you'd get into a rocket and fly off to another place to live. And I asked you, what if there were no rockets, and you got upset and started crying and it took me a long time to get you to calm down and your mum gave me a hard time for it, but I cuddled you and you stopped, you fell asleep in my arms and I held you for ages. I was going to put you to bed, we were on the stairs, and you woke up and smiled at me and gave me a kiss, and you said to me, Stan, you said to me that it would never be One, because we were together all the time. You said we'd been meant to be together all the years I'd been me without ever knowing you. And it's true. Ever since you came into my life I can't remember before it. Which sounds silly. I mean, I know I lived for thirty-odd years before we had you, but they seem so pale and pointless. I came into being at the same time you did, my gorgeous boy, my Stan. And you are always with me. You kept me alive for so long. You keep me going.

So we're here and it's now, maybe ten years since I last saw you, you a big boy now, already at the end of school and thinking about sixth form, maybe, and we're playing One for real. Well, it's not properly One, because there are some of us left. You too, I'm hoping. You and Mum, I'm praying every day that's the case. Things are dangerous, Stan.

And sometimes I hope you went fast. Right at the start of things. With no danger of ever being alone and afraid, your innocence being torn to meaninglessness. I hope you did not suffer.

Jane's pen hovered above the journal; he was unable to form into words what he doubted his son would ever understand anyway. Instead, he returned to his survey of this corner of the city. For maybe the thousandth time he counted the cars and buses that were ranged around Trafalgar Square. Forty-eight cars, including taxis; nine vans of varying size; one coach (what a day trip that turned out to be); twelve buses. Seven motorbikes. He remembered photographs he had seen of various parts of London, miraculously free of traffic. Dogs and horses and carts. One or two automobiles driven by people who had nowhere to go and few roads on which to take their shiny toys. Sheaves of mud and dung peeled to one side by thin wheels. Now, unless you were walking at night and alert to possible hiding places, you could easily miss the vehicles that cluttered the streets. Even if somebody could be bothered to shift them, their ghosts would remain in the parts of the road shielded by metal and cellulose like the outlines of bodies at the scene of a crime.

There were twelve buses ranged around Trafalgar Square. One of them was on its side. Four of them were black where fire had turned them to shells. A Brixton bus for ever veering left to travel down Whitehall had been turned into an armoured safe house. Steel braces had been bolted onto the sides of the bus and dug deep into the earth under the tarmac, to prevent anything from pushing it over. Steel shutters protected the empty frames of the windows. During the daylight hours, when few Skinners were seen, the people who lived in this tank would come out to fortify the braces where they had begun to be excavated, and reposition the thickets of barbed wire that had been pulled away in the night. Jane envied them their stoicism, but could not have done the same thing. All those weeks of walking down to London had instilled in him a fear of standing still, even for a short time. Although he liked this spot, he grew itchy after just quarter of an hour, and had to quell the instinct to get back on the road. This was orange. This was safe. For now.

Cold was creeping through the blanket and the fleece of his coat into his legs. Jane stopped writing and stood up, wishing for a flask of something hot. He did some exercises, unhappy with how quickly he grew tired and breathless. He made himself cough into his fist and inspected his sputum. Each time he did this he was braced for flecks of blood but they never came. His breath smelled rotten, though, and he knew this was due to some failure in his teeth, the decay he had felt working its way through his mouth for years. As for the rest of him, sometimes when he moved he caught a whiff of how ripe his flesh was, but that was true of everybody. Washing was a luxury. Sometimes he took cold showers if he could find a working spigot and a compliant pump. Mostly he went without. His hair hung in damp ropes. He'd tried to cut it once, but there was no point. You felt you could never get dry. Dirt was ingrained in the contours of your fingers, these fingers that had once touched the pulse in the wrist of a sleeping child. Your hands became maps of all the places you'd been, digging through the filth to get to something or get away from it. You lost sight of who you were and where you came from. You failed to recognise things and they began to matter less.

He tended to keep many of his clothes on these days; he had enough to worry about without the shock of his own emaciation. Resources among the Shaded were growing scarce; soon they would not be able to offer any kind of reward for this work. He foresaw a future of blank pages. Hunger eventually blotted out all other thought. You couldn't write if you were going blind with the need for sustenance.

Jane knew he was following a dark path with all this negativity. He could see where it was leading him. It was a case of how far he was likely to travel. How much distance was there between forgoing basic hygiene and swallowing the pill of Stanley's death?

He spent three hours on the rooftop of the ENO building – hoping that Aidan might stop by this way – before the rain came back and he spotted the tiger, drifting like smoke out of Northumberland Avenue. He saw it pad across to Canada House, where it sat and washed its paws, gazing at its frozen brethren. Jane clenched his teeth and felt the gums in his jaw shift like a thumb pressed into sponge. He delved for positive images, the bright, shiny packages wrapped up with string that he turned to when it seemed he must go under. He wanted to believe that he always felt like this during Library duty; not because of the bad memories that it necessarily forced you to dredge up, but because it always presaged the worst job he had ever had. Plodding through frigid, alien fathoms in utter darkness in order to weld closed any number of fatigue cracks was a doddle compared to incineration duty.

But nothing he could fasten on, bar Stanley, ever repelled the misery. Peacock feathers found under a slurry of ash and black slush in Holland Park. A tray of glittering butterflies rescued intact from the looted squalor of the Natural History Museum. A can of Guinness discovered inside one thigh-high PVC boot in a BDSM dungeon in Kentish Town. It was all just a different kind of dust. It was as if, resorting to his son – every day, every hour, every other minute – was diminishing him. He was using Stanley up, like a pencil. There was nothing but a stub left, it seemed. He dreamed sometimes of his boy and he appeared so tired, so exhausted by his father's demands that every rise of his ribcage had to be his last.

He watched the tiger slowly, almost lazily, pull itself on to all fours once more. He saw the great head swing his way, making hesitant curlicues as it sniffed the air, the jaws hanging open to aid its sense of smell. The wind was blowing up from the Thames today; his scent was being pushed in a different direction. Still, it terrified Jane to see the muscled hulk of three hundred pounds of big cat – or whatever filled the space it had once owned – working hard to draw Jane's taste into its flavour chambers, pausing as if unsure of what the weather was telling it.

The tiger slunk away, the frayed rope of its tail trailing behind it.

Jane exhaled slowly and rubbed his face with his hands. The smell of ink and soil and dust. He pressed the heels of his hands into his closed eyes for so long that he saw motes of colour spawn from the black. It reminded him of the weird light show he had seen all those years ago, standing at the bottom of the sea.

Jane opened his eyes. He blinked, but everything was blurred. Eventually, the soft edges regained their shape, except for one. Stopper sat next to him. Jane stared at his old friend, leaning forward over his forearms, which had withered to useless air-dried limbs, like Parma hams carved back to bone. Severed tendons had caused his hands to contract into famished fists. Stopper's face had been sucked clean by marine life. There was little left to distinguish him. The perished yellow Henrikson Subsea logo clung to the tatters of his jacket; it could be nobody else. He smiled, or grimaced, and black water drizzled from between his teeth. Something churned in the wet black reaches of his left eye socket, something with cilia. Something that made hard little *skritting* noises as it scraped parts of itself against Stopper's orbit.

'He warn't delivered t'me,' Stopper managed, and his voice was little more than the hiss of fossil-fuel ghosts released from ancient pockets in the seabed. His hair danced as if slowly animated by deep water. 'None of your kin fell t'me. S'all right, big man. S'all righhhh.'

Jane leant into his old friend, feeling his tears come. He wondered if he would ever cry himself dry, if that were at all possible. Stopper threatened to topple over, but managed to right himself. Jane smelled marine, deep water, the high ruin of matter that has fermented to oil over millennia. There was beauty in it, Jane supposed, as he felt the familiar weariness drag him down. You could be the ugliest, nastiest, most miserable piece of shit known to man, but if you had a beating heart there was always a chance you'd turn into a diamond after a million years. Everyone was composed of stardust, the random, immeasurable collision of atoms. We'd return to it again one day. He'd be reunited with Stanley then, that was for sure.

He fell asleep to that thought and woke up, seemingly seconds later, more refreshed than he had been for months.

He gazed down at the spot where Stopper had been sitting and saw a thin film of oil on the waterproof surface of the roof, a rainbow shifting through it.

His head was thumping; he remembered to breathe.

Stupid, though. A stupid thing to do, to fall asleep on duty. He was glad of the rifle as he crept down through the opera house, pausing at the mouth of the auditorium as if there had been some minuscule sound, that just yards away in the vast black space were hundreds of people in the slashed, scorched seats, the wings and the gods, staring back at him in silence, waiting for the heavy velvet curtains to peel open and reveal the future.

He stepped, shaking, on to Saint Martin's Place. The dark was something almost solid between the buildings; moving through it was slow business. It clung to the lungs like tar. His head was craned out in front of him; he strained for any and every sound. All he could think was *orange*. He tried to recall the safe houses nearby but drew blanks at every remembered alley and aisle on the *A–Z*. There would be help in his bible if only he had a flame to read it by.

Cautiously, for want of any better idea, and in need to keep moving, Jane walked south. He might as well deliver the recent pages of his letter to the safeboxes at the hotel. He tried to remember which roads he was walking along, knowing that to get lost at night was to feed yourself to the Skinners. As long as he continued in this direction he would hit the water, and then things would become a little easier.

The things we know, he thought to himself as he hugged the walls. *The things we don't.*

We know you came from the Event, with the Event. You spread yourself wide and we thought you were dust. You settled in the damp folds of dead bodies. You found the deepest parts of lungs that would never breathe again. You coated everything in the way ash from a catastrophic volcanic eruption that travels around the globe does. You were both seed and preservative; after all, what use is a body without meat on it for a newborn to hatch into?

Everything indoors, untouched by your dust, your seed, decayed. You exploded into life within the husks of the dead. You exploded into life within the bodies of the living. You assumed the shape of the thing you grew inside. I have seen horses, dogs, a crocodile. A tiger. No birds.

You fed well, although you do not eat skin. Perhaps its taste is repellent. Perhaps you are incapable of digesting it. You fill the skins of your victims so that you wear them like the shell of a hermit crab, or maybe it's to do with decoration, or bragging rights. A modern-day scalp. In London, and no doubt in towns and cities all around the planet, millions, billions have been resurrected to seek food, to bring down the survivors.

You cannot see. You cannot speak. You are afraid of nothing, save fire. You are bioluminescent, like some fish. You are translucent. Sometimes it is possible to see clearly into you, to look at what you are digesting.

You kill and eat males on the spot. You incapacitate women and take them away. Why? Do you store them for later? Does female flesh taste better after it has been hung?

What will you do when we are all gone? Will you turn to dust and blow away again on solar winds at the end of our planet's life? Will you travel for light years in stasis, waiting until you happen upon another paralysed Earth?

Jane had hoped that distracting himself with facts might help his progress, but now he saw it was hampering it badly. He was almost crippled with terror. The thought, entertained on countless occasions, that Stanley had been riven by one of these creatures, either directly as a snack or via the unholy germination of its seed, never lost its potency. It gutted him every time. To stumble upon his son one day and find not the Stanley he loved but some shambling, pyjama-clad scarecrow was enough to make him want to leap from any of the tall buildings he favoured staying in. He would kill Stanley, quickly, if that was the case. Kill his son and then commit suicide. He almost fainted and had to slap himself awake in the middle of what he was sure was Northumberland Avenue to even briefly consider allowing his son – what his son had become – to feed on his dad, to get a head start. *Eat up Stan, get big and strong for Daddy. This is protein. This will give you muscles.*

He reached Victoria Embankment and could just make out the patterns of the current in the skin of the river. Things floated past that he was glad – even now, after so many years of disgust – he could not see. He turned left, heading east. Waterloo Bridge within stumbling distance. Everything was dark apart from the occasional candle in a high-rise window. It reminded him of midnight train journeys through the Pennines when there was little around but the suggestion of hills, a slightly deeper shade of black against that which they rose before. A distant brief orange brick was a farmhouse window. Then nothing but black again.

No figures he could see or hear on the bridge. No animal smell. No stripes. He picked up his pace and by the time he reached the steps up to the bridge he was sprinting. Left up Lancaster Place to the Strand. Now he saw Skinners. He almost stumbled into a party of them trying to separate a figure from its skin but they were having trouble getting it over the angles of its hips. They were quiet, intent. The silence always dismayed Jane. Even when there was a struggle of some sort they did not display any evidence of effort. One of the Skinners had given up peeling and had buried its face into the shining membrane on the figure's lower back that contained the fatty kidneys.

They were too engrossed to register Jane. He backed away and hit Aldwych at full tilt. He was inside what remained of the swing doors of the hotel before he could meet a phalanx of Skinners coming the other way, from the direction of Kingsway. A cocktail bar to the left of the foyer resembled the scene of a water-pistol fight played out with gallons of blood. To the right, the reception desk was spotlessly clean.

Jane took the stairs to the top floor. The Dome Suite was locked; he had a key. He let himself in and felt the tension of the last half an hour fall from him. He felt safe here, one of a few places he had claimed for himself, or that other survivors had not yet become aware of. He'd fight off any challenger to this place. From the boardroom you could look out over the Strand and Waterloo Bridge. Windows to the east of the room gave you an unhindered view of the area around Temple, while to the left you could check along Wellington Street as it sloped into Theatreland.

He unlocked one of two dozen safeboxes lined up in the boardroom and carefully placed the pages of his letter to Stanley inside. On the lid was a number indicating that this was the latest collection. He placed his journal notes for the Shaded on top – they could go to Heathrow with him in the morning – and took off his clothes. In the expansive sitting area, he poured himself a drink and wished he had one of Plessey's radios with him. He wished for sound of any sort. He remembered how, before Stanley had been born, he would come home from a shift and fix himself a drink and listen to vinyl while he waited for Cherry to come through the door from work. They'd hold each other in the dark and dance for a while to Frank or Dean or Sammy. Sometimes he'd put on Chuck Berry or Fats Domino. It was difficult to remember those songs now, though at the time it felt as though they were as much a part of him as the colour of his eyes.

He checked that the windows were secure and that the fire escapes were still destroyed. The only way in would be through the door and that was a five-inch firecheck. He had access to the roof and could make his way as far as Drury Lane if need be. Safety ensured, he felt exhaustion come on.

He went to bed and fell instantly to sleep. When morning came he turned over to find the polished skull of a hobby on the pillow next to him.

20. THE HINDMOST

Jane made it as far as Ealing before the blisters on his feet caused him to put an end to his march. He found a hotel on The Broadway near the Tube station. None of the rooms were habitable, though, suffering from mould or awash with dirty water or host to families of huge rats that turned and regarded him insouciantly like street gangs looking for any excuse to rumble.

In the kitchens behind a dining room where no furniture remained, Jane made a bed on a long stainless-steel work surface by wadding his coat on top of his backpack. He fell asleep almost immediately, the rifle, safety off, clasped between his legs and arms, the barrel pressing against his cheek.

He dreamed of Stanley wiping orange chalk from his skin faster than Jane could apply it. He woke up after twelve hours feeling no more refreshed than when he had gone to sleep. He sat on the edge of the work surface feeling bad, feeling unsure of everything.

Jane checked the cupboards and chest freezers. He found nothing to eat. He drank from the bladder in his backpack and wondered about the half-moons of filth under his nails;

was there food in that? He closed his eyes and listened to his breathing. He felt he had been worn away, eroded like rocks in hard weather. He felt like rind.

Outside he waited for a long time for some kind of sign that he was doing the right thing. He kept looking back to the bruise of the city but there was no curled finger in the smog above it. He carried on along the Uxbridge Road. He found orange chalk on the outer wall of St Bernard's Hospital. Inside, everyone had been slaughtered. A big kill, maybe over a hundred survivors huddling in the wards, waiting for some kind of signal, some indicator of hope. Skinners had swarmed all over the place. He came out fast, his nostrils stinging with the smell of recently shed blood, crossed the orange with slashes of blue, and cut south-west through Osterley Park, joining up with the Great West Road which took him to the airport's surrounding roads.

Six hours had passed since he'd wakened and he'd walked them as if in a trance. He broke into houses abutting the airport grounds west of Waggoners Roundabout, mindless of the risk: there were many stories of desperate hunger driving survivors into the arms of the Skinners who had turned millions of houses into death-traps. In a house on Byron Avenue, after he'd checked all the kitchen cupboards and found everything turned bad, Jane stumbled upon a plastic container of bird seed, presumably forgotten, behind a bag of charcoal and a punnet of woodchips. He sat eating and choking on handfuls of this until his jaws hurt too much to continue. He stuffed his pockets and headed back to the melted perimeter fence, spitting out bloody husks and resigned to a following day of agony for his teeth and gums.

He strode through the downed barriers and stared at the immense airfield. Jets, bleached and corroded, were still standing in the terminals or on the approaches to the great two-mile runways. Some of them appeared slumped, their wings having begun to part from the fuselages, tips lowered like sea-birds trying to pull free from an oil slick. He could see no living person. Ancient bodies lay around the aircraft like sunbathers, or pilgrims genuflecting at the feet of giants.

Jane hurried across the taxiways and toasted grass verges. More than once he slipped in the oil that had sweated from the engines of the airliners. The ghosts of other aircraft, long gone, existed as shadow lines in the tarmac. Suitcases littered the bays. A stuffed toy was a black framework of wire. Blistered signs on the retractable passenger tunnels bid Jane *Welcome to Heathrow*. There was a sound of deep metallic cracking, the kind of fatigue that he recognised in his own body. His sighs and groans were really not that much different.

He called out: 'Aidan!'

The control tower was a gaping, deeply runneled fist of shapeless concrete. He thought he saw movement inside, but there were all kinds of dark grains sifting across his vision these days and, anyway, it would be too obvious to run things from there.

He found a way into the terminal and headed for the baggage carousels. The rubberised conveyors were long gone, but the smell their burning had left behind was still detectable. He walked along featureless corridors that seemed to have been designed for days such as these. Places like this were meant for queues. Without them, they seemed unfinished. Bodies piled up at the end of moving walkways clutched boarding passes and hand luggage. They appeared to be sinking into, or emerging from, the floor.

Jane found no edible food in the coffee islands dotted on his way through to the duty-free zones. Once there he saw how the fast-food restaurants had all been raided already, perhaps by rats, and not that long after the Event. Everything bore an impression of age about it. Everything smelled stale.

Once he might have been taken aback by the crowds he encountered at the security screening area, but other than a reflex glance at the slumped dead to check there was nobody breathing he ignored them. Skinners sometimes attempted to blend in with the dead in the hope of snaring the living but it was easy to spot them. They couldn't stay still, fidgeting constantly as if uncomfortable within the shells they had invaded. Jane despised them, the way they were so unsubtle in their appetites and their methods of assuaging them. He hated them for assuming that human beings were stupid and for their utter lack of compassion. He hated them for what they had reduced him to. Searching for his son was the thing that kept him alive and the thing that prevented him from progressing. He lived for his son, but was not living. He supposed nobody was. People were still alive only because they feared death. He was a machine whose built-in obsolescence had refused to kick in.

Very clearly, he heard the *chunk* of a closing door.

He stopped, feeling the chill breath of all these surrounding corpses flutter upon him. He gazed down at the stained paper mask of a child whose expression, in death, might almost have been one of bemusement. He looked like Stanley just after waking up. Kind of stupefied. Kind of cross. *What will you do?* He could almost see the question squirm from between gritted, grinning milk teeth. The shadow of his eye might have turned a little to regard him better. *It's your move.*

He realised he had been following the routes any passenger might when entering an airport, albeit in a reverse direction. But there was another territory at Heathrow unknown to the civilian and Jane had unconsciously been respecting its boundaries, a throwback to those days of heightened security and the sheep mentality immediately assumed once you found yourself in a world of cordons, channels and arrows.

He checked that the rifle was loaded and pushed through a door badged with the words *Staff Only*. There was a brief moment when he felt he might be granted some glimpse of nirvana, but there was no mystique to this prohibited area, just a grey, quotidian continuation of what he'd left behind. Offices, storerooms, corridors. He felt the dead echo of the closed door hanging in these smothered heights. The impression that what had caused the sound had passed by this way recently was strong.

He moved past a canteen where he pickpocketed a security guard for a caramel wafer that was as tough as cardboard but brought Jane to the edge of tears while he devoured it. There was nothing else but broken crockery and pans coagulated with inedible plaque. A newspaper offered headlines from a time he couldn't believe he had lived through. He was distracted from its fragile pages by a sound like a broom handle clattering to the floor.

As soon as he resumed his journey he felt a change, as if in the mood of the building. Prior to this moment he had not experienced any sense of wrongness, just the disorientation of an unfamiliar building and a mystery to be solved. Now came a foreboding similar to any number of awful events that had followed him down through the years. He was thinking about retreating, getting back out into the vast wilderness of the airfield where he would be able to see danger encroaching for miles in every direction, when he heard the grinding cry of hinges clotted by dust and years. And then a voice, muffled by the proximity of walls and ceiling, that called his name. It didn't matter that that could only be a good thing. He screamed anyway.

Their voices scrambled over each other, trying to disguise fear and relief with news and gossip and apologies. Aidan kept putting a hand to his belly and Jane kept meaning to ask if he was all right, but then there'd be a pause and a look and another hug and the question had missed its cue and could wait. In their collision of stories, Jane heard something that slapped him out of his excitement at seeing Aidan again. He had to ask him to repeat himself. Now that they were allowing each other to speak, fear crept back in, aware of the little moments of quiet, the space that was inveigling itself between them.

'Plessey is dead. I mean, he died. Was killed, is what I mean.'

'An accident?' Jane asked, knowing full well.

Aidan shook his head. 'I arrived at the market in the morning. Nobody in the shop, even though I used a secret knock. I didn't know what to do, so I was going to get over to one of the places you told me to find if I was in trouble or, you know, scared. Not that I was scared, but I was worried about Becky.

'But then I found him. He hadn't even made it out of the market. The Skinners had been at him, but his throat had been slit.' He suddenly grabbed Jane's arm, appeared unsure. He was fifteen – a wispy beard was a mask under which a man was being formed. But at moments like this, he was still just a boy. You looked hard enough, you could see the baby in him. 'Skinners . . . they don't do that, do they?'

'No,' Jane said. 'It would be kind of nice if they did, compared to their usual MO.'

'So maybe the same person who caught up with Fielding, you think?'

'Or someone in league.' Jane peered into Aidan's eyes. They were dark brown, so dark it was hard to discern their pupils. The rest of his face was open, fresh. He'd have had an innocent look about him if it weren't for those eyes and the soft frown above them. He'd seen a lot, Jane supposed.

More than he ought. 'Where have *you* been, Aidan? You're your own man, I know, but we care about you. We're not your mum and dad, but we're your friends. It doesn't stop us from worrying.'

Aidan pressed his lips into a flat line. When he spoke again, it was with forced brittleness. Jane saw behind it immediately; he knew him too well by now. His hand at his belly again. Hungry, probably. Jane wished he hadn't snaffled that wafer.

'Just ... hanging out with friends. Experiments, you know. Down at the river. Checking the air quality. Someone has to.'

'And how is the air quality?'

'Epic fail,' Aidan said. 'Major no.'

'Doesn't look like the HQ's moving in, does it?'

'No.'

Jane scratched at his beard. The sound seemed enormous. 'Fielding gave me the envelope ...'

'An envelope.'

'Sorry?'

'Fielding gave you an envelope. It wasn't *the* envelope.'

'You mean I was given false information?'

Aidan didn't say anything. He couldn't meet Jane's gaze.

'Why are you here, Aidan? You get the same dodgy map?'

'Something like that,' he said.

'Something like that.'

The hand on the belly. A prickle of sweat drawing attention to the frown.

'You OK, Aid?' His mind went back to the first time they'd met. Becky's concern. The thought of his blood conspiring against him.

'Yeah. Just tired. Just hungry. You promised me a roast dinner once.'

'Shit. You didn't forget that, did you?'

'Can I have it now?'

They had picked through the debris of countless restaurants and bars to no avail. Everything worth eating had been carried off. What remained were the bones of people who had decayed where they'd dropped many years before. No chocolates or fudge in the duty-free boutiques. No snack packs dangled in the vending machines.

'What about out there?' Aidan asked.

'There's nothing out there,' Jane said. 'You mean the houses beyond the perimeter?'

'No. I mean the planes.'

They found a self-propelled passenger stairway in a maintenance hangar and trundled it out to a Virgin Atlantic 747 that had pushed back from its ramp at the moment the Event hit it, peeling off much of its paint and tearing the tail section clean off the rear of the aircraft. The flap canoe fairings had been snapped away from the underside of the wings like model parts, and the main jet-core shrouds were torn, revealing the intestinal squirm of the machine beneath. A telegraph pole had become a javelin, thrown by 200 mph winds from outside the perimeter fence, puncturing the fuselage above the sagging portside wing. Both wings had given up their yield of fuel; maybe 120 tons had poured out of the cracked tanks and evaporated, leaving a dark stain that reached out almost as far as the main runway. It was a wonder there had not been an explosion. The roof of the cockpit had been crunched in, a hard-boiled egg beneath a spoon, by something that was no longer in evidence. Jane thought he could see a white shirtsleeve, an arm thrown back on the flight deck, above a face that was nothing but shadow.

'Maybe we should try a different plane,' Jane said. 'I mean, this one was just setting off. There'll be a lot of bodies on it.'

'Then there'll be a lot of food too. They wouldn't have started serving until they got into the sky, would they?'

Aidan was right. A smaller plane taxiing towards the terminal would have had an empty galley. What was the point of protecting him from bodies when they were everywhere you looked? Jane sighed. Just to give him a break, he supposed. It would be nice not to have all that *grinning* in your face all day, every day.

The doors were sealed; the holes pitting the skin of the jet too small to climb through. They pushed the stairs around to the back of the plane. There was a ragged hole where the empennage had been.

'Big enough for you?' Jane asked. Aidan nodded.

Jane raised the stairs to the hole; they rattled in the spanks of wind gusting in from across the wide, open airfield.

'See if you can open that rear exit for me once you're in,' Jane said. 'Don't fanny about.'

Aidan skipped up the stairs and hoisted himself into the Jumbo. A few moments later his face appeared at one of the windows. He gave Jane a thumbs-up. He ducked clear of the window and a few seconds later the door folded outwards. Jane withdrew the stairs and repositioned them at the doorway. Inside he drew the door to, not closing it completely. A sudden snapshot in his head: Rae and Carver exploding through the crack in a door. He couldn't get on with doors any more. Closed, open, they would never stay still in his thoughts.

'All right?' Aidan asked.

'Yes,' Jane said, a little too stiffly, and looked beyond Aidan's shoulder to the ranks of dead sitting strapped into their seats. They had died primly, hands clasped in front of them, watching a stewardess at the front of this section of the cabin who had collapsed in the middle of performing her safety procedures. There were children with colouring books and iPods and hand-held game consoles. Everyone was thin in their clothes, dwindled into seats. Oxygen masks hung from the cabin ceiling, octopoid creatures reaching for prey. Punkah louvres in the overhead units had melted and hardened before they could drip to the floor. They resembled waxy stalactites. One of the bulkheads had been split by the telegraph pole that now blocked the portside aisle leading to the front of the plane; part of the vacuum-moulded wall panel had sheared free; insulation was a frozen cloud seeping from behind it. Rainwater had poured in through the fissure, warping fixtures, swelling the bodies it touched.

Jane said, 'Let's check the galleys.'

They ransacked the six galleys and found meal-tray trolleys loaded with spoiled food that had rotted away to a crisp film on the plates, like dried algae, over the years. But there were plenty of packets of nuts that, although past their use-by date, seemed fine. The two of them sat on the cabin floor gobbling snacks so quickly that there wasn't much tasting going on. Minutes later, the floor strewn with empty wrappers, they were too full to speak. Jane picked crumbs from his sweatshirt and fed them to himself. Aidan pressed his hand to his belly and slowly lost his expression of satisfaction as it became one of harrowed concern.

'We should have taken it easy, shouldn't we?' Jane asked, patting his own stomach. 'We'll probably cramp up something chronic.'

Aidan nodded. 'We should get some stuff for Becky,' he said. His voice wavered for a second, as if he was going to start crying. *Nothing strange about that*, thought Jane. *A young lad who finds something tasty for the first time in many months, maybe a year or two. Even I'm filling up*. And all the while, beneath that, *Something is wrong, something is very wrong*.

He followed Aidan to the next galley, stepping over withered limbs sticking out into the aisle; his feet turning tacky in whatever had washed and set upon the floor. They unloaded the bagged snacks from the trolleys and stashed them in Jane's backpack. They found miniatures of gin, rum, vodka and whisky; tins of mixer. There was Coca-Cola and 7-Up and Carlsberg lager.

'Let's get sloshed,' Jane said, and mixed himself a gin and tonic. 'No ice, no lemon. Hardly a civilised drink.' But it sluiced through the desert of his mouth like a monsoon. 'Bubbles,' he sneezed. 'Jesus, that's good.'

Aidan refused the alcohol, sipped instead at a can of lemonade. Jane felt bright, alert, refreshed, but Aidan did not look as though he was returning from his enervated state. His eyes retained their dull lustre; they resembled glass eyes. They almost fooled you, but they lacked that essential something.

'Are you OK?' Jane asked, hating the wheedling in his voice; he'd asked the question already a dozen times since they'd met.

'I'm fine,' Aidan said.

'Becky was worried about you,' Jane said. 'She misses you when you're not around.'

Now the gloss came to his eyes. He was crying and trying to hide it, his small chest barely able to keep from jerking. Jane was conscious of the small boy still within Aidan, and when he dropped his head he could almost believe that this was how Stanley might look. It was gloomy in the passenger cabin. He might be standing here with his own son; his boy needed him.

Jane put out a hand, whispered, the words barely denting the air as they slipped from his lips: *Stan*.

'Don't you!' Aidan screamed, whipping his head up and fixing Jane with a hot stare. He shook his head, nodded, shook his head again. A knowing smile deepened the shadows in his face.

'I'm sorry,' Jane said. 'I meant nothing by it.'

'Ever since I saw you. That first day in the hospital. You've been looking at me like you love me and you hate me at the same time.'

'That's not—'

'It *is* true. You want me to be Stanley. And you hate me for not being him. You hate me for surviving and you wish he had lived and I was dead.'

Jane reached for him again, but Aidan flinched, stepped back. His foot landed on a shin which crumbled like chalk. 'Stanley's alive, Aidan,' he said.

'See?' Aidan yelled, gesturing wildly, as if he were beseeching the passengers around him. 'See? You can't leave him alone. When it's the two of us alone in a room? It's actually three.'

'You can't condemn me for that, Aidan. It's not my fault. You—'

'HE'S DEAD! HE'S FUCKING DEAD!'

Jane only realised he had hit the boy when he felt the raw sting in the knuckles of his right hand. Aidan was on the floor, one hand covering his mouth, the other scrabbling against an armrest as he tried to pull himself upright.

Jane held up his hands. 'Aidan. God, I'm sorry. I'm . . . I was bang out of line. I should not have done that.'

The spark was gone from Aidan. The matte eyes blinked at Jane. He wiped blood from the corner of his lip, regarded it for a long time with some fascination, as if he were looking at a rare jewel. He stared back at Jane and his voice was no longer edged. 'He is dead.'

21. SOMA

They spent the next few hours at separate ends of the aircraft. Aidan would not leave, despite Jane's pleas. It was getting dark. Figures were moving around the edges of the airstrip, stopping, and turning their way. Even if they could not see Jane and Aidan maybe they were nonetheless baffled by the new scents. It was early enough, and there were sufficiently few Skinners around, for Jane and the adolescent boy to make a getaway, but they had to go now.

'Why did you bring me out here, Aidan?'

Aidan wouldn't answer.

The dark came on, creeping through the fuselage like black ink drawn into the reservoir of a fountain pen. The emptied windows provided soft charcoal shapes against the jetblack. Jane heard the shuffle of feet on the runway apron. After a while he could hear the phlegmy breath of them beneath the aircraft. Something barged against the stairs, causing them to rattle massively. Jane remembered he had left the door open. He ran to it now and shut it, locked it. Hissing and howling from outside; they knew there was something to be had in here.

Jane glanced at the ragged hole in the tail. If they moved

the stairs and came up there they would not fit through, but they would shred the thing wider within minutes. He had to hope that their being unable to see the hole was enough. You couldn't *smell* what wasn't there, surely. But then they did move the stairs. Jane heard them being wheeled away from the door. He cast around for a weapon, expecting them to attack, but they were returning the stairs to the main building.

'Just great,' he murmured. 'Three storeys up now, Aidan. What are we going to do? Jump down in the morning? We going to carry each other back to the centre with broken legs?'

Aidan wasn't saying anything. Jane looked down the aisle at him; he could just make out his shape, limned by the palest ambient light, sitting in the dark like a Buddha. His head was down over his chest, his hands resting on his crossed legs. He might have been asleep, but Jane didn't think so.

He wanted to say something, but there seemed to be no way back from what had happened. Aidan was right. All this time he had looked at Aidan and seen his own son. He wondered if he shouldn't be excused for that. But then he realised that Aidan had lost everyone too: his father, his mother, his sister; a worse scenario than Jane's in many ways, but he had been too wrapped up in the epic scenes of his own mind – the eventual reunion with Stanley chief among them – to show even a rudimentary empathy. Becky had been the gauze on his wounds, the kiss goodnight, the arms to fall into during the worst of the nightmares. Jane had either been turned in on his own reveries or trying to measure Aidan for a body cast that would never fit, and should never have been tried on in the first place.

He looked out at the night. Tow tractors crouched low at the edge of the airfield, as if trying to dodge out of view.

Shreds of a windsock rippled violently against the sky like an escaped, frantic thought.

'Why did you bring me here, Aidan?'

He thought of Becky at Plessey's shop, sorting through batteries or touching an alligator clip to the crystal radio, listening to voices hundreds of miles away offering hope or some bastardised version of it. He thought of a raft so great that you could build villages on it. He thought of fetching up on Normandy beaches lined with a welcoming party of skeletons in their millions, or Skinners sharpening blades on strops made from the hides of children.

He dismissed the image and turned away from the window, disgusted with himself. The grim thought had never been far from his mind, even during the days of normality. Evenings sitting on the balcony with his wife, sharing a bottle of wine, listening to Johnny Mercer or Bobby Darin, the bricks, the roads, the sky touched by that soft pink stain of summer, he'd envisage, suddenly, Stanley falling from the heavens to impale himself on railings. He'd imagine a gas pipe shearing and igniting, hosing his son in the face with thousands of degrees centigrade. The balcony crumbling, sending him to unforgiving concrete twenty yards below. The worry could never be confined, it was never something over which he held sway. It was always a wild uncontainable panic that had so many strands to it that he could not keep track. It was like trying to put an eel in a jam jar with greased hands.

Another thought cut across all this, unbidden, unconnected: *What if Becky is dead?*

It was no effort, really, to imagine her being peeled while something drooled above her, staring into her with black sockets, its teeth manifold, curved, like the spines you might find within an exotic carnivorous plant if you pushed it inside out. Beyond those rows of canines, something like the grinding bits at the business end of tunnelling machinery. He had heard that bizarre mouth working on occasion, mincing the life out of whatever it came into contact with.

Jane did not realise he was dreaming by now. The shadow line between real life and unconsciousness seemed to be growing softer by the day, a charcoal border smudged by a thumb almost to invisibility. He was aware of the bodies sitting all around him in their cramped rows. A Japanese woman in the next seat turned her head on the grinding apex of her barebone neck and leered at him. Her jacket yawned as she leaned nearer; he saw mould spots on the cup of her bra, the grey, sagging puffball within it. Flakes of her snowed on him as she struggled to speak.

Much more leg room now, don't you think? It's the ultimate diet.

Jane started awake. He was holding the famished claw of the woman next to him. He bolted out of the seat, disorientated. He had thought of his flare-up with Aidan, and was now convinced that when Aidan had screamed *he's dead* he had meant himself, not Stanley.

'Aidan?' he called out. But there was silence. 'Aid?'

For a second he thought the boy had left him, monkeying out of the aircraft and down to the tarmac, abandoning him here. But then he saw him where he had been all along, tipped forward, hands curled into his lap. The ghost of Stopper seemed to shimmer at his shoulder, a suggestion that this was the classic position of the vein-opener, and he rushed to Aidan, convinced he had killed himself. But the truth was far worse.

Jane stopped six feet short of the boy. Already he could see that Aidan, or what had once been Aidan, was near death if not dead already. The dull sound of gristle popping, like someone jointing a chicken, was a queasy explosion in the base of Jane's head. He put his hands to his ears, but it was as persistent as a bad tune heard on the radio.

He could do nothing to save Aidan. By the youngster's side he saw perhaps two dozen duotone capsules: protein-pump inhibitors that Aidan had saved but not ingested over the past three weeks or so. He was allowing himself to be hollowed out. He saw the physicality of what was invading him move through his bones, dissolving him, absorbing him, filling his shell. Aidan's slender muscles bulged and deflated. His eyes, filling with red, sank into his face as his head tilted back.

'Why?' Jane asked it. Aidan's shoulders jerked back, a violent shrug. His lips grimaced and pursed; blood pulsed from between them. The ring of his teeth was ejected; his jaw and soft palate slithered down the slick on the front of his jumper. Jane moaned, covered his mouth. Aidan's hair jumped and danced as if it were teeming with lice. His hand turned from a fist to a star: a Stanley knife popped clear of it. Jane snatched it up. The blade was black with dried blood, the edge uneven where it had blunted itself against bone. A rag of cleanly shaven flesh had jammed in the slot where the blade could be retracted. Jane could almost smell Fielding's cologne upon it.

He threw the tool away. He had maybe fifteen minutes before the Skinner emerged; already there were strains appearing in the thinned cyanotic flesh of the boy. He would begin to tear soon. Perhaps Aidan had come out here having duped Jane into making the trip. Perhaps he had intended to apologise. But it was too late; he had been doomed long before this moment, probably at the time he stopped taking the drugs. Possibly earlier, in the second they clapped eyes on each other in a Newcastle hospital.

Jane went back to the door at the rear of the 747. Long way down. He heard the splash of Aidan's internal organs as the picky Skinner evicted them. There was a deep grunt, deeper than anything Aidan had ever said. Like the rest of him, his voice was broken for good.

Jane unclasped the overhead storage bins and swept through the luggage, looking for something that might help. Too late, he realised there would be an axe in the cockpit, but he would not be able to get past the Skinner in the starboard aisle now. The flight deck would be secured from the inside anyway.

He had to accept that Aidan was gone for good. What hulked and slobbered in his place, though it resembled the boy, was one hundred per cent meat-head. No reasoning. No compassion. No guilt. Aidan, at least, at last, had been unable to live with what he had done. It didn't matter that he had put Jane in a dangerous position; he hoped that, *in extremis*, Aidan had failed to grasp that. He couldn't believe he could be so calculating, no matter how thoughtless and unsympathetic Jane had been towards him over the years.

The wet sounds had stopped. The Skinner, recently born, was hungry. It was pulling Jane's smell into its head, trying to differentiate his scent from the dead bodies arrayed around it. This was it; he was going to have to jump and risk a shattered ankle or a compound fracture of the shin. Crazily he thought of school, when a friend had told him that you had to bend your knees during a parachute-jump landing, otherwise your spine would come ramming through the top of your skull.

Thanks for that, he thought, peering through the window and trying to assess the severity of the drop. It must be twenty feet, straight down onto cold, hard concrete. He levered open the door and looked for handholds of any kind, but the skin of the jet was smooth. No vehicles nearby that he could leap onto. The nearest were a mobile belt conveyor and a commissary truck, both fully thirty yards away.

Jane glanced back and saw Aidan looking directly at him, the skin of his face flat, the frown ironed out of it, sheened with sweat or leeched fat or some other serous leakage. Not tears, though – Christ, never that. *It can't see you.*

Jump. Use the box-cutter on your own throat. Something. Do something.

He sat on the edge of the doorway and propelled himself forward. The wind caught him and tried to suck him out. No way. No shitting way. Where was there a rope when you needed it?

He swung his legs back in and stood up. A body in the seat nearest his was shrugging herself out of her cardigan. He helped her. Then he was frantically tearing clothes off everyone within reach, tying crude knots into cuffs and hems; attaching belts, attaching ties. He had about fifteen feet of improvised line when the Skinner, attracted by the noise of his excited breathing, and the exotic dust he was causing to puff up from the bodies around him, came shambling over the seats diagonally towards him.

Jane cinched one end of his makeshift rope to an underseat baggage-restraint unit. He jerked on it twice, hard, and the knot only shrank, tightening itself. He stood on the edge of the doorway and leaned back, gripping the clothes, feeling the dust and grease of human decay seep out of the fibres. He wrapped one leg around the rope and began to lower himself as the face of the Skinner emerged from the darkness. He went so quickly that instead of being able to set himself at the end of the rope for the drop of five or six feet that remained, as he had planned, he fell to the floor awkwardly. For a second he thought he had twisted his ankle, but there was no damage to bone or ligament. He'd have a bruise. He could walk through the pain of that.

He glanced back at the jet but the Skinner was no longer facing his direction. Perhaps, his scent dispersed into the air, it had lost interest in him, had switched off. It was turned towards the north. He felt a pinch in his heart when he saw the Skinner wipe its nose with the back of its hand, a mannerism that Aidan had not been able to shake from childhood. Perhaps he was not yet fully absorbed. Perhaps Skinners assimilated little tropes of behaviour from their victims. It just made it all the more sad.

The shape of the wind changed. He heard screams on the edge of it, carried from the other end of the airfield, beyond Terminal 5. They were women's screams. Pained, almost bestial. Howling. Something in the sound made him want to go to them.

He found himself striding across the tarmac, and it was only when the screams began to assault his ears without the sonically softening buffer of the wind that he hesitated. A thin red light trembled on the horizon, staining the lowest part of the sky. He could hear something else now, but his mind would not allow him to identify what it was. *Know this and you shut down for good. There is no coming back from something so dark.*

Jane turned and fled.

The journey back to the city centre was achieved in a fug of disgust and regret and pain. Despite the shutters coming down in his mind the previous night, Jane kept trying to tease them open. It was like a facial scab. Your fingers kept gravitating towards it without you realising. The pain in his foot helped. He had had to cut his bootlaces in the morning, the flesh having swollen during a night spent wrapped around his beloved rifle in a crumpled heap of groaning containers that had been blasted into the garden of a house backing onto the Longford river, just south of the airport. He'd wrapped a triangular bandage around the swelling, making sure he could still waggle his toes when it was tied off. He ate a packet of nuts and spat bloodily into the earth. His teeth felt as stable as decorations pushed into a cake. Two of them were loose, an incisor and a pre-molar. His gums bled at the slightest pressure. If he ran his tongue across his teeth he'd be spitting red for a good twenty minutes. The menace in the air was catching up with him after all this time. He wondered, if Becky could get any of her X-ray machinery to work, if his body would be riddled with black stains.

He walked towards the suggestion of the sun as it dawned behind the thicket of bronze permacloud. He barely registered the topography as it altered around him. He was shivering, despite his thick waterproofs.

East Bedfont. North Feltham. Spring Grove. Brentford. Kew. Turnham Green. Shepherd's Bush.

Jane felt at one point as if he was not so much walking towards as being sucked into his destination. London was a plughole drawing anything down that was not tethered fast. When the sawtooth architecture at the river's edge emerged it reminded him of nothing other than the crippled shape of his own jaws. He didn't feel as if he had returned or arrived. He didn't feel at home. It wasn't places that did that for you, he understood now, way, way too late. It was people.

It was getting dark. The sun had leapt over him and was at his back now, sinking into that part of the country that was a red rim of terror in the pit of his thoughts. The howling of the women. He thought he could never have felt anything but shock for a woman who screamed like that, but he had smiled into the face of one, once, long ago. He had kissed it, gently brushed away the damp hair that latticed it, whispered his love to it.

Her hand had gripped his so hard that they were like white ice statues. She didn't have the spit to keep her lips dry. They were stuck to her bared teeth, cracking, a pain smile. Eyes slitted, turned to him, confused, afraid. He'd squeezed her hand as hard as she had gripped his and urged her on, told her how amazing she was, how much he loved her. Stanley had burst from her with the cord wrapped around his neck, a meconium-streaked shock. Jane had reared back at the violence and mess of it all. For one brittle second he feared his son and resented him for what he had done to his wife. But it all dissolved into concern and love. Love so pure and deep that it seemed to make a mockery of what he felt for Cherry.

He made it back to Spitalfields in a gloom so dense he thought he must get lost. He forced his way through the razor-wire barricades and hammered on the door. Nobody came. He tried the handle and the door opened. Mothballs and soup. A smell of age. 'Becky?'

No reply. He shrugged the rifle from his shoulder and followed its muzzle into the shop. He closed the door behind him. He checked each room but could find no Skinners, no evidence of a struggle or a death. Becky was gone.

He went back outside and repositioned the razor wire. He locked and bolted the door and pressed his head against it. Safe now, for a while. *Darling, I'm home.* He could feel an ache pulsing behind his skull, transmitting through to the wood, almost knocking at it. A cough was hatching in his chest. Cold had reached deep into him. What was it Stopper used to say? *I feel like seven different kinds of shite all knocked into a one-shite thimble.* He moved through to Plessey's workshop, thinking of listening to some broadcasts, but the crystal radio was gone. He couldn't find it in any drawer or filing cabinet. He thought about where it might be; who might have taken it. He wished Becky was around. He missed her terribly.

Jane lit candles and put a flame to the wood stove in Plessey's cosy little kitchenette. There was a water butt labelled *Lavage* at the heavily barred fire escape at the back of the shop. He knocked his hip against it, listened. Plenty. He carried countless pans of water to the stove and to the bath. When it was full and steaming, Jane undressed, closing his eyes against the dips and hollows and shadows, and slid into the water. He shampooed his hair and clipped his fingernails. He massaged the blood back into his toes. When he got out, the bath revealed a tidemark of dark grey scum. He towelled himself dry in front of the warm stove. He cut his hair with a pair of sharpish barber's scissors from one of Plessey's chests of wonders and shaved, carefully, with a cut-throat razor and some rose-scented cream whisked onto his bristles with a shaving brush made from badger hair.

He ate warm chicken soup with stale water biscuits crumbled into it. He sat in Plessey's leather armchair in a towelling bathrobe sipping cognac, his other hand on the stock of the rifle lying across his lap. He felt reborn. When he slept, he dreamed of a black lake, still and deep, surrounded by black mountains and a sky bluing at its edges, brimful of stars. He dreamed of Cherry's body, the way it had been when they met, not towards the end when she refused to be naked in the same room as him. She had been slender, almost athletic. She liked to squeeze her breasts when he made love to her. It turned him on to see her so thrilled by her own body. He dreamed of her now, beneath him, moving to his rhythm, her fingers snagging and tickling at her nipples. She looked up into his eyes and there was nothing there. No recognition. No love. No sense of who she was herself. He was looking up at himself through her eyes. No sweat, no expression of mounting excitement. They both stopped fucking. They both deflated, like rubber dolls under a knife. There was nothing to them whatsoever.

Knocking at the door.

Jane wakened feeling drowsy and unfamiliar. He was hot. He wiped sweat from his brow. The room was baking. He got up from the armchair and slopped cognac over the bathrobe. He got his finger behind the trigger of the rifle, the butt under his armpit, and scurried to the door, the muzzle of the gun pointing at the ground by his foot. He held his breath and placed his ear to the door. He heard something shuffling outside. He heard a muttered oath and knew this was no Skinner.

'Who is it?' he called.

'It's Simmonds.'

He opened the door a crack and her lachrymose expression dipped into view.

'What's going on?' he asked.

'You've scrubbed up well,' she said. 'Hot date?'

He waited, staring at her.

'We're on the move,' she said.

'What? Where? How do you mean?'

Simmonds looked behind her. 'You think you might let me in? I know it's daytime and all that, but I still get the heebie-jeebies being outside.'

He let Simmonds in and put a kettle of water on the stove.

'Nice place Plessey sorted himself out with here.'

Jane nodded. 'Some people feel safer locked in, having just one place. Not for me, though. I don't know how he manages.' He stopped preparing cups of tea and glanced back at Simmonds. 'Managed, I mean.'

'Yes,' she said. 'Most unfortunate, that.'

'So who's on the move?'

'Becky came to us. She brought the radio. We heard the broadcasts.'

Jane handed her a cup. 'And you think it's worth exploring?'

'Of course,' she said. 'Anything has to be better than this. It's like being a cured ham hanging in a room for months, waiting for someone to come and select you. I'd rather take my chances out in the wilds than have slices taken off me by some churning mouth with a sac attached to it.'

'Well, when you put it like that,' Jane said.

'There are some hot zones in need of a messenger. We've got Harris, MacCreadle and Barrett on it at the moment. You up for a mercy mission?'

'Where's Becky?' he asked.

'We're hiding her. Priority case. Wrapping the poor dear in cotton wool.'

'Why?'

The sad eyes grew larger. A crack appeared in Simmonds's niggardly mouth, the closest she would ever get to a smile. 'You don't know? Oh, my dear sir. There's congratulations in order, clever boy. She's pregnant.'

22. FEARFUL SYMMETRY

J ane saw two or three knots of people heading for the A20 out of London that day. He wished he could go with them, but he was committed to this task. He couldn't leave knowing that Harris, MacCreadle and Barrett, all older than him, all family men, were dashing around the London survivor hot spots, disseminating information, getting people up onto their feet for the long march south. He checked each face that floated owlishly by, though. He could not and would not stop searching. It was difficult, trying to imagine how Stanley might have changed over the past ten years. There had been a marked alteration in Aidan's features; he had been hardened by experience. He guessed Stanley would have been too. But nobody he saw fit the identikit portrait in his mind.

The numbers of people thinned out soon. It was disheartening to think that so few had made it. In terms of percentages dead, he couldn't know for sure, but after the ninety-nine and the decimal point, he was willing to bet there were lots more nines involved. By the time he reached the City Road he was on his own again, his shoes slapping echoes from a thin gruel of slush and ash. A pipe had burst underground; water was geysering from a crack at the southern end of Upper Street. He splashed through a small river at the mouth of the Tube station, struggling to pull back the barrier gates, their runners snagged in years of accumulated litter. He stood in the entrance hall, water sluicing past him, roaring down the escalators. It would be dark, properly dark, before he'd made it halfway down there. He thought there might have been a mistake. Of all the places people could choose to live, why here, in permanent night? He wondered if his exhortations to leave might not be understood. Too long out of the real world and everything shut down.

Chalk marks adorned the walls, all of them orange. Someone had scrawled *Come and play*. Jane went to the mouth of the escalators and peered down. He supposed the tunnel network offered a freedom that wasn't necessarily available on the surface. But he still would not swap the skin of the earth with the veins beneath it. Like veins, the tunnels would become more and more furred. There was structural collapse occurring all over the city. He didn't fancy being marooned between stations with flood water hammering towards him from both ends. Or a ceiling giving way. Or a fire breaking out. There was nobody to maintain the upkeep of the system any more. People choosing to come down here, he thought, descending the longest escalators in the entire network, were out of their minds.

At the base of the escalator he was groping blindly. His foot reached level ground and he stood still for a while, head cocked, listening for signs of life. Shapes began to become known to him: the edge of a wall, the outline of a maintenance doorway, the familiar London Underground roundel against white tiles. His scalp crept as he considered the possibility of Skinners, lots of them, standing mere feet away. But popular wisdom spoke of Skinners rarely sinking below street level. They didn't like the stink, some said. Or maybe there was some kind of interference with their internal compasses, an anomaly in the magnetic flow. Maybe they were confused by the various scents barrelling around the tunnels, pushed and pulled from unknowable sources any number of miles away. Maybe they were just smart, biding their time, knowing that the inevitable collapse of the honeycomb would send people running into their arms.

Jane gripped the rifle, holding it out in front of him as if it were a torch. As he neared the broad southbound platform, though, he saw that there were lights down here, albeit crude and lacking in power. Candles were dotted between sleeping bags and tents pitched all along the platform. Their uncertain light reflected in the scarred curve of the ceiling, showing how it had crumbled back to its supportive ribs. Posters on the trackside wall had peeled to the extent that nothing could be made out in their messages. Water sheened the walls; nitre was a series of slow white blossoms. A stench rose up from the latrine that the tracks had been turned into. He had to zip his coat up over his nose and mouth. 'Jesus,' he whispered. 'Mind the crap.'

People began to unfold from their beds, like insects shedding their chrysalides. Thin, shivering figures approached him, every one of them with eyes so large they seemed painful to carry in the cross-hatched wastelands of their faces. A woman touched his arm; the light of the candles gave her skin a pale, waxy sheen, as if she were assuming the form of what illumined her.

'Have you seen my little boy?' she asked. 'He's my only boy. I lost him a couple of months ago. He vanished in the night. I woke up and it was all I could do to convince myself I'd ever had a boy in the first place. Have you seen him?'

Jane shook his head and backed away. Scurvy was sinking her eyes, paling her skin; her hand on her lower stomach clutched at blood – the reopening of a Caesarean scar, he supposed. He could read chapters of pain on every face. They regarded him as if he was here to deal them the *coup de grâce*. Fear and resignation mixed to a pathetic uniform look.

He said, 'People are leaving London. You should too. There's a raft . . . a boat off the south-east coast that can take you across the Channel to France.'

His reading of the general mood was misplaced. A man with a white beard, his right arm bandaged and smelling of rot, thrust his chin at him. 'Why would we want to go to France?'

'There's the possibility that what happened was restricted to these shores,' Jane said. Hoots of derision. He didn't believe what he had said either, but it was his job to put the option on the table. 'We're running out of places to hide. They're closing the net. In France we might be better positioned. More options. If you were to get on the raft you might find a better life.'

White Beard spat at Jane's feet. 'We might find a worse one, too,' he said. 'You just want us to leave so you can have the tunnels for yourself.'

'I'm not interested in tunnels,' Jane said. 'I'm here to pass on information, that's all. What you do with it is your business. You're looking at eighty miles. Cross the river at Tower Bridge. Head for the A20. Maybe you'll join up with the rest, hundreds of them, before you get there.'

He was turning to leave when someone called out, asking about the others.

'What others?' Jane asked.

'There's more of us,' the voice called. 'In the crossover passages at City Road. The old disused station.'

'Can't you pass it on?'

'You pass it on, pal. It's your job. We're leaving.'

Jane stood on the platform as roughly two-thirds of the platform dwellers hastily packed up their things and streamed by him. One or two shook his hand and thanked him. A man wearing a trilby over a mass of sweaty rat-tails told him he should get going himself and fuck the City Roaders or he'd end up being the last pretzel in the Skinners' snack bowl.

He watched their backs fade through the exit, heard them swearing and stomping and splashing up the escalators. About twenty men remained. Already they were repositioning their gear, seemingly happy with the grand space they had inherited.

'Fucking mugs, the lot of them,' White Beard said. 'Fucking raft? Who'd go out on the sea? I'll take my chances with the Smoke. My grandad lived here in the Blitz. Didn't get a fucking scratch.'

Jane loped down to the end of the platform and squinted into the tunnel's throat. A constant breeze shifted his hair, chilled the flesh of his arms. It was like the final protracted breath of a giant. It carried every scent you could associate with death upon it. It was a stew of bad things, dirty water run from the tap leading directly to the well of your nightmares.

He dropped down into the gulley of sewage and allowed himself to be swallowed.

It wasn't far to the defunct City Road section of the Northern Line tunnel but Jane's constant stumbling on the rails and the fragments of wall collapsing into the passageway lengthened his journey considerably. There were no platforms at the station any more, but candles had been left here too, lighting the way to the passage arches, seemingly hanging in the wall, five feet above the floor. Soot clung to every surface; it was as if everything had been carved from it. The floor seemed to shiver as he hauled himself up from the rails; his hands sank into inches of soft matter. Dead cables slinked around him, hanging from their routers like snakes sleeping in branches, roughly following the shape of the architecture as though they were its preliminary pencil sketches.

Jane called out but his voice died immediately in the granular acoustics. Pieces of unrecognisable machinery lay by the tracks. A dust-veiled sign from the 1940s warned people not to leave their belongings behind after the all-clear. He saw a figure at the central corridor leading to the stairs. A child holding a toy, a stuffed animal. It looked like a lion. The slight figure was wearing pyjamas. He was barefoot. Jane's heart lurched as if it were making a break for freedom. He almost laughed out loud.

'Stanley?' he called.

The figure instantly turned and ran away, as if it had been waiting only for Jane's voice to trigger it. Jane stood in the passageway staring at the skirls of dust the figure had kicked up at the moment of its exit. Not Stanley. Stanley would not be five years old still. Stanley would be wearing a scowl and a hoodie and bumfluff on his upper lip. Stanley would not run away. He'd stand his ground and ask Jane, 'What's it to you, fuckhead?'

Jane took off after him.

He managed a couple of flights before the walls started to move. Figures detached themselves from the murk as if they had animated themselves from the soot. Soon he found himself trying to move through a corridor packed with black flaking bodies. He couldn't think beyond the character of Pigpen in *Peanuts*, who seemed to be constructed from dirt. All he could see were wild white eyes and teeth; a smell of humus and brackish water. It was as if the shored-up earth, failing now, deep beneath the capital, was shedding ghosts at every turn.

'Stanley?' he called out again, a reflex that he seemed to have no power over. When it came to his son, those moments when he felt close to Stanley, either during these mirages or in dreams, it was as if he could not rein in his excitement. It could only be a memory, or a wish, but the ever-hopeful part of his brain lit up, burning so brightly that no other function could be considered.

Now he had reached the ancient locked-in ticket barrier. How long had this station been closed to the public? A good seventy years, surely. People were huddled together under their shifting blanket of dust as though resigned to death. Jane imagined them never moving, just sitting, waiting, waiting for a moment such as this, a person to release them from a stasis they had not noticed arriving and did not know how to shake off. They looked at him with a mixture of puzzlement and relief.

Jane told them about the raft. He said they would have to go back through the tunnels because these doors had been locked so long they might well have sealed themselves shut. They stood and applauded him, and he began to cry, surrounded by shades, all of them weeping with gratitude, all of them missing somebody. Everyone was the same. Everyone sought solace of one kind or another.

He looked around for Stanley as they filed past him, but he knew there would be nobody here who reminded him of his son. He had seen a ghost, that was all, a bruise in his memory. Stanley was still with him, in one way or another. There was no point in getting excited every time it happened. It was just his way of saying hi. It was the son in his blood. He would never leave him to be on his own.

But then he saw him again a couple of hours later. A little boy, in blue-striped pyjamas plated with dry mud. A soft toy clutched in one hand. Hair mussed as if he'd just got out of

bed. He was running along Primrose Hill Road, just north
of Regent's Park, legs barely bending as he ran, leaning over
so far it seemed he must trip and fall headlong, just the way
that Stanley ran when he saw his dad approaching the house
from a long shift on the rigs. Jane pursued. It could not be
Stanley. Stanley had not been trapped at the age of five all
this time. It didn't matter. The child still needed to be taken
care of.

He lost sight of the boy as he reached Albert Road. One
moment he'd been there – Jane was sure he wasn't aware
that he was being followed, he hadn't seen his head turn,
he would have loved to glimpse the face, just to convince
the old romantic, the gullible sap wishing for the impossible, in him – the next moment he was gone. There were
plenty of hiding places. Jane didn't know where to start.
He could be looking for him for an hour and the boy
would be on the south side of the park, heading down
Portland Place.

Jane crossed the road and nipped through the park's
exterior to the Outer Circle where the main entrance to
London Zoo was located. He walked straight through the
open gates. In. Pass on the details. Out. Job done. On to the
next and then find Becky and scram.

He marched along the zoo's paths trying to work out
where everyone would be congregating. Every cage he
walked past bore a sign that had been burned clean of
information. Sometimes there was a body, an animal carcass
beyond identification, trapped inside the bars, passed unsuit-
able for Skinner invasion or devourment. More often than
not the cages were empty, whatever had lived within having
bent the bars open in order to escape, once consumed by
their Skinner hijacker. Behind him the great nets of the
Snowdon aviary had collapsed; scorched patches of it lay
flapping around like failed spiders' webs. Cairns of dried shit

were the only pointer to any kind of animal habitation now. Jane wondered where they had all gone.

He checked the vivarium and aquarium, but both were empty, their glass tanks smashed, the animals within now gone, perhaps taken for food. He headed south-east, towards a shattered fountain, past areas where African birds had been kept, pygmy hippos, bearded pigs. He dug in his memory for what these creatures looked like.

He stopped, his heart suddenly reminding him it was still beating, as a filthy, limping rhinoceros plodded across the wasteland of a former picnic area, its head swinging around as if trying to rid itself of a pain or a cloud of irritating insects. It paused and turned Jane's way. There was a Skinner inside it, he was certain of that. The poor animal was a shadow of what its genes had meant for it to be. Its face was slack, the tough hide turned in places to elastic bars, showing glimpses of the awful thing that dwelled within. Its great horn had sheared through like a lopped branch; the stump was cracked and sore-looking, surrounded with a collar of crusted pus. The black dinner plates of its eyes seemed without edge, a shadow that might keep on growing until it was totally consumed. Jane tensed himself, ready to make a run for it if the Skinner considered charging, but clearly it was unhappy within the body it had invaded; it turned its back on him and staggered away.

Jane waited, watching the animal move slowly past the sinkhole of the old flamingo pond. He thought that maybe there was nobody left here now. Orange zone suddenly turned blue. It gave him a nasty jolt. He'd been stupid, brazen, to come here without checking the perimeter first. He resumed his walk through the grounds, but now his eye was caught by something to his left, a shapeless mass on an area of pathway between a children's cratered playground and the dry, weathered edifice of the penguins' fake iceberg.

Jane approached, leaning over slightly as if he might be able to identify what it was before he got too close. He saw the flap and curl of torn clothing. He saw a separated blue-white hand lying on its knuckles like a dead crab, a few feet away from the main salmagundi of body parts. He thought he saw a swatch of striped pyjama in there but closed his mind to it, turned away. He was close enough now to see steam rising, to smell the rich, sour odours of fear and adrenaline that seamed the meat. He thought of his own teeth slicing through cooked flesh, tattooed skin crisped on a griddle. He put a brake on his bile before it could leap from his throat.

He heard the guttural, drool-laced rattle of something big nearby. It came again, each breath transformed into a wet snarl of aggression, catching in the throat. It sounded like the starter motor to some velvety engine. It was a beautiful, terrifying sound.

Jane backed away from the butchery as the tiger emerged from the collapsed north wall of a café, twenty yards away. It was deteriorating. Its once proud, blocky head was a cheap Halloween mask. The ears might have been flattened back in a classic intimidatory pose but they had frayed to nubs of gristle. Its fur was losing the stripe of a man-eater, gradually fading back into the insipid, featureless colour that death preserves for all. Its chipped, split claws scratched at the path, reminding Jane of the sound of skipping ropes in school playgrounds. The tail had long since worn away to a chewed, twitching stick barely two inches long.

It padded towards him, steam wreathing a grimace filled with black teeth. Its hollowed eyes were mesmerising; Jane could almost believe they were Jane-shaped, designed at the very moment of conception only to focus on him. They were full of him now, despite the blindness of the Skinner. The tiger was locked on.

Jane backed away. Nowhere to go. The zoo was an open arena. He raised the rifle and flicked off the safety catch. He shouldered the weapon and drew a bead. He shot the tiger in the centre of the chest when it lifted its head to check his scent. The tiger staggered back onto its haunches, a *phut* of complaint whiffling its chops. Its teeth oozed into view again, the eyes screwing up in a blind reflex of hatred and rage. The black corkscrews of its whiskers turned towards him as he was drawn into its olfactory glands. If the tiger was in pain, it wasn't showing it. A fresh sheet of drool unfolded itself from the open mouth. The wound was bloodless.

The tiger found its feet again and came on.

Jane ran. He did not look back, despite the roar, despite the spattering claws now sounding like grit tossed on an ice-covered pavement. He ran to the southern point of the zoo and clambered over and through what remained of the perimeter wall. The park beyond it was a morass of churned mud. He felt sudden, massive heat across the back of his left thigh, and then he was jumping. He was caught in the mud almost immediately. One boot was sucked from his foot. He turned to try to retrieve it and went down on his side, his arm disappearing almost to the shoulder. The tiger was struggling too. It was twelve feet shy of him; Jane could smell the baking, rancid heat that powered from its jaws. It lurched, trying to spring, but succeeded only in burying its hind legs more deeply. Jane forced himself flat on his stomach and wriggled clear, trying to swim across the surface of the mud, wriggling like a soldier, his gun held in front of him, across no-man's-land.

He chanced a glance over his shoulder and saw that the tiger was failing to close the gap. Its snarls grew ever more frustrated. At one point it seemed to try to take a bite out of its own flank. Gradually the mud turned drier and Jane was able to get to his feet. He ran past the festering waters of the Boating Lake and reached relatively solid ground at the Inner Circle road. Ten minutes later and he was on Marylebone Road, certain that he could hear the frustrated screams of the tiger, certain that at any moment it would come skittering out of York Gates and bring him down within seconds.

He ran for an age without thought of where he might be heading. The shock of the pursuit, the sadness of finding an orange zone massacred, the pain in his leg – blood was filling his remaining boot now; it rose out of the lace holes with each sickening step – was conspiring to cloud his mind. He must stop soon and rest, get himself patched up, or risk fainting.

Jane forced himself to study his surroundings. Maiden Lane, was this? He recognised it from a time in the 1990s when he'd met Cherry for a drink in some dark, poky little pub down an alley through which you'd have struggled to walk two abreast. Thoughts of Cherry, bizarrely, revived him a little. Something about the sass of her in those days, how she could get his prick hard within seconds of their meeting just in the way she'd nip his ear with her teeth after a kiss hello, or the way she'd look at him, a naked desire in her cool green eyes. Something about the bitch in her. Whatever it was, it slapped him awake as he limped into Southampton Street.

On the Strand he checked both ways before continuing, conscious of the heavy Skinner traffic that had been in evidence the last time he had ventured this way. Empty now, thank God. He must smell like an abattoir skip. He looked back at the blood trail and dreamt he saw Skinners following on their knees, sucking up his vital fluids as they inched after him. He could not risk compromising his safe house. He crossed to the south side and crunched through the broken glass of a shoe shop. In the storeroom he found a boiler bolted to the wall. A tray next to it held cracked mugs, an empty tea caddy and a bowl of congealed sugar with a spoon trapped inside it. He chipped some of the sugar off and sucked it as he worked at the seized tap. It gave a little. He held a rag under the spigot and forced it open. About a pint of rusty water gurgled from it. He soaked the rag and gingerly removed his jeans. The tiger's claws had slashed through the denim and left three deep gouges in his upper thigh. Blood oozed freely from them. Jane almost blacked out at the prospect of a vein having been opened. Death would be a long time coming. He'd feel it settle on him by degrees as his life pulsed from him. There was no point in shoving a finger in there, putting pressure on the severed blood vessel. He couldn't suture it closed. He wouldn't find anybody with the requisite skills to do so before his heart stopped.

Me and you, both, Stopper. Just a little slower than you copped it. Typical me, eh?

He dug in the rucksack for the First Aid pack. He took out the stapler and some sealed squares of antiseptic tissue. He wiped the wounds clean, gritting his teeth against the pain. The blood was still coming, but it was less free-flowing. He pinched the edges of the wounds together and, swearing copiously, stapled them shut. Once all three slashes were gathered, he snapped off the end of an ampoule of antibiotics and drew them into a syringe. He plunged the needle into his thigh, just above the wound. Then he wrapped a clean bandage around the whole sorry mess and secured it with a tubular bandage pulled up over his leg. He stood up, testing the leg with his whole weight. It hurt like a bastard, but it felt supported, secure.

Jane thought of the filthy claws of the tiger and what might have been swarming on their points. He couldn't believe he had isolated all possibility of infection, regardless of how careful he had been in washing the wound. He was dead if his leg required amputating.

He turned to go and heard a crunch of glass in the shop front. He saw a Skinner standing among the overturned displays like a man who has forgotten his shopping list and is trying to summon the items back from memory. Fire in a bank of shops across the road leapt at its shoulders, enhancing its silhouette. Jane wiped his hands on a fresh antiseptic wipe and pocketed it; he toed the bloody rags of the used ones into the far corner of the room. It landed with a splat. He saw the Skinner cock its head like an inquisitive dog. Jane backed into the other corner and made his breathing shallow.

The Skinner came. It moved into the room, blocking the entrance with its bulk. In another life it had been a woman in a suit; her black leather briefcase was still snagged on one arm. Her blonde hair had once been a styled, angular cut. Now it was tangled with all kinds of street debris: old litter, soot, blood. There was a finger in there. Her face was the colour of pastry, riddled with tears as though kneaded by a child. Thick saliva had poured from the jaws of the Skinner and hardened against its chin, like melted drips from a candle. Dirt was a cracked glaze across its chest. Its head was a pendulum swinging first his way, then the rags'. Death hung on a simple decision. Jane was not frightened any more. It had been dogging him for so long that it didn't seem to possess the finality it once had. He imagined himself being clawed inside out, turned to a pulp, and then sitting up once the Skinner had moved on, pulling himself back into some kind of order and getting the old stapler out again.

The Skinner shuffled towards the rags and started sucking them dry. Immediately, Jane shot past it and headed for the exit. The Skinner ignored him. Jane paused to snatch what looked like a size nine from a tumble of leisure shoes. When he lifted his head, there was another figure standing in the doorway, backlit by the fire.

She raised her hand. Six fingers. She closed her hand to a fist. A forefinger emerged. She pointed east. She stepped down from the doorway. She left. Fast; he could not pursue. He did not know what he would say could he have caught her.

Stumpily, stiff-legged, he tottered to the hotel. Orange marks on the wall. Not that that meant anything any more. He was more cautious this time, mindful of his mindless charge through the zoo. He took each floor slowly, making sure the corridors were clear. Checking for any evidence of Skinners having moved in. There was nothing.

He climbed to his favourite room and locked the door. He lit candles. The weather had booked in too, through a crack where the window frame had pulled away from the wall, turning one corner of the suite into a peeling, crumbling wreck. But it was a large suite; he could sleep in the boardroom. Jane stared at the locked cases lined up against the wall. He couldn't bring these with him. His letter remained unfinished. Never mind. He could save the last paragraphs for the day he saw Stanley again.

He opened each case and took out the papers. He carried fully two reams to the window. The wind tore past the gap when he opened it. Jane fed handfuls of love to the wind and watched them sail away into deep night. When the last of the pages had gone

Dear Stanley, I hope you are well. I miss you so much. Do you know, there's a little Stan-shaped hole right in the middle of my heart? Maybe there's a Daddy-shaped one in the middle of yours . . .

he closed the window and bolted it. He took his gun to the boardroom. A sleeping bag was open on the grand table, waiting for him. He fell upon it. In the night, as he slept, three teeth oozed clear of his lips and danced across the varnish like strange dice.

23. EXODUS

Jane said goodbye to his hotel room. He would not be back. He stood at the north end of Waterloo Bridge remembering how beautiful everything had looked when he had first moved down to London with Cherry. They would make a point of visiting the bridge, especially on summer evenings when everything seemed to be honey-coated, softened. Cherry was so beautiful; her face had yet to take on the creases and frowns that drew everything into a tight, resentful pucker. The light seemed drawn to her. They watched the tugs and barges on the river, talking about everything and nothing, waiting for the darkness and the lights. It had seemed there was nobody else around, despite the frantic foxtrot of pedestrians, the endless laps of cars and buses. London was there just for the two of them.

One, now.

Beauty was erased from this world. Perhaps for ever. He stopped at the middle of the bridge, looking down at the fragmented skulls and the shrivelled skins, wondering if this spot was where the two of them used to stand all those years ago. There was no warm ghost of recognition. No magical exclamation mark making itself known in the air. His heart beat normally. Some of the skyscrapers along the waterfront were slowly sliding into the river. The tugs and barges were burnt-out shells floating on a scum of clothes and driftwood. Fires burned in more and more regions of the city; a pall of black smoke formed an underscore to the metallic ceiling of cloud. When the wind changed direction he might hear a scream or the concussion of an explosion as a gas pipe ruptured. He shot one last look back over his shoulder at Aldwych, certain he would see the figure in the striped pyjamas, but there were just the same old grim tumbleweeds of skin and soot, dust devils of peeled white faces, rising into the sky.

Hope had wormed so many openings in him that he felt honeycombed. At any moment he might collapse in on himself. More dust to add to the drifts already shifting along the roads and pavements. Dunes of regret. A shattering desert.

He felt old beyond his years. His thigh pulsed hotly as he walked. There was a hand of pain at the very centre of the wound and it had long fingers. His flesh was sensitive as far south as his knee and north just to the edge of his ribs. Not a good sign. He chewed painkillers and eyed the remaining ampoules as if they were golden chalices. They were, he supposed. He had to use them sparingly. Becky had slipped them into his palm with a kiss.

Medic's perks. Just to prove that I like you, that I think you're a bit of all right.

He pulled his hood up over his head and zipped the coat closed. His pockets clinked with four stoppered bottles of paraffin. His tongue took a tour of his mouth, squirming in the soft dips of his undressing gums. His remaining teeth seemed too long, too loose, his jaws receding from them as if they were foreign bodies to be ejected. But at least there was no blood in his fist when he coughed. No hair loss. He regularly checked his testicles for lumps, but nothing doing there either. No hard masses beneath the skin of his stomach. No fits, no blackouts. He was as healthy as he could expect to be. So just periodontal disease, then? Just the unlucky caries that come from too many sweets and not enough flossing.

At the South Bank he got down off the bridge and followed the obstacle course of the Queen's Walk as far as Bermondsey and it was just him and his bad leg and the same old sound of his breath rasping inside the bicycle mask. As he passed beneath Tower Bridge he thought he heard laughter and song. But he also heard gunfire and screaming, further south. The laughter and song died pretty quickly after that.

He stood on the pier and looked out at the lapping river. Rat Island rose out of it like a swollen belly from cold bathwater. He saw people moving over the great built-up mound of wreckage, looking for food, or for relatives. Bivouacs dotted this artificial island; people emerged from tunnels like maggots from bad apples.

Jane called out: 'Hey!'

Faces turned to the river bank. Most went back to their rooting; one man cupped his mouth and asked for a name.

'Richard Jane. I have news.'

The man untied a simple boat from a post and rowed his way over to where Jane stood. He was short and bald, his head strangely large on top of his wasted body, like an unsucked lollipop. He introduced himself as Jon Petersen, a printer from Bergen, Norway who had moved to London to live with his English wife who owned a luggage shop in Nunhead. His wife had disappeared during the Event while Petersen had been in the centre of town, travelling on the Tube, shopping for her birthday presents.

'How many are you?' Jane asked.

Petersen looked back at the island. 'There are a few hundred here,' he said. 'It's a hellish stink, but we feel safe. Skinners don't go swimming. And the rats we can cope with. They make good eating, if you can catch them. You have to fast them first, though, for a few days or they're bitter.'

Jane saw the rats moving briskly across the skin of the island, surefooted and sleek, as if they were on rails. They did not seem as fat or aggressive as they used to be. Everything that had survived was losing weight. He was coming to see the raft as a last chance.

He told Petersen what he knew and the other man listened without speaking, constantly licking his already wet lips so that Jane could not take his eyes from them; they resembled the flesh of cherries.

'A raft,' Petersen said, when Jane was finished. 'In the water?'

Jane nodded. 'There are people on the way now.'

'I saw them. I wondered what was happening.'

'Head for the south-east,' Jane said. 'Tell your people.'

'The water,' Petersen said again. He seemed troubled as he pushed the boat off for the island. He kept looking into the river around him, as if it contained things that he found suddenly unpalatable.

Jane felt liberated. He had done what had been asked of him. Everyone in London who hadn't struck out on their own had been made aware of the existence of the raft. The city was emptying. Now he hoped that the screams and howls he could hear belonged to the Skinners as the streets turned lonely and the houses grew used to the ageing echoes of human voices.

He watched Petersen tie the boat off at the platform. A crowd quickly grew around the Norwegian. Jane waved once to them, turned his back, and headed for the Old Kent Road.

* * *

After about an hour he heard little footsteps slapping through the wet, struggling to keep up.

'Hello, Stanley.'

'Hiya, Dad.'

'Where've you been?' He was tempted to look to his side, but he didn't want the illusion to vanish just yet. It was enough to see the blue stripe of Stanley's pyjamas in his peripheral vision, the arc of his arm as he swung Walter up and down. He had walked the length of the A2; New Cross Gate was ahead, then Lewisham and the A20 that would take him into Kent. The crippled expanse of superstores lay around them like so many crushed sardine cans.

'You sticking to the road, Dad?'

'Yeah, why? I'll probably catch up with more people before long. It'll be safer then.'

'Safer? How?'

He wanted to reach out and plant his hand on the boy's hair, feel the heat of his scalp run through his fingers. Drop his hand to Stanley's slender neck, feel the muscles shift against each other under the impossible soft skin.

'You've heard of safety in numbers haven't you?'

'No.'

'Well. It means the more of you there are, the less afraid you need to be.'

'I think that's a load of rubbish.'

Jane stopped. He checked behind him, but there were no refugees. The road was empty. It had been preying on his thoughts; he believed that by now he would either have caught up with a convoy, or been assimilated by one joining the A2 at any of the main junctions.

He no longer wanted to look down at Stanley, but not because he was concerned the boy would fragment and drift apart, like desert cloud. He was scared. Stanley's eyes, what he could make out from the corner of his own, were too large for his head, too dark. His voice had faltered, but it was not the change in vocal cords you would expect from a boy who was in his fifteenth year. It was slurred, scorched, splintered. It had been interfered with in some way. Now he suspected that the way Stanley kinked his neck to look up to his father was no longer some endearing facet of his behaviour but an enforced failing in his physicality, a terrible injury.

'Are you all right, Stanley?'

'Fine,' came the voice. It was no longer that of his son. It was filled with fluid. The boy's face vibrated; he could hear the chomp and smack of his own lips as he chewed through the flesh of his cheeks and mouth. Shadows descended. Jane thought it might be unconsciousness but it was a dozen or so birds – vicious grey shrikes – fluttering down to tear strips from his boy's face. He scattered them with his fists and turned to sweep Stanley into his arms.

There was little left of him. He was an effigy, a voodoo-doll death threat. Spurs of bone shone through where the hard beaks had drilled him. Jane could see through the plundered sockets of his eyes to a part of his son that had once flickered with happy memories of chases in the park and cuddles on a sofa watching cartoons. The boy turned to nothing under his fingers. He was sure he could hear the creak and caw of airborne birds but when he looked above him there was only the iron-plaited insult of the sky.

He turned his attention back to the road ahead. What had Fielding said that day? Something about a cordon? A slip-knot tightening. The wind gusted into him like the over-affectionate shoulder charge of a drunken friend. Danger was in it. He was sure he heard cries and shouts from up ahead, although he'd hoped he might have left that behind. Screams in the daytime. 'Get off the road, Dad,' Stanley said. His voice. His good voice. Jane heeded the advice. He got onto the railway line at New Cross and followed the track along the backs of schools and works and supermarkets. The embankments wore a second skin of fly-tipped rubbish, machinery and cadavers eroded by the weather almost to nothing. He hurried beneath those bridges that still stood, aware of their weakness, or manoeuvred a route through those that had crashed to the rails, sometimes topped by cars bearing occupants who bore the same gritted expression he'd seen everywhere for the past ten years. The look of death was the look of someone concentrating, or grimacing in pain or embarrassment, or concealing a hilarious secret.

The track wound through Lewisham, bypassing depots and shuttling under the high street. He hurried by ruptured, stinking stock at the Hither Green sidings without bothering to look at what was inside. No food here. No hope of help. Human bones had sifted to the surface of the embankment outside the cemetery, sprawling over the rails as if left there by some untidy scavenger. The land opened up. The arid span of a former golf course. The spent matchsticks of a wood.

As the day lengthened, Jane felt London's grip on him loosen. He felt like a finger tracing a route in the *A–Z*. It had reached a section where there were no more arrows pointing to the next pages. He was falling off the map. He was leaving the city where his child used to play, used to stand on the balcony and watch out for his return. He looked back at the miles he had covered and wondered about his boy. Maybe he and Cherry had heard about the raft too and were making their way out here. Maybe they had reached the coast already, and were hunting for Jane among the others lying exhausted on the beach.

The hope would not lie down in him.

* * *

Jane spent the night in an overturned coach in the south-east corner of Orpington. All the windows were smashed. Nothing else shared the space with him. Various fluids on the ceiling of the vehicle had dried to a homogeneous black glaze. The coach was so old that it had shed any smells that might have identified the stains, or the cause of its accident.

He was tired to his bones, but he couldn't sleep. Worry gnawed at him. He wanted to see Becky again, despite accepting that she was safer with the others. He wanted an end to the wearisome plodding that his life had become. He measured his days in how many miles he had clocked up. There was no humour in him or for him, no tenderness. All he looked forward to was the face of his boy; he hoped he would remain tear-free for long enough to register his first expression. Not gritted. No. Death could not find its way into a boy with such laughter inside him. Death would mope away, shamefaced for even trying.

He was up and within view of the M25 before the bastardised dawn congealed around him. The previous night he had happened upon a camp that the Shaded had pitched about a mile north of the ring road. Skinners moved up there, a great wall of them stretching away in each direction: part of the noose that Fielding had talked about. There had been much talk about what to do. Some were for the long trek back to London: stick with what you know. But most of them – Jane could see it in the tension bunching their shoulders – were itching for a fight.

Now, to his left, ranged south of the A20, were dozens of the Shaded, like him ducked low into the dusty countryside abutting the fractured strip of road. Everyone hefted some kind of weapon. There were shivs and gardening forks and heavy-duty motorbike chains with shackles swinging on the end, knurled so that steel burrs stuck out of them. Shotguns and butchers' cleavers. Bottles of hydrochloric acid. One man held a Heckler & Koch semi-automatic carbine in each fist, his chest criss-crossed with bandoliers, his cargo pants stuffed with magazines. Jane had to believe that the cordon of Skinners was only one figure deep. He didn't want to rush any breach they might be able to enforce only to find legions of the monsters waiting to mop them up as they poured through. He saw some of the Shaded carrying guns that looked far more powerful than his own. There were others who carried axes and knives. He saw someone with a hand resting on the scabbard of a sheathed samurai sword, another holding *nunchaku*, another holding what looked like piano wire between fists protected with grey bandage.

Jane watched as heads began to turn and bodies unfolded from their hiding places. He felt the crackle of electricity in the air, the thrill and relief that aggression brought, the liberation of positive movement. He understood immediately why people went to war, were prepared to die. It wasn't *Pro Patria Mori* – Wilfred Owen's 'old lie' – it was to do with the people you knew and loved. It was the fear that they would suffer if you did not come through.

Jane rose with the others and put a match to the wick of his petrol bomb. Once it was burning, he hurled it as hard as he could at the Skinners. The explosion as the bottle shattered was drowned out by a roar from the Shaded as they stormed the motorway. Jane was roaring too. Jane was smiling, fit to split his face in half.

He didn't remember much about what happened after that and was still so pumped up with excitement that he couldn't feel the extent of his injuries. His right arm was burned as far as his elbow. Not too bad, but the skin was tender and pink and hairless. He'd had to shrug himself out of his coat fast and slap the flames out with the part that wasn't on fire.

It was an injury worth sustaining; he'd taken down three Skinners with the Molotov cocktail that had almost killed him. He'd been grabbed from behind at the moment of launching the bottle and had dropped it to the ground, igniting himself and his attackers as he bent to try and catch it before it smashed.

Others were less lucky. Roughly fifty per cent of the Shaded who had charged the Skinners had been over-powered. In the thick of the fighting he'd watched men dismantled as easily as wasps trapped on a floor of ants. The few women that had been in the group were dragged away. Even above the smell of the paraffin flames the musk of the creatures hung heavy, a wardrobe of mouldy winter coats opened after a long time. There was something deeply unnerving about grabbing hold of a hand or a face and feeling it come away in your fingers like a swatch of fabric. He had to keep reminding himself that these were no longer people, that they had been subjugated, replaced. If you kept your eyes away from the mangled, silently agonised faces and on the alien posture of their bodies you could avoid the question.

The Shaded broke through somehow, and the land on the other side of the Skinners seemed green and vital, although it was no different to the swidden they had travelled up to that point. The Skinners did not pursue them; they closed ranks and waited for the next wave of migrants. There was a slow, confident intelligence about them, the knowledge that they had time to mop up. Jane thought with a jolt of panic that they were aware of what things were like all over the globe. You didn't have to fight quite so valiantly if you knew you were going to overwhelm your enemy later when they'd had all hope crushed from their weakened bodies.

From a safe distance Jane watched the Skinners scrapping over the men who had fallen. He gritted his teeth against the raging pain in his arm and suspected that the injury was more serious than he had first diagnosed. He needed cold running water and there was none. He needed to wrap the limb in cellophane, and there was none. Already blisters were inflating under the skin, its colour deepening.

Thirty of them struck out along the road to the sea. He found someone who was willing to share his painkillers. Another who had an aerosol of burn spray in his rucksack. It would have to do. He held the arm out, naked, in front of him like a diviner.

They peeled off on occasion, little groups of them, to forage for food in the factories and houses that formed a broken guard of honour on either side of the motorway. They ate while they walked. They talked little. Jane asked if anybody had seen or heard of a woman, Becky. Nobody replied, but the faces he inspected turned darker, more inward. Everyone had a woman who was gone from their lives.

They walked through the night and through the day and through the night. The land grew flatter and less built-up. The wind cleared its throat and lashed them. Rain was a dreary, dismal constant. On either side of him, men were staggering, wearing masks and goggles of every description. Their hair was long and unkempt, their beards like those of fakirs. It was like being part of a nightmare army staggering towards death having developed a real appetite for it. Every form of horror and degradation was in their wake. They'd bumbled through it all, passed every examination, and now, struggling to stay on their feet, they approached the edge of the world, knowing that death, if it was waiting for them here, the final joke, the ultimate irony, well, it would be welcome; it would be greeted with a deep smile and arms held out.

24. CAST-IRON SHORE

Jane knew he was at the end of himself. He was a car that had been badly cared for, run into the ground, its odometer clocked. No amount of repairs was going to rescue him from a date with the crusher. Eating did not lift his spirits. Thoughts of Becky carrying the shred of his genes in her womb could not lift him out of his torpor. Worst of all, he could not concentrate for long enough to summon Stanley to the forefront of his thoughts. He was weak and tired beyond what he understood those words to mean. His soul was like an animal run over on a busy road. It had been flattened over time by so many tons of traffic that it resembled a dirty outline of what he was, who he had been. He was a memory in his own lifetime. He was dust, shadowless; he was shutting down.

The beach described a flat arc from north-east to south-west. It curved before him and it did not appear to incline towards the sea, nor erase itself against a different kind of landscape behind him. The sea seemed to join the beach at a random point, sewn on like a dark hem. It did not seem to have any depth to it. The violence that he had seen in the North Sea was gone here, as if it had spent itself. The sea was flat and black and indolent. Stiff gusts of wind drew some motion from its surface – frail, corpse-grey combers – but it was reluctant, tacked on, almost, like some remembered reconstruction of how oceans ought to behave. The fruits of a decade's worth of slow tides lay on the sand, a scruffy, impromptu market. Orange barrels. Endless lengths of timber. Bleached streamers of plastic. Bodies face down into the sand as if trying to burrow, to escape the embarrassment of scrutiny. Buy one, get one free.

Jane rolled over onto his side, his good side. Despite the flare of pain along his arm, the flesh purpuric and angry, and the dull throb in his savaged thigh, it was comforting to sit in the shingle. He pushed his fingers through the flint pebbles, enjoying the feel of the cool stones against his skin. There was hard work going on all across the headland. The raft itself was a trembling disc of pale blue sitting on the water. It was hard to see, but it seemed to be buoyed by a series of floats lashed to its outer rim. Someone had talked of how it was necessarily open at the centre, so that more floats could be added as a counterbalance to prevent the raft collapsing.

'We're going to sea on a blue Polo mint,' someone had called out, incredulous.

The peninsula was dotted with the remains of fishing boats. Beachcombers sifted through the wreckage, looking for workable pieces of wood. Sometimes Jane looked in a direction where there were no people, no buildings, and it was like viewing a moonscape. The end of the world was desolate and grey. You couldn't see the coast of France. He thought that maybe much of the rest of the world had dissolved into the oceans. It wouldn't take long for the same to happen here.

Jane drew himself up to a sitting position. He was with maybe twenty other wounded. Medical volunteers were slowly tending to the injuries, on a sliding scale of need. A badly burned arm and slashes to the arse were low priorities compared to the man with half his head caved in, or another with an arterial bleed. Jane watched the life puddle out of that one, turning the stones crimson. When he died, nobody cried. There was no sighing or oaths to God. Nobody turned away. The medics covered him up and moved on to the next. Two other men died before they could receive treatment, rattling away into the stones, their faces smoothing as death claimed them. It seemed almost preferable.

Eventually the medics turned their talents to Jane. He had seen one of them before, a wiry man in his forties with a tattoo of an octopus, its tentacles winding around his muscles on his forearm. Edwards, he thought his name was. He and his colleague, a younger man with black skin and alopecia, peeled away Jane's dressings, bathed his wounds and gave him injections. The world drifted away a little. Warmth washed through him. They bandaged his thigh with clean dressings and slathered a cream on his arm that turned it chill. They put a pillow under his head and he lay down on it. Nobody had said a word. There was no need for comfort, or reassurance. You died or you lived. Everyone was beyond the niceties that once accompanied such attention.

Jane slept.

It was growing dark when he revived. The drugs had worn off and he was shivering, his arm laced with pain. Someone had tucked a blanket around him, but it was no good now. The shingle he had enjoyed the feel of earlier was now a relentless sharp digging in his back and buttocks.

'Goes it?'

Jane jerked his head in the direction of the voice. A grainy shape folded into the shingle. Green clothes crusted with black blood.

'I'm all right. A bit stiff, but then I've been feeling like that for years. Edwards, is it?'

''Tis.'

'How long have you been here?'

'Months. Since they began building the fucker. This is the busiest we've been for a while. The worst injuries we had before this were splinters and sprains.' The voice sounded so tired that Jane thought it might simply fade out. He supposed everyone sounded like that now. Tired, strung out. Maybe just giving up the ghost without even realising it.

Jane scrambled to his feet and stretched, keeping his arm tucked in against him. The raft was no longer visible on the water and he thought it might have left without him, or been sunk, but his panic was short-lived. Labourers were huddled together checking plans and drinking hot water from metal cups. Fires had been started all along the beach. He heard laughter from somewhere and it almost scared him. It was such an alien sound, like the sudden cry of an attacking animal. Gradually he allowed himself to relax, to feel safe for the first time in a long time.

'So what's it like, back in London?' Edwards asked him.

'Not great,' Jane said. 'You got anyone there?'

'London? No. Never set foot in the place me entire puff. Nearest I got was Leatherhead, Surrey. Grew up in Leeds. Everyone dead.'

Jane didn't know what to say. As in most cases, he allowed the silence to build a wall between them. Then he turned and walked along the beach, his movements ungainly in the deep, shifting pebbles. Forgotten angles of machinery poked out of the ground like relics from an alien era unearthed by archaeologists. Chains and cogs and pistons and gears, larger than lorries. He felt a little like these submerged weird machines. Machines needed people to work them. Once they disappeared, or the knowledge of their purpose was lost, they became redundant, useful only for scrap. He had felt more and more rudderless in recent weeks. He felt like someone who has aged to a point where he no longer feels relevant, someone pale and lined who drifts around the periphery of things, who escapes attention because he has come to the end of his life.

He supposed that the future would come to resemble the past. Hundreds of years ago, you outlived your usefulness to the planet once you'd procreated. Life expectancy was mid-thirties. He felt another tooth coming loose. Lower incisor. Once your teeth were gone, it became harder to take in the nutrients you needed. Aches and pains everywhere. It didn't matter any more that he knew how to weld, could determine how long to stay underwater on a tank of heliox. These were skills the world no longer needed. He was a shot bolt. He sat down again, weary, sapped to the bone.

An old woman with beautiful hair, silver and soft and long, leaned over him and asked if he was all right. He smiled at her and he saw her wince; blood in the teeth, he thought, and shut his lips. He turned away, looking at the nuclear reactors to the south, the dome of the decommissioned Sizewell A. Jane remembered his concern over these plants, but nothing had come of the threat. He remembered Becky rubbing his shoulder when he became upset that they had survived only to face an impossible future, one fraught with danger at every turn.

'I know a girl,' he said. 'Her name's Becky. She . . . she's pregnant.' He turned back to the old woman. Her eyes were bright blue; remarkably there was no corona edging the iris to speak of her age. She had the eyes of a teenager.

'I know Becky,' she said. She averted her gaze and Jane knew there was something wrong.

'I'm the father,' he said. 'I . . . well, I think. I hope. A woman called Simmonds. She said she was being looked after. Protected.'

The old woman nodded. She sat next to Jane and put a callused hand on his knee. He stared at the liver spots on her skin and thought he'd never seen anything so beautiful in his life. Her nails were long and pretty. He thought he might have fallen in love with her, a little.

'Becky's gone,' she said.

'Gone.' He was finding it hard to imbue anything he said with any emotion.

'She was taken.'

'She was being protected.'

'There was an attack,' she said.

'She was taken.'

'That's right.'

'Where?'

The old woman raised her head and pointed beyond the power station, to where the peninsula swept back to the west and Camber Sands.

Jane stared at the workers in their overalls, hair tied back with bandanas. 'Has anybody tried looking for her?'

The woman looked at him as if he had just made a pass at her. 'Nobody has seen her since she was taken. We just assumed . . .'

'People survive,' Jane said.

'There's nothing we can do.'

The old woman drifted away, so slowly that he thought he could still feel her fingers leaving him even though she now had her back to him and was moving off towards other loners, other groups of crying survivors at tether's end. He stayed where he was for a while, thinking about women and why the Skinners took them. He assessed the damage to his body and realised that while he was in no fit state to play frisbee, he could maybe walk a few miles and see what was what. He imagined talking to Stanley about it, the complication of explaining Becky to him. The concept of a new mummy, a second mummy. Getting him to understand that they were having a baby. Trying to make him see that this was a good thing. He believed he would not have to talk him around that much. Stanley was a good boy. He liked people. Although he had only been at school a short time, he seemed to make friends easily, much more easily than Jane had when he'd been that age. School in the 1970s was difficult, especially at the rough northern comprehensive he'd had to survive.

He wandered down to the shore, standing a good distance back from the treacly tide. The ancient bones of fish lay all around him. Now he could see the raft, a darker shape, lenticular on the surface. How many people had died in the building of that thing? He doubted he would have the guts to go wading through that caustic soup, and he was mildly amazed by the thought, given that he had spent so much of his adult life submerged in water. He turned back and walked up the shingle to a group of men hunched over square billycans, Sporks clenched in grimy fists. They glared up at him guardedly, shoulders drawing in, protective of their food.

'I'm going to find Becky,' he said. 'I wondered if you might come with me.'

'Where is she?' asked one of the men. He had shaved his head badly; it was blue, nicked and slashed all over with cuts that had become infected. The swelling had wormed down across one eye. Lines of gravy on either side of his mouth gave him the look of a ventriloquist's dummy. The rain began to fall again. Another man, deep within his fur-lined hood, began swearing, covering his can with a gloved hand.

'We're eating, friend,' he said.

'There's a woman been taken by those bastards,' Jane said. 'She's pregnant.'

'She's gone,' the man said, scooping thin brown liquid into his mouth. 'You the father?'

'Yes.'

He shrugged. 'You ought to take care of your women better,' he said.

Jane made to swipe at him but the bald man stood up and put a hand on his injured arm, squeezed, dug his nails in. Jane cried out.

'Want me to set fire to your other arm? Give you barbecued wings?'

Jane turned away. Didn't anybody care any more? He tried talking to the medics, but they shooed him from the forest of sucking wounds and slashed limbs. Everyone was staggering around, or so exhausted that they were lying in shingle, many of them partially submerged, as if the beach was steadily, stealthily, sucking them down. He saw two men pull free of some people wearing medical aprons and pound across the shingle, aiming for the sea. The medics went to pursue, but they gave up pretty soon. You ran only when you had to; it was better to preserve your energy. Everyone stood and watched the men as they crashed into the surf, one slightly ahead of the other. The man at the rear surfaced fast and back-pedalled out of the water, spitting and hawking, wiping his hand repeatedly across his mouth. The man in front of him did not come up.

The survivor stood yelling the other man's name – it sounded like 'Paul' – and made to re-enter the water a few times. But then he gave up and sat down on the shingle. After a while, when it was clear that the medics had given up on him and that his friend was gone for good, Jane crunched through the gravel towards him.

The man was crying. His clothes were soaked on his body, the colour leaching out of them on to his skin.

'What happened?' Jane asked. He sat down carefully a couple of yards away. The man didn't seem to register his presence. He was sobbing quietly, his eyes screwed up, wet. He had an injury. His shoulder was a shining curve where something had scraped it. It was sore-looking. Infected, too. It was kind of encouraging to know that microbes had lived on, no matter how damaging they might be to the body. It pointed to a future of returning life. Maybe.

'He's gone,' the man said. The way he said it made him sound as if he was ten.

'Who's he?'

'My dad,' the man said. He wore jeans with an ID patch on the left thigh. It read: *Sutton*.

'He drowned?'

'I don't know. He just slipped out of sight.'

Jane put his hand to his face and swore softly. He didn't know how many hours had passed since he'd woken up. He felt it could have been days.

'We were going to swim to the raft,' the man said, his eyes strafing the shore. 'We were going to cut it free and fuck the fuck off. Sick of hanging around. Waiting for people to turn up. Too many people get here, they said they'd start some fucking lottery to decide who was in the first bunch to leave. Fuck that. We were here first. Me and Dad. First.'

His voice became strangled. He screamed and pounded his fists into the shingle. He collapsed into it and quietened down. Jane thought he might have gone to sleep. After a while, he pushed himself up into a sitting position and stared out at the water.

Jane talked to him. They talked for a long time. They talked about fathers and sons. They both cried. Sutton was known as Loke. His real name was Eddie, but he'd always been called The Bloke by his dad and gradually, as all names seemed to do, it got whittled down over time.

'I don't know if the raft is the answer, Loke,' Jane said. 'It's given people hope. Maybe that's the thing that matters. I just can't see what it can offer. You untie it. You launch it. You go where?'

'Anywhere is better than this,' Loke said.

'Is it?'

Loke nodded, wiped the tears away from his face. He was gradually cleaning his hands with that water. 'I don't want to be pissing into the pebbles when the Skinners finally suck all the meat off the bone of the big cities and come down here to pick their teeth with what's left of us.'

'What if you go to France, or Holland, or wherever, and it's the same? If it's worse?'

'Dad's gone. It doesn't fucking matter. I don't care one way or the other any more. I just want some kind of result. I want to force the issue. I want to be a catalyst.'

He looked out to the water as if he was considering charging back in to make some attempt at rescue. Perhaps it bothered him that he'd given up so easily. Jane wanted to put an arm around him, to tell him that it was all right. Things had changed so much, it was hard enough to keep track of it, to keep ahead mentally, let alone react quickly enough when something horrible happened right in front of your eyes. Everyone had a tale to tell. Tragedy had not spared a single person. He didn't need to say a word.

'So you'll stay?' Loke asked him.

Jane found himself nodding although he had not come to any kind of decision. He had walked all this way to be with Becky. Maybe because there was some decision brewing to try to persuade her to stay in the UK. The thought of her on some rickety floating island with a baby inside her was unbearable.

If it's a boy ... and it is *a boy, I know that, I know ...
we'll call him—*

'But what will you do?' Loke persisted.

'We'll keep going. It's all we've ever done. We'll fight
them on the beaches.'

'Jesus. You *must* have kids. You *must* be a dad.'

Jane nodded again, and was able to smile. 'I was, I am.
And will be again,' he said.

'I never had kids,' Loke said.

'It changes you,' Jane said. 'You lose your ego. You realise
that life isn't just all about what you want, what you can
have, or take. It's a good feeling. You slowly pull your head
from out of your arsehole. You make sacrifices, and you do
not resent it. Not one bit.'

'Yeah, well. Maybe now's not the best time to become a
dad.'

Jane nodded. He hadn't really thought a great deal about
that. The shock of the news had blinded him to what it
actually meant. Becky giving birth would be hard enough.
Where were the paediatricians, the midwives? What if the
baby was born as Stanley had been, limp and grey, the
umbilical cord wrapped around his neck? And what kind of
world was this in which to bring up a child?

25. THE FARM

The beach grew chill and dark. Jane recalled a bluff in Keri, on the south-west tip of Zakinthos, a Greek island that he had visited with Cherry. It had been renowned for its sunsets. He remembered Cherry leaning against him as they sat on the rocks watching the sun sink. A girl of around nineteen took off her clothes and stood with her arms outstretched towards it, smiling broadly. Her skin had been dark pewter. When the sun vanished, they stayed on to watch the colours in its wake, amazed by the range it shifted through, as if someone were applying ever more dramatic filters to the sky.

He didn't know if it was the girl, or the way Cherry's body yielded against his, or the soft heat of the sun. He didn't know if it was the cool, spiced ruffle of dusk air against their skin as they drove back to the hotel in the open jeep. He didn't know if it was the ouzo, or Cherry's inky eyes, or the kiss she gave him as they stood on the balcony. But their lovemaking seemed to take on a fresh intensity that night. It was as if the dying of the sun had acted as some kind of omen. A reminder that life was no more than a blink of the eye in the grand scheme of things. She held him inside her and it was like desperation, or fear. They made love a lot on that holiday, but with nothing like the same intensity of that one night. Jane liked to think that Stanley was conceived then.

Now he searched the sky for some clue as to where the sun had set. He couldn't believe that beyond that layer of cloud was blue sky and a gorgeous blazing yellow star. It came to him, in dreams, as a cold steel sphere. It was hard to recall the colour of it. The colour was life but there was nothing, other than the beggared remainder of the human race, to remind him what that meant.

'PAUL!'

Jane started. He had been drifting into sleep, the drugs that the medics had given him removing the pain in his arm and reminding him of his tiredness. Now he felt fully awake. Loke was down by the shore, scurrying towards the oily tide as it retreated, withdrawing when it surged back up the sand. There was a body tumbling in the push and pull of the surf; Loke was trying to fish it out. Jane hurried down to the water. Loke clearly didn't want to feel the sea on him again. He had talked of it burning like bleach, and feeling greasy, a sensation he couldn't get out of his skin, no matter how many dry baths he took in the shingle. Jane was looking around for a piece of driftwood when the sea seemed to tire of playing with the body, and pushed it further up the beach where Loke was able to grab hold of it under the arms and pull it clear of the water's edge.

Jane could see that it was a dead man, but Loke was too pumped up to acknowledge it. 'Paul!' he kept crying. 'Dad!'

There were massive injuries to the torso. Something had taken bites out of him the size of serving platters. His legs ended at the knee; the rags of his trousers prevented any scrutiny of what remained. The face was clogged with shards and scraps of itself. Livid, bloodless wounds were carved into him like a poor Halloween pumpkin. He flapped and sagged in too many places to even be in one piece, let alone still be alive.

Jane put out his hand to restrain Loke, who was checking his father's mouth, and tilting his head back to open his airway. Something gritted inside.

'Loke,' Jane said.

'Shut up.' Loke started performing cardio-pulmonary resuscitation. He laced the fingers of one hand into the other and rhythmically pumped them into Paul's sternum. He seemed oblivious to the black seawater pulsing from the jaws with each downward thrust.

Jane left him to it. He walked back to the little hollow he'd dug himself. Fires had been built up and down the beach. It was encouraging to see so many. He had a vision of more fires, hundreds and hundreds, burning on the beaches and in the hills of the country. Maybe there would be a way back from this. Maybe the Skinners could be defeated. Maybe the clouds would part and the sun would heal the planet. Green shoots and a nation of pregnant women.

He was so engrossed in his reverie that he didn't hear Loke approach. He slumped to the shingle like a sack dumped from a weary shoulder.

'This woman of yours,' Loke said in a voice that was resigned but also, it seemed to Jane, relieved. 'This Becky. Do you know where the Skinners took her?'

Jane turned his head to the south. The edge of his country. The lowest part of it. The world was fringed with a trembling red light there. He hoped it was just the colour of the fires that had been stoked all around, but he knew it was not.

'That way,' he said. 'Past the power station. I don't know how far.'

'And you're going? You're going to try and get her back? Even though you'll probably die?'

Jane turned back to the sea. Becky was carrying his child. It ought to have been a question that didn't need airing. Loke would know, one day, when he was staring down at a big raw mouth with a bunch of skinny limbs attached. Death was nothing when your child's safety was at stake. Death was a puny streak of piss. Beneath contempt.

'You know the answer to that.'

Loke nodded. He was wiping his hands on his jeans. He had done his best to bury his father in the shingle. 'I'll come with you,' he said.

They left the camp when the last of the fires had burned down. The rain returned, that soft, insistent mist that had blurred virtually every day of Jane's life since the Event. Loke helped him put on his coat, pausing every time Jane winced when the fabric caught on the blistered, bubbled length of his forearm. They walked south, heading for the black bulk of the nuclear reactors. The shivering line of red light was like a skin on the ground far in the distance. Jane remembered how a similar light had cowed him at the western edges of Heathrow airport. He wondered how long it would be before the screams reached their ears. He thought too of how tardy he was; what if she was dead already? He pictured her shaking with cold and terror in some awful Skinner idea of prison, a long way from the comforts of the Shaded's base at Pentonville. He turned away from thoughts of miscarriage brought on by trauma. The body protecting itself by self-aborting. That would not happen. Becky was strong. She was resourceful. His spirits lifted when he considered that she might have escaped already.

'Keep your wits about you, Loke,' he said. 'If someone got away, we might walk right past them.'

Loke grunted in return, and Jane knew he had instantly dismissed the idea, but Jane clung to the story of the woman who had fled from the Skinners encamped at Wembley stadium. She might have died later, her brain stalled with whatever barbarity she had been put through, but she got away. She got away.

Jane found the going became easier after a while as his muscles warmed up and the stiff feeling in his wounded leg was worked out. He had kept the cuts scrupulously clean and sought advice from the medics. They'd pulled some classic faces when he'd showed them his thigh, but they were satisfied it was not infected and gave him pills to cope with the pain that those wounds and his burnt arm were feeding him.

The peninsula was broader than he'd thought. He had never been out this way before, although he had read about Derek Jarman's cottage and its weird garden of stones and iron and claws. The skeletons of fishing boats lay in the shingle along with that strange machinery, like unearthed fossils from an alien age. Occasionally they would trip over some rusted girder or spar, or see the shape of a cog half-submerged in the beach. Jane wondered how deep it reached and whether it was really discarded, or if it was part of some arcane Heath-Robinson contraption that served the coastline in some secret way.

The mutter of the camp faded behind them and dead silence fell. Jane felt much as he used to in the diving bell travelling between the Ceto and the seabed. A time when you collected your thoughts and focused yourself on the job. All the banter of the DSV was behind them. The hours of noisy respiration and the headache of high-pitched voices, the roar of the blowtorch was to come. It was the eye of the storm. And it had always been the time that scared him more than any other. He couldn't help but think, while the various aspects of the job impinged and the gauges were read and adjusted, that this journey would be his last. Once he was in his gear and tramping towards the coalface he was fine. It was the pause to take breath beforehand, the catalogue of things that might go wrong that caused his will to falter.

So it was now. He thought that despite all his best intentions, if Loke had not been walking alongside him he would not have been able to do this. The pain in his arm was too great. He was so tired that he thought he might begin to crumble. He feared that he would find Becky dead, and that would be the final black underscore to his chances of happiness, or hope.

It took some time to work their way around the nuclear reactors – Jane was expecting to hear some kind of hum, but all was silent – because of a number of downed pylons and security fences obstructing their path. Once on the other side they made better time. The sand was mired with deep pits and runnels; occasionally they stumbled upon items of clothing, or single shoes. It looked like the haphazard disrobing of suicides. The red line leapt in streaks of orange as they got closer.

'What's the fire for?' Loke asked.

Jane shrugged. 'I don't know. Maybe they're cooking. Or it's a sacrifice or something.'

'Nice. Wish I hadn't asked.'

Jane clenched his jaw; another tooth popped loose. He spat it out. Dull fire was spreading deep in the angles of his face. Bone cancer, he thought.

'Loke, are your teeth all right?'

He sensed the other man turning to him in the dark. 'They're OK. I mean, they could be better. I haven't been to a dentist in ten years. But they're not giving me any gyp.'

Jane fell silent. He must be dying. Much of the time, talking to other survivors, he had surreptitiously checked out their mouths, and, other than the occasional abscess or absence, most people's teeth had been intact. He had noticed the way people snatched glances at his own ruined gums and then looked away, like rubberneckers at a fatal crash who have seen more than they bargained for. The taste of blood was always in the back of his throat, the rust smell of it trapped in the mask all hours. He would lie awake at night, prodding and palpating his flesh, feeling for fibrous lumps, or for any too soft, bruised parts of him that suggested decay.

He ran his tongue delicately over his remaining teeth. How many? Ten? Twelve? All of them waggled in their sockets at the faintest touch. He shuddered with disgust and tried to push the thought of what it meant from his mind; a job needed doing.

Loke said, 'Oh no.'

The beach fell away. It was blasted open, as though it had been hit by some immense bombshell or meteorite. They crawled on their bellies to the lip of the crater and peered in.

You believe, once you've grown up, that you're hardened to the worst things the planet and its people can throw at you. You form a skin around you so tough it's like horn. You watch the footage of Katrina, of the Boxing Day tsunami, of 9/11 and you struggle to cope with it, to understand it; you find it hard to continue. But you do. You go on. You layer the pain around you and feel it become absorbed. Next time it doesn't hurt quite so much. You kind of begin to expect bad things.

What's the worst thing you've ever seen, Dad?

He thought of the abattoir and the mirror carp. But it was nothing. It was a confection. It was almost cosy.

Never mind, Stanley. How about you? What's . . .

But he couldn't finish the question. His boy had seen the worst thing in the world, and Jane had not been there to hold him while it blazed all around.

'Loke,' he whispered. He could see his companion to his left, lying on his back staring up at the sky. He seemed not to be breathing. For a second Jane thought he might have committed suicide. The lure of it hung thickly in the air like the remembered scent of summer flowers. 'Loke?'

'OK,' Loke said. 'I'm all right.'

Jane couldn't ask him about what was down there. To mention it was to confirm it and Jane had to cling on to the possibility that it was all a mirage, something dreamed up by his poisoned subconscious.

'I need to find Becky,' he said. The simplicity of it bolstered him. Everything else was scenery.

'What do you want me to do?' Loke asked.

'Just keep an eye on me,' Jane said. 'If it looks as though I'm getting into trouble, cause a distraction. Get them to come after you. And get the fuck away.'

'I love those no-risk strategies,' Loke said.

Jane took a deep breath, shut his eyes. Stanley was there. Nothing that happened to Jane could equal what his boy must have gone through. What he had seen beyond the crater's lip replayed itself against the black screen of his closed eyelids. He rolled over the edge and into the abyss.

What's the worst thing you ever saw, Daddy?

Oh, Stanley. Oh my God.

There were no Skinners to be seen. He walked among the ribcage prisons, wondering if one of the malformed babies screaming within them belonged to Becky. It didn't seem to matter that she was less than two months pregnant. Logic had no place here. He didn't want to see, but he had to watch where he was putting his feet; the babies were packed together so tightly. Some of them were dead. Others had stopped crying or had never started, and looked out through the gaps in the bones with black eyes, open faces. Some of them were bloated to the point of featurelessness, others bore spare limbs, vestigial or fully formed. The pit stank of meconium and vomit and the ever-present civet-like musk of Skinner. It was like some monstrous collection of lobster pots.

Up ahead was an enormous linear bonfire, stretching a hundred yards or so between the headland and the water, the source of the quaking red light. The ribcages stretched as far as he could see. There must be fifteen hundred, maybe as many as two thousand, he thought. He felt the centre of himself deliquesce. The fire picked out the half-submerged wreck of a ship in the water, its skid fin peppered with rust-holes that gleamed like eyes. He thought he could hear the waves beating against the hull, but knew it was only the tumult of his own heart. To his right, where the beach rose up to meet the low wall of a promenade, he could see movement. He crouched, grimacing as a hand put out to balance him cracked a rib and brought a fresh sustained volley of protests from the blighted thing trapped within. He saw Skinners, fully three dozen of them, churning through the sand towards the upper ranks of the cages. The way they behaved itched at Jane. Something was not right in their movements. There was a desperation there, a motivation other than hunger.

Jane averted his gaze as they began plundering the ribcages. He covered his ears to the sounds of feasting, the horrendous glissando of screams and greenstick dislocations, and hurried on, moaning, shaking so hard that he thought he might simply vibrate to dissolution, like a cast of sand.

More Skinners were tripping and sprawling over the promenade wall, rolling down to the beach larder. There was nothing Jane could do. He had no Molotov cocktails in his coat pocket. The rifle was a toy. It made no difference. All his act of defiance would bring was his own death and that of Becky and all of these by-blows.

He angled down to the tide and approached the fire, feeling it, blowtorch-hot, from as far as fifty yards away. When the heat grew so intense that he could feel the hair on his face begin to singe, he inched into the sea, holding on to the sloping banister of a groyne. The water was more like warm grease; he felt it seep through his clothes and nestle against his skin as if enamoured of his flavour. He hurried, eager to be free of it, and almost fell headlong. He doubted that he'd have been able to drag himself clear. He rounded the end of the firewall; it hissed and sputtered where the tide tongued it. He didn't stare too hard at what was at the heart of the flames, fuelling them.

On the other side he saw the mothers, or what remained of them. He thought the screaming might have been worse here, but then he knew that trauma was an excellent soporific. Those who had died had been picked clean. Those that were pregnant sweated and thrashed in the sand, chained or nailed or becalmed by razor-wire garrottes. Some were giving birth as he scrambled up onto the beach, the emerging newborns delivered by surrogate midwives that smacked their chops over the emerging mooncalves.

They were visible far off into the distance, as far as the light from the fire reached. Skinners were pouring over the partition wall at the head of the beach now. He felt one at his back before he had time to do anything about it, but it ignored him. He caught a glimpse of panic behind the foul pretence of its former face.

He screamed Becky's name and felt his voice crack in the middle of it. What erupted from his throat felt at once both the most poisonous and the most pure thing that Jane had ever heard. He thought he saw a shadow pass over him, a bird of such immense proportions that its wingspan might eclipse the beach. And then it was gone, chased away by the shriek that came powering from his lungs.

26. THE RAFT

He saw the Skinners fleeing and being brought down by fast-moving figures in hoods. They used long curved knives to reach inside the bone-armour of their prey. They moved with purpose, aggression. They locked onto a target and did not falter until it was brought to ground. This close to a chance of freedom, the Shaded were behaving like cornered rats. The killing fields had altered. These weren't the narrow jack-in-a-box horror traps of London. The Skinners could not rely on darkness and dense architecture to help snaffle their prey.

Open land, common ground: it was all up for grabs now.

The Skinners were backing away from Jane, despite the swelling of their numbers. They charged towards him from the foot of the beach only to rear up like horses before snakes when they saw him. He thought it must be the wave upon wave of men and women at his shoulders, armed with wrenches and billhooks and cleavers, or the threat of the black sea, but no, they were recoiling from *him*. It was exhilarating to feel in power for a change.

Jane concentrated on moving deeper into the farm. Wherever he could, he helped to free the women who were unable to help themselves. He scored his hands on the razor wire locking them into the beach and tore his nails on the brackets and shackles that kept their hands immobile. Intent on a slaughter before they could be stopped, some of the Skinners had taken to pulling the women up against their restraints, throttling them, a prelude to escape. Others were simply opening up the victims that remained, scooping this human caviar into their claws, final meals for the condemned.

The wall of fire came down. A great cloud of sparks and smoke swept across the sand, befogging the bodies and blood. Jane was too frantic in his search for Becky to be grateful that he could no longer see the atrocities committed by the Skinners, or the dismantling of them by his people as they came pouring over the promenade wall. It was a hell of noise. Of screams and howls and awful wet tearing. The wind would occasionally steal in to whip these sounds away, only to return them as if too disgusted by what it had taken. The smoke turned the shoreline into a besieged beachhead, a too-true re-enactment of some terrible wartime battle. Something exploded; a car, a drum of fuel. Jane heard, then felt shards of metal whizz past his ear. One of them embedded itself in his shoulder and he felt no pain, only an increasing heat. He patted and pawed at his clothes, ripping off his coat. A smoking rind of metal, two inches across, had buried itself in him. There was no blood; the foreign body had cauterised the wound before it had a chance to weep. He made to remove it but managed to quell that instinct. He would be no use to Becky if he pulled that clear only to find, in the most spectacular way, that one of his arteries had been punctured.

He staggered on, thinking of Stopper, thinking that for a moment he had seen his old friend keeping time with his uncertain step, twenty yards or so to his left, a shadowy, pale figure loping through the sea. It bolstered him – though he knew it could only be an illusion, or wishful thinking – to imagine his old buddy here, at the end of the world, as madness descended all around him. He cried out Becky's name, but the pain in his throat was too great to usher forth anything stronger than a bruised rush of air. He tripped and sprawled on a limb sticking out of the sand. Whoever it was attached to was dead, smothered by the beach – if indeed the limb was attached to anything.

Someone let off a magnesium flare. Out to sea, hundreds of bodies dipped and rose in the oily swells. The Skinners were being pincered. The Shaded were massing at the western edges of the arc of light cast by the flare. Hundreds of them were pounding past Jane now from the east. The promenade wall writhed: a physical cordon. A dozen women lay to Jane's left. He hurried to them as the spectral light began to fail. One of the women was giving birth. Her throat was a necklace of rubies where the razor wire had sawn against her contractions. She was choking on blood, trying to stay alive long enough to get the baby out of her. But then he saw that wasn't what was happening. She was trying to kill herself on the ligature before the baby could emerge. A Skinner was between her legs, trying to get hold of the baby's head. Its hands were streaked with blood. It couldn't gain purchase. The dying light glistened on its slavering chops.

Jane strode over to it and hooked his fingers into the desiccated peepholes of its eyes. What inhabited that bone carcass shrank back from him, lifting famished claws in defence. Jane grabbed its left hand and ground the bones to so much dust within his fist. He yanked back on its mask and the boss detached. Something soft and malformed quivered within, a sac with a centre of spiny teeth. It reminded him of exotic food. Trips to the Chinese supermarket with his father where he would be allowed to choose something he had never tried before. Soft fruits you sliced open with a nail and turned inside out, disgorging pulp and seed and fibre that smelled of mushrooms or meat but tasted of nectar.

He had his face in there before he realised it. When the body had stopped twitching around the suck and maul of his mouth he staggered back, disgusted, exhilarated. He dropped to his knees by the body of the woman and saw that she was dead. The baby had died too. He sat back in the sand and pushed his hands through his damp, sticky hair. Sand coated him. He felt that it might penetrate him, turn him to the cold, granular being that seemed to have been some silent promise to himself ever since Cherry and he had begun to fragment.

Jane felt drifting over him a sleepiness that he had not felt for years. It was a feeling of contentment, the warmth of a good meal sitting in his belly. Almost immediately, he rolled over and was copiously sick. He felt his stomach heave as if it was eager to be out of his body and on the beach alongside his waste. He lost sight of what he was, where he was for a while. Dark grains shifted behind his vision. He felt that by vomiting he had loosened a little of what made him who he was supposed to be. He felt unhinged, dislocated. So much of his life had slid away from him, it was as if what he needed to make himself solid and real had been removed. He was like a computer without any software loaded into it. He was something awaiting instructions. He was potential – less than that.

He raised himself to his feet, weak now, his legs shaking as if he had risen from a long coma. The sleepiness had not faded, it had simply changed into a nastier version of itself. This was bone-tired. This was an exhaustion that people just did not return from. It preceded the suicide note and the pills.

The women stretched away from him along the beach like appalling sunbathers. Somehow he managed to get moving again. The Skinners were being overwhelmed. Bodies lay around like shellfish shucked of their fruits. Jane tried to ignore the churning of hunger in his sore guts and put one foot in front of the other. He saw a hairband dividing a sweep of dirty blonde hair. A still head nestled in the beach; she did not flinch when fans of sand were kicked across her face as the combat unfolded around her. He ran to her. She was breathing. Her hands and throat were laced with barbed wire, but she had not shifted against it. He said her name, his voice still little more than a wheeze. He checked her pulse. For a moment he thought he could feel two: hers and the strong, fast code of her baby underpinning it. Then her eyes were open and she was staring at him and it was like the day he first saw her. That wild, untrammelled look just before she had assaulted him. He knew she would be all right. She was a survivor in more ways than one.

Jane freed her hands and then loosened the noose so that she could wriggle under it. He held her and asked if she was all right but his voice was so breathless that she couldn't have heard him.

'Yes, yes, I'm OK,' she said. 'They didn't touch me. I'm not . . . I wasn't ready yet.'

He shushed her and helped her to her feet. Her, well and unharmed with him, gave him strength. They hurried as fast as the sand would allow them.

'Where's Aidan? Did you find him?'

'Aidan's dead.'

Becky didn't say anything, but he sensed a change in her movement and posture. He felt the need to back up his statement, but he didn't know how. To tell her how it had happened was to condemn Aidan. Better she should remember him how she preferred. His betrayal, his threat no longer mattered.

'He stopped taking his pills,' she said.

'You knew that?'

She nodded. 'I should have made him, but what can you do? He was sick. I think he understood that. I think he believed he was dying.'

Or changing, Jane thought. It struck him that maybe Aidan had embraced his own internal demolition by the Skinners, favoured it over the auto-cannibalism of whatever disease lurked in his bones. Maybe the Event had tweaked his genes in some way. Maybe death wasn't so inevitable, for Aidan, for some others. Maybe futures too terrible to entertain lay in store. He thought of the girl in the scarf, the ghastly knowledge that gleamed in her eyes, and he shuddered.

'Where are we going?' Becky asked.

'The raft,' he said.

'It's real? You saw it?'

Jane nodded. It was hard not to smile, not to be infected by the sudden tremor of excitement in her voice. Fear too, he supposed. Death was settling in bodies all around them and it was a fair distance to the peninsula yet. Traps lay in wait, as they had done day after day, down all the miles, all the years.

At the barrier they kicked sand into the fire until a cold path was cleared. They rushed through and Jane touched her on the shoulder, told her not to look, but of course she did and he felt her change beneath his fingers. It was a strange tensing and relaxing, as if she might implode in an arthritic drawing-in of fear and revulsion, or simply collapse, fade away where she stood.

'We can help. We can save them,' she said, but the quavering in her voice was its own acknowledgment of the truth. She did not resist him when he drew her on.

'There's nothing we can do,' he said. 'All we can do is save ourselves.'

An ecstasy of tripping and stumbling and sprawling. Every foot of beach seemed to have been taken up by a body. Dead or close to death or screaming as though volume alone might ward it off. They breasted the lip of the crater; Loke was nowhere to be seen. The ancient, rusted angles of Dungeness returned to the beach. The bodies thinned out. The noise of fighting receded.

He saw the girl.

She had made herself known to him by peeling away from the stream of fighting bodies. She was a sudden stillpoint in the current. She raised her hand and he saw now what it was about her that had itched at his mind for so long. The alien meld of her hand against his; the misted imprint of her fingers on the motorhome window. He understood the significance of the drawing he had seen, of the six-fingered hand enclosing the stick figure within. He thought of protection and assistance. Of species intertwined, inter-weaved, interdependent. Of mutualist relationships. Of pilot fish and sharks. Of the jaws of the fates.

He thought, perhaps, that she must have chosen him as her little project. A way to maybe convince herself that there was a shred of humanity left in her. Like Aidan, she was fighting against a stacked deck. He wondered if she was the girl whose house he had invaded in Burnmouth, a hundred thousand years ago. A bedroom filled with the accoutre-ments of the seriously ill. Stuffed toys and sleeping draughts. Posters of Disney characters and a diary filled with appoint-ments to see specialists. Nobody could say how a failed physique might react when bombarded by the special chemistry of the cosmos. A trillion photons passing through the flesh were bound to have some kind of impact. Time bombs and slow releases. The savagery of the mutated cell.

Maybe she had witnessed his tender interment of her No. 1 Grandpa – no matter how tokenistic the act – and it had helped her to ignore the death knell of her own heart. For Jane, it was something to cling to, at least.

A Skinner came pounding across the sand and the girl turned and floored it with the heel of her hand. Very clearly, Jane heard the crack of its host's sternum upon instant deceleration. The girl looked back towards Jane, as if seeking approval, and hooked a finger over the edge of her scarf. She pulled it clear of her lower face. The glands in Jane's mouth squirted sour enzymes on to his tongue in some kind of recognition. Her jaws were deep, powerful. The ring of her teeth was too great for her lips to close over them. He felt a wave of love for her. She had seen on or around him some shade that he could not recognise in himself. A scar on race memory, some brief verse from DNA's long lament. The dedication he showed for his son was echoed in her looking out for him. They were nesting parts of the same Russian doll. She was the outer figure; Stanley was the baby at the core that could not open. He was somewhere between, rattling around, seeking closure.

'Come on,' Becky urged.

He turned away from the girl when she bent to the body, a long, curved knife sliding out of the sheath of her hand and opening the Skinner with the deep Y-cut of a pathologist. He ran with Becky and he couldn't give voice to his fear that the raft might, in the face of the vicious fighting, have cut loose its mooring ropes and be scudding across the Channel. They had said they would return, but he didn't believe that. He knew that the boat was making one journey and it was more about getting away than arriving.

They reached the broad curve of the peninsula. The fires along the shore had burned down to embers; they looked like the sullen eyes of great lizards basking in the shingle.

Jane thought he saw a swatch of striped fabric, the blue and white of Stanley's pyjamas in the mad criss-cross of bodies, but he couldn't be sure. His mind would not banish the illogicality. He wanted to believe anything and everything that his desperation sowed in him. Pain was unfolding in his shoulder now; no matter how still he kept his arm, it was as if he could feel the ball of his humerus being ground into a socket lined with glass splinters. The deep beat of heat around the shrapnel gave the illusion that his heart had shifted location.

He still wasn't certain he could get onto the raft knowing his boy remained on this soil. He understood that this might mean a lifetime of picking through rubble and entering buildings of shadow that harboured beings that wanted him dead, but all other alternatives possessed no attraction for him. A life free from threat in another country would be hollow; he would barely register what happened from day to day. He would be thinking only of the UK, and his boy squirrelled away in some alley or attic, wishing for his dad, wondering why his dad had not come for him.

The raft was there. It had been hauled to the beach and now drifted in the shallows, anchored with mooring irons, a great white standard whipping around on a mast rising from its centre. People were already on board. The raft seemed to hang a few feet above the ground like a disc of shadow. The people appeared to float in mid-air. It was a disconcerting, disorientating sight. Jane could not be excited by it. Becky too seemed to hang back, despite the howling conflict at her shoulder. He knew that designers and tradesmen had grafted hard over that vehicle for months, but it seemed too flimsy for the water it rested upon. They found themselves approaching it almost against their will; their hearts eager to fling themselves into the void even as their minds threw up all manner of warning signs.

Again Jane was distracted by some subtler movement than that going on across Romney Marsh and the weatherboard cottages along the Dungeness Road. He peered into the shadows and thought he could see the flicker of blue and white stripes; a small body struggling against the tide of inhumanity, a shuttle in some ghastly loom.

'Stanley?' he called out.

'This way, Richard,' Becky said. Her arm was around him. Suddenly he was aware of how terrible he felt. It was as if the fire and smoke, the sand in his throat and the awful mealy smell of bodies strewn across the beach had taken him out of himself to the point where he was unaware of what he was feeling. Even the agony of his shoulder had gone away to some extent, had some distance about it, as if it was remembered – or imagined.

He had to rest by a coil of chain that rose up from the shingle like some weird snake. To his left, a giant anchor had lost its shape to the creep of oxidant. Machinery emerged from or immersed itself into the beach, metalwork so large it might have some sway over how the world turned. Jane thought he could hear the spit and crackle of static barking from the radios in a fishing-boat wheelhouse but it was his unsteady feet on the chips of stone.

'Stanley,' he gasped, trying to focus on Becky's features. She leant down towards him and the face he had fallen in love with found clarity. It was stippled with sweat that clung like small beads to skin greased with diesel. Her eyes were wide and brimful of concern. She kissed Jane and held him. 'We're close,' she said, but he didn't know if she meant their relationship, or their proximity to some kind of end. 'Don't leave me now.'

'I saw Stanley,' he said. The boy's name was like a living thing on his tongue. It reanimated him. He hurried Becky towards the raft. Someone was blowing a horn. Fighting was breaking out at the water's edge. People were being dragged off the raft, or pushed on. Human chains clung to it, desperate to be a part of this maiden voyage.

'They're going to leave.' She sounded panicky; relieved.

'Not without you,' he said. 'I promise.'

They splashed through the surf, Jane grimacing inwardly at the warm, viscous beat of the tide against his legs. Someone swung an arm his way; he pushed Becky to one side and ducked. His attacker bowled over into the water and was lost under dozens of thrashing limbs. Jane didn't see him resurface. They kept being repulsed at moments when it seemed he might get Becky onto the raft. Her boots squealed against its lip – 'Hook a leg on!' – but others scrambled over her, causing her to cry out as her knee threatened to bend the wrong way. She tumbled back against him, her head dipping under the waves. He bent to retrieve her and almost lost his footing as more people charged into him. He felt himself crushed against the edge of the raft, and it, drawn by the tide, was dragging up the shingle, rising out of the sea. Screams from the far edge of the raft. He imagined people tipping off the end. The balance was screwed. It was going to come ramming down on his head and that would be that. Something would have to give and Jane saw it would have to be him. He sucked in his breath and ducked underwater. He had not let go of Becky and could feel her thrashing beneath his fist. The raft came back down and jerked to the right. The hull tore into his back and he cried out. Panic leapt around inside him as he sought the surface again, but the raft had slid across his exit routes.

He readjusted his grip on Becky, and on his dread, and struck out deeper, away from shore and the forest of legs blocking his progress. He turned left and kicked. Feeling above him with his free hand for the edge of the raft. He thought it might never come, but it did, and he hauled Becky coughing and spluttering from the water. It filmed his eyes like oil; he could feel it in his mouth like the residue of a pastry saturated with lard. They were both sick as they splashed from the water, around fifteen yards away from the worst of the squabbling. People were dying. Jane shouted at them, an incoherent bellow of anger and frustration.

He wheeled around at the sudden crunch of approaching footsteps, ready to launch his forearm into whatever face came at him, but it was Loke, his nose and mouth bloodied. He looked tired, hunted. Jane supposed they all did.

'I couldn't stay,' he said. 'It was getting very, very nasty out there.'

'It's all right,' Jane said. 'Mission accomplished. Becky? Meet Loke.'

They all turned to watch the raft. Another horn blared through the grey nets of retreating dark; Jane couldn't see the player. It would be dawn in an hour or two. He envied them their place on the raft at the same time that he was secretly thanking whatever invisible guardian had kept him from that insane binding of waterproofed wood and tarpaulin. He heard the '*chunk*' of an axe as it bit through the ropes attaching the raft to land. There was a great cheer, subsumed by an even greater caterwauling of dismay. The raft slid slowly away from the shore.

Becky began to cry.

'It's all right,' Jane said, without conviction. He placed a hand on her belly, imagined it swelling, becoming a curve that arrived almost by stealth but then could not be ignored. He imagined the baby's hands reaching for them, the knock of its limbs and the faint tremor of its heart.

'They'll come back. They'll come back.' He kissed her cheek, the top of her head.

He stepped away from Becky, drew Loke in towards her.

He touched Loke's arm. 'Look after her for a moment,' he whispered.

He turned towards the headland and the cottages that dogged the coastline for half a mile or so. The figure had moved this way. He crunched towards the flimsy buildings. Many had been turned to so much driftwood by the Event, or the winds that it had created. His ears were pricked, listening out for Becky's voice. If she called him back, he would go to her. This would stop, if she decided it. But she didn't call him. He did not look back.

Over the years he had tried to project the babyish face of his son on to a fifteen-year-old boy. A manchild. He had never been able to do it. Trying to imagine that face without its remnants of baby fat, the pudgy cheeks and wide eyes, the trim, pouting bow of his mouth, was beyond him. Further, he didn't like to do it. It was negating who his boy really was for some fantasy that could never even approach the truth. The likelihood, although he baulked whenever he confronted it, was that he would walk straight past Stanley in the street. The difference between the baby and the five-year-old was greater than he perceived. Add another ten years and you had a new person, in effect. Maybe the shape of the eyes remained, but there was a change in the bone structure, a moving away from the infant that made you strangers, no matter how tight these factions of the family.

Movement now, up ahead. A shifting of shadow around the edges of a stoved-in cottage, window frames gone, door blown in by the wolf that was the wind.

A whimper turned his head. He saw someone duck out of sight beyond the dry gardens and their blasted configurations of sea kale and yellow horned poppy, santolinas and crambes. Starfish lay around his feet as if the heavens had turned to stone at the insult to the world and had fallen on this spot. He had to step over a wreckage of railway sleepers and shattered floorboards, downed telegraph poles and great cairns of bleached crab carapaces. It was like walking a moonscape infected by dreams of violence and perversion.

There was a slight incline up ahead, a dip that exposed the rear of the cottage and a hole dug into it, leading to deep shadow beneath the building itself. He saw the figure hunker down and wriggle into the hole. He felt a jerk in his chest at the sight of blue and white striped pyjamas, his son's favourite pyjamas. He was sure of it.

I luff these jim-jams, Daddy, they're all warm and soft and make me look like toofpaste . . .

'Stan?' he called out, and he ignored the thickening pain in his jaw, the fresh seep of blood from his ruined gums. The swelling had puffed his left eye almost completely shut. He could still see through the right, just, a blurred, splintered view. He supposed he would have to cut into an eyelid to reduce the swelling if it blinded him completely.

'Stanley?' He strode towards the house, ignoring any pretence he'd made at caution. 'It's me, mate. It's Dad. Don't be scared.'

He slithered down the shingle into the dip and leant close to the hole. He could see nothing in there but the pure black of childhood nightmares. But then there was a flurry of movement. The grimy striped swatch of his pyjamas shifting back and forth beyond the edge of the hole, settling now, his back to Jane. The whimpering continued. Cold, afraid, alone for so long.

'Hey,' Jane said. Tears were forming. He could almost feel the slender bones under his fingers, the shivering of his boy. 'I'll make you warm. I'm here, Stan. Dad's here. I never left you, you know. I'd never let you go. Come on.' He was finding it hard to keep his voice level.

He bent to the hole, resting one hand on the cold shingle, reaching his other towards his boy.

'Stanley, it's time to go.' His fingers touched the cotton. It did not feel right.

The whimpering stopped. The shivering of his boy stopped.

The tiger turned around within the black circle of the hole and showed Jane what properly rotten jaws ought to look like.

'Stan,' Jane said, and his voice was nothing but an old man's breath, tired, played out, defeated. He kicked back against the shingle but managed only to dig his heels deeper into the loose stones. He was going nowhere. The strength was gone from him. The tiger clawed a path towards him, muscling out of the hole like something born of darkness. Its ragged, matted cloak stank of death. It placed one massive paw on the centre of Jane's chest, pinning him back against the cold ground. The pitted box of its muzzle wrinkled as it bared its black fangs. The shrivelled tubes of its eye sockets told of distances that Jane could never comprehend. How many millennia had these things drifted through the stars, waiting to find food? How many dead planets had they impacted upon, waiting for an atmosphere, a primordial scenario, an evolution that would never come?

He was thinking this as the tiger almost nonchalantly swatted a claw across his throat. Jane felt an instant numbing chill there and found that he could not swallow. He tried to say something, but his mouth only filled with blood. He jerked against the weight of the rotting animal but it did not budge. Jane couldn't breathe. He was vaguely aware of footsteps in the shingle slowing. He couldn't see who it was.

Light.

A gap as the clouds parted. The moon appeared, gibbous; osteal white. The tiger raised its great head towards it, growling, unsure. Jane put his hand to his own shoulder and withdrew the long shard of shrapnel. He didn't feel a thing. He drove it deep into the tiger's eye. The tiger made no sound but slumped against him, like Stanley used to as a baby when he was tired. His sweet, warm head on Jane's chest. The passage to sleep, so swift as to be almost seamless.

Jane felt like that now. He could close his eyes and drift into oblivion and it would not be any effort. He placed a hand against his throat and there was nothing but pumping wetness.

A snuffling noise.

But he felt no pain. He saw the girl and behind her, coming up the beach, Loke with his arm around Becky, who was steadfastly looking out to sea. The girl raised her hand. Protection. He knew the baby would be cared for. He knew there could be a future.

That snuffling noise.

Jane turned his head and Stanley was standing there in his pyjamas, at the edge of the dip, Walter dangling from his hand.

'Hiya, Dad,' his boy said. 'Where've you been? I'm freezing.'

Jane struggled free of the tiger's dead weight and stood up. He moved slowly towards his son. He was cautious, unsure. He didn't want to be tricked again. He clambered up to level ground and Stanley reached out a hand, slid it through the gap between Jane's thumb and forefinger.

'Make me warm, Dad. I've been cold for such a long time. Waiting for you.'

Jane wiped away tears, eager after all this time to have Stanley clear in his sight. 'I'm here. I've always been here.'

'Me too, Dad. Come on, it's this way.'

Jane allowed himself to be led. He did not look back. After a while, he reached down and picked his boy up. He closed his eyes to his magical, unique smell, the soft measure of his breath, his strong, regular heartbeat. He closed his eyes and it was as if nothing had changed.

Read more dark fiction from Virgin Books

The Unblemished

by Conrad Williams

Enter the mind of a serial killer who believes he is the rightful son and heir to an ancient dynasty of flesh-eaters.

Follow the frantic journey of a mother whose daughter is infected with the stuff of nightmare.

Look through the eyes of Bo Mulvey, who possesses the ancient wisdom a bloodthirsty evil needs to achieve its full and horrifying potential. A man upon whom the fate of the human race depends.

One of the most powerful horror novels of our time, *The Unblemished* is an epic tale of history and destiny, desperation and desire, atrocity and atonement. It is a savagely beautiful tale of a mother's determination to rescue her daughter, which plunges you into the monstrous world of serial killers and a cannibalistic apocalypse that rips through modern Britain.

ISBN 9780753513514

Primal

by Robin Baker

No clothes, no shelter, no hope of rescue. How did they survive the dark side of Paradise?

A group of naked and ragged survivors emerges one year after going missing on a field trip to an uninhabited Pacific island. All but one of the women have conceived and three of the party, including the group leader, are missing and presumed dead. In the glare of the world's media, each survivor sticks to the same unconvincing version of events.

Through one man's determined investigation the true story emerges of what happened on the island – a *Lord of the Flies* scenario of regression, tribalism and suspected murder. But are there signs of something more monstrous at work to confirm the group leader's theory that there is no beast more savage than man?

ISBN 9780753518267

My Work Is Not Yet Done

by Thomas Ligotti

When junior manager Frank Dominio is suddenly demoted and then sacked, it seems there was more than a grain of truth to his persecution fantasies. But as he prepares to even the score with those responsible for his demise, he unwittingly finds an ally in a dark and malevolent force that grants him supernatural powers. Frank takes his revenge in the most ghastly ways imaginable – but there will be a terrible price to pay once his work is done. Destined to be a cult classic, this tale of corporate horror and demonic retribution will strike a chord with anyone who has ever been disgruntled at work.

ISBN 9780753516881

Teatro Grottesco

by Thomas Ligotti

In this peerless collection of dark fictions, Thomas Ligotti follows the literary tradition that began with Edgar Allan Poe: portraying characters that are outside of anything that might be called normal life, depicting strange locales far off the beaten track, and rendering a grim vision of human existence as a perpetual nightmare. Just by entering his unique world where odd little towns and dark sectors are peopled with clowns, manikins and hideous puppets, and where tormented individuals and blackly comical eccentrics play out their doom, is to risk your own vision of the world.

ISBN 9780753513743

Thieving Fear

by Ramsey Campbell

Who could have believed that a night's camping on Thurstaston Common would lead to a haunting of such power and reach. After ten years Charlotte Nolan and her cousins unwittingly disturb something that should never have seen the light, their very dreams are filled with a suffocating darkness and each is pursued by an undefined figure that seems to have slipped straight out of a nightmare. Together, they must investigate an occult mystery stretching back one hundred years and confront the malevolent force that was once a man.

ISBN 9780753518113

The Grin of the Dark

by Ramsey Campbell

Tubby Thackeray's stage routines were so deranged that members of his audience were said to have died or lost their minds. When Simon Lester is commissioned to write a book about the forgotten music hall clown and his riotous silent comedies, his research plunges him into a nightmarish realm where genius, buffoonery and madness converge. In a search that leads him from a twilight circus in a London park to a hardcore movie studio in Los Angeles, Simon Lester uncovers a terrifying secret about Tubby Thackeray and must finally confront the unspeakable thing he represents.

ISBN 9780753513811

Banquet for the Damned

by Adam Nevill

Few believed Professor Coldwell was in touch with an unseen world – that he could commune with spirits. But in Scotland's oldest university town something has passed from darkness into light. And now the young are being haunted by night terrors. And those who are visited disappear. This is not a place for outsiders, especially at night. So what chance do a rootless musician and burnt-out explorer have of surviving their entanglement with an ageless supernatural evil and the ruthless cult that worships it?

ISBN 9780753513583